The Omega Prophecy:

*Threads of the Ancients
to Unlock Humanity's Future*

ROBERT MALDONADO

THE OMEGA PROPHECY
THREADS OF THE ANCIENTS TO
UNLOCK HUMANITY'S FUTURE

By Robert Maldonado

All rights reserved. This book, or parts
thereof, may not be reproduced in any form
without written permission from the publisher.

ISBN: 979-8-89766-894-6

Copyright
June 2025
Printed in USA

Dedication

To all Starseeds, Lightworkers, and Guardians of Ancient Wisdom—

You are the luminous threads weaving the past, present, and future into a greater tapestry of awakening. Your courage to remember, your love to heal, and your vision to uplift humanity are the beacons guiding our world toward its next great transformation.

May this story honor the journey of all who walk between worlds, carrying the wisdom of the ancients and the dreams of the future. May it remind you that you are not alone—that across time and space, we are connected in the great unfolding of humanity's destiny.

With gratitude and hope for the new dawn.

Also by Robert R. Maldonado

Conversations with Earth: Wisdom in an Era of Crisis
Walking in Your Light: Essential Tools for the Ascension
The Impact of the Universal Energies and How to Use Them
Flying with My Higher Self: Awakening to Self Mastery
Children of Atlantis: Keepers of the Crystal Skull
The Calling of the Heart: A Journey in Self-Healing

Available from Amazon.com

When the Earth is ravaged and the animals are dying, a new tribe
of people shall come unto the Earth from many colors, creeds, and
classes, and who by their actions and deeds shall make the Earth
green again. They will be known as the Warriors of the Rainbow."

Hopi Prophecy

After the fall of Atlantis, surviving groups scattered across the globe, seeking refuge in areas where the Earth's energy was still strong and untainted. One such group traveled to the Andes, drawn to the sacred energy of Lake Titicaca and the surrounding mountains. They settled near Tiwanaku, establishing a hidden civilization beneath the surface to protect their advanced knowledge and preserve their way of life. Over time, they merged aspects of their Atlantean culture with the indigenous traditions of the region.

Table of Contents

Introduction

The Omega Prophecy: Threads of the Ancients to Unlock Humanity's Future explores humanity's potential for an evolutionary leap—a transformation into a new species of heightened consciousness known as *Homo Omega*.

The term *Homo Omega* has its roots in both 20th-century philosophy and esoteric thought, as well as ancient extraterrestrial teachings. French philosopher and Jesuit priest Pierre Teilhard de Chardin introduced the concept of the *Omega Point*, an evolutionary culmination where humanity transcends individual limitations and merges into a higher collective consciousness unified with the cosmos and the divine. While Teilhard did not use the term *Homo Omega*, later thinkers and spiritual teachers expanded on his ideas, envisioning an advanced human state characterized by unity, love, and wisdom on a universal scale.

In the shamanic and esoteric traditions, particularly the teachings of the Q'ero shamans of the Andes, it is called *Homo Luminous*, an enlightened, heart-centered human evolving beyond the current Homo sapiens state, where individuals radiate light, embody unity consciousness, and live in harmony with the cosmos. Interestingly, the concept of *Homo Omega* is rooted in Arcturian teachings, which describe the next phase of human evolution—a quantum leap into a multidimensional existence aligned with higher frequencies of consciousness. In this view, humanity's transformation is not only a philosophical or spiritual ideal but part of a cosmic process guided by the Arcturians, benevolent interstellar beings assisting Earth's awakening.

This idea forms the foundation of *The Omega Prophecy*, which continues the story of Atlantis—not as a tragic end, but as a key to humanity's future. My earlier book, *Children of Atlantis: Keepers of the Crystal Skull*, explored the energies at play in Atlantis' final hours, focusing on the profound duality between the spiritual "Law of One" and the dark forces of the Brotherhood of Belial. Atlantis, at its zenith, achieved a harmonious golden age unparalleled in Earth's history. Yet even their spiritual advancements could not prevent the shadows of fear, power, and disconnection from creeping in, leading to their downfall.

Many of us carry within our souls the unresolved pain and guilt from that time. This book seeks to illuminate the Atlantean wisdom of balance and harmony, offering it as a guide for navigating today's crises. The Atlanteans envisioned a future where humanity could evolve into *Homo Omega*, transcending fear and division, to embody unity and higher consciousness. But how do we bridge the gap between our tumultuous present and this utopian vision of the future? This book offers a roadmap—one that combines personal transformation with collective awakening.

In writing this book, I embarked on an adventure to uncover the hidden connections between sacred sites, ancient civilizations, and cosmic forces. I explored places around the world with deep links to Atlantis, including Tiwanaku, Stonehenge, Avebury, Machu Picchu, and others. Through these explorations, I uncovered ley lines—a global energy grid essential to the Earth's harmony. These lines, compromised by dimensional rifts, have allowed lower astral energies to disrupt our world, causing war, disease, and environmental collapse. Healing these ley lines is vital to restoring balance, both to the planet and human consciousness, and healing Mother Earth—Gaia.

The Angels of Atlantis and the Arcturian-Pleiadean alliance play a significant role in this narrative. These higher galactic beings act as guides and protectors, reminding us that we are not alone in this journey. They, along with ancient wisdom keepers, are sacred allies in humanity's transformation, helping us unlock our latent evolutionary potential.

A central theme of *The Omega Prophecy* is the ongoing tension between spirituality and technology. In Atlantis, the Law of One embodied harmony with nature and the cosmos, using technology to serve the greater good. In contrast, the Brotherhood of Belial pursued unchecked technological power, leading to disconnection, exploitation, and ultimately the fall of Atlantis.

This ancient conflict mirrors the dilemmas we face today. As we navigate an unprecedented era of technological advancement—artificial intelligence, genetic engineering, and the rise of digital realities—we must ask ourselves: Will technology serve humanity's evolution, or will it lead to greater division and control? It is my contention that our survival as a species and the planet depends on its answer. The Atlanteans foresaw this challenge, and their experiences and wisdom offer a guiding light as we seek to balance these forces in our time.

The journey to *Homo Omega* is not merely about technological or physical advancement. It is personal—about expanding our consciousness, integrating intellect with heart, and aligning authentic power with compassion. This delicate balance holds the key to humanity's evolution and the restoration of harmony on Earth. In the process, we are transformed.

As you read this novel, ask yourself: What role will you play as the story unfolds and as it will be told? Will you be a passive observer, or will you take an active part in shaping humanity's destiny? The journey to *Homo Omega* is not a story that belongs solely to the past or to fiction—it is alive in the present, waiting for each of us to answer the call.

Although a work of historical fiction, *The Omega Prophecy* delves into these profound questions, weaving together ancient wisdom, spiritual awakening, our galactic heritage, and the lessons of Atlantis. It challenges readers to reflect on their relationship with technology, spirituality, and the evolving world around them. Ultimately, the story reveals that humanity's destiny lies in our ability to embody unity and wisdom—unlocking the future of *Homo Omega* and fulfilling the legacy of Atlantis.

Robert Maldonado

The Scrolls of Light

The air inside the Crystal Temple of Atlantis hummed with an almost imperceptible vibration, the resonance of energy pulsing through the towering quartz walls. The luminous blue glow of the great central crystal cast shifting patterns across the polished floor, bathing the gathered initiates in an ethereal light. At the temple's heart, the High Priestess, Amara knelt in deep meditation, her flowing silver robes pooling around her like liquid light. The air was thick with the scent of burning sacred resins, their smoke curling toward the domed ceiling where golden constellations mirrored the celestial dance above.

Tonight, the veil between worlds was thin.

As Amara's breath deepened, her consciousness expanded beyond the temple, beyond the city, beyond the very limits of time. A vision engulfed her—a revelation so profound it shook her to her core. She saw the fate of Atlantis hanging by a fragile thread, its people standing at a precipice. The brilliance of their civilization, the pinnacle of human achievement, teetered on the edge of ruin. The Brotherhood of Belial, hungry for power, sought to harness the limitless potential of Atlantean technology, forsaking the sacred balance that had sustained them for millennia. Yet, amidst this turmoil, she glimpsed something else—a beacon of hope glimmering in the distant future.

She was no longer in Atlantis. She stood among a different humanity—beings of radiant energy, their forms shimmering with an iridescent glow. These were not ordinary men and women; they had transcended the confines of fear, ego, and division. They were the next evolution of humankind, a species that had awakened to its true potential. Through pure intention, they shaped reality itself. They spoke not with words but through the silent communion of the mind. They moved effortlessly between dimensions, in harmony with the universe, the Earth, and each other.

The vision deepened. Amara saw that this golden future was not inevitable—it was a path forged through trials, through the choices of those who would come after Atlantis. She saw the conflict that would divide her people: the Law of One, the wisdom of unity and heart-centered consciousness, pitted against the growing corruption of those who sought to dominate through knowledge stripped of its soul. She saw Atlantis crumble beneath the weight of its own arrogance, its once-magnificent temples swallowed by the ocean. Yet, the prophecy could not be lost.

With urgency, Amara emerged from her trance, her eyes shimmering with the afterglow of what she had seen. Taking up a Scroll of Light, she began to inscribe the vision in flowing Atlantean glyphs, the sacred symbols pulsing with their own quiet luminescence. The scrolls would become a guide—encoded within the Vesica Piscis, carved into sacred temples, and woven into the crystalline artifacts that held the keys to the future. The Crystal Skulls—repositories of wisdom and memory—would be hidden, waiting for those who would one day seek them.

Her voice, strong yet tinged with sorrow, echoed through the temple as she spoke to her gathered disciples.

"Atlantis may not survive, but humanity will. And one day, when the stars align and the ancient memory awakens, a new race will rise. Homo Omega—the Great Ascension of humankind—will come when the world is ready to remember."

Outside, the city shimmered beneath the twin moons of Atlantis, unaware that its final days had already been written in the stars.

Prologue

The rhythmic clack of the loom filled the small, warmly lit room as Andres Paredes sat cross-legged on a woven mat, his dark eyes fixed on his grandmother's weathered hands. Abuela Kallfü's fingers danced across the vibrant threads, weaving together a tapestry that seemed to shimmer with an otherworldly light.

Andres leaned forward, his brow furrowed in concentration. "Abuela, how do you make the colors dance like that?" he asked, his voice barely above a whisper.

Abuela Kallfü's eyes twinkled as she glanced down at her grandson. "Ah, my little one, it's not just about the colors; it's about the stories they tell." Her silver braid swung gently as she worked, the intricate Mapuche jewelry adorning her neck catching the flickering firelight.

Andres's mind raced with questions, his curiosity burning as brightly as the flames in the hearth. He had always known his grandmother was special, but lately, he sensed there was so much more to learn. The loss of his parents still ached deep within him, a wound that never quite healed. But here, in this moment, he felt a connection to something greater.

"What stories, Abuela?" he pressed, scooting closer to the loom. "Can you tell me?"

Abuela Kallfü's hands paused, hovering over the threads. She fixed Andres with a penetrating gaze that seemed to look right through him. "These are the stories of our people, Andres. Of the earth and sky, of powers beyond our understanding." She resumed her weaving, her movements fluid and purposeful. "They are the stories that have shaped us, and the ones that will guide us into the future."

Andres's heart quickened. He had heard whispers of these tales before, but never like this. "Is that why you always say our traditions are so important?"

"Yes, my dear one," Abuela nodded solemnly. "Our ways connect us to the wisdom of our ancestors. They prepare us for the challenges that lie ahead."

A shiver ran down Andres's spine, though he could not explain why. He watched as his grandmother's tapestry took shape, patterns emerging that seemed to pulse with hidden meaning. In that moment, he felt the weight of something profound settling upon his young shoulders.

"Will you teach me, Abuela?" he asked, his voice filled with a mixture of excitement and trepidation. "I want to understand."

Abuela Kallfü's hands stilled once more. She turned to face Andres fully, her eyes shining with an emotion he could not quite name. "That, my brave one, is why I've called you here tonight. It's time you learned the true history of our people—and the role you may yet play in it."

Andres's breath caught in his throat. He sensed he stood on the precipice of something monumental, though he could not begin to grasp its scope. All he knew was that his grandmother's words stirred something deep within him—a calling he had always felt but never understood.

As Abuela Kallfü began to speak, her voice low and melodious, Andres felt the world around him fade away. The room seemed to expand, filled with the echoes of ancient wisdom and the promise of adventures yet to come.

Abuela Kallfü's voice wove a tapestry of sound, as rich and vibrant as the threads she had just been working on. "Long ago, when the stars sang different songs, there existed a vast network of sacred places, each pulsing with cosmic energy."

Andres leaned forward, his eyes wide. The flickering candlelight cast dancing shadows across his face, mirroring the images forming in his mind.

"Tiwanaku," Abuela continued, her words painting vivid pictures, "a city that held the key to time itself. Stonehenge, a celestial gateway. And the Great Pyramid, a pillar of light connecting earth to the heavens."

Andres's breath quickened. "Were they built by aliens, Abuela?" he whispered, thinking of the fantastical stories he had heard at school.

Abuela's eyes twinkled. "No, my curious one. These were the work of our ancestors— humans who understood the symphony of the cosmos in ways we have forgotten."

As she spoke of hidden cities and battles fought across dimensions, Andres felt a curious warmth spreading through his chest. It was as if some part of him recognized these tales, not as fiction, but as a heritage he had always known but never remembered.

"But why were they built, Abuela?" he asked, his voice barely above a whisper.

"To maintain balance," she replied, her tone grave. "These nodes form a grid, Andres. A network of power that sustains our world and connects us to realms beyond imagination."

Andres's mind raced, piecing together the fragments of a cosmic puzzle he was only beginning to glimpse. "And now?" he pressed, sensing there was more to the story.

Abuela's face grew solemn. "Now, many lie dormant. The knowledge to awaken them, scattered. But there are those who seek to control this power for their own ends."

A chill ran down Andres's spine, not of fear, but of an awakening purpose. He felt, in that moment, that his life would never be the same.

Abuela Kallfü's voice took on a more solemn tone, her eyes fixed on Andres with an intensity that made him shiver. "There is a prophecy, mi niño," she said, her words carrying the weight of ages. "A chosen one with roots in two worlds, destined to bridge the ancient and the new."

Andres's breath caught in his throat. He ran his fingers through his hair, a nervous habit that betrayed his inner turmoil. "What do you mean, Abuela?"

She reached out, taking his hand in hers. Her touch was warm and comforting, yet it carried an electric energy that made his skin tingle. "You, Andres. The prophecy speaks of you."

His mind reeled. "Me? But how... why?"

"Your blood carries the wisdom of the Mapuche, the guardians of the Earth's spiritual balance," Abuela explained, her voice gentle but firm. "And through your father, you are connected to the world that seeks to uncover the mysteries of the past."

Andres's thoughts raced to his parents, their lives cut short by political violence. His father, Sebastián Paredes, had been a historian and professor at the University of Buenos Aires, dedicated to uncovering the truths buried beneath layers of colonial narratives. His mother, Elena Antillanca, a Mapuche activist and anthropologist, fought to preserve the traditions and language of her people. Together, they had instilled in him a deep reverence for history and lineage—both the written and the forgotten.

But their convictions had placed them in the crosshairs of Argentina's military regime. One night in 1978, they were taken—vanished into the shadows like so many others. No bodies, no answers. Only the deafening silence of an unmarked grave.

He had always felt caught between two worlds, never fully belonging to either—his father's European lineage tied to the conquerors, his mother's indigenous roots tracing back to the conquered. Could this be why? Was he always meant to stand at the crossroads of history, trying to bridge what had been torn apart?

"But what am I supposed to do?" he asked, his voice barely above a whisper.

Abuela's eyes softened. She cupped his face in her weathered hands, her touch as familiar and comforting as the Andean breeze. "You must learn, and grow, and when the time comes, you will know. The path of the chosen one is never easy, but you will not walk it alone."

Andres leaned into her touch, feeling the strength of generations flowing through her. "I'm scared, Abuela," he admitted.

"Of course, you are, mi valiente," she said, pulling him into an embrace. "But remember, fear is just the shadow cast by great courage. You carry the strength of our ancestors within you."

As they held each other, Andres felt a profound connection not just to Abuela but also to something larger—a legacy stretching back through time. He thought of the sacred sites, the hidden knowledge, the cosmic battles that shaped the world. For the first time, he felt like he might have a place in that grand tapestry.

"Will you help me understand?" he asked, his voice muffled against her shawl.

Abuela's laugh was warm and reassuring. "Every day, every moment. That is why I am here, to guide you as you discover your path."

And then he was no longer in the dimly lit room but back in the forests of southern Chile, a boy once more, standing beside his grandmother. The scent of damp earth and woodsmoke filled his senses as Abuela Kallfü's laughter rang in the crisp morning air.

"Every day, every moment," she had told him, her voice like the river—soft yet unyielding. *"That is why I am here, to guide you as you discover your path."*

Abuela Kallfü had been no ordinary woman. She was the most powerful and revered machi—a shaman and spiritual elder—of her village in the Quepe region of Patagonia. Her blood carried two legacies: Mapuche and German. From her Mapuche ancestors, she inherited the sacred knowledge of the land, the spirits, and the hidden forces that shaped reality. From her German lineage, she drew upon an old and esoteric power, blending both traditions in a way no one else could. She understood how to bridge worlds—spiritual and physical, past, and future, seen and unseen.

Her family had a long history of ethnic intermingling, dating back to the 19th century when a Mapuche machi from her village had married a Spanish settler's daughter. That merging of bloodlines continued across generations, forging a unique lineage of warriors, healers, and visionaries.

Andres's mother, Elena, had carried that legacy forward in her own way. An activist and anthropologist, she fought tirelessly to preserve the traditions and language of the Mapuche people, documenting sacred practices before they faded into history. She had believed in balance—the harmony between modernity and tradition, reason, and spirit.

But both she and his father had been taken too soon.

After their passing, Abuela Kallfü became Andres's guide, sheltering him in the old house nestled among the whispering forests. When grief and doubt had threatened to consume him, she had steadied him with stories of their ancestors, of spirits that walked among them, of a wisdom older than time itself.

"Your path is already within you, André. You only need to remember."

He saw it now—the way she had always known. The way she had been preparing him, not just for survival, but for something greater. As their hands parted in the memory, he caught the shimmer of love, pride, and something else—something unspoken, yet deeply felt.

Sadness.

Back in the present, André blinked, his breath uneven. "Thank you," he whispered, his words barely reaching the silence around him. But in the depths of his heart, he knew they had already been heard.

Abuela, as if reading his mind, simply nodded, her smile speaking volumes.

Abuela Kallfü's weathered hands moved with practiced grace towards a small, intricately carved wooden chest nestled in the corner of the room. Andres's breath caught as she lifted the lid, revealing a soft gleam within. His heart raced, sensing the weight of the moment.

"This, mi niño," Abuela said, her voice low and reverent, "has been in our family for generations."

She withdrew a stone, its surface etched with swirling patterns that seemed to dance in the flickering candlelight. Andres leaned forward, mesmerized by the intricate design—spirals and geometric shapes that hinted at cosmic alignments and hidden wisdom.

"It's beautiful," he whispered, unable to take his eyes off the object.

Abuela nodded, her silver braid catching the light as she turned the stone in her hands. "More than beautiful, Andres. It carries the very essence of our ancestors, of the land itself."

As she spoke, Andres could have sworn he felt a faint vibration in the air, as if the stone was resonating with some unseen energy. He reached out instinctively, then hesitated.

"Can I...?" he asked, his voice barely audible.

Abuela's eyes crinkled with a mixture of love and solemn purpose. "Of course, mi valiente. It is time."

With infinite care, she placed the stone in Andres's outstretched palms. The moment it touched his skin, a warmth spread through his fingers, up his arms, settling in his chest like an ember.

"It's warm," Andres gasped, his eyes wide. "How is that possible?"

Abuela's smile was enigmatic. "The stone recognizes you, Andres. It carries the wisdom of ages, and now, it calls to you."

Andres cradled the stone, feeling its surprising weight—both physical and metaphorical. He thought of his parents, taken too soon by a brutal regime, and of the stories Abuela had shared of their people's struggles and triumphs. This stone connected him to all that history, all that pain and resilience.

"What am I supposed to do with it?" he asked, a tremor in his voice betraying his mix of excitement and trepidation.

Abuela placed a gentle hand on his shoulder. "For now, listen. Feel. The stone will guide you when the time is right. But remember, with great power comes great responsibility."

Andres nodded solemnly; his young face etched with determination. "I won't let you down, Abuela. I won't let our people down."

As he held the stone, images flashed through his mind—towering pyramids, shimmering portals, battles waged across time and space. Andres knew, with a certainty that both thrilled and terrified him, that his life would never be the same.

They walked outside. The highland night descended swiftly, draping the world in a velvet darkness pierced by countless pinpricks of starlight. Andres sat on the worn wooden porch of his grandmother's small house, the ancient stone still clutched tightly to his chest. His dark eyes, wide with wonder, swept across the vast expanse above.

"Abuela," he whispered, "the stars... they're so bright. I've never seen them like this before."

Abuela Kallfü settled beside him, her weathered hand resting on his shoulder. "The spirits of our ancestors shine down on us, mi niño. They guide us, just as they guided the great civilizations of old."

Andres's gaze fixed on a particularly bright cluster. "Like the Atlanteans?"

"Sí," Abuela nodded, her voice taking on a reverent tone. "And the Tiwanaku. They understood the language of the cosmos, the sacred geometries that connect all things."

The boy's fingers traced the intricate patterns on the stone's surface, feeling a subtle vibration beneath his touch. "Do you think... do you think I'll understand it too someday?"

Abuela's eyes gleamed with a mixture of pride and concern. "You carry their blood, their wisdom. But remember, Andres, with great knowledge, comes great responsibility. The path ahead may not always be easy."

Andres's brow furrowed, thinking of his parents—their passion for uncovering hidden truths, and the price they paid for it. "I'm not afraid," he said, his young voice filled with determination beyond his years.

"Good," Abuela murmured, pulling him close. "Now, it's time for sleep. Let the stone's warmth guide your dreams."

As Andres drifted off in his small bed, the stone nestled against his heart, images began to swirl in his mind. Towering crystal spires pulsed with ethereal light, while shimmering portals yawned open, revealing glimpses of other worlds, other times. A sense of exhilaration coursed through him, but beneath it lurked a shadow of foreboding.

In his dream, Andres found himself standing before an enormous Vesica Piscis, its curves etched in glowing lines across the fabric of reality itself. A voice, ancient and powerful, echoed in his mind:

"The key awakens, young one. The time of convergence approaches."

Andres tossed in his sleep, the stone growing warmer against his skin as if responding to the cosmic dance unfolding in his unconscious mind.

Andres's dream shifted, and he found himself standing atop a colossal pyramid, its stone surface thrumming with hidden energy. The night sky above was a tapestry of unfamiliar constellations, their patterns pulsing in rhythm with the earth beneath his feet.

"Look, mi niño," Abuela Kallfü's voice whispered in his mind. "See how the stars align with the sacred sites."

Andres's gaze swept across a vast landscape dotted with towering structures—pyramids, temples, and standing stones. Each seemed to glow with an inner light, connected by shimmering threads of energy that crisscrossed the earth like a luminous web.

"The global energy grid," Andres murmured, the words rising unbidden to his lips.

Suddenly, the ground trembled. A portal of swirling light materialized before him, its edges shimmering with prismatic hues. Through it, Andres glimpsed fleeting images: a sprawling underwater city, its crystal spires piercing an alien sea; a mountaintop sanctuary where robed figures performed intricate rituals; a subterranean chamber filled with humming machinery of impossible complexity.

"Atlantis," he breathed, his heart racing with a mixture of wonder and apprehension. "Tiwanaku. The hidden temples."

As if in response to his recognition, the portal pulsed, growing larger. Andres felt an irresistible pull, urging him to step through.

"Wait!" he cried out, his dream-self hesitating at the threshold. "I'm not ready!"

Abuela's voice came again, gentle but firm. "You are more ready than you know, Andres. Your parents' courage flows in your veins, and our ancestors' wisdom guides your steps."

The mention of his parents sent a pang through Andres's chest, even in the dream. He remembered their passionate debates about hidden histories, their determination to uncover truths long buried. And then, the terrible day when they did not come home...

"But what if I fail?" Andres whispered, the weight of destiny suddenly feeling very heavy on his young shoulders.

The dream world around him seemed to pause, the starlight dimming as Abuela's presence enveloped him like a warm blanket. "Failure is not our greatest fear, mi pequeño guerrero. It is the failure to try that would truly dishonor their memory and the path that lies before you."

Andres squared his shoulders, drawing strength from her words and the comforting weight of the stone against his chest. He took a deep breath and stepped towards the shimmering portal.

"Remember," Abuela's voice echoed as the dream began to fade, "the Vesica Piscis is the key. Balance, harmony, the union of worlds. This is the wisdom of Atlantis and Tiwanaku, the path to awakening humanity."

As Andres drifted deeper into sleep, the stone pulsed with a soft, reassuring warmth. The whispers of ancient stories mingled with the hum of cosmic energies, weaving a tapestry of destiny around the sleeping boy—a destiny that would bridge past and future, earth, and stars, in ways he had yet to imagine.

Above the sleeping form of young Andres, the night sky blazed with an otherworldly intensity. Stars flickered and pulsed, their light seeming to reach down towards the small hut where the boy lay dreaming.

Andres's eyes fluttered open, drawn by an inexplicable pull. He sat up, still clutching the carved stone to his chest, and made his way to the window. The highland air was crisp and charged with an electric anticipation.

"Abuela," he whispered, his voice filled with awe, "look at the stars!"

Kallfü stirred from her mat, joining her grandson at the window. Her weathered hand rested gently on his shoulder. "Ah, mi niño. The cosmos speaks to us tonight."

Andres's gaze swept across the celestial tapestry, his mind racing with the stories Abuela had shared. "Are they... watching us?"

Kallfü's eyes twinkled. "They are guiding us, Andres. Just as they guided our ancestors in Tiwanaku and the great civilization of Atlantis."

The boy's fingers tightened around the stone. "I can feel it, Abuela. It's... singing."

"What does it tell you?"

Andres closed his eyes, concentrating. "It's like... a map. But not of places. Of time, maybe? And... other worlds?"

Kallfü nodded solemnly. "The path ahead of you is long and filled with wonders, mi pequeño guerrero. But also, great challenges."

"I'm scared," Andres admitted, his voice small.

"Fear is natural," Kallfü said, pulling him close. "But remember, you carry the strength of those who came before. Your parents--"

"I miss them," Andres whispered, a familiar ache blooming in his chest.

"They are with you always," Kallfü assured him. "In here," she tapped his chest, "and out there," she gestured to the star-filled sky.

As they stood in silence, a shooting star blazed across the heavens, leaving a trail of shimmering light. Andres gasped, feeling a surge of energy pulse through the stone and into his very being.

"Abuela!" he exclaimed. "I saw... I think I saw the future!"

Kallfü smiled, a mixture of pride and sadness in her eyes.

Chapter 1

Dr. Andres Paredes jolted awake, his heart pounding in his chest. He sucked in a breath, struggling to ground himself as the dream shattered like glass, leaving shards of its vividness embedded in his mind. The sheets clung to his sweat-dampened body as he sat up, eyes darting around the dimly lit bedroom. For a moment, he half-expected to see the ethereal blue walls of the crystalline city still glowing around him. Instead, the familiar clutter of his apartment came into view—augmented reality displays blinking faintly from a holographic projector, articles on ancient civilizations overlaying the books and journals scattered across his workspace.

"What was that?" he whispered, his voice hoarse.

The dream hadn't felt like a dream at all. It clung to him, as if some part of him was still there, amidst the spiraling staircases, pulsating murals, and the Vesica Piscis—a symbol that had burned itself into his consciousness with an almost magnetic pull.

And then, the figure.

Andres's chest tightened. He could still feel those eyes—deep, ancient, and knowing—boring into him, their intensity cutting through the shimmering veil of energy that surrounded them. They carried a weight he couldn't explain, as though they had pierced the layers of his soul.

He swung his legs over the side of the bed, his feet meeting the cool floor, grounding him momentarily in reality. But his thoughts raced, refusing to let go of the dream's haunting fragments. "It felt so real," he murmured to himself, running a hand through his damp hair. "More than a dream. Like... like a memory."

A memory of what? He had never seen a place like that before—a city pulsating with living energy, its impossible architecture defying even the latest simulations archaeologists had been using to reconstruct ancient sites. The most advanced imaging from Tiwanaku or Göbekli Tepe didn't come close to what he had just experienced. And yet, it resonated with him, stirring echoes of his grandmother's teachings about hidden truths and sacred places.

His gaze drifted to the framed photograph on his nightstand. His abuela's weathered face smiled back at him, her wise eyes seeming to hold answers he desperately sought. "What are you trying to tell me, Abuela?" he whispered, his fingers brushing the edge of the frame. "Is this what you meant when you talked about dreams that come as messages?"

Outside, the faint hum of autonomous delivery drones cut through the silence, mingling with the distant whirr of the city's new mag-lev commuter trains. The Bolivia of 2036 felt worlds away from the country he had grown up in, its skyline now dotted with solar towers and vertical farms. Yet, for all its modernity, ancient mysteries still called to him.

Unable to stay still, Andres paced the room, his thoughts spiraling. The Vesica Piscis. The figure's commanding presence. The city's humming energy. Each detail felt woven into something far larger than himself, something that transcended explanation. He paused at the holo-terminal on his desk and, with a quick gesture, summoned a news feed. Headlines about the upcoming *Global Summit for Cultural and Planetary Renewal* scrolled across the screen, alongside updates on the anticipated celestial alignment—an event astronomers and spiritual leaders alike were calling humanity's next great turning point, a harmonic portal they were calling it.

"If it's a message," he muttered, "what am I supposed to do with it? Why now?"

His steps faltered by the window. The pre-dawn city sprawled before him, its skyscrapers softly illuminated by bioluminescent lighting. The sight reminded him of something he had read about the ancient Andean belief that cities were reflections of the heavens. Was that what the dream city had been—a celestial map, or something more?

An urgency gripped him. Andres grabbed his journal from the desk, flipping to a blank page. "I need to write this down," he said, his hand trembling as he gripped the pen. Words poured out of him as though they had a life of their own. He wrote feverishly, capturing the city's radiance, the spiraling staircase, the living murals, and the Vesica Piscis. The figure's eyes—piercing and eternal—were etched in his mind as clearly as the voice that had spoken:

"This is not a dream, but a doorway. Your journey begins here. The Year of Destiny approaches. Prepare the Earth for the Great Alignment. The forces

of light and shadow are gathering. You must choose... step through the gateway or wake into uncertainty."

Andres froze, the memory of those words reverberating through him. The gateway. He could see it now—the Vesica Piscis, alive with pulsing blue light, shimmering like liquid reality. He caught his breath. He had studied the symbol countless times in his research, but never like this. This was not just sacred geometry; it was a key, a threshold, he thought.

The two interlocking circles formed a radiant mandorla, the almond-shaped portal where opposites merged—spirit and matter, past and future, the seen and the unseen. In ancient traditions, it was the womb of creation, the union of divine forces. Here, before his eyes, it was no longer just an abstract concept. The space between the circles pulsed with an intelligence of its own, a living membrane between dimensions.

His pulse quickened. The Vesica Piscis had been carved into temples, encoded in cathedrals, and whispered in mystical teachings for millennia. It was the shape of light itself, the geometry of manifestation. And now, as its luminous energy rippled before him, Andres understood—this was more than a symbol. It was a doorway, waiting to be crossed.

"The symbols," he murmured, sketching crude renditions of the intricate designs that had adorned the murals. "The Vesica Piscis... it was everywhere."

As he wrote, a memory surfaced—a research paper he had reviewed on the carvings at Tiwanaku. The similarities were uncanny, and Andres felt a sudden, inexplicable urge to visit the site he had studied for so long but never seen in person.

He opened a calendar app with a swipe, his gaze narrowing on the date of the upcoming celestial alignment. Two weeks. He could not explain why, but he knew he had to be there. The dream had left him with more questions than answers, but one thing was clear: the answers would not be found in his apartment.

Unbeknownst to him, the journey ahead would challenge not just his understanding of the world but his very identity, calling upon him to unite the truths of his heritage with the logic of his profession in a quest that would transcend anything he had ever imagined.

The insistent chime of an incoming video call jolted Andres from his reverie. He blinked, momentarily disoriented, as he reached for his laptop. Dr. Evelyn Carter's name flashed on the screen, and he felt a mix of anticipation and trepidation as he accepted the call.

Her familiar face appeared, framed against the background of her meticulously organized study. Bookshelves lined with ancient texts and neatly labeled research notes surrounded her—a reflection of the razor-sharp mind behind them. Despite the early hour, her sharp eyes sparkled with an intensity that always seemed to transcend time zones.

Evelyn had an almost uncanny ability to cut through ambiguity, a skill honed from years spent deciphering lost languages and unraveling the intricacies of forgotten civilizations. With her mixed British and Egyptian heritage, she carried an innate appreciation for the past, yet she never allowed sentimentality to cloud her judgment. Every claim, no matter how extraordinary, had to withstand her relentless scrutiny.

Andres had seen her debunk myths with ruthless precision, but he had also witnessed something else—a quiet curiosity beneath her skepticism. While others dismissed the impossible outright, she lingered at the edges of wonder just long enough to test its reality. That was what made her invaluable. She was both gatekeeper and bridge between logic and the unknown.

"Couldn't sleep either?" she asked, arching a knowing brow. Her voice carried its usual dry wit, a subtle warmth hidden beneath her methodical exterior.

Andres exhaled a breath he hadn't realized he was holding. "Something like that."

"Andres, I hope I'm not interrupting," she began, her voice clipped yet warm. "But something came up that I thought you'd want to see right away."

Andres straightened, trying to shake off the lingering haze of his memories. "Not at all, Evelyn. What is going on?"

Evelyn glanced to the side, her expression tense. "Have you been following the news out of Cairo? Another artifact has surfaced—like the Atlantean scroll you received last year. But this one..." She trailed off, her brows furrowing as if searching for the right words.

"What about it?" Andres leaned forward, his pulse quickening.

"It contains markings we believe align with the planetary alignments predicted for 2038. The kind of alignments your dream mentioned." Evelyn's voice dropped as if sharing a secret. "And there is something else. The artifact was found embedded in what appears to be... well, the remnants of an ancient energy grid."

Andres felt a chill run down his spine. "You think it's connected to the Vesica Piscis coordinates?"

"Yes," Evelyn confirmed, her voice taut with urgency. "It is more than a possibility—it is almost a certainty. This changes everything. And I have already secured clearance for you to examine it, but you will need to come to Cairo immediately."

The weight of her words settled on him, and for a moment, the room seemed to shrink. His mind raced. The dream, his grandmother's voice, and now this revelation—it was all converging into a singular, inescapable point.

"When would I need to leave?" he asked, his voice steady, despite the whirlwind within him.

"By tomorrow morning," Evelyn said. "I will send you the details. But, Andres, there is one more thing. The artifact—it is emitting low-frequency vibrations. The kind that resonates with geological and magnetic anomalies. It is... active."

Active. The word reverberated in Andres's mind like the hum of the city in his dream. For a moment, he was back in the underground corridors, the energy surging around him. The visions were not just echoes of the past—they were a roadmap, leading him to this moment.

"I'll be ready," he said firmly, the hesitation that had plagued him earlier now dissipating. "Thank you, Evelyn."

She nodded, her expression softening. "I knew you would understand the importance of this.

A sharp knock at the door startled Andres, cutting through Evelyn's excited chatter. His heart leaped, a mixture of anticipation and unease coursing through him.

"Evelyn, hold on a second," he said, his voice tense. "There's someone at my door."

"At this hour?" Evelyn's brow furrowed with concern. "Be careful, Andres."

Andres approached the door cautiously, his footsteps muffled on the worn carpet. As he opened it, he found not a person, but a package resting on his doorstep. Its unexpected presence sent a shiver down his spine.

"It's... a package," he called back to Evelyn, still visible on his computer screen. "No one's here."

Bending down, Andres lifted the parcel. Its weight surprised him, as did the faint, earthy scent emanating from it. He turned it over in his hands, searching for a return address or any identifying marks.

"That's odd," he muttered, more to himself than to Evelyn. "There's no sender information."

As he examined the package more closely, his breath caught in his throat. There, barely visible in the dim light of the hallway, was a faint symbol etched into the wrapping. It resembled a Vesica Piscis, the very same shape he had seen in his dreams and studied in the carvings at Tiwanaku.

"Andres?" Evelyn's voice snapped him back to reality. "What is it? You look like you've seen a ghost."

He returned to his desk, package in hand, his mind racing. "Evelyn, you're not going to believe this," he said, his voice barely above a whisper. "This package... it's connected to everything we've been discussing. I can feel it. It is..."

Andres's fingers hovered over the wrapping, hesitating. Opening this package felt like stepping off a cliff into the unknown. Whatever was inside, he sensed it would irrevocably change the course of his research—and perhaps his life.

"Should I open it now?" he asked, both seeking Evelyn's advice and voicing his own internal debate.

Evelyn leaned closer to her camera, her eyes intense. "Andres, whatever's in that package, it found its way to you for a reason. Trust your instincts."

Andres took a deep breath, steeling himself. "You're right," he said, his resolve strengthening. "Here goes nothing."

His fingers trembled as he carefully unwrapped the package, revealing an ancient scroll encased in a protective cylinder. His heart raced as he gently removed it, the parchment crackling softly under his touch.

"It's a scroll," he breathed, his eyes wide with wonder. "Evelyn, this is... incredible."

As he unrolled it, intricate symbols and diagrams sprawled across the aged surface, their meaning tantalizing yet just out of reach. The Vesica Piscis appeared prominently, intertwined with unfamiliar glyphs and geometric patterns.

"What do you see?" Evelyn leaned forward, her excitement palpable even through the screen.

Andres squinted, his breath fogging the window as he peered closer. "It's unlike anything I've ever encountered. There are symbols here that resemble Tiwanaku script, but others... they're completely alien to me."

A chill ran down his spine as his gaze drifted to the street below. There, bathed in the flickering light of a streetlamp, stood a figure in a long, flowing coat. Motionless. Watching.

"Andres?" Evelyn's voice sounded distant. "What's wrong?"

He blinked, his pulse quickening. "There's someone outside. Just... standing there."

The figure shifted slightly, and Andres caught a glimmer of reflected light—eyes locked on him. His breath hitched.

"I need to go," he muttered, unable to tear his gaze away from the ominous presence below.

As he reached to end the call, the streetlamp sputtered. In that brief moment of darkness, the figure vanished.

Andres blinked rapidly, his heart pounding as he scanned the now-empty street. Had he imagined it? The eerie stillness outside only heightened his unease.

Turning back to the scroll, a realization dawned on him. The vivid dreams, this cryptic artifact, the looming threat—they were all connected. He was at the center of something far greater than he had ever imagined.

"What have I gotten myself into?" he whispered, his scientific skepticism warring with the spiritual teachings of his Mapuche grandmother. For the first time, he truly understood: he was the bridge between these two worlds, and the weight of that responsibility settled heavily upon him.

Andres's fingers traced the intricate symbols on the scroll, his grandmother's voice echoing in his mind. "Dreams are messages, niño. They guide us to the truths we need, even if we're not ready to hear them."

He closed his eyes, the memory of her weathered face and wise eyes as vivid as if she were standing before him. "Abuela," he whispered, "I think I understand now."

The scroll beneath his fingertips seemed to pulse with an energy he could not explain. It was more than just an artifact—it was a key to unlocking secrets buried deep in time.

"The global energy grid," he breathed, recalling legends of Atlantean technology. "It's real."

A surge of determination coursed through him. Whatever forces were aligning against him, whatever dangers lay ahead, he knew he had to see this through.

Andres straightened, a newfound resolve hardening his features. "I won't let you down, Abuela," he said to the empty room. "I'll find the truth—for both of us."

Suddenly, his laptop chimed with a new email.

Subject: URGENT—Need to Discuss Findings
From: Dr. Jacqueline Hart
To: Dr. Andres Paredes

"Andres, I just returned from a field study in Malta, and you won't believe what I found. There are inscriptions beneath the Hypogeum that match the symbology you described in your last paper on pre-Diluvian languages. This is bigger than either of us thought. If you're still in Bolivia, we need to compare notes. When can we talk?"

Andres's mind raced. If the inscriptions beneath the Hypogeum of Hal Saflieni matched the script on the scroll, the implications stretched far beyond Tiwanaku. This wasn't just a localized anomaly—it was a global link to an ancient, forgotten past. And Evelyn was one of the few people who could help him decode it.

Dr. Evelyn Hart had grown up in a household that revered both science and art. Her mother, an astrophysicist, had taught her to see the universe as a vast, intricate puzzle, while her father, an art historian, had instilled in her a deep appreciation for ancient civilizations. Their combined influence had ignited Evelyn's fascination with the stars and humanity's past, pushing her to explore the connections between the two.

Determined to bridge the gap between archaeology and astronomy, she pursued a dual Ph.D. in archaeology and astrophysics, becoming a pioneer in the emerging field of astro-archaeology. Her research had revealed how civilizations like the Egyptians, Sumerians, and Maya aligned their monuments with celestial phenomena—sometimes with staggering precision. To Evelyn, this was more than coincidence; it suggested an ancient understanding of the cosmos, one deeply embedded in spiritual and cultural traditions.

Her groundbreaking work had earned her respect, but also skepticism. Many in academic circles dismissed her theories as straying too close to the esoteric, but that only fueled her determination. She wasn't chasing myths—she was uncovering truths that had been lost or deliberately ignored. And now, if the symbols she had found in Malta truly mirrored the ones on this scroll, it could be the missing piece of a puzzle she had been assembling for years.

This was too important for email. He had to bring her in. His fingers hovered over the keyboard before he started typing.

Subject: Change of Plans—Come to La Paz
From: Dr. Andres Paredes
To: Dr. Jacqueline Hart

"Jackie, thank you for reaching out, but I need you in La Paz as soon as possible. I've come into possession of something extraordinary—an ancient scroll with markings that might predate known civilizations. If what you found in Malta aligns with this, then we're looking at something far bigger than either of us anticipated. A global pattern. Something buried in our past that's finally resurfacing."

"We need to compare our findings in person. This is too important for email. Let me know how soon you can get here."

Before he could close his laptop, his phone vibrated. Dr. Evelyn Carter.

"Andres, I forgot to tell you—there's something anomalous beneath Tiwanaku," Carter said, her voice edged with urgency. "The latest satellite scans show a massive, buried structure beneath the site. I had to pull some strings to get access to the data, but I think we're looking at something ancient, possibly predating the known ruins."

Andres frowned. "You think it's connected to—"

"I don't know what to think yet," Carter cut in. "That's why I'm flying in. If what you found has any bearing on this, we need to piece it together before certain institutions start getting involved."

A buried structure. A scroll with an unknown script. Possible connections spanning continents. The weight of discovery pressed on Andres once more, but this time, he wasn't alone in carrying it.

He exhaled and glanced down at the scroll one last time before saying, "I will see you in La Paz, Evelyn."

Chapter 2

Dr. Evelyn Carter entered Andres' office with brisk energy, her heeled boots clicking against the wooden floor. She paused only for a moment, her gaze sweeping across the room before locking onto the scroll unfurled across the desk.

"Oh, it's here!" she exclaimed, the words tumbling out as she moved toward it, brushing a stray lock of auburn hair from her face. The scroll seemed almost surreal under the dim glow of the desk lamp, its intricate symbols catching the light.

The office itself was organized chaos that spoke to a life steeped in exploration. Shelves groaned under the weight of dusty tomes, some spines cracked with age. Maps, peppered with faded annotations, were pinned haphazardly to the walls, and relics from Andres's expeditions lay scattered across the desk—a fragment of a clay tablet here, a chipped obsidian blade there, a human skull and a Mapuche "Thunder Stone" from Abuela...

Evelyn hovered over the scroll, her fingers twitching as though resisting the urge to touch it directly. "Look at this," she murmured, her voice filled with wonder. "The craftsmanship... the precision of these symbols. Andres, this is extraordinary!"

Andres leaned back slightly in his chair; arms crossed as he observed her. His dark eyes followed her movements, his expression unreadable. Evelyn's excitement filled the room, but he remained grounded, his analytical mind reluctant to leap to conclusions.

"Careful," he said evenly. "We don't even know what we're dealing with yet."

Evelyn shot him a quick look, her sharp gaze both amused and exasperated.

Smiling, she said, "Come on, Andres. You do not need to be so cautious. This could be the find of a lifetime." She straightened, brushing the air with her hands as though framing a thought. "The symbols... they look like a cross between Linear A and something entirely alien. And the material—have you noticed? It is not papyrus or vellum. It is…" She hesitated, bending closer. "…It feels metallic but organic. Almost alive."

Andres raised an eyebrow, his skepticism flickering through his otherwise stoic demeanor. "Alive?" he echoed, his tone bordering on incredulous.

"Yes! Or at least, it's something we've never seen before." She glanced at him, her excitement undiminished. "Imagine what this could mean. If we can decode it—"

"Evelyn," he interrupted, his voice steady but firm, "let's not get ahead of ourselves." He uncrossed his arms and leaned forward, resting his forearms on the desk. "Do you really think this is what it claims to be? Something… Atlantean?"

Her eyes narrowed thoughtfully as she studied him. "I do," she said, her voice softening but losing none of its conviction. "And I think you do too, whether you want to admit it or not."

He did not respond immediately. Instead, his gaze shifted to the scroll, its symbols seeming to shimmer faintly under the lamplight. His mind wrestled with the artifact's implications—an intersection of history, myth, and something far beyond his comprehension.

Finally, he sighed, a faint smile tugging at the corner of his mouth. "I suppose we'll find out," he said, his voice carrying a mix of skepticism and reluctant intrigue.

Evelyn grinned, already reaching for her notebook. "Exactly. Now, let us get to work."

Evelyn's fingers danced across the scroll, her eyes darting between the ancient glyphs and her notebook. She muttered softly to herself, her brow furrowed in concentration. "These symbols… they're unlike anything I've seen before. There's a fluidity to them, almost as if they're… pulsing."

Andres leaned in, his skepticism momentarily forgotten as he watched her work. Her methodical approach was mesmerizing, each movement precise and purposeful. He knew that she had an eidetic memory for languages and symbols, which makes her a phenomenal codebreaker, able to connect patterns and fragments others might overlook.

"Look here," Evelyn said, her voice barely above a whisper. She pointed to a series of interlocking circles and spirals. "This glyph keeps repeating. It's… it's almost like a key."

She began to read aloud, her voice filled with wonder. "The great... no, the cosmic wheel turns. Cycles of... rebirth? No, ascension. The Crystal... Skull? Yes, Skull... awakens the dormant... spark?"

Andres's eyes widened. "Crystal Skull? That can't be a coincidence."

Evelyn nodded, her excitement palpable. "It's all connected, Andres. The Skull, Tiwanaku, the energy grid—"

A gentle knock on the door caught their attention. Andres Paredes glanced up from the ancient scroll he was examining, his sharp eyes lighting up with recognition. The door creaked open, and a poised figure stepped in. Her calm presence filled the room with an air of quiet confidence.

"I hope I'm not interrupting," she said with a hint of amusement in her melodic voice.

Andres stood, offering her a warm smile, and gestured toward a seat. "Not at all, Jackie. Thank you for coming on such short notice."

Dr. Jacqueline Hart stepped further into the room, her long auburn hair cascading over her shoulders, a few strands tucked neatly behind her ear. Her green eyes, sharp and inquisitive, swept over the scroll and artifacts on the table, her curiosity already piqued. She moved with a balance of grace and purpose, her practical yet refined attire underscoring her scholarly demeanor.

"Jackie, I'd like to introduce you to Dr. Evelyn Carter," Andres said, motioning toward the woman seated across from him. "Evelyn has been instrumental in helping us uncover some of the mysteries surrounding this site."

Evelyn extended a hand, her expression a mix of curiosity and warmth. "It is an honor to meet you, Dr. Hart. Andres speaks highly of your work."

Jacqueline took her hand with a firm yet polite grip. "Please, call me Jackie. And the honor is mine. Andres's invitation had me intrigued the moment I received it. The convergence of ancient history and celestial alignments is my passion."

Andres nodded, stepping between them. "That is precisely why I called Jackie here. She is not just an archaeologist or an astrophysicist; she is a pioneer in astro-archaeology and has spent years studying how ancient civilizations aligned their monuments with celestial phenomena. Her insights might be the key to understanding the greater purpose of what we have found."

"It's a fascinating field," Jacqueline added, her voice carrying an undertone of passion. "The Egyptians, the Maya, even the Sumerians—they all seemed to share a profound connection to the stars. Their knowledge of astronomy was far beyond what many give them credit for, and I have dedicated my career to unraveling how their understanding shaped their cultures."

Evelyn leaned forward, her interest evident. "Do you believe that connection extends beyond just practical uses, like agriculture or navigation?"

Jacqueline's eyes brightened, her freckles catching the light as she smiled. "Absolutely. For many of these civilizations, the stars were a bridge to the divine, a way of aligning their lives with the cosmos. They believed their purpose and destiny were written in the heavens, and their monuments were as much spiritual tools as they were scientific marvels."

Andres chimed in, his voice steady. "That is why I wanted Jackie to join us. If anyone can help us decode the celestial alignments and their connection to the artifacts and inscriptions we have found, it is her."

Evelyn glanced at the scroll on the table, her curiosity sharpening. "If what you've uncovered here aligns with what I've seen elsewhere, we might be looking at something truly extraordinary—a piece of humanity's cosmic heritage."

Andres nodded. "Exactly."

Jacqueline smiled warmly at Evelyn. "May I?" she asked, gesturing towards the scroll.

Evelyn hesitated for a moment, then nodded, stepping aside.

Jacqueline leaned over the desk, her eyes scanning the glyphs. "Fascinating," she murmured. "These symbols... they speak of a great awakening, a convergence of energies."

Andres watched her intently. "What do you mean?"

Jacqueline's fingers hovered over the scroll, never quite touching it. "The ancients believed in cycles of consciousness, periods of spiritual evolution. This scroll... it seems to be describing such a cycle, one tied to the activation of sacred sites across the globe."

Evelyn's eyes widened. "The global energy grid," she breathed.

Jacqueline nodded. "Exactly. And if I'm reading this correctly, Tiwanaku plays a central role in this awakening."

As the three of them huddled over the scroll, the air in the room seemed to thicken with possibility. Andres felt a shiver run down his spine, his skepticism warring with a growing sense of wonder. Whatever they had stumbled upon, he realized, was far bigger than any of them had imagined.

The energy in the room pulsed with excitement as the three scholars exchanged rapid-fire observations, each building on the others' insights.

"Look here," Evelyn pointed, her finger tracing a series of intricate glyphs. "These symbols suggest a convergence of celestial bodies. Could it be referring to a specific astronomical event?"

Andres leaned in, his brow furrowed in concentration. "Possibly. But what is this recurring motif?" He indicated a symbol resembling two intersecting circles. "It appears at key points throughout the text."

Jacqueline's eyes lit up with recognition. "The Vesica Piscis," she breathed. "A sacred symbol representing the union of heaven and earth, the gateway between worlds."

As they debated the implications, Andres felt a shift in the air, a sudden chill that raised goosebumps on his arms. He looked up, his instincts on high alert, just as the door to his office swung open.

Dr. Elera Voss stood in the doorway, her silver hair gleaming in the lamplight, her piercing gaze sweeping the room.

"Well, well," she said, her voice as cold and precise as a scalpel. "Quite the gathering we have here."

Andres tensed, acutely aware of the sudden shift in atmosphere. Voss's presence seemed to suck the warmth from the room, replacing excitement with wary suspicion.

"Dr. Voss," he said, straightening up. "This is... unexpected."

Voss's lips curved in a razor-thin smile. "Is it? I would have thought you'd anticipate my interest in such a... significant discovery."

"How on earth did you find out?" Andres asked, eyes narrowing.

A knowing smirk spread across the other's face. "Come on, Andres. News flies faster than the wind—you of all people should know that."

As she moved into the room, Andres noticed Evelyn and Jacqueline exchange uneasy glances. He felt a knot forming in his stomach. How much had Voss overheard? How did she know about this? And more importantly, what did she intend to do with that information?

Voss glided across the room, her lab coat rustling softly as she approached the desk. Without asking for permission, she leaned over the scroll, her eyes narrowing as she scanned the ancient text.

"Fascinating," she murmured, her long fingers hovering just above the fragile surface. "The intricacy of these glyphs... they're not just writing; they're a form of technology."

Andres watched her warily. "What do you mean?"

Voss traced the air above a series of interconnected symbols. "See how these lines converge? It is a schematic, Dr. Paredes. A blueprint for channeling energy."

Despite his misgivings, Andres could not help but be intrigued. He leaned in, following Voss's gestures. As he did, a fragment of his recurring dream flashed through his mind—a towering crystal structure, pulsing with blue-white light.

"The crystal towers," he whispered, almost to himself.

Voss's head snapped up, her grey eyes locking onto his. "What did you say?"

Andres hesitated, suddenly aware of the weight of everyone's gaze. He took a deep breath, deciding to trust his instincts. "I've been having these dreams... visions, maybe. Of massive crystal structures, harnessing some kind of energy."

As he spoke, the images became clearer in his mind. "They're connected to the earth somehow, drawing power from it. But also... reaching up to the stars."

Voss's expression was unreadable, but Andres sensed a flicker of something—surprise, maybe recognition in—her eyes? "Interesting," she said, her tone carefully neutral. "And how long have you been experiencing these... visions?"

Andres felt a chill run down his spine. There was something predatory in Voss's gaze, a hunger that made him deeply uneasy. Yet he could not shake the feeling that his dreams were somehow key to understanding the scroll's secrets.

"Since we discovered the artifact," he admitted, struggling to maintain his composure. "They've been getting more vivid, more frequent. It's like... like the knowledge is trying to surface."

As the words left his mouth, Andres realized with startling clarity that it was true. These were not just dreams—they were memories, ancient wisdom rising from the depths of his consciousness. But how? And why him?

Suddenly, a low hum filled the room, vibrating through the floor and up into their bones. The air seemed to thicken, shimmering with an otherworldly energy that made the hairs on Andres's arms stand on end.

"What's happening?" Evelyn gasped, her eyes wide with a mixture of fear and exhilaration.

Before anyone could answer, the world around them dissolved into a kaleidoscope of swirling colors. Andres felt a tugging sensation as if his very essence was being pulled from his body. He tried to resist, panic rising in his throat, but the force was inexorable.

In an instant, they were somewhere else entirely. Andres blinked, struggling to process the scene before him. They stood atop a great stone pyramid, overlooking a vast city that pulsed with life and energy. Gleaming structures of impossibly smooth stone reached towards the sky, interconnected by intricate canals, and raised walkways.

"Tiwanaku," Jacqueline breathed, her voice filled with awe. "But not as ruins—but rather as it once was."

Andres's mind reeled. This was no mere vision; it felt startlingly real, as though he had been transported to another world. The warmth of the sun pressed against his skin like a comforting embrace, and he could sense the soft resistance of the earth beneath his feet. The air carried a heady mix of scents—rich, loamy soil mingled with the faint perfume of unfamiliar flowers, their fragrances vibrant and intoxicating. A gentle breeze brushed past him, stirring the foliage, and bringing with it the distant sound of rustling leaves and melodious bird calls. Every detail felt vivid and alive, overwhelming his senses, and making him question where the vision ended, and reality began.

"Look!" Evelyn pointed, drawing their attention to a central plaza below.

There, atop an ornate pedestal, sat the Crystal Skull. It pulsed with an inner light, sending out waves of energy that seemed to harmonize with the very earth itself. Andres could feel the resonance in his chest, a deep thrumming that spoke of balance and connection.

"It's... it's maintaining everything," he murmured, understanding dawning. "The crops, the water systems, even the air feels charged with its energy."

Voss stepped forward, her usual aloofness replaced by an almost childlike wonder. "Incredible," she whispered. "A perfect symbiosis of technology and nature."

But even as they watched, the sky began to darken. Storm clouds gathered with unnatural speed, and Andres felt a sense of impending doom settle over him like a shroud.

"Something's wrong," he said, his voice tight with anxiety. "We need to—"

His words were cut off by a deafening crack of thunder. The ground beneath their feet began to tremble violently. In the plaza below, the Crystal Skull's glow flickered and dimmed.

"No!" Voss cried out, her mask of indifference shattering completely. She reached out as if she could somehow prevent what was unfolding before them.

The city around them began to crumble. Buildings toppled, canals overflowed, and the very earth seemed to tear itself apart. Andres watched in horror as the vibrant civilization they had just witnessed was reduced to ruins in a matter of moments.

As abruptly as it had begun, the vision ended. They found themselves back in Andres's office, gasping and shaken. The silence that followed was deafening.

The air in Andres's office crackled with tension as the group emerged from their shared vision, each processing the weight of what they had witnessed. Dr. Paredes was the first to break the stunned silence, his weathered face etched with a mix of awe and urgency.

"We have to go to Tiwanaku," he declared, his voice carrying a gravity that left no room for argument. "What we've seen... it changes everything."

Evelyn nodded vigorously, her eyes alight with determination. "The scroll, the vision—it's all connected. We can't ignore this."

Andres cast a wary glance at Dr. Voss, who stood unnaturally still, her earlier vulnerability now masked behind her usual cool facade. "And what about you, Dr. Voss? Are you still with us on this?"

Voss met his gaze, a flicker of something—regret or determination?—passing across her face. "My expertise will be crucial for understanding the technology we encountered in the vision. You need me."

Jacqueline Hart stepped forward, her calm presence a balancing force. "We may not trust each other fully, but we're united in this quest. Tiwanaku's secrets won't reveal themselves easily."

As the group began to disperse to gather supplies, Andres found himself lost in thought. *Are we really ready for what we might find? And can we trust Voss when the stakes are this high?*

Andres's relationship with Voss was fraught with complexities, shaped by their shared history and the unresolved betrayal that lingered like a shadow. Once, they had been allies—even friends. Voss's idealism had been infectious, her belief in the transformative power of knowledge a source of inspiration for Andres. But that faith had been shattered, and Andres could not escape the guilt that he might have played a role in her disillusionment. Whether through a failure to stand by her when she needed him most or an unintentional slight that she had taken as abandonment, the fracture in their bond was undeniable.

Now, as Voss's ambition drove her closer to the Sons of Belial, Andres saw glimpses of the person she used to be—the one who sought truth for humanity's betterment. Yet, the bitterness born from her betrayal clouded her judgment, pushing her toward power as a means of control and validation. Despite it all, Andres could not ignore the moments of hesitation he caught in her, the way her eyes softened when they spoke of the past. Perhaps there was still a part of her that longed for redemption, even if she could not yet admit it to herself.

He shook off his doubts and focused on the task at hand. "We'll need both traditional and modern tools," he announced, moving to a locked cabinet. "Trowels, brushes, sieves – the archaeologist's standard kit. But also..." Andres pulled out a sleek, compact drone. "This will give us aerial surveys and access to hard-to-reach areas."

Evelyn appeared at his side, her arms full of field notebooks and digital tablets. "I've got our reference materials covered. Ancient Andean languages, astronomical charts, anything that might help us decipher what we find."

As they packed, the atmosphere in the office shifted from shock to a palpable sense of anticipation. The weight of their impending journey hung in the air, a mixture of excitement and trepidation that Andres could feel in his very bones.

We are on the verge of uncovering truths that could reshape our understanding of history, he thought, carefully stowing a set of delicate measuring tools. But at what cost?

Andres paused, his hand resting on an ancient Mapuche stone tucked away in his desk drawer. He closed his eyes, allowing the familiar weight of the carved stone to ground him. The voices of his ancestors seemed to whisper in his ears, a comforting reminder of his heritage and the wisdom it carried.

"Everything alright, Andres?" Jacquleine's gentle voice broke through his reverie.

He opened his eyes, offering her a slight smile. "Just... centering myself. There's so much at stake."

Jacqueline nodded, understanding in her eyes. "Your grandmother's teachings?"

"Yes," Andres replied, his voice softening. "Abuela Kallfü always said that true wisdom comes from listening to the earth and the spirits of those who came before us. I can't help but feel they're guiding us now."

He slipped the talisman into his pocket, its presence a constant reminder of the balance between the physical and spiritual worlds he sought to maintain.

"We're ready," Evelyn announced, hefting her backpack. "The van's packed, and Voss is already waiting outside."

Andres took a final look around his office, his gaze lingering on the maps and artifacts that had defined his life's work. "This journey... it's more than just an archaeological expedition. We're stepping into something far greater than ourselves."

"Scared?" Evelyn asked, a hint of challenge in her voice.

Andres shook his head, a determined glint in his eye. "No. Humbled. And ready."

As they filed out of the office, Andres was the last to leave. He paused at the threshold, his hand on the light switch. The weight of the moment wasn't lost on him—they were leaving behind the familiar world of academia and stepping into the unknown.

"May the wisdom of the ancients guide our path," he murmured, switching off the light and closing the door behind him.

The Next Day

Outside, the team assembled around the van under the pale light of dawn, their faces painted with a mixture of anticipation and resolve. Andres approached, his boots crunching against the gravel, a deep sense of unity settling over the group. Whatever personal conflicts simmered beneath the surface, they were united by a singular purpose—a discovery that could redefine their understanding of humanity's past and its cosmic destiny.

Evelyn leaned against the van, her arms crossed, a faint smile tugging at her lips. "So, are we ready for this?"

Jaqueline adjusted her satchel, her green eyes scanning the group with quiet determination. "Ready as we will ever be. But let us not forget—we are stepping into the unknown. Caution will serve us as much as courage."

Andres placed a hand on the van's door, nodding to each member of the team as they prepared for the two-and-a-half-hour journey. "This is it. Whatever lies ahead, we face it together. Keep your wits about you, and remember, this is not just about what we discover—it is about what we preserve."

The team murmured their agreement, their excitement tempered by the gravity of Andres's words. As the engine roared to life, the van began its journey toward the excavation site, carrying its passengers toward the threshold of ancient secrets and untold revelations.

Chapter 3

The ancient stones of Tiwanaku rose before them, silent sentinels guarding the secrets of a long-lost civilization. As Dr. Andres Paredes stepped out of the dust-covered SUV, a shiver ran down his spine. The Andean wind whispered through the ruins, carrying with it faint echoes of chanting voices, the clash of stone tools, and the rhythmic beat of ceremonial drums—sounds long buried beneath centuries of silence.

Tiwanaku's capital sprawled across the high-altitude plains like a masterpiece etched into the Andean landscape, strategically situated near the sacred waters of Lake Titicaca. This monumental city was not only a hub of advanced engineering but also a spiritual axis deeply connected to the myths of creation and cosmic balance. Towering stone blocks, some weighing more than 100 tons, were carved, and assembled with such precision that not even a blade of grass could slip between them, hinting at knowledge that rivaled—or perhaps surpassed—that of their contemporaries. Structures like the Akapana Pyramid and the Kalasasaya Temple were aligned with celestial events, marking solstices and equinoxes with astonishing accuracy. Tiwanaku's design reflected a profound understanding of sacred geometry, astronomy, and energy flows, integrating the principles of the Vesica Piscis to connect the city to a global energy grid. The proximity to Lake Titicaca, revered as the birthplace of the sun and humanity itself, imbued the site with mystical significance, positioning Tiwanaku as both a ceremonial center and a gateway to higher dimensions.

The Akapana Pyramid dominated the skyline, its eroded steps still conveying the grandeur of its original design. Believed to symbolize a sacred mountain, it had been a focal point for rituals that connected the heavens and the earth. Nearby, the Kalasasaya Temple stood in silent majesty, its massive stone walls and carved pillars aligned with celestial phenomena. The Gateway of the Sun, with its intricate reliefs of deities and celestial symbols, captured the first rays of the morning light, its carvings said to encode the cosmology of an ancient people whose understanding of the stars bordered on the divine.

Sophisticated drainage systems snaked beneath the city, an often-overlooked marvel of engineering that allowed this civilization to thrive in the harsh Andean highlands. Ceremonial plazas, now partially reclaimed by the earth, stretched wide with an air of solemnity, their sunken designs inviting visitors to descend into spaces that blurred the line between the physical and the spiritual.

Evelyn walked up to Andres, her expression one of reverence. "It's not just a city," she murmured. "It's a living map of their understanding—a reflection of the cosmos etched into stone."

Andres nodded, his gaze sweeping across the ruins. The scale, precision, and spiritual depth of Tiwanaku had an undeniable power, a magnetism that stirred something ancient within him. As he inhaled the crisp air tinged with the scent of wildflowers and the earthy musk of ancient stone, he felt an unshakable certainty: this was not merely a relic of the past. Tiwanaku was a gateway—to understanding, to transformation, and perhaps to something far beyond their comprehension.

"It's... calling to me," Andres murmured, his dark eyes scanning the weathered structures. He could almost hear his grandmother's voice, telling stories of their Mapuche ancestors and their connection to this sacred land.

Jaqueline emerged from the vehicle, her auburn hair whipping in the wind. "Fascinating," she breathed, already reaching for her equipment. "The Gateway of the Sun should provide crucial data on the site's celestial alignments."

Andres nodded, watching as she began setting up a portable laser scanner and theodolite. His gaze was drawn to the massive stone archway looming before them, its intricate carvings still visible after millennia.

"The Gateway," he said softly. "Our ancestors believed it to be a portal between worlds, connecting the earthly and the divine."

A rustling sound drew his attention, and he turned to see a figure emerging from the shadow of the Akapana Pyramid. Amaru, the elder of Tiwanaku, approached with the steady gait of one who had walked these lands for countless years. His lined face was a testament to his age and wisdom, but his eyes sparkled with a vitality that defied time. He was draped in traditional Andean attire, his vibrant poncho fluttering in the breeze, and his staff—a simple yet intricately carved piece of wood—clicked lightly against the stones as he walked.

"Andres," Amaru called out, his voice tinged with warmth and relief.

The elder reached out, his weathered hand resting firmly on Andres's shoulder. "It is good to see you again, my friend," he said, his voice deep and steady, carrying the weight of generations.

Andres embraced him, the bond of years spent exploring the mysteries of this land evident in the simple yet profound gesture.

"It's been too long," Andres said, pulling back to meet Amaru's gaze.

Amaru smiled faintly, his eyes searching Andres's face. "And yet, time is but an illusion here. The stones remember you."

Amaru, known as Yachayni among his people, was more than a guardian of Tiwanaku—he was its living memory. Born into a lineage of spiritual leaders stretching back to the last great keepers of Tiwanaku's wisdom, he carried the sacred responsibility of preserving the oral history and protecting the land's spiritual integrity. Some whispered that his ancestors held knowledge of Tiwanaku's connection to Atlantis. Others believed he was the last keeper of a prophecy foretelling the city's reawakening.

From childhood, Amaru was immersed in the ancient traditions of his people. He learned to read the signs in the wind, the whispers in the water, and the language of the stars. The elders taught him the sacred chants that aligned one's spirit with the cosmic forces and trained him to walk the line between the seen and unseen worlds.

As he grew, Amaru's wisdom deepened, and his role evolved. He became a bridge between past and future, a guardian of Tiwanaku's hidden truths. The world outside changed, forgetting the old ways, but Amaru remained steadfast, knowing that one day, the seekers of truth would return.

And now, standing before Andres, he knew this moment was another turning point in the great cycle of destiny.

As the team gathered near the edge of the ancient ruins, the distant cry of a condor echoed across the vast Andean plains. Andres glanced skyward, his breath catching as the majestic bird appeared, its massive wings slicing through the crisp air.

The condor soared overhead, its shadow momentarily casting a dark silhouette over the group. It began to descend, circling them in graceful, deliberate arcs. The movement was hypnotic—first wide loops, then narrowing until its flight pattern resembled the sacred Vesica Piscis. Each pass seemed to weave a message into the very air around them. The group stood in awe, their silence broken only by the whisper of wings and the faint rustle of grass beneath their feet. The condor's final arc brought it so low that they could see the sharp clarity of its eyes before it ascended again, vanishing into the bright horizon.

Andres turned to the team, motioning for them to step forward. "Amaru, these are my colleagues—Dr. Hart, Dr. Carter, and the rest of the team. They have come to uncover the truths Tiwanaku still guards."

Amaru stood at the threshold of the ruins, his weathered face illuminated by the soft, golden light of the setting sun. His gaze swept over the group, lingering on each person as though he were reading not just their faces but their very souls. His expression was unreadable, yet his eyes shone with an ancient wisdom that made each of them feel exposed, as though standing before a mirror reflecting their truest selves.

"You are welcome here," Amaru said at last, his voice carrying the cadence of the mountains, both firm and gentle. "Tiwanaku is a place of truths—some ancient, some yet to be revealed. But know this: its secrets are not given freely. The answers you seek will test your spirits as much as your minds."

He paused, his words hanging in the air like an unspoken challenge. "Beware—truth can be both a gift and a burden. It will ask of you more than you know."

The team exchanged uneasy glances, the weight of Amaru's words sinking in. Yet beneath the trepidation, a spark of determination flickered in their eyes. They had come too far to turn back now.

Andres stepped forward, placing a hand over his heart in a gesture of respect. "We understand, Amaru. We are ready."

Amaru's gaze softened just enough to hint at approval. "Then let the journey begin."

Evelyn stepped forward, her reverence palpable. "It is an honor to meet you, Amaru. Andres has spoken of you often."

Amaru's lips curled into a faint smile. "And he has spoken of you, Dr. Carter. The paths we walk are woven together, even when we cannot yet see the pattern."

Andres turned to the group. "Amaru and I go back many years. He has guided me through the mysteries of this place and others like it. If anyone can help us navigate what lies ahead, it is him."

Amaru gestured toward the towering ruins behind him, the majesty of Tiwanaku unfolding in the golden light of late afternoon.

"Come. The stones are waiting," Amaru's gravelly voice carried on the wind, commanding their attention. "Let me show you the heart of Tiwanaku."

As they walked, Amaru's measured steps seemed to fall in rhythm with an unseen pulse of the earth. The group trailed behind, captivated by the magnetism of his presence. His voice took on a lyrical quality, weaving a tapestry of legend and history as the Andean sun cast a golden light over the ruins.

"Here, in the ceremonial center," he began, sweeping his arm across the vast expanse before them, "our ancestors communed with the gods. The Akapana Pyramid," he pointed to the massive, terraced structure in the distance, "was our sacred mountain, bridging earth and sky. Its waters purified not just the body, but the soul. When the rain fell, it was seen as the gods' blessing, flowing through these channels to nourish the land and its people."

Dr. Hart, the analytical astro-archaeologist, studied the pyramid with awe. "The engineering required to build this... it is remarkable. Look at the symmetry and the terracing. It is as if it mirrors the Andean peaks around it."

Amaru nodded, a hint of pride in his smile. "The Tiwanaku understood balance in all things. Their structures reflected the cosmos itself. They were not just architects; they were guardians of harmony."

He led them toward the Kalasasaya Temple, a space imbued with solemnity even in its weathered state. "This is the Temple of the Standing Stones," Amaru explained, gesturing to the stone pillars that marked its edges. "During the solstices, this place came alive with light and shadow, aligning humanity with the rhythms of the stars. It was here that offerings were made to ensure the cycles of life continued unbroken."

A man approached joining the group, his piercing eyes fixed on the monolithic structure. "Quite the feat of engineering," he remarked coolly, running a hand along the precisely fitted stones. "These joints are still nearly seamless after all this time."

Andres fought a twinge of unease at the man's clinical assessment. There was something in his demeanor that set him on edge, a hunger that seemed at odds with the site's spiritual significance.

"Yes… and you are?" asked Andres sternly."

Julian Blackwood turned his gaze toward Andres, his expression unreadable. "Julian Blackwood. I am here with the same purpose as you, Dr. Paredes," he replied smoothly. "To uncover the secrets of Tiwanaku. To bring its ancient wisdom into the light of modern understanding."

Andres, surprised, asks," Have we met before?"

Julian's lips curved into a faint smile, his tone remaining calm yet carrying an undercurrent of calculation. "You may remember I was the one who asked about the possible alignment between Tiwanaku's ceremonial structures and the Earth's energy grid at the World Archaeological Congress in Lima last year."

Andres's brow furrowed as the memory surfaced. "I do remember," he said slowly. "You asked if I thought these alignments were intentional or coincidental—if the ancients understood the energy grid as we theorize it today."

Julian nodded, his gaze steady. "Your answer intrigued me. You spoke of patterns that repeat across ancient civilizations, how their knowledge might have been more unified than we realize."

Andres studied him, feeling the tension between his words and his demeanor. "I also mentioned that understanding those patterns requires humility, not just curiosity. These sites aren't just artifacts of history—they're alive, and their wisdom needs to be approached with respect."

Julian's smile widened slightly, though it did not reach his eyes. "A sentiment I deeply admire, Doctor. After all, reverence is the first step toward unlocking true potential, wouldn't you agree?"

Andres's jaw tightened. Something about Julian's measured words and the way he avoided direct answers raised his defenses. "And what, exactly, do you consider true potential, Blackwood?"

Julian chuckled softly, turning his gaze back to the towering stones of Tiwanaku. "Potential," he said, "is the ability to transform the world. To bridge the gap between what was and what could be."

"I see," Andres answered, stepping closer. "Are you here to study Tiwanaku or to exploit it?"

Julian's expression grew serious, his piercing gaze meeting Andres's. "I'm here to ensure its secrets are not wasted," he said quietly. "Some knowledge is too important to remain buried, wouldn't you agree?"

Andres crossed his arms, his instincts screaming caution. "That depends on who decides how that knowledge is used."

"Indeed," Julian replied, a cryptic edge to his voice. "And that's why I intend to make sure it's used wisely."

"I see," Andres answered.

As the tension between them grew, Evelyn approached cautiously, her expression wary. In a wary and calm but firm voice, she said," Perhaps we can table this philosophical debate until after we've actually uncovered something."

Julian smiled again, the tension seemingly dissipating. "Of course. Forgive me, Dr. Paredes. It seems my enthusiasm got the better of me."

Andres did not reply immediately, his sharp gaze tracking Julian's every move. Finally, he gave a curt nod. "Let's focus on the work, then."

But as Julian turned away, Andres felt a knot of unease tightening in his chest. There was something about Julian's presence—a quiet, insidious ambition lurking beneath his polished demeanor—that set off warning bells in Andres's mind. It reminded him of the very forces he had spent his career uncovering and opposing, hidden in the shadows of history. His instinct whispered that Julian did not belong with them, that his presence could jeopardize everything. Andres hesitated, torn between speaking up and trusting the process, unsure whether to ask him not to join the group.

"What do you sense here, Andres?" Evelyn asked, pausing in her work to study his face. "Your connection to this place could prove invaluable."

Andres closed his eyes, allowing the energy of Tiwanaku to wash over him. "There's... power here," he said slowly. "But also balance.

The Tiwanaku people understood harmony with nature in a way we've forgotten."

Overhearing, Julian scoffed lightly. "Charming folklore, but hardly scientific."

"Science isn't everything," Andres countered, a hint of steel in his voice. "Our ancestors possessed wisdom we're only beginning to rediscover."

As the team continued to set up their equipment, Andres found his gaze continually drawn back to the Gateway of the Sun. Its weathered face seemed to hold countless untold stories, waiting to be unlocked.

"We're on the cusp of something monumental," he thought, a mixture of excitement and trepidation coursing through him. "But at what cost?"

The wind picked up, carrying the faintest hint of whispers in an unknown tongue. Andres shivered, sensing that Tiwanaku held far greater mysteries than any of them could imagine.

As the group took in the magnificence of their surroundings, Evelyn broke away, drawn to the intricate carvings on the Gateway of the Sun. She crouched before the glyphs, pulling out a small notebook, her pen flying across the page as she muttered to herself.

"These glyphs," she called out, excitement tinged with disbelief, "they are unlike anything I've seen before. Andres, Dr. Hart, come look at this."

Andres and Jaqueline joined her, curiosity ignited by her urgency. Amaru lingered nearby, his expression unreadable, as though he were watching a story unfold for the second time.

"What do you make of it?" Andres asked, his voice hushed with reverence as he studied the carvings.

Dr. Carter's brow furrowed in concentration. "It is clearly a calendar of some sort, but the complexity... it is astounding. Look here," she pointed to the central figure, "this could represent Viracocha, the creator god."

"Or perhaps," Jacqueline interjected, "it is a map of cosmic alignments. See how the rays emanate outward? This could represent the position of celestial bodies during significant events."

As the scientists debated, Andres felt a familiar tingle at the base of his skull. The stone seemed to pulse with an inner light, visible only to him. Drawn by an unseen force, he reached out and placed his hand on the carving. The air shifted around him, growing heavy yet electric. For a moment, the world fell away.

Andres's vision blurred, and for a fleeting moment, he was elsewhere. Tiwanaku unfolded before him, not as the ancient ruins they stood among, but as a thriving, vibrant city in its prime. The ceremonial center was alive with activity, its polished stone plazas filled with people in garments of brilliant reds, golds, and deep blues. Their chants resonated through the air, a harmonious symphony that seemed to ripple through the very fabric of existence. Golden light poured through the Gateway of the Sun, illuminating the intricate carvings, and casting ethereal patterns on the ground. Priests and priestesses moved gracefully, their movements synchronized with the rhythms of the cosmos, performing rituals that seemed to bind the heavens and the earth.

The Akapana Pyramid rose in the distance, an imposing yet elegant structure that radiated an almost tangible energy. Streams of water cascaded down its carefully engineered terraces, reflecting the sunlight in dazzling patterns. Surrounding the pyramid, the Kalasasaya Temple stood as a monument to the civilization's mastery over stone and sky, its massive blocks fitted so perfectly that no mortar was needed. The carvings on its walls pulsed with life, their astronomical precision speaking to an unparalleled understanding of the stars.

The vision faded as quickly as it had come, leaving Andres standing amidst the silence of the ruins. His heart raced, not from fear, but from the profound sense that Tiwanaku's spirit still lingered, whispering its truths to those who would listen.

A voice, soft but commanding, echoed in his mind. "Remember, you are the bridge between the past and the future. The answers lie not in what you see, but in what you feel."

Andres gasped and stumbled backward, the vision fading as quickly as it had come. Amaru's steady hand caught his arm, grounding him.

"You have felt it, haven't you?" Amaru asked quietly, his tone almost conspiratorial.

Andres nodded, still trying to process what he had experienced. "There's something here... something alive."

Amaru smiled knowingly. "Tiwanaku is not just stone and history. It is a heartbeat, a message waiting to be understood. And it has chosen you to hear it."

The moment left the team shaken yet resolute. Even the skeptical Julian Blackwood, standing apart, seemed momentarily humbled. They gathered, unified by an unspoken understanding that their mission had become more than just uncovering ancient secrets—it was about protecting something timeless and sacred.

Dr. Elera Voss's piercing gray eyes scanned the weathered stones of Tiwanaku, her tall, gaunt figure casting a long shadow across the ancient site. She moved with measured grace, pausing periodically to scribble notes in her leather-bound journal.

"Fascinating," she murmured, her voice carrying a hint of clinical detachment. "The stonework here shows evidence of advanced tool use far beyond what we'd expect for this period."

Andres approached; his curiosity piqued. "What are you seeing, Dr. Voss?"

Elera's lips curled into a thin smile. "These precise angles, the seamless joins—they suggest a level of technological sophistication that challenges our current understanding of human evolution in this region." She ran her fingers along a perfectly smooth edge, her touch almost reverent. "This isn't just craftsmanship; it's a window into a civilization that may have been far more advanced than we've given them credit for."

Julian Blackwood scoffed from nearby. "Or perhaps they simply had exceptional stonemasons. Not everything needs to be a grand mystery, Elera."

Elera's eyes flashed with irritation. "And not everything can be explained away by conventional thinking. We must be open to all possibilities."

As the team gathered around the Gateway of the Sun, the air crackled with intellectual tension. Jacqueline spoke up, her voice filled with wonder. "The astronomical alignments here are incredibly precise. This wasn't just a religious site—it was an observatory of incredible sophistication."

Andres nodded, feeling a deep connection to the ancient wisdom surrounding them. "Maybe it was both. A place where the physical and spiritual realms intersected."

Amaru's eyes lit up. "Yes! Our legends speak of Tiwanaku as a bridge between worlds, a portal to other dimensions."

Julian rolled his eyes. "Portals and dimensions? We're scientists, not science fiction writers."

Elera surprised everyone by coming to Amaru's defense. "Actually, Julian, recent theories in quantum physics suggest the possibility of intersecting dimensions. We shouldn't dismiss local knowledge so readily."

As the debate intensified, Andres found himself caught between the competing viewpoints, each perspective adding depth to their understanding of Tiwanaku's enigmatic purpose. He closed his eyes, trying to make sense of the swirling theories and the strange vision he had experienced earlier.

What are you trying to tell us? 'he thought, reaching out with his mind to the ancient stones around him. *What secrets are you protecting?*

As the team explored the ruins, the air around Tiwanaku seemed to grow heavier, thick with an energy that Andres could not quite place. Suddenly, a sharp, searing pain shot through his temples. He staggered, gripping the side of the Kalasasaya Temple for support as the world around him blurred and distorted.

"Andres?" Evelyn's voice called out, faint and distant.

Before he could respond, the landscape around him shifted. Andres found himself plunged into a vivid, terrifying vision. The Earth's ley lines, usually invisible to the naked eye, glowed an ominous, sickly green, pulsating with unstable energy. Cracks formed along the grid, spreading like a spiderweb across the globe. Ancient structures—Stonehenge, the Great Pyramid, Tiwanaku itself—shook violently, their foundations crumbling. Above, the sky darkened as storm clouds swirled, lightning illuminating scenes of chaos.

In the vision, Andres saw hazy, spectral figures locked in combat. Their forms were indistinct, but he recognized their movements—the grace and power of the Atlantean priest-warriors of the Law of One clashing with the dark forces of the Brotherhood of Belial. Each strike in their battle sent shockwaves rippling through the grid, further destabilizing it. A final, catastrophic tremor erupted, shattering the vision. Andres fell to his knees, gasping for breath, as the world around him came rushing back.

"Andres! Are you okay?" Evelyn at his side, gripping his shoulder with concern.

"What happened?" Julian Blackwood demanded, his voice sharp with what might have been worry—or something else.

Andres struggled to his feet, his head pounding. His eyes darted between his companions. "I saw... the grid. It is collapsing, just like in Atlantis. If we don't act, everything will fall apart again."

Elera frowned, her expression skeptical but not dismissive. "The global energy grid? Andres, that is purely theoretical. We have no concrete evidence to—"

"No," Andres interrupted, his voice steadier now. "It is real. And it is in danger. We are running out of time."

As the team exchanged uneasy glances, Andres's instincts flared. He noticed something subtle but telling: Julian and Elera shared a brief, loaded look. Julian's jaw tensed, and Elera's hand twitched as though she were reaching for something in her pocket.

Andres's grandmother's voice echoed in his mind: "*Trust your intuition, mijo. It will guide you through the darkness.*"

He straightened, his gaze fixed on Julian and Elera. "What aren't you telling us?"

Julian raised an eyebrow, his expression carefully neutral. "I am not sure what you mean, Andres. We are all here for the same purpose, aren't we?"

"Are we?" Andres pressed, his voice hardening. "And because I'm starting to wonder if there might be other agendas at play here."

The tension in the air thickened, almost tangible. Evelyn and Jacqueline exchanged worried glances, while Amaru stood silently, his sharp eyes observing the unfolding confrontation.

Julian's lips curved into a faint, disarming smile. "Let us not jump to conclusions, Andres. Tensions are high, but we are all here to uncover the truth about Tiwanaku."

"Then why do I feel like you're not telling me everything?" Andres shot back, his instincts screaming at him to push further. "And ...you just appeared out of thin air!"

Elera finally spoke, her tone calm but clipped. "We all have our specialties, Andres. Not everything needs to be shared until we have something definitive to report."

Andres's eyes narrowed. "Or until it serves your purpose."

For a moment, silence hung over the group like a storm cloud. Andres could feel the weight of their mistrust and the crackling undercurrent of secrets.

"Enough," Amaru's voice cut through the tension like a blade.

His weathered hand rested on Andres's shoulder, grounding him. "Tiwanaku has witnessed many struggles—some of power, some of truth. Do not let this place see another. If there are secrets, they will reveal themselves in time. Trust the earth. Trust the signs."

Andres reluctantly nodded, but his unease did not abate. The vision of the collapsing grid still burned in his mind, and his growing suspicion of Julian and Elera gnawed at him like a thorn. Whatever they were hiding, he was determined to uncover it before it was too late.

Andres took a deep breath, feeling the ancient stones beneath his feet pulse with energy. He ran his fingers through his hair, centering himself, before addressing the team with renewed purpose.

"Amaru's right," he said, his voice carrying a quiet strength. "We can't let our differences divide us. Tiwanaku has called us here for a reason, and we have a responsibility to uncover its secrets—and protect them."

Jacqueline's eyes met his, a silent understanding passing between them. She stepped forward, her face shimmering in the fading sunlight. "The wisdom of this place is both a gift and a burden," she intoned. "We must approach it with humility and unity."

Evelyn pushed her glasses up, her skepticism evident. "And how do you propose we do that, exactly? We've just witnessed something that defies scientific explanation."

Andres felt a surge of determination as the tension in the room grew palpable. He could sense the team teetering on the edge of discord, and he knew his next words would be crucial in uniting them.

"By embracing both our scientific minds and our intuition, we'll uncover what's hidden here," he said, his voice steady and resolute. "Evelyn, your expertise in decoding the inscriptions is invaluable. Jacqueline, your deep understanding of celestial alignments and ancient languages will help us unravel the layers of meaning embedded in this place. Elera, your evolutionary perspective might reveal how Tiwanaku fits into the broader tapestry of human history."

Andres's gaze shifted to Julian, who had been leaning casually against the wall, his sharp eyes betraying a hint of skepticism. "And Julian…" Andres hesitated, searching for a way to frame the man's enigmatic role. "Your insights will be useful.

Amaru, who had remained silent until now, finally stepped forward. His presence was grounding, his calm demeanor a stark contrast to the group's growing unease. "We must also honor the spirit of this place," Amaru said, his voice rich with conviction. "Tiwanaku is not just stone and history—it is alive. The ancestors whisper here, guiding those who will listen. The path forward will demand more than knowledge; it will demand humility and balance."

Andres nodded, grateful for Amaru's timely words. "Exactly. This is not just an academic puzzle—it is a journey of trust, intuition, and respect for the wisdom that came before us."

He noticed Julian's faint smirk, the flicker of something unreadable in his expression. Andres's gut churned with unease; the same instinct that had flared the moment Julian joined the team. Andres could not shake the feeling that he was playing a game of his own. For now, Andres decided to keep his concerns quiet, hoping that whatever agenda Julian carried would not unravel the fragile unity they were trying to build.

As the group absorbed his words, Andres felt the tension ease ever so slightly. But deep down, he knew this was only the beginning. The mysteries of Tiwanaku—and the secrets each of them carried—would test them all in ways they could hardly imagine.

He turned, meeting each team member's gaze. "But we must also be open to what we can't immediately explain. The energy here is palpable. The visions we've seen are real, even if we don't yet understand their source."

Dr. Carter sighed but nodded reluctantly. "I suppose there's no harm in considering... unconventional explanations, as long as we maintain our scientific rigor."

Andres felt a glimmer of hope. "Exactly. Now, let us prepare for tomorrow. We will need to—"

A sudden gust of wind interrupted him, carrying with it the faintest whisper of an unfamiliar language. The team exchanged uneasy glances.

"What was that?" Julian asked, his usual composure slipping.

Andres's hand instinctively went to the pouch of sacred herbs his grandmother had given him. "A reminder," he said grimly, "that Tiwanaku isn't finished with us yet. We need to be ready for anything."

As the team dispersed to gather their equipment, Andres could not shake the feeling that they were being watched. He caught Amaru's eye, and he gave him a slight nod. Whatever challenges lay ahead, they would face them together— even as the web of trust and suspicion around them grew ever more complex.

Chapter 4

The fading light of dusk cast long shadows across the ancient stones of Tiwanaku, their surfaces slick with the damp kiss of the Andean mist. Dr. Andres Paredes knelt beside the wall, his fingers brushing against the cold, weathered surface. The faint markings he had been searching for danced just out of reach, concealed beneath layers of grime and moss. His breath quickened, and he rubbed at the stone frantically, feeling a growing desperation in his chest.

"This has to be it," he muttered, glancing at the scroll clutched in his trembling hand.

The faded Atlantean glyphs whispered possibilities, their meaning tantalizingly close. He traced a faint symbol hidden beneath the grime—a circle intersected by another. His heart leaped.

"The Vesica Piscis," he whispered, his voice trembling with equal parts triumph and disbelief. "It is here. The gateway is here."

Evelyn straightened, her brow furrowed, the dim light of her scanner flickering on the stone. "Andres, we have combed this site for days. Are you sure you are not grasping at shadows?"

He did not answer, his focus razor-sharp on the faint geometry beneath his hands. "It is not shadows. It is ancient concealment," he said, voice tight. "The symbol is designed to mislead the eye."

Amaru stepped closer, his weathered face unreadable in the gloom. He placed a steadying hand on Andres's shoulder, then pressed his other palm against the wall. "These stones have lived many lifetimes," he said softly. "Let them speak."

As Amaru closed his eyes, his deep voice began to hum a low, haunting melody, the sound ancient and resonant. It grew louder, filling the air with a vibration that seemed to seep into the bones of the ruin.

The ground trembled faintly beneath their feet, and Evelyn staggered back, her scanner emitting frantic beeps. "I'm picking up massive seismic activity—what the hell is happening?"

Andres pressed closer to the wall; his breath caught in his throat. A deep groan of shifting stone echoed through the ruins, and then, with a heart-stopping crack, a fissure appeared in the wall. Dust and debris rained down as a section of the ancient structure split apart. The opening was jagged and narrow, revealing only darkness beyond. Andres and Evelyn froze, awe overtaking caution. Amaru stood unmoved, a small, knowing smile playing on his lips.

"Did you know this would happen?" Andres asked, his voice a mix of disbelief and exhilaration.

"The old ones hide their paths well," Amaru said simply. "But they welcome those who listen."

Andres moved first, stepping into the passage, his flashlight slicing through the pitch-black void. The air was cool and heavy, carrying the faint tang of minerals and something else—something almost electric. Evelyn and Amaru followed closely, the rest nearby, their movements cautious but eager.

As they descended into the narrow passage, the walls began to shimmer faintly, a soft blue glow emanating from carvings and symbols that seemed to come alive under their touch. Andres's breath hitched as he ran his fingers over the intricate patterns, his mind racing with recognition.

"This is..." He stopped, unable to find words. His voice cracked with emotion. "This is more than I ever imagined."

Evelyn stared in wonder, tears welling in her eyes. "Andres, we have found it. We have really found it!"

For a moment, all three stood together, suspended in awe. After years of searching and endless setbacks, they had pierced the veil of Tiwanaku's greatest mystery. And somewhere, in the depths of the ancient passage, something was waiting for them—something that would change everything.

Their reverent silence was shattered by the sudden roar of helicopter blades. Andres exchanged a worried glance with Amaru as they hurried back to the surface. The low thrum of rotor blades grew louder as the sleek, black helicopter descended onto the makeshift landing pad near Tiwanaku's outskirts. The Airbus was as polished and imposing as Sebastian Thorne himself, its gleaming surface reflecting the golden hues of the setting sun. Dust swirled in the air, the force of the blades creating a vortex that seemed to momentarily disrupt the stillness of the ancient site.

Thorne stood at the edge of the site, his tailored suit somehow immune to the chaos of wind and dust. His expression was unreadable, a mask of calm composure that belied the urgency with which he had insisted on his sudden appearance.

Andres watched from a distance, his arms crossed, unease gnawing at him. Thorne had been unusually cryptic in their last conversation, offering only vague reassurances that he would return soon with "resources to advance their work."

"Dr. Paredes! Dr. Carter! What a marvelous discovery," he effused, shaking their hands enthusiastically. "When I heard you'd made a breakthrough, I simply had to come see for myself."

Andres's brow furrowed. "Mr. Thorne, I wasn't aware we'd informed anyone of our findings yet."

Sebastian waved a hand dismissively. "Oh, word travels fast in archaeological circles. Now, tell me everything! The symbol... the Vesica Piscis, is it not? Fascinating use of sacred geometry by the ancients."

As Sebastian continued to charm the team with his apparent knowledge and excitement, Andres felt a prickle of unease. Thorne's charm was disarming, but something about his timing—about *him*—felt too precise, too deliberate. Andres caught Amaru's eye, seeing his own wariness reflected in the shaman's gaze. He stepped back, his posture tense as if Thorne's arrival had disrupted the sacred energy of the site.

Amaru leaned close and whispered, "Andres, that man walks with too much certainty for someone who just stumbled upon us."

Andres nodded.

Thorne clapped his hands together, breaking the tension. "Well then, shall we proceed? I would not miss the next chapter of this adventure for the world."

Andres observed Thorne closely as Andres led them back through the passageway into the chamber. Thorne walked with a confidence that felt unnatural. He seemed to know where to step, which ancient symbols to avoid, and even how to activate subtle mechanisms etched into the walls, Andres thought.

"Fascinating, isn't it?" Thorne said, his voice smooth as polished marble. He gestured toward an intricate mural depicting a celestial alignment. "The Atlanteans had such an advanced understanding of the cosmos. Imagine what humanity could achieve with this knowledge."

Andres nodded but kept his thoughts guarded. "It's remarkable, but also a bit overwhelming. We still don't fully understand the purpose of this chamber."

Thorne smiled, but there was something predatory in his expression. "That's precisely why I'm here—to help. My resources are at your disposal, Dr. Paredes. Together, we can unlock these secrets and ensure they're used for the benefit of all."

The words were generous, yet they carried an edge that set Andres on high alert. He could feel the weight of Thorne's gaze, like a predator assessing prey.

"Your interest in this project is... unexpected," Andres ventured, keeping his tone neutral. "You've been very supportive of funding many of our projects, but I have to wonder—what drew you to Tiwanaku in the first place, Mr. Thorne?"

Thorne's expression did not waver. "Curiosity, Dr. Paredes. And a sense of duty. Humanity is at a crossroads, and I believe the past holds the key to our future. Don't you agree?"

Andres hesitated, sensing the veiled challenge in Thorne's words. "I do. But I also believe that knowledge like this must be approached with caution and respect."

"Of course," Thorne said smoothly, but his eyes betrayed a flicker of impatience. "Which is why it's fortunate you have someone like me to guide the process. You are a brilliant archaeologist, Andres, but this discovery requires more than academic expertise. It requires vision. And courage."

Andres felt the tension between them crystalizing, a subtle battle of wills beneath the surface of their conversation. He did not trust Thorne—his presence was too convenient, his knowledge too precise, and his motives too opaque. He remembers also his tendency to be controlling, abrupt, and demanding.

As they continued deeper into the chamber, Andres noticed how Thorne seemed drawn to specific artifacts and symbols, lingering over them as if they held personal significance. At one point, Thorne paused before a series of interlocking symbols shaped like the Vesica Piscis. His fingers traced the carvings with an almost reverent touch.

"This is it," Thorne murmured, more to himself than to Andres.

Andres stepped closer. "What do you mean?"

Thorne's expression shifted, a flicker of something unguarded—determination, perhaps, or obsession. "Nothing. Just admiring the craftsmanship."

But Andres was not convinced. There was no mistaking the intensity in Thorne's gaze, as though he had uncovered something he had been searching for a very long time. The encounter left Andres deeply unsettled. Thorne was undeniably charismatic and persuasive, his words weaving a vision of progress and discovery that was hard to resist. Yet, there was a shadow behind his polished exterior—a driving force that hinted at deeper, possibly darker motivations.

This was not the first time Andres had felt a pang of distrust toward his enigmatic benefactor. A memory surfaced, unbidden, from their expedition in Egypt a year earlier. Thorne had funded a dig near the Giza Plateau, claiming it would unearth artifacts that could rewrite history. At first, it had seemed like a noble cause, one aligned with Andres's passion for uncovering humanity's forgotten past.

But as the excavation progressed, Andres had witnessed troubling behavior. Thorne had pressured local workers into longer hours, dismissing their complaints of exhaustion and unsafe conditions. He had even dismissed warnings from conservationists about the fragile state of the ancient structures they were exploring.

One particularly glaring incident stood out in Andres's mind—a chamber containing delicate wall carvings that had survived millennia. Against Andres's protests, Thorne had ordered the carvings to be forcibly removed, citing their "critical importance" to the mission. The operation had damaged the artifacts irreparably. When Andres confronted him, Thorne brushed it off with a cold, calculated response: "History only remembers the results, Dr. Paredes, not the methods."

That moment had planted a seed of doubt, but it had been overshadowed by the dazzling opportunities Thorne offered. Now, in the dimly lit chamber, with the weight of the Atlantean prophecy hanging heavy in the air, those doubts grew into a gnawing certainty. There was a pattern to Thorne's actions—a willingness to cut corners, to manipulate, to sacrifice ethical boundaries in the pursuit of his goals.

As they exited the chamber, Andres resolved to keep a closer eye on his benefactor. He could not afford to let his guard down—not when so much was at stake. The ancient scrolls, the Crystal Skull, the interdimensional portal—these were not just relics of the past; they were keys to humanity's future. And in the wrong hands, they could lead to devastating consequences.

Andres's grip tightened on the journal he carried, its pages filled with his notes and observations. He silently vowed to document everything, to uncover Thorne's true motivations before it was too late.

Andres's eyes narrowed as he watched Sebastian effortlessly command the team's attention, his charisma as polished as his leather Oxfords. There was something off about the man's enthusiasm, a hint of calculation behind the dazzling smile.

"Remarkable craftsmanship," Sebastian mused, running his fingers along an ornate carving. "The precision rivals even Machu Picchu."

Andres's jaw clenched. "Interesting comparison. I wasn't aware you had expertise in Pre-Columbian architecture."

Sebastian's laugh was smooth as silk. "Oh, just a passionate amateur, Dr. Paredes. I find all ancient mysteries utterly captivating."

"Indeed," Andres murmured, noting how Sebastian's gaze lingered a beat too long on certain artifacts. *What are you really after?* he thought to himself.

Evelyn's crisp voice cut through Andres's brooding. "Mr. Thorne, your insight on the Vesica Piscis was quite astute. Perhaps you would care to examine these inscriptions with me?"

Andres watched as Evelyn led Sebastian to a far wall, her usual skepticism seemingly set aside. He tried to quell his rising anxiety. *Am I being paranoid, or is there truly something sinister at play?*

"These glyphs," Evelyn was saying, her green eyes alight with intellectual fervor, "they're unlike anything I've encountered. See how this symbol repeats? It could be a phonetic marker, or perhaps..."

She trailed off, fingers tracing the intricate carvings. Sebastian leaned in close, his breath stirring her auburn hair.

"Fascinating," he purred. "What do you make of this circular pattern here?"

Andres's fists clenched involuntarily. He forced himself to breathe, to focus. Stay alert. Watch for any slip in his mask. The truth always reveals itself, if you know where to look.

As Evelyn's linguistic expertise began to unravel the chamber's secrets, Andres kept a wary eye on their unexpected guest, determined to uncover Sebastian Thorne's true motives—before it was too late.

Evelyn's eyes widened as she deciphered more of the intricate symbols. "This... this is extraordinary," she breathed, her voice trembling with excitement. "These inscriptions speak of a 'golden city beyond the sea.' It is... it is unmistakably referring to Atlantis!"

Sebastian's eyebrows arched. "Atlantis? Are you certain?"

"As certain as I can be," Evelyn replied, pushing her glasses up her nose. "Look here—this glyph represents a great wave, and beside it, a symbol I've only seen in supposed Atlantean artifacts. The connection is... it's unprecedented."

Andres moved closer, his curiosity momentarily overriding his suspicion. "What else does it say, Evelyn?"

She ran her fingers over the inscriptions, her brow furrowed in concentration. "It speaks of 'brothers across the waters,' and 'shared wisdom of the stars.' It seems Tiwanaku and Atlantis weren't just aware of each other—they were allies, or perhaps even sister civilizations."

Sebastian's eyes glittered with an intensity that made Andres uneasy. "Fascinating," he murmured. "And what of their... capabilities? Any mention of advanced technologies or... evolutionary leaps?"

Evelyn hesitated, her excitement dimming slightly. "It's... difficult to say. There are references to 'powers beyond mortal ken,' but that could mean anything in a spiritual context."

Andres noticed Sebastian's jaw tighten almost imperceptibly. *Why is he so interested in their power?* he wondered. *What is his angle here?*

"Perhaps," Sebastian said smoothly, "we should explore further. Who knows what other secrets this chamber might hold?"

As the team moved deeper into the ancient space, Andres could not shake the feeling that they were treading on dangerous ground. Sebastian's gaze kept darting to specific artifacts, his expression hardening whenever evolution or advanced abilities were mentioned.

A sudden chill swept through the chamber, causing the hairs on Andres's arms to stand on end. He glanced at Amaru, whose weathered face had gone taut with tension. The elder's eyes darted to the shadows beyond their light, his grip tightening on his wooden staff.

Evelyn's voice cut through the eerie silence, her typically measured tone tinged with unease. "Did anyone else hear that? It sounded like... whispers."

Andres strained his ears, catching the faintest rustle of movement in the darkness. His heart began to race. "We're not alone," he murmured.

Amaru's gravelly voice carried a weight of foreboding. "The Sons of Belial. They watch us from the shadows, Andres. Agents of the Brotherhood, here to interfere with our work."

A cold dread settled in Andres's stomach. He had heard whispers of the Brotherhood before, but to have them here, now... "How can, you be sure?" he asked, his voice barely above a whisper.

Amaru's eyes met his, filled with ancient wisdom and grim certainty. "I feel their presence. The air itself grows heavy with their dark intentions."

Jaqueline placed a comforting hand on Evelyn's arm. "Perhaps we should—"

Her words were cut short by a muffled sound from a secluded corner. Andres turned to see Sebastian, his back to the group, speaking in hushed, urgent tones into a sleek satellite phone.

"...critical juncture... need to move quickly... Yes, I understand the stakes." Sebastian's voice was barely audible, but the tension in his posture spoke volumes.

Andres's mind raced, grappling with the surreal tension in the chamber. *Who—or what—was he talking to? And what "stakes" could possibly be at play here?* The air felt thick, almost charged, and the room, once alive with the thrill of discovery, now seemed oppressive, its towering walls closing in.

He glanced back at Amaru, who stood as still as a statue, his face lined with both resolve and worry. The elder's silence spoke volumes.

We are in over our heads, Andres thought, his stomach twisting. *And I fear we have only glimpsed the edge of the abyss.*

The dimly lit chamber seemed to hold its breath. Shadows pooled unnaturally in the corners, shifting in ways that defied logic, and a low, almost imperceptible hum began to vibrate through the air. It was not the sound of machinery or stone grinding—it was something deeper, something primal.

Andres felt a sudden coldness in the pit of his stomach as an overwhelming sensation washed over him—a presence, dark and unyielding, bearing down upon them. It was as if the very essence of the Sons of Belial had seeped into the room, turning the atmosphere heavy and electric.

"Do you feel that?" Evelyn's voice broke the silence, her usually steady tone now trembling.

Andres nodded, his hand instinctively tightening around the flashlight. "It's them," he murmured, his voice barely audible. "The Sons of Belial. Their energy... it's here."

Amaru took a step forward, his staff tapping softly against the stone floor. He closed his eyes, his lips moving in a silent prayer or incantation. The oppressive energy seemed to push back against him, an invisible force testing his resolve.

And then, like a dagger slicing through the tension, a deep voice echoed through the chamber.

"You've gone too far, Dr. Paredes."

The words were disembodied, their origin impossible to pinpoint. They reverberated off the ancient walls, carrying an authority and menace that made Andres's skin crawl. He turned sharply, his eyes scanning the shadows for the speaker, but there was no one.

"Who's there?" Evelyn demanded, her voice breaking under the strain of the moment.

No answer came, only a palpable increase in the energy swirling around them. The shadows seemed to shift again, and for a moment, Andres thought he saw a pair of glowing red eyes staring out from the darkness. But they vanished as quickly as they had appeared, leaving behind only the echo of a cruel, mocking laughter.

"Andres," Amaru said sharply, his voice cutting through the tension. "We must move. Now."

Andres tore his gaze from the shadows, his heart pounding. "What was that?" he asked, his voice low.

"The Belial," Amaru replied, his face grim. "The Sons of Belial. They know we are here, and they are watching. Their power grows in this place. If we linger, we risk more than we understand."

Andres exchanged a glance with Evelyn, who looked pale but resolute. Whatever forces were at work here, they were no longer just exploring history. They were walking into the heart of an ancient conflict, one that threatened to consume them all.

What have we stumbled into? Andres thought, his hand unconsciously tracing the Vesica Piscis symbol etched into his pendant. *And how in the world are we going to navigate it?*

As the sun dipped below the horizon, casting long shadows across the ancient ruins, Sebastian Thorne led Dr. Voss and General Kaine to a secluded alcove hidden from prying eyes. The air was thick with tension, matching the gravity of their clandestine meeting.

Sebastian's voice was low and measured, his eyes gleaming with calculated intensity. "Our patience is about to pay off. Andres's team is closer than ever to uncovering the Crystal Skull."

Dr. Voss's lips curled into a sneer. "And the Vesica Piscis symbols. Do not forget those, Sebastian. They're the key to everything."

Kaine's scarred face tightened, his red eyes glowing in the dim light. "We're taking unnecessary risks. Why not simply take what we need by force?"

Sebastian raised an eyebrow, his tone dripping with condescension. "And risk damaging the artifacts? Or worse, alerting the world to our presence? No, General. Subtlety is our strength."

Dr. Voss paced, her movements sharp and agitated. "Andres is no fool. He will figure it out eventually. We should act now, before—"

"Before what, Elera?" Sebastian interrupted smoothly. "Before your personal vendetta clouds your judgment?"

Voss whirled on him, her eyes flashing. "Don't you dare question my commitment to the Brotherhood! You have no idea what that man cost me."

Kaine growled, "Your petty grievances are irrelevant. The global energy grid—"

"… is precisely why we must proceed with caution," Sebastian finished, his voice a steel trap of finality. "One wrong move, and we risk premature activation. The consequences would be... unfortunate."

Dr. Voss clenched her fists, her voice trembling with barely contained rage. "You weren't there, Sebastian. You did not see how Andres stole my research, how he took credit for breakthroughs that should have been mine. He destroyed my career, my reputation—everything I had worked for!"

Sebastian's gaze softened fractionally, a calculated show of empathy. "And you'll have your revenge, Elera. But we must be patient. The Brotherhood's goals come first."

Kaine scoffed, "Patience? While we wait, Andres's team grows closer to the truth. We should strike now, before—"

"Before the time is right?" Sebastian cut in, his voice sharp. "No. We wait. We watch. And when the moment comes, we'll be ready to seize everything we've worked for."

The trio fell into an uneasy silence, the weight of their conspiracy hanging heavy in the air. As darkness fully enveloped the ruins, Sebastian's lips curled into a predatory smile. "Trust me," he purred. "When the time comes, Andres and his team won't know what hit them. And the world... the world will never be the same."

As the sun dipped below the horizon, casting long shadows across the ancient stones of Tiwanaku, Sebastian's piercing gray eyes locked onto Andres from across the excavation site. The weight of his gaze felt almost palpable, a silent promise of conflict to come.

Andres, oblivious to the predatory stare, bent over a newly uncovered inscription, his weathered fingers tracing the intricate patterns. "Dr. Carter," he called out, excitement coloring his voice, "I think we've found something significant here."

Evelyn hurried over, her eyes widening as she examined the symbols. "This could be a key to understanding the Vesica Piscis," she breathed, her analytical mind already racing with possibilities.

As the team continued their work, Andres could not shake the feeling of being watched. His dark eyes scanned the deepening shadows at the edge of their work site, sensing more than seeing the hidden figures lurking there. The Sons of Belial, preparing to strike.

"Something wrong, Andres?" Evelyn asked, noticing his distraction.

He forced a smile. "Just thinking about the implications of our discoveries. The potential here is... staggering."

Internally, Andres's thoughts raced. *There is so much at stake. The knowledge here could change everything... or destroy it all if it falls into the wrong hands.*

As the team packed up for the night, Andres lingered behind. He knelt, pressing his palm against the cool stone of the ancient ruins. He closed his eyes, drawing strength from the connection to his Mapuche ancestors and the timeless wisdom of Tiwanaku.

"Give me strength," he whispered in his native tongue. "Guide me to protect this knowledge, to use it for the good of all."

Rising, Andres squared his shoulders, a newfound determination settling over him. Whatever challenges lay ahead, whatever unseen threats lurked in the shadows, he would face them. The fate of humanity's past—and its future—hung in the balance, and Andres Paredes was ready to fight for it.

Andres watched from a distance, his arms crossed, unease gnawing at him. Thorne had been unusually cryptic in their last conversation, offering only vague reassurances that he would return soon with "resources to advance their work."

Before boarding his helicopter, Thorne turned back, his eyes locking onto Andres with an intensity that made the archaeologist's stomach twist. "Keep digging, Dr. Paredes," he called over the noise, his voice carrying effortlessly. "You're on the brink of something extraordinary. I'll be in touch."

And then, with a fleeting but enigmatic smile, Thorne climbed into the helicopter, the door shutting behind him with a metallic click.

As the helicopter lifted off, its shadow passed over the ruins, casting an ominous silhouette against the ancient stones. Andres squinted up at it, the growing distance between them doing nothing to dispel his unease. Thorne's departure felt less like an exit and more like the beginning of something far larger, as though the man carried the secrets of Tiwanaku with him, leaving Andres to grapple with questions that only seemed to multiply in his absence.

The helicopter disappeared over the horizon, leaving behind only the fading echo of its rotors. Andres stood in the stillness, staring at the empty sky, wondering not just where Thorne was headed—but what he truly intended to do next.

Chapter 5

Dr. Evelyn Carter's fingers danced across the intricately carved wall, her touch light yet purposeful. The cool stone seemed to pulse beneath her skin as she traced the celestial symbols etched into its surface. Her keen eyes darted from glyph to glyph, her mind racing to connect the dots.

"It can't be," she murmured, tucking a wayward strand of auburn hair behind her ear. "But it is."

The silence of the underground chamber shattered as Evelyn's voice rang out, echoing off the ancient walls. "It's a map! A map of a global energy grid!"

Jaqueline's head snapped up, her eyes wide with disbelief. "A what?"

Evelyn's hands trembled with excitement as she gestured to the intricate carvings. "Look here," she said, pointing to a series of interconnected lines. "These aren't just random patterns. They're ley lines—powerful energy currents that crisscross the entire planet."

Andres stepped closer, his dark eyes reflecting a newfound understanding. "Like the meridians in the human body," he murmured.

"Exactly!" Evelyn exclaimed. "But on a global scale. And look at these points where the lines intersect—they align perfectly with known sacred sites around the world. Stonehenge, the Great Pyramids, Machu Picchu... and others."

As the implications of their discovery sank in, a mix of awe and disbelief washed over the team. Jaqueline let out a low whistle, while Andres ran a hand through his hair, his expression a blend of wonder and contemplation.

Evelyn's mind raced with possibilities. Could this be the key to unlocking the mysteries of ancient civilizations, the bridge between science and spirituality they had been searching for? Her heart pounded with the thrill of discovery, tempered by a cautious voice in the back of her mind, warning her not to jump to conclusions.

"If this is real," Jacqueline began, her voice hushed with reverence, "it could change everything we thought we knew about human history."

Andres nodded slowly, his eyes never leaving the wall. "And our understanding of the Earth itself," he added. "If these energy lines truly exist, imagine the implications for geology, physics, even consciousness studies."

Evelyn felt a surge of validation at her colleagues' reactions. This was not just her imagination running wild—they saw it too. The weight of their discovery pressed upon her, a mix of exhilaration and responsibility.

"We need to document everything," she said, reaching for her camera with shaking hands. "Every symbol, every line. We can't miss a single detail."

As she began to photograph the wall, Evelyn's mind whirled with questions. *How had the ancients known about this energy grid? What was its purpose? And most importantly, what secrets might it still hold, waiting to be unlocked after millennia of silence?*

The chamber hummed with possibility, the ancient stones seeming to whisper of long-forgotten wisdom. Evelyn knew, deep in her bones, that they stood on the precipice of something monumental. Whatever lay ahead, their world would never be the same.

Amaru's weathered hand brushed against the carved wall, his touch reverent. The old man's eyes, deep pools of ancient wisdom, fixed on the intricate symbols Evelyn had just deciphered. His gravelly voice broke the awed silence, carrying the weight of generations.

"The legends speak of this," Amaru intoned, his words measured and rhythmic. "Our ancestors, the Tiwanaku, were entrusted as guardians of the Earth's sacred knowledge."

Evelyn's breath caught. "What kind of knowledge, Amaru?"

The elder's gaze swept across the team, settling on each face in turn. "The kind that shapes worlds, Dr. Carter. The Tiwanaku understood the delicate balance of energies that flow through our planet, connecting all living things. They had conversations with the spirit of the earth, *Pachamama*."

Andres stepped closer. "Like ley lines?"

Amaru nodded slowly. "Yes, but far more complex." He gestured to the intricate lines and symbols etched on the ancient wall. "This grid," he said, his voice reverent, "is a map of the Earth's very spirit. *Pachamama*—our Mother Earth—breathes through these lines, and her heartbeat resonates through the sacred sites connected by them."

He let those words sink in, the group standing in awed silence. Then, as if calling upon a deeper wisdom, Amaru added in Quechua, "*Kay pacha, hanaq pacha, ukhu pacha.*" His voice was soft yet powerful, the words rolling like an ancient chant.

"The layers of existence—the world we walk upon, the heavens above, and the depths below—all converge through this grid. It is not merely a map; it is a bridge, a sacred design that links all realms."

Amaru turned to Andres, his gaze steady. "To understand this, you must see beyond what your eyes tell you. These lines are not simply coordinates. They are currents of life, woven into the fabric of the universe. *Tupananchiskama,*" he said, his tone carrying both a blessing and a challenge, "until we meet the truth within ourselves, we cannot unlock the truth of the Earth."

The air in the chamber felt charged, as though the ancient carvings themselves were alive, pulsing with the energy Amaru described. Andres felt a shiver run through him, a deep resonance with the words. Amaru's wisdom seemed to awaken something within him, something that had been dormant but was now stirring, eager to be understood.

As Amaru spoke, weaving together strands of myth and history, Evelyn found herself captivated. The academic part of her mind raced to categorize and analyze, but another part—one she usually kept tightly contained—thrilled at the mystical implications.

"Our people believed that this knowledge was too powerful for any one civilization to control," Amaru continued. "So, they became its protectors, safeguarding it here, in the heart of Tiwanaku. We are the original Earth Keepers and feel her pulse."

Andres's eyes widened, a spark of recognition igniting within them. "My abuela," he murmured, almost to himself. "She used to tell me stories... I always thought they were just legends."

Evelyn watched as Andres's usual scientific detachment gave way to something deeper, more personal. His hand unconsciously reached for the small stone he always wore—a gift from his Mapuche grandmother, she realized.

"What kind of stories, Andres?" Evelyn prompted gently.

Andres's voice was soft, tinged with wonder and a hint of disbelief. "Of an ancient people who could speak to the Earth itself. Who understood the language of the stars and the secrets hidden in stone." He looked up, meeting Amaru's knowing gaze. "I never imagined... could it be true?"

Amaru's lined face creased into a smile. "The wisdom of our ancestors flows through your veins, Dr. Paredes. Perhaps it is no accident that you find yourself here, at this moment."

Evelyn observed the interplay between the two men, sensing a profound shift occurring. Andres's usual skepticism seemed to be melting away, replaced by a tentative acceptance of something greater than himself.

As the weight of Amaru's words settled over the chamber, Evelyn felt a mix of excitement and trepidation. They stood on the threshold of something monumental, poised to uncover secrets that had lain dormant for millennia. But with that knowledge came responsibility—and danger.

"If this energy grid is real," she mused aloud, "what does that mean for us? For the world?"

Amaru's eyes met hers, filled with both hope and caution. "That, Dr. Carter, is the question we must now answer. The path ahead is treacherous but also filled with possibility. Are you prepared for where it may lead?"

As Evelyn opened her mouth to respond, a subtle tremor rippled through the chamber, causing loose pebbles to skitter across the floor. The team exchanged startled glances, their bodies tensing instinctively.

"Did you feel that?" Andres whispered, his eyes darting around the room.

Amaru's weathered hand gripped his staff tighter, his gaze fixed on a far corner of the chamber. "The earth speaks," he murmured, his voice barely audible. "It reveals its secrets to those who listen."

Evelyn followed Amaru's line of sight, her heart racing. "There," she breathed, pointing to a section of wall that seemed to shimmer in the dim light. "Do you see it?"

As if responding to her words, a hairline crack appeared in the stone, slowly widening to reveal the outline of a concealed passage. Evelyn's scientific mind raced, trying to rationalize what she was seeing. Could there be some sort of mechanism triggered by the vibrations? Or was this something beyond her current understanding?

"Incredible," Andres muttered, taking a tentative step forward. "How did we miss this before?"

Amaru moved with surprising agility for his age, approaching the hidden entrance. His fingers traced the edge of the opening, his eyes closed in concentration. "The guardians of old have deemed us worthy," he said solemnly. "We must proceed with reverence and caution."

Evelyn felt a mix of excitement and apprehension as she joined Amaru at the threshold. "What do you think lies beyond?" she asked, her voice hushed.

The old guide turned to her, his eyes twinkling with a hint of mischief. "That, Dr. Carter, is what we are about to discover. Shall we?"

With a deep breath, Evelyn nodded. "Lead the way, Amaru. We're right behind you."

The team moved forward, their footsteps echoing in the narrow passage. Evelyn's mind whirled with possibilities. What ancient marvels awaited them? And what dangers might they face? As they ventured deeper, the air grew thick with anticipation, each step bringing them closer to unveiling the mysteries of Tiwanaku.

As they emerged from the narrow passage, the oppressive darkness gave way to a breathtaking spectacle that none of them could have prepared for. The team froze, their collective gasp swallowed by the vastness of the scene before them. An entire underground metropolis stretched into the distance, its sheer scale and grandeur defying comprehension.

Towering crystalline spires spiraled impossibly upward, their surfaces shimmering with an inner light that shifted through every hue of the spectrum. Each tower seemed alive, pulsating with an otherworldly energy that danced in time to an ethereal melody, felt rather than heard. The ceiling, so distant it appeared as an endless cosmos, shimmered like a star-studded night sky, casting a soft, celestial glow over the city.

For a moment, they stood there transfixed, their breath caught in their chests as the scene before them seemed to shimmer with an otherworldly energy, each detail pulling them deeper into a spellbinding sense of awe.

Andres took an involuntary step forward, his breath catching in his throat. "This… this isn't just a city," he said, his voice trembling with awe. "It's a living organism; a symphony of light, energy, and form."

Evelyn's eyes darted across the intricate patterns etched into the streets, the walls, and even the spires themselves. "The geometric precision…" she murmured, almost to herself. "Every structure aligns perfectly with the golden ratio. It's as though the city itself is a manifestation of universal harmony." Her fingers traced invisible lines in the air, connecting the fractals that rippled outward in infinite, mesmerizing patterns.

Amaru's gaze swept the metropolis, "This place," he said with reverence, "is a nexus. A bridge between worlds, where time and space converge. The energy here… it feels ancient, but alive, as though waiting for something—or someone."

As they moved cautiously down a pathway carved from translucent crystal, the air around them began to hum with a gentle, resonant vibration. Glowing symbols, faint at first, flickered to life along the walls and ground. They pulsed in a rhythm that seemed to synchronize with their heartbeats, responding to their mere presence.

Evelyn extended a hand, hesitant but unable to resist the magnetic pull of one of the symbols. Her fingertips hovered over its luminous surface, and as she made contact, the symbol shifted and shimmered, transforming into a cascade of golden light that spiraled upward. A soft, melodic chime resonated through the air, reverberating deep in their chests.

Andres watched, his heart pounding. "These symbols," he said, his voice filled with wonder, "aren't just decorations. They are keys. Messages encoded in light, waiting to be unlocked."

Ahead of them, the path opened into a massive plaza, dominated by a monolithic structure that dwarfed the spires around it. The central edifice glowed with a brilliance that seemed to pierce their very souls. Its facade was adorned with carvings that shifted and rearranged themselves as they approached, as though responding to their consciousness.

"Look at that!" Jacqueline exclaimed, pointing to a massive archway at the structure's base. It was engraved with the Vesica Piscis, the interlocking circles radiating light in hypnotic waves. "This must be the heart of the city—the source of its power."

The air grew warmer, charged with a palpable energy that made their skin tingle. The closer they came to the central structure, the more the city seemed to awaken. Faint echoes of voices—not quite human—drifted through the plaza, their tones melodic yet incomprehensible.

Andres stopped, overwhelmed by the sheer magnitude of what they had uncovered. "We're standing in a place that shouldn't exist," he said, his voice breaking with emotion. "This isn't just an archaeological discovery. This is a gift from another world, another time. And it's waiting for us to understand its purpose."

For a moment, the team stood in silence, their eyes wide with wonder and their minds struggling to absorb the enormity of the truth before them. They were not just explorers—they were witnesses to something extraordinary, something that had the power to change everything they thought they knew about human history, about the universe itself.

"Do you hear that?" Jacqueline asked suddenly, her head tilted as if listening to something beyond human perception.

Andres nodded slowly, a shiver running down his spine. "Whispers... like voices carried on the wind, but we're underground."

Evelyn frowned, straining her ears. "I don't hear anyth—" She stopped abruptly as a faint, melodic whisper brushed past her consciousness, gone almost as soon as it had come. Her scientific mind reeled, searching for a rational explanation.

As they continued their exploration, an unsettling sensation crept over the group. Evelyn could not shake the feeling of being observed, as if countless unseen eyes were tracking their every move. She glanced at her companions, noting the tension in their postures. "Does anyone else feel like we're being watched?" she asked hesitantly.

Andres met her gaze, his expression a mix of wonder and unease. "It's not just you, Evelyn. There is something... alive about this place. It's as if the city itself is aware of our presence."

Amaru nodded solemnly. "The ancient ones are stirring," he said, his voice carrying a weight of ancient wisdom. "We stand at the threshold of knowledge long forgotten. Tread carefully, for every step we take echoes through time itself."

As they pressed on, Evelyn's mind raced with questions. *What forces had created this marvel? And more importantly, what secrets did it hold that could change their understanding of human history forever?*

Evelyn's fingers traced the intricate patterns etched into the wall, fully immersed. Amaru stood silent, his weathered face a mask of calm contemplation. The air hummed with an otherworldly energy, making the hairs on the back of Evelyn's neck stand on end.

"These glyphs," Evelyn murmured, her voice barely above a whisper, "they're not just decorative. They're a blueprint, a schematic of sorts."

Amaru nodded slowly, his eyes never leaving the wall. "The ancients spoke of the Earth's veins, channels of power that flowed like rivers beneath our feet. What you see here, Dr. Carter, is the map to that power."

Evelyn's heart raced. "An energy grid? But how could they have known–"

"Some truths," Amaru interrupted gently, "are beyond the reach of your science. Our ancestors understood the language of the Earth itself."

As they worked, Evelyn's analytical mind clashed and merged with Amaru's intuitive wisdom. She found herself translating complex mathematical equations into the elder's metaphorical narratives, and vice versa. It was an exhilarating dance of knowledge and instinct.

"Look here," Evelyn pointed excitedly, "these convergence points. They align perfectly with known sacred sites around the world. Stonehenge, the Great Pyramid, even–"

A low rumble interrupted her words. The ground beneath their feet began to tremble, and a faint glow emanated from the etched lines on the wall. Evelyn's eyes widened in realization and alarm.

"Oh no!" she breathed. "We've triggered something."

In an instant, lines of brilliant blue-white light burst forth from the walls, crisscrossing the chamber in a dazzling display. The team watched in awe as the luminous web expanded, connecting every structure in the underground city.

Evelyn's mind raced. "It's activating. The entire network... it is coming online!"

Andres stood transfixed, his eyes wide with wonder as the web of light pulsed and danced around them. The luminous threads wove through the ancient structures, revealing intricate patterns and hidden geometries that had been invisible moments before.

"Incredible," he whispered, his voice barely audible over the low hum that now filled the chamber. "It's... it's beyond anything we could have imagined."

Evelyn struggled to comprehend the scene before her. "The energy output must be astronomical," she murmured, her fingers twitching as if longing for instruments to measure the phenomenon. "And yet, it seems to be drawing power from... from the Earth itself."

As they watched, speechless, the light began to pulse in rhythmic waves, as if the entire city was breathing. Each surge sent ripples of energy through the team, leaving them tingling with a strange mixture of exhilaration and unease.

Andres turned to his colleagues, his expression a mix of awe and growing concern. "This discovery... it changes everything we thought we knew about ancient civilizations, about human potential."

The light began to fade, the brilliant web dimming until only a faint, pulsing glow remained. As stillness settled over the underground city once more, the weight of their discovery pressed upon them like a physical force.

Evelyn broke the silence, her voice uncharacteristically hesitant. "What do we do now? This kind of power... in the wrong hands..."

Andres nodded gravely. "We have a responsibility here. To unlock these secrets, yes, but also to protect them. To ensure they're used for the betterment of humanity, not its exploitation."

Jacqueline's serene voice cut through the tension. "Remember, this technology was not just about power, but balance. The Atlanteans sought to harmonize with the Earth's energies, not dominate them."

As the team stood in contemplative silence, each grappling with the enormity of their discovery, Andres could not shake the feeling that they stood at a crossroads of human history. The path they chose from this moment would shape not just their own destinies, but potentially the future of the entire world.

Andres's gaze drifted back to the fading grid, his mind awash with conflicting thoughts. The pulsing energy seemed to resonate with something deep within him, calling forth memories of his grandmother's stories and the ancient wisdom of his Mapuche heritage.

"My abuela," he began, his voice barely above a whisper, "she used to speak of the Earth's sacred energies, of hidden knowledge passed down through generations. I always thought they were just legends, but now..."

Jacqueline stepped closer, her dark eyes reflecting understanding. "The lines between myth and reality are blurring before our eyes, Andres. What your grandmother taught you, may be more vital than we could have imagined."

Evelyn's analytical mind was already racing ahead. "If we could decipher the mechanisms behind this grid, the applications could be revolutionary. Clean energy, advanced communication, perhaps even..."

"Careful, Evelyn," Jacqueline interjected, her tone gentle but firm. "We must approach this discovery with reverence, not just scientific curiosity. These energies were meant to be in harmony with nature, not exploited."

Andres nodded, feeling the weight of responsibility settling on his shoulders. "Jacqueline is right." We need to proceed with caution. This isn't just about scientific breakthrough; it's about stewardship of something far greater than ourselves."

As the team fell into contemplative silence, each member's face reflected a unique mix of emotions. Evelyn's eyes sparkled with intellectual excitement, tempered by a hint of apprehension. Jacqueline's serene expression belied the profound sense of purpose stirring within her. Amaru's face was a mask of reverence, his connection to the ancient energies palpable.

Andres felt a surge of anticipation, tinged with a sense of foreboding. "Whatever lies ahead," he said, his voice steady despite his inner turmoil, "we face it together. The path forward won't be easy, but the potential for understanding, for growth... it's unimaginable."

The air in the ancient chamber seemed to thicken with possibility, the team's collective breath held in anticipation of the journey that lay before them. As they stood on the precipice of a new era of discovery, the fading glow of the energy grid served as a poignant reminder of the profound mysteries still waiting to be unraveled.

Andres took a deep breath, his eyes scanning the faces of his team. The weight of their discovery pressed upon him, a mix of exhilaration and trepidation coursing through his veins. He cleared his throat, his voice carrying a newfound resolve.

"We've unlocked something extraordinary here," he began, gesturing to the dimming energy grid. "But with this knowledge comes great responsibility. We're not just archaeologists anymore; we're guardians of a power that could reshape our understanding of history and humanity itself."

Evelyn nodded. "Andres is right. The implications of this discovery are... staggering. We need to approach this with the utmost care and discretion. "But how do we even begin to study something so far beyond our current scientific understanding?" she interjected, her voice tinged with a mix of awe and frustration.

Amaru's serene voice cut through the tension. "We must listen to the wisdom of the ancients. The answers lie not just in your scientific methods, but in opening our hearts and minds to the teachings this place holds."

Andres nodded, feeling a strange resonance with Amaru's words. He turned to face the team, his expression serious. "We'll need to combine our expertise—archaeology, anthropology, physics, and yes, even the spiritual insights we've gained. This isn't just about unlocking the secrets of the past; it's about safeguarding the future."

As he spoke, a subtle tremor ran through the chamber, as if the very earth was responding to their presence. The team exchanged glances, a mixture of excitement and apprehension evident in their eyes.

"Whatever challenges lie ahead," Paredes continued, his voice strong and determined, "we face them together. The road won't be easy, but the potential for understanding, for growth... it's beyond anything we could have imagined."

The air in the ancient chamber seemed to pulse with possibility, the team's collective breath held in anticipation of the journey that lay before them. As they stood on the precipice of a new era of discovery, the fading glow of the energy grid served as a poignant reminder of the profound mysteries still waiting to be unraveled—and the tremendous responsibility they now carried.

Chapter 6

The team had relocated to a bustling makeshift camp atop the underground chamber, the area transformed into a hub of activity. Large, weather-resistant tents were pitched in a loose semicircle around the excavation site, their fabric flapping gently in the sporadic gusts of the Andean wind. Heavy-duty stakes anchored them securely to the rocky ground, ensuring they withstood the elements. At Amaru's direction, a group of local helpers had been contracted to assist with the excavation, their expertise invaluable in navigating the rugged terrain and handling the delicate artifacts emerging from the depths. Their presence infused the camp with a steady rhythm of coordinated effort, blending modern archaeological techniques with generations-old knowledge of the land.

The largest tent, serving as their central command, was illuminated from within, its soft glow spilling out into the twilight. Inside, the air buzzed with a hum of technology and quiet voices exchanging theories and observations. A folding table at the center was strewn with cutting-edge equipment: UV scanners with sleek, glowing interfaces; compact 3D imaging tools projecting holographic renderings of artifacts into the air; and a portable spectrometer emitting a soft, rhythmic beep as it analyzed minute samples.

Several laptops lined the table, their screens displaying scrolling streams of data and vibrant holographic models of the underground city's layout. An adjoining side table bore neatly labeled specimen containers, each holding fragments of crystalline material and ancient carvings retrieved from the site below.

Against one wall of the tent stood a portable whiteboard, now a chaotic collage of equations, sketches, and hastily scrawled notes. Evelyn had taken to drawing detailed fractal diagrams of the underground city's layout, her handwriting looping elegantly around the symbols and annotations.

To the side, a smaller tent housed the lab's power source: a generator humming steadily, connected to a network of cables that snaked out like a web to the other tents. The generator was supplemented by a series of solar panels, their polished surfaces catching the last rays of the Andean sun.

Outside the main tent, a secondary shelter was dedicated to artifact storage, its interior meticulously organized with shelves and crates. The shelves held delicate instruments for cleaning and preserving the finds, while a temperature-controlled container safeguarded the most fragile items.

The camp itself was alive with motion. Jacqueline stood near the excavation site, poring over a holographic map of the underground chamber on her tablet. Nearby, Andres conferred with one of the team members, gesturing toward a drone equipped with high-resolution cameras. It sat perched on a portable landing pad, ready to descend into the chamber to capture more data. A smaller tent housed their makeshift rest area, equipped with foldable cots and a propane heater for the chilly Andean nights. A communal table outside held a scattering of thermoses and meal packets, the faint aroma of coffee mingling with the crisp mountain air.

Above it all, the Andean sky stretched vast and unbroken, its deep blue fading to indigo as evening approached. The camp felt both temporary and timeless, a fleeting human presence set against the ageless grandeur of the surrounding landscape, where ancient mysteries lay waiting to be unveiled.

The canvas tent fluttered in the crisp Andean breeze as Evelyn hunched over the ancient codex, her dark eyes darting across the weathered pages. The soft glow of LED lights illuminated the makeshift research station, casting long shadows across the faces of her colleagues.

"It's here," Evelyn breathed, her finger tracing a line of intricate glyphs. "The Atlantean Crystal Skull—it's not just a myth. According to this, it's a central node in a vast energy grid that spans the entire planet."

Jacqueline, who had been quietly photographing the codex with a high-resolution camera, chimed in. "The scroll we found aligns with this theory. It's almost like they're meant to be read together, one unlocking the other." She unrolled the scroll carefully, setting it beside the codex. The symbols from both texts appeared to resonate, their designs interlocking in a way that suggested a deeper meaning.

Jacqueline leaned in; her brow furrowed. "Dr. Carter, look at this passage in the scroll. The imagery, the symbols—they are mirroring the codex. It is as if..."

"... as if they were meant to be read in tandem," Evelyn finished, a thrill of excitement coursing through her. She felt the weight of discovery pressing down on her shoulders, a familiar mix of exhilaration and trepidation. What secrets had they stumbled upon in the depths of Tiwanaku?

Amaru's weathered voice broke through her reverie. "In the stories of my people, there is talk of a great crystal that bridged the gap between the heavens and the earth. A conduit for divine wisdom and cosmic energy."

Evelyn nodded, her mind racing. "These ancient cultures, separated by vast distances, all speak of similar concepts. It can't be coincidence."

She reached for the UV scanner, her hands trembling slightly. As the blue light swept across the pages, hidden text blazed to life.

"Coordinates!" Evelyn gasped. "But these... they don't correspond to any known geographical location. It is as if they are pointing to..."

"... another dimension," Jacqueline interjected, her green eyes alight with curiosity. "Evelyn, what you've uncovered here aligns perfectly with some of our most cutting-edge theories in quantum physics."

Evelyn felt a surge of respect for her colleague. "Go on. How so?"

"These ancient texts," Jacqueline explained, gesturing to the codex and scroll, "describe what modern science is only beginning to grasp—the interconnectedness of all things, the potential for interdimensional travel. The global energy grid they reference? It's remarkably similar to quantum entanglement."

She paused, her eyes gleaming with insight. "Quantum entanglement is one of the most astonishing phenomena in physics. When particles originate from the same source, they remain intrinsically linked, no matter how far apart they drift across time and space. They do not just maintain a connection—they shed their individual quantum states and adopt a unified one. Any change in one particle instantaneously influences all the others it is entangled with. Now, imagine if entire sacred sites, or even human consciousness itself, operated on this same principle. The ancients may have understood that activating these energy nodes could awaken a network of entangled forces spanning dimensions."

Evelyn's mind reeled. *Could it be possible? Had ancient civilizations possessed knowledge that modern science was only now rediscovering?*

"But how?" she asked, voicing the question that burned in her mind. "How could they have known?"

Jacqueline's response was measured, tinged with a hint of awe. "Perhaps the better question is: how did we forget? These ancients weren't just building monuments—they were cosmic engineers, working with energies we're only beginning to comprehend."

As the implications of their discovery sank in, a heavy silence fell over the tent. Evelyn felt the weight of responsibility settling on her shoulders. They stood on the precipice of something monumental, something that could change the course of human understanding.

"We need to proceed carefully," she said, her voice low and determined. "Whatever secrets this crystal holds, whatever power this energy grid possesses—it's clear we're dealing with forces beyond our current understanding."

Andres turned toward Jacqueline. "Dr. Hart," he asked, his voice steady but curious, "what exactly was the significance of the Crystal Skull to the Atlanteans? Why would they create something so extraordinary?"

Jacqueline paused, her eyes glinting with a mix of awe and determination. "The Crystal Skull of Atlantis," she began, her voice resonant in the quiet chamber, "was no ordinary artifact. It was both a tool and a treasure—crafted not just from physical materials but imbued with the very essence of Atlantean wisdom and consciousness. Its crystalline matrix was encoded with knowledge that spanned millennia.

She continued, "Legend says the Atlanteans were masters of crystal technology, using it to power their cities, enhance their spiritual practices, and even manipulate space and time. This particular skull—the thirteenth of its kind—was known as the Gatekeeper Crystal. It resided in the Temple of Poseidon, the heart of Atlantis, and was the most sacred of all."

Amaru stepped closer, his expression solemn. "And what was its purpose, Dr. Hart?"

Jacqueline nodded at him. "The Gatekeeper Skull acted as a unifier. It harmonized the energies of the other twelve skulls, creating a frequency so powerful that it could open portals to higher dimensions. Through these portals, the Atlanteans received guidance from celestial beings—knowledge about the cosmos, spiritual evolution, and the delicate balance between technology and nature. The Skull was the key to their greatness, but also..." Her voice faltered briefly. "... their downfall."

Andres asked, "What do you mean?"

"The Atlanteans were a divided people," Jacqueline continued, her voice tinged with sorrow. "On one side were the followers of the Law of One, who sought harmony and spiritual enlightenment. On the other were the Sons of Belial, who desired dominion and the unchecked use of technology. The skulls became a point of contention. The Law of One wanted them safeguarded, hidden until humanity was ready. The Sons of Belial wanted to exploit their power for control."

Amaru nodded gravely. "The energies of the Belial are still tied to such ambitions," he said.

Jacqueline nodded. She picked up the thread. "When Atlantis fell, the Gatekeeper Skull was hidden away, protected by generations of guardians who understood its importance. It was said that only when humanity was ready—when we stood on the brink of transformation into Homo Omega—would the skulls reveal their full potential."

"And Homo Omega?" Andres asked.

"The next stage of human evolution," she explained. "A balance between technological advancement, spiritual wisdom, and expanded consciousness. The Atlanteans believed the skulls could guide us toward this destiny. But only if they were reunited and used with the purest intentions. Otherwise..."

She trailed off, but Andres understood the implications. The skulls could either uplift humanity or lead it down a darker path of destruction.

"Why thirteen?" Andres asked.

Jacqueline smiled faintly. "In esoteric traditions, the number thirteen symbolizes completion and transformation. The Gatekeeper Skull was the master key, amplifying the energy of the others and creating a resonance that linked the grid of sacred sites around the world. Together, they could activate the planetary energy grid, uniting humanity with the cosmos."

Andres's mind spun with the implications. "And if the Sons of Belial got their hands on it?"

Jacqueline's face hardened. "They would use it to create their vision of a new humanity—synthetic beings merged with AI, devoid of the very essence that makes us human. They tried it in Atlantis through genetic experiments, and they are trying it again now."

A heavy silence filled the chamber as the team absorbed her words.

Andres turned to Evelyn and Amaru. "This Skull… it holds the key to more than we ever imagined. The future of humanity might depend on what we do with it."

Evelyn said, "Then we must ensure it's used as it was meant to be—a beacon of light, not a weapon of darkness."

Amaru nodded solemnly. "The wisdom of the ancients is not to be taken lightly. It has the power to elevate or destroy."

As the team exchanged glances, a mixture of excitement and apprehension palpable in the air, Evelyn could not shake the feeling that they had set in motion events that would reshape the world as they knew it. The journey ahead was fraught with danger and promise in equal measure, and she silently vowed to see it through, wherever it might lead.

Julian Blackwood moved with practiced nonchalance through the tented campsite, his keen eyes darting from artifact to artifact. His fingers traced the edge of an ancient ceramic shard, but his focus was elsewhere. With a fluid motion, he slipped a compact camera from his pocket, angling it discreetly towards the open pages of the codex.

Click. Transmit. Delete.

The process was swift, almost mechanical, yet each image sent to the Brotherhood left a bitter taste in Julian's mouth. He swallowed hard, pushing down the knot of guilt that threatened to rise in his throat.

This wasn't what he had envisioned when he first aligned himself with them. Once, he'd believed their promises—that knowledge was power, that some secrets were too dangerous for the world, that he would be part of something greater. But the years had eroded those convictions, replacing them with quiet doubts and an increasing sense of entrapment. He had seen too much, learned too late that the

Brotherhood's true purpose had little to do with preservation and everything to do with control.

And yet, they owned him. A debt, a mistake, a past miscalculation—whatever it was, it had bound him to their cause with chains he could not yet break. The price of defiance was steep, and Julian had no illusions about what would happen if he stopped delivering what they demanded.

His fingers lingered over the codex for a second longer before he turned away, exhaling softly. One day, he told himself, one day, he would find a way out.

"Fascinating markings on this piece," Julian remarked casually, holding up the shard for Dr. Carter to see. "Any theories on its significance?"

As Evelyn began to explain, Julian's mind raced. The weight of his betrayal pressed against his chest, a constant, suffocating presence. He thought of the team's passion, their dedication. For a fleeting moment, he allowed himself to imagine being part of something greater than the Brotherhood's machinations.

The sound of raised voices snapped Julian from his reverie. Across the camp, Amaru and Evelyn r were locked in heated debate, their words carrying on the cool mountain air.

"You cannot simply dissect these sacred texts like some academic puzzle!" Amaru's usually calm demeanor had given way to barely contained frustration. "There are forces at work here beyond your scientific instruments."

Evelyn's response was equally passionate. "And we cannot blindly accept mystical explanations without empirical evidence. The coordinates, the references to the energy grid—these are tangible leads we must pursue!"

Julian watched the exchange with growing unease. The team's cohesion, so vital to their mission, was fracturing before his eyes. He felt a twinge of something almost like concern.

"Perhaps," he ventured, surprising himself, "there's value in both approaches. The ancients clearly bridged the scientific and spiritual. Shouldn't we attempt the same?"

His words hung in the air, met with startled looks from both Amaru and Evelyn. Julian's heart raced. Had he overstepped? Revealed too much?

As the tension in the camp continued to simmer, Julian retreated to the shadow of a nearby tent. His fingers brushed against the camera in his pocket, a cold reminder of his true purpose. Yet the seed of doubt had been planted, and Julian found himself questioning, for the first time, which side of this cosmic chess game he truly wanted to be on.

A figure emerged from the twilight, silhouetted against the dying embers of the sun. Sophia Blackwood approached with measured steps, her boots crunching softly against the rocky terrain. The crisp morning air carried the faint scent of herbs from the provisions she had brought, mingling with the earthiness of Tiwanaku's ancient stones. Her presence was unassuming yet purposeful, the kind of energy that rarely demanded attention but often commanded respect.

"I've brought the additional equipment you requested," she announced, her voice soft yet carrying an undercurrent of carefully controlled emotion. "And some fresh provisions."

As she set down her burden, Sophia's gray-green eyes swept across the camp, taking in the tense atmosphere with a single, penetrating glance. Her gaze lingered on Julian for a moment, a mixture of love and apprehension flickering across her features.

Andres looked up from the array of maps and artifacts scattered before him. His dark eyes flickered with a brief recognition, but his expression remained distant, unfocused. He nodded in acknowledgment, offering a distracted thanks as his thoughts continued to churn in some far-off place.

Sophia observed him for a moment. She was no stranger to this version of Andres—absorbed, consumed by his work, his mind tethered more to the past he sought to unravel than to the present moment. She had known him long enough to recognize when to press and when to hold back.

Sophia had first joined the expedition months ago, brought in as an expert in logistics and communications. A former field operative with a shadowy past in intelligence work, she had a knack for navigating high-stakes environments and had proven invaluable to the team. But her reasons for being here went beyond professional interest. There was a personal connection—one that she kept well-guarded, much like the enigmatic journals she always carried.

Andres's focus on Tiwanaku had drawn them together in more ways than one. For Sophia, this place was more than a site of historical significance. It was a crossroads, a key to mysteries that resonated deeply with her own search for answers. She suspected Andres knew this about her, even if he never said it aloud. Their conversations often danced around their shared sense of urgency, their unspoken acknowledgment of something much larger at play.

"I've also included the celestial charts for the upcoming solstice," she added, her tone professional yet warm, trying to ground him in the task at hand. "I thought they might help with your calculations for the alignment."

Andres's gaze finally settled on her, his distracted demeanor giving way to a flicker of gratitude. "Thank you, Sophia. I... I had not thought to ask for those. That's... thoughtful."

She gave him a small, knowing smile. "You've got enough on your mind. I'll take care of the rest." But as she turned to organize the supplies, her own thoughts lingered. Whatever secrets Tiwanaku held, they were pulling all of them deeper into its enigmatic orbit. And Sophia knew, perhaps better than most, that when one peered into the mysteries of the past, the past often stared back.

Sophia began unpacking, her movements deliberate and measured. As she worked, her thoughts churned. *How much does Julian know? How far has he gone?* The weight of her divided loyalties pressed down upon her, heavier than any physical burden.

As the team pored over the codex and scroll in the tented campsite, Andres found his attention wavering. While the others immersed themselves in decoding symbols and uncovering hidden meanings, Andres wrestled with a growing unease.

Visions flashed before his eyes, unbidden and jarring: shadowy figures locked in battle, ancient cities consumed by fire, and a crushing sense of betrayal from unseen forces. He clenched his fists, willing the images away, but they persisted, whispering doubts and fears into his mind.

Jacqueline, seated nearby, noticed his distracted glances and furrowed brow. "Andres," she said gently, her tone carrying both curiosity and concern. "You seem a million miles away. Is something bothering you?"

He forced a tight smile and nodded. "I'm fine," he said, though his voice betrayed the turmoil within. "Just... trying to process everything."

But the truth weighed heavily on him. The codex's revelations about the global energy grid and the Crystal Skull only amplified his inner conflict. Memories of his grandmother's wisdom resurfaced— her stories about balance, shadow, and light. She had often spoken of the need to confront one's darkness to find harmony, yet Andres had always avoided facing his own.

Now, with the cosmic significance of their mission becoming clear, Andres felt the burden of his role more acutely than ever. His mind replayed moments of doubt—decisions he second-guessed, opportunities lost to hesitation. The fear of failure, the fear of leading his team astray, gnawed at him.

The intensity of his visions escalated, blurring the lines between past and present. He saw Evelyn, Amaru, and the others among the shadowy battles, their faces etched with betrayal and despair. The whispers in his mind grew louder, urging him to distrust even those closest to him.

Andres stepped outside the tent, the cool Andean air hitting his face like a balm. He closed his eyes and took a deep breath, trying to ground himself. His grandmother's voice echoed in his mind: "The shadow is not your enemy. It is your teacher. Face it, and you will find your strength."

Jacqueline followed him out, her gaze steady but kind. "You've been distant," she said. "Whatever's going on, you don't have to carry it alone."

Andres hesitated, torn between opening and guarding his fears. "I've been seeing... things Jackie," he finally admitted. "Visions of betrayal, battles—us. I cannot tell if it is a warning or just my mind playing tricks on me."

Jacqueline folded her arms, thoughtful. "Sometimes the mind reveals what we are afraid to face. But you have always been someone who looks for meaning in the chaos. Maybe these visions are not just warnings—they could be a call to action."

Her words struck a chord. Andres realized that his doubts and fears reflected his deeper insecurities. If he were to move forward— if he were to truly embrace his role in this cosmic plan—he had to stop running from his shadow and instead integrate it as part of his strength.

Amaru emerged from the shadows, his weathered face illuminated by the soft glow of the campfire. The old man's presence seemed to bring a sense of calm to the turbulent night air.

"The spirits speak to you, young one," Amaru said, his voice a low, melodious rumble. "But do you know how to listen?"

Andres felt a flicker of hope. "I'm trying, Amaru. But the visions are so chaotic, so... overwhelming."

Amaru nodded sagely, leaning on his intricately carved staff. "The chaos is but a veil. To see beyond it, you must look with your heart, not your eyes."

As Amaru spoke, Andres felt a shift within himself, as if pieces of a cosmic puzzle were slowly falling into place. The old man's words resonated with a truth that transcended mere language.

"Your visions," Amaru continued, "they are like the waters of Titicaca—turbulent on the surface, but beneath, they hold great wisdom. You must learn to dive deep."

Andres closed his eyes, letting Amaru's metaphor wash over him. In his mind's eye, he saw the chaotic visions not as a threat, but as a tapestry of possibilities.

"I think I understand," Andres said slowly, opening his eyes. "These visions aren't just about warning us of danger. They're showing us the path we need to take."

Amaru's eyes twinkled with approval. "Now you begin to see, young one. The wisdom of the ancients flows through you. Embrace it."

He returns to the tent with renewed determination, his mind clearer, though the weight of his visions remains. As the team continues decoding the codex and scroll, Andres begins to see their discovery not just as a mission for humanity, but as a personal calling to transcend his own limitations.

The night sky stretched like an obsidian canvas above the campsite, pinpricked with stars that seemed to pulse with an otherworldly energy. Andres Paredes stood at the edge of the tented area, his weathered face etched with lines of concern as he gazed into the darkness. Suddenly, his vision blurred, and the world around him dissolved into a kaleidoscope of images.

"No," Andres whispered, his voice hoarse with dread.

Before his eyes, he saw the global energy grid—a shimmering network of light encircling the Earth—begin to fracture and collapse. Brilliant lines of energy snapped like overstretched rubber bands, each break sending shockwaves across the planet. Cities crumbled, oceans roiled, and the very fabric of reality seemed to tear at the seams.

As quickly as it began, the vision faded, leaving Andres gasping for air. He stumbled back toward the main tent, his mind reeling. "It's happening again," he muttered, running his fingers through his graying hair. "Just like Atlantis."

Inside the tent, the team huddled around a table strewn with artifacts and papers. Andres's eyes darted from face to face, searching for any sign of deceit or hidden agenda.

Evelyn looked up from the codex, her brow furrowed. "Andres? You look like you've seen a ghost."

"Worse," Andres replied, his voice tight. "I've seen our future if we fail."

Jacqueline set down her tablet, her dark eyes narrowing. "What do you mean?"

Amaru stepped closer, his expression a blend of urgency and reverence. "The grid is alive, Andres," he said, his voice low but charged with conviction. "It breathes with the Earth's pulse, connecting sacred sites across the globe. For centuries, it has slumbered, awaiting the moment when humanity is ready to remember its purpose. That moment is now—the Year of Destiny."

Andres studied the faint, glowing lines on the map before him. The interconnected web of energy nodes shimmered like veins of light coursing through the planet. "But it's fracturing," he said, his voice heavy. "The pressure is building at the weak points. If we can't stabilize it before the harmonic portal opens during the alignment, it could unleash forces beyond our control."

Amaru nodded solemnly. "Precisely why the ancients encoded their knowledge into these sites—Stonehenge, Tiwanaku, Giza, and the others. They foresaw this moment and left us the tools to repair the grid. But it is not just about technology. The grid responds to consciousness, to intention. Balance must be restored not only to the Earth but within ourselves."

Jacqueline added in her steady voice "This isn't just about preventing collapse. The grid's reactivation will unlock the harmonic portal, a gateway to dimensions beyond our current understanding. It is a chance to realign humanity's path, to evolve. But if we fail—if the grid fractures further—it could amplify the chaos and destruction."

Andres ran a hand through his hair, grappling with the enormity of the task. "How do we even begin? The ancient texts, the alignments—they're fragments of a puzzle, and time is running out."

Amaru placed a hand on Andres's shoulder, grounding him. "We begin by preparing ourselves. The grid mirrors our collective state. Fear and division weaken it, but unity and purpose strengthen it. The rituals, the alignments, the harmonic frequencies—they are as much about transforming us as they are about the Earth."

Andres exhaled, the weight on his chest easing slightly as he felt the resolve of those around him. "Then we need to move quickly. Every site, every node must be activated. And we will need everyone—scientists, mystics, healers—working together. The Year of Destiny does not just belong to the few. It's a call to all of humanity." The grid was preparing, awakening, but its fate—and the portal's opening—rested in their hands.

Julian Blackwood scoffed, but Andres noticed a flicker of something—fear or guilt maybe—in his eyes. "Come on, mate. You cannot seriously believe—"

"I've seen it," Andres interrupted, his gaze boring into Julian. "And I think someone here might be working to make it happen."

A heavy silence fell over the group. Amaru shifted uncomfortably, while Sophia avoided eye contact altogether. Jacqueline cleared her throat, clearly unsettled.

"Andres," she said softly, "are you suggesting one of us is a traitor?"

The tension in the tent was palpable, thick enough to cut with a knife. Andres's eyes swept across the faces of his companions once more, searching for any hint of betrayal.

"I don't know," he admitted, his voice barely above a whisper. "But I intend to find out."

Chapter 7

The flickering glow of their headlamps cast eerie shadows on the weathered stone walls as the team snaked through the subterranean labyrinth. Amaru's staff tapped a steady rhythm against the ground, each impact sending ripples through the air thick with anticipation.

Evelyn's keen eyes darted from symbol to symbol etched into the corridor, her mind racing to decipher their meaning. "These glyphs," she murmured, tracing her fingers over a spiraling pattern, "they're unlike anything I've seen before. It's as if they're... alive somehow."

Amaru paused, his wizened face inscrutable in the dim light. "The ancestors speak through stone," he intoned, his gravelly voice barely above a whisper. "We must listen with more than our ears."

Evelyn felt a shiver course down her spine, equal parts excitement, and trepidation. She tucked a stray lock of hair behind her ear, a nervous habit she'd never quite shaken. "I'm trying, Amaru," she replied, her scientific mind grappling with the mystical implications. "But how can we be sure we're on the right path?"

As if in answer, a faint blue glow pulsed ahead, casting the team in an otherworldly light. Julian Blackwood pushed forward; his eyes gleaming with barely contained greed. "There! Do you see it?"

Evelyn placed a cautionary hand on his arm. "Wait," she warned, her gaze fixed on a series of interlocking triangles that seemed to shimmer and shift as she watched. "These markings... they're changing."

Amaru nodded solemnly. "The veil grows thin," he murmured. "We approach the threshold."

The air around them seemed to crackle with unseen energy, raising the hairs on Evelyn's arms. She fought to quell the rising panic in her chest, reminding herself of the scientific marvels that awaited discovery. Yet as they pressed deeper into the heart of the ancient city, a nagging doubt gnawed at her resolve. *What forces had they truly awakened, and at what cost?*

Evelyn's fingers traced the intricate patterns on the wall panel, her breath catching as the symbols beneath her touch began to glow with an ethereal blue light. "This is it," she whispered, her voice a mix of awe and trepidation. "The entrance to the Atlantean Temple."

The ornate wall panel, adorned with swirling glyphs and geometric designs, pulsed with energy. As if responding to Evelyn's touch, a seam appeared in the seemingly solid rock, widening to reveal a passage beyond.

"Incredible," Andres breathed, his eyes wide with wonder. "After all this time..."

Sophia stepped forward, her usual skepticism giving way to curiosity. "How do we know it's safe?"

Amaru's calm voice cut through the tension. "The ancients have deemed us worthy. We must trust in their wisdom."

Julian scoffed, but his eyes gleamed with barely concealed excitement. "Wisdom or not, we didn't come this far to turn back now."

Evelyn hesitated at the threshold, her scientific mind racing to categorize the impossible scene before her. The entrance was marked by pulsating Atlantean symbols, each one seeming to hold a universe of meaning. "These markings," she mused aloud, "they're not just decorative. They're... alive somehow."

With a collective breath, the team stepped into the temple. The atmosphere shifted instantly, enveloping them in an aura of ancient power. The air inside the temple felt heavy with the presence of ancient forces. A deep, resonant hum permeated the space, vibrating at a frequency only those attuned to Atlantean energies could sense. The temperature seemed to fluctuate—one moment cold, the next warm—affected by the energy currents flowing through the crystalline structures. A faint glow emanated from the walls, casting eerie shadows that seemed to move and shift, as if the temple itself were alive, watching and waiting.

Evelyn's eyes darted around, trying to take in every detail of the awe-inspiring architecture.

Sweeping arches of an unknown, pearlescent material stretched overhead, meeting at a central apex that seemed to glow with its own inner light. Organic columns, reminiscent of towering trees, supported the vast chamber, their surfaces etched with complex, flowing patterns that seemed to move when viewed from the corner of one's eye. In the center of the room, there is a towering, pyramid-shaped structure, crowned with a glowing orb that hums with latent power.

This orb is connected to the portal system, acting as a focal point for the temple's interdimensional capabilities.

"Look at the crystals," Sophia gasped, pointing to clusters of shimmering, multi-faceted gems embedded in the walls. They pulsed with a rhythm that felt oddly familiar, like a heartbeat.

Evelyn's analytical mind raced to make sense of it all. "These aren't just ornamental," she realized. "They're part of some kind of... energy network."

As they moved deeper into the temple, the air hummed with potential, as if the very molecules around them were charged with ancient knowledge. Celestial carvings adorned the ceiling, depicting star systems and cosmic events that both fascinated and perplexed Evelyn.

"What do you make of these symbols, Evelyn?" Andres asked, gesturing to a series of intricate glyphs that seemed to float above the surface of a nearby wall.

Evelyn shook her head, both exhilarated and overwhelmed. "They're trying to convey concepts our language doesn't even have words for."

The walls of the temple are inscribed with Atlantean symbols and pictograms that recount their civilization's history. There are depictions of Atlantean sages, intricate star maps, and diagrams of energy fields radiating from sacred sites around the world. As Andres and the team move deeper, they see murals showing the clash between Atlantis and Tiwanaku, their energy conflict spanning dimensions. The murals depict advanced machinery channeling cosmic energy, representing the two civilizations as opposites: Atlantis, a master of technology, and Tiwanaku, a guardian of natural, spiritual power.

They can see that the entire temple is infused with a complex network of crystalline veins embedded within its walls and floors. These crystals are connected to ancient Atlantean power sources, which harness energy from interdimensional planes. Scattered throughout the temple are relics of Atlantean technology—strange devices that seem dormant at first but begin to stir to life. There are large, disc-like mechanisms mounted on the walls, possibly used to focus energy or manipulate dimensional gateways.

As the team spread out to explore, Evelyn could not shake the feeling that they were being watched, evaluated. The temple seemed to pulse with anticipation as if it had been waiting millennia for this moment.

"We need to be cautious," she warned, her voice echoing in the vast chamber. "We don't fully understand the forces at work here."

But even as she spoke, Evelyn knew they had crossed a threshold from which there was no turning back. Whatever secrets this Atlantean Temple held, they were about to be revealed—for better or worse.

Evelyn's eyes darted across the intricately carved glyphs adorning the temple walls, her fingers tracing the contours of ancient symbols. She muttered to herself, "Fascinating... these patterns."

"What do you make of them, Dr. Carter?" Julian asked, his voice tinged with barely concealed eagerness.

Evelyn, her analytical mind racing. "They're not just decorative. There's a logic to them, a... language." She paused, her scientific skepticism warring with the undeniable evidence before her. "It's as if they're describing energy flows, interdimensional gateways, portals. But that's..."

"Impossible?" Andres finished, a knowing smile playing on his lips as he approached.

Evelyn's dark eyes met his, a flicker of uncertainty crossing her face. "I was going to say 'extraordinary'," she admitted. "These symbols, they're bridging concepts I've only theorized about. It's like looking at the blueprint of the universe itself."

As she spoke, her fingers brushed against a particular glyph, and to her astonishment, it began to glow faintly. A gasp escaped her lips. "Did you see that?"

Andres nodded, his expression serious. "The temple is responding to us, Evelyn. It's alive in its own way."

Evelyn's scientific mind reeled at the implications. How could she reconcile this with everything she thought she knew? And yet, the evidence was undeniable. "It's... beautiful," she whispered, a newfound sense of wonder creeping into her voice.

While Evelyn grappled with her paradigm shift, the chamber seemed to vibrate with a power older than time itself, as if the very air carried the echoes of a forgotten civilization. Andres's gaze was irresistibly drawn to the center of the room.

There, he noticed a crystalline altar that floated a mere inch above the ground, suspended by an unseen force. Upon it rested the Atlantean Crystal Skull, a relic of indescribable majesty.

The Skull was unlike anything Andres had imagined, its surface a mosaic of translucent brilliance, refracting light in an endless kaleidoscope of colors. Deep hues of azure and violet swirled like liquid galaxies within the crystal, while veins of molten gold ran through it, as though it pulsed with the lifeblood of the Earth itself. Every angle revealed a new dimension of its beauty—facets that shimmered with emerald and sapphire undertones, a crown that caught the light and cast prismatic rainbows against the chamber walls. It seemed alive, breathing in energy and exhaling it back into the ether. The hollows of its eyes glowed faintly, like twin portals to the unknown, drawing Andres closer with an almost magnetic allure. The jaw was slightly parted, as though whispering secrets in a tongue no mortal could understand, and the entire Skull emanated a soft, rhythmic hum—a symphony of cosmic resonance that thrummed through the chamber like a heartbeat.

As Evelyn and the team stepped beside him, her breath caught. The Skull was not merely an artifact; it was alive with purpose, a fragment of a civilization that had once commanded forces beyond comprehension. In its presence, the weight of their discovery pressed on them with an almost divine significance. This was no ordinary relic—it was a conduit of unfathomable power, an anchor to a world lost to myth.

"Andres," Sophia called out, her voice tight with concern. "Be careful."

But Andres barely heard her. He felt an irresistible pull toward the artifact as if it were calling to him across the millennia. With each step, the air around him seemed to thicken, charged with ancient energies.

As his hand hovered over the Skull, he hesitated for a heartbeat. Then, driven by an instinct he could not explain, he touched its smooth surface.

Suddenly, the world exploded into light and sound.

Andres gasped as visions flooded his mind—two mighty civilizations locked in conflict, energies beyond comprehension clashing in the skies. He saw Atlantis, resplendent and terrible in its power, facing off against the humble yet formidable forces of Tiwanaku.

"My God," he breathed, his voice barely audible over the sudden hum that filled the chamber.

The moment Andres's fingers touched the Skull; the entire temple came alive. The crystalline network embedded in the walls and floor blazed with light, bathing the room in shifting hues of blue, purple, and gold. The air vibrated with a harmonic frequency that seemed to resonate with the very essence of creation.

Evelyn stumbled back, her eyes wide with awe and a touch of fear. "What's happening?"

But Andres could not answer. He was lost in the vision, witnessing the ancient energy war that had shaped the course of human history. The raw power, the stakes of the conflict—it was almost too much to bear.

As the temple pulsed with awakened energy, the team exchanged worried glances. They had unlocked something profound and potentially dangerous. And as the vibrations intensified, they all sensed that this was only the beginning of their journey into the heart of an ancient mystery.

Andres's hands trembled as he pulled away from the Crystal Skull, his eyes wide and unfocused. The vision's intensity left him reeling, struggling to process the immense weight of his Atlantean heritage.

"Andres?" Sophia's voice cut through his daze. "Are you alright?"

He blinked, trying to ground himself in the present. The temple's crystalline network still hummed with energy, casting dancing shadows across the ancient walls. "I... I saw it all," he mumbled, his voice hoarse. "The war, the destruction. Our legacy."

Amaru stepped closer, his weathered face etched with concern. "What did you see, my friend?"

Andres ran a hand through his hair, a nervous habit surfacing as he grappled with the implications. "The power they wielded... it was incredible but also terrifying. What if—" he hesitated, voicing his deepest fear, "What if I'm not strong enough to control it?"

Julian's smooth voice cut through the tension. "Control what, exactly?" His piercing gaze fixed on Andres, a calculating glint in his eyes. "What kind of power are we talking about here?"

"I'm not sure," Andres replied cautiously. "It's all jumbled. I need time to process it."

Julian's lips curled into a thin smile. "Of course. Take all the time you need." His eyes darted to the Crystal Skull, then back to Andres. "But surely you must have some idea of what this artifact is capable of?"

As Julian spoke, Andres noticed the man's fingers twitching slightly, as if itching to reach for the Skull. A seed of suspicion began to take root in Andres's mind.

"We should focus on securing the site," Andres deflected, trying to steer the conversation away from the Skull's power. "Evelyn, what else can you tell us about these symbols?"

But even as Evelyn launched into an explanation of the glyphs, Andres could not shake the uneasy feeling that had settled over him. He caught Julian casting furtive glances at the artifact, his expression a mix of hunger and calculation.

"Jacqueline, your thoughts," Andres asked.

Her gaze shifted to the Crystal Skull.

"And that... It is the key, isn't it? This Skull is not just an artifact; it is a conduit. It is meant to unlock the full potential of this place, perhaps activating energies we cannot fully comprehend yet. But this also means that if it falls into the wrong hands..." She let the warning hang in the air, the weight of it adding tension to the room.

"Andres, this site is more than we imagined," she concluded. "We're standing on the threshold of something extraordinary—and potentially dangerous."

Andres's mind raced. Could he trust his instincts about Julian? Or was his newfound connection to Atlantis making him paranoid? As the team continued to explore the temple, Andres felt the weight of his dual heritage more acutely than ever, torn between embracing his destiny and fearing the consequences of the power now within his reach.

The atmosphere in the chamber was thick with unease, every eye fixed on the glowing Crystal Skull. Julian lingered at the edge of the group, his hands clasped behind his back. Slowly, he stepped closer under the guise of admiring the intricate carvings on the walls.

"This truly is a marvel," he murmured, his tone casual yet tinged with something unreadable.

Before anyone could react, his hand darted forward, the gleam of a sleek metallic device catching the light as he pressed it against the Skull. "For the Sons of Belial," he hissed under his breath, his words barely audible but sharp as a dagger.

Andres's reflexes kicked in, his body moving before his mind could process the betrayal. He dove, arms outstretched, shielding the Skull with his own body. "Julian, stop!" he yelled, his voice raw with shock and anger.

The temple trembled, ancient mechanisms whirring to life. Eerie whispers filled the air as pulses of blue-white energy crackled along the walls. Andres's skin tingled, the hair on his arms standing on end.

Evelyn's eyes widened as she frantically scanned the glowing symbols. "It's a defense system!" she shouted over the rising hum of energy. "Andres, we need to—"

Her words were cut short as Amaru sprang into action, his weathered hands gripping Julian's arm with surprising strength. "You fool!" the elder hissed, his usually calm demeanor shattered. "You know not what forces you tempt."

Andres's mind raced. How could he have been so blind? He locked eyes with Julian, seeing the man's desperation and fear. "Why?" he demanded, struggling to his feet, the Skull cradled protectively against his chest.

Julian sneered, still wrestling against Amaru's grip. "You're all so naïve. The Brotherhood understands true power. We will reshape the world, not cower before some ancient prophecy!"

The Skull pulsed in Andres's hands, sending a wave of energy that short-circuited Julian's device. The betrayer cried out in pain, dropping the smoking gadget.

Chunks of crystal began to fall from the ceiling as the temple shuddered violently. Andres's heart pounded. They had to get out, but he could not let the Skull fall into the wrong hands. He looked at his team—Evelyn's determined face, Amaru's unwavering strength, even Julian's defeated form—and made his decision.

"Everyone, listen up!" Andres's voice cut through the chaos. "We're getting out of here together. Evelyn, Sophia, Jacqueline, secure any data you can. Amaru, help me with Julian. We leave no one behind, understood?"

As the team scrambled to follow his orders, Andres felt a surge of clarity. The weight of leadership settled on his shoulders, but for the first time, it did not feel like a burden. He was bridging worlds — Atlantean heritage and modern reality, individual power, and collective strength.

"Move, now!" Andres commanded, guiding the group towards the exit. The Skull hummed in his grasp, a reminder of the power and responsibility he now carried. As they raced through the crumbling temple, Andres's resolve hardened. They would face whatever came next as a united front—the only way to confront the challenges that lay ahead.

The moment they crossed the temple's threshold, a blinding flash erupted behind them. Andres whirled around, his eyes widening as he witnessed an incredible sight. The entire chamber pulsed with an otherworldly blue light, emanating from the intricate network of crystals embedded in the walls and ceiling.

"My God," Evelyn gasped, her scientific mind struggling to comprehend the spectacle. "It's like the whole place is... awakening."

The energy surge rippled outward, causing the ground beneath their feet to tremble. Ancient Atlantean symbols etched into the stone walls began to glow, their patterns shifting and rearranging in a hypnotic dance.

"We need to move," Andres urged, his voice tight with urgency. "This pulse could alert every enemy within miles."

As they sprinted through the labyrinthine corridors, the reverberations grew stronger. The Crystal Skull in Andres's hands seemed to resonate with the awakening technology, its surface shimmering with an inner light.

"Andres," Sophia called out, her voice strained, "what's happening?"

He shook his head, feeling the weight of his incomplete knowledge. "I'm not sure, but I think we've triggered some kind of ancient defense system. Or worse, a beacon."

The team pressed on, their footsteps echoing through the cavernous halls. Julian, supported by Amaru, stumbled along with them, his face a mask of conflicted emotions.

As they neared the exit, Andres's mind raced. The betrayal, the Skull, the awakening technology—it was almost too much to process.

He glanced at his team, noting the mix of fear, determination, and uncertainty on their faces.

"Everyone alright?" he asked, trying to keep his voice steady.

Evelyn nodded, clutching her tablet. "I managed to download some data before we left. It might help us understand what we've unleashed."

Andres's jaw clenched. "Good thinking. We'll need every advantage we can get."

Finally, they burst out of the underground city, the cool night air a stark contrast to the charged atmosphere they'd left behind. The team huddled together, catching their breath and taking stock of their situation.

"What now?" Amaru asked, his eyes fixed on Julian.

Andres felt the weight of their expectant gazes. He looked down at the Crystal Skull, its enigmatic presence a constant reminder of the immense responsibility he now bore.

"Now," he said, his voice low and determined, "we figure out our next move. And quickly."

Miles away, in a dimly lit command center, General Kaine stood rigidly before a wall of flickering monitors. His steel-gray eyes narrowed as he processed the sudden surge of data flooding his screens.

"Sir," a young technician called out, "we've detected a massive energy spike in the Tiwanaku region. It matches the signature we've been tracking."

Kaine's jaw tightened, a muscle twitching beneath his skin. "Paredes," he muttered, his voice a low growl. "Triangulate the exact location and prepare a strike team. We move in 10."

As his subordinates scrambled to obey, Kaine allowed himself a moment of reflection. The stakes had just risen exponentially. Whatever Paredes and his team had uncovered, it was clear they were dangerously close to upsetting the delicate balance the Sons of Belial had worked so hard to maintain.

"Not this time, Doctor," he murmured, his fingers tracing the outline of an ancient symbol etched into his tactical vest. "Your misguided quest ends here."

Meanwhile, back at the entrance to the underground city, Andres and his team huddled in the shadows, their breath visible in the cool night air. The Crystal Skull pulsed faintly in Andres's grip, a constant reminder of the power they now possessed—and the danger that came with it.

"We need to move," Evelyn said urgently, her eyes darting around the darkened landscape. "That energy surge will have every Sons of Belial operative in the area converging on this spot."

Andres nodded, his mind racing. "Agreed. But where? We can't risk leading them back to our base camp."

Amaru stepped forward, his expression grim. "I know a place. An old sanctuary used by my people, hidden in the mountains. It's not far, and it's well-protected by both natural and... other means."

"Other means?" Sophia asked, her eyebrow raised.

Amaru's lips quirked in a humorless smile. "Let's just say my people have ways of staying hidden that even the Sons of Belial can't penetrate."

Andres weighed their options, acutely aware of every second ticking by. The weight of leadership pressed down on him, each decision potentially the difference between success and catastrophe.

"Alright," he said finally. "Lead the way, Amaru. But we need to be smart about this. Evelyn, can you use that data you downloaded to mask our trail?"

Evelyn nodded, already tapping away at her tablet. "I think so. It'll take some doing, but I should be able to create a false energy signature to throw them off our scent."

"Do it," Andres commanded. He turned to Julian, who had been unnaturally quiet since their escape. "And you. I do not trust you as far as I can throw you, but right now, we need every hand we can get. Are you with us, or do I need to leave you tied up in a cave somewhere?"

Julian met Andres' gaze, his eyes a swirl of conflicting emotions. "I... I am with you. For now. But don't think this changes anything between us, Paredes."

Andres's lips tightened. "Wouldn't dream of it. Now let us move. We've got a long night ahead."

As the team melded into the darkness, following Amaru's lead, Andre could not shake the feeling that they were being watched. Somewhere out there, Nathaneal Blake and the Sons of Belial were closing in. The real battle, he knew, was just beginning.

Chapter 8

The trek to the hidden sanctuary was grueling, the mountain trails steep and treacherous under the cover of night. Andres's mind raced as they climbed, every rustle in the forest a potential threat, every shadow a reminder of the relentless forces hunting them. Amaru moved with ease through the terrain, his connection to the land palpable, while the others struggled to keep up. Despite Evelyn's efforts to mask their trail, Andres's unease only grew. The sanctuary would offer temporary refuge, but it was clear to him that they could not afford to stay hidden for long. Answers awaited them in the underground city—answers they desperately needed if they were to survive the trials ahead.

The next morning, they gathered back in the Temple. The air in the ancient chamber crackled with energy, sending goosebumps racing across Andres's skin. The rhythmic hum of the Crystal Skull seemed to resonate with his very heartbeat, an almost hypnotic pull that made every detail of the chamber sharper, more vivid. Shadows danced across the crystalline walls, their fluid movements suggesting something alive and watchful.

Andres's team fanned out behind him, their expressions a mix of awe and trepidation. Jacqueline adjusted her glasses, her eyes fixed on the glowing glyphs etched into the walls. "These markings—" she began, her voice tinged with wonder.

"Later," Andres cut her off softly, his focus unbroken. His instincts screamed that something pivotal was about to unfold.

Suddenly, the atmosphere shifted. A faint vibration rippled through the ground beneath their feet, followed by a low, melodious hum that seemed to emanate from the very chamber itself. The light dimmed, and then a figure emerged from the shadows, bathed in an otherworldly glow.

Andres's breath caught in his throat. The figure was unlike anything he had ever seen—tall and regal, with flowing garments that shimmered as though woven from starlight. It appeared to be a woman, and her features were otherworldly, yet unmistakably human. She was ethereal, with long brown hair cascading down her back, framing a face of haunting beauty. But it was her emerald eyes that captivated Andres—luminous, radiating both wisdom and sorrow, as if they held the secrets of the universe. A brilliant diamond-like light shone from her forehead, pulsing gently with a rhythm that matched the quickening beat of Andres's heart.

Then, something stirred deep within him—an echo from a time long past. The moment their eyes met, a rush of fragmented memories flooded his mind—flashes of a lost civilization, whispers of a forgotten love, hands reaching for each other across the ages. He staggered slightly, overwhelmed by the sudden wave of recognition. He *knew* her. Not just in this moment, but across lifetimes.

A name hovered on the edge of his consciousness, just beyond reach. His lips parted, but no sound came. Yet, in the depths of her gaze, he saw the same recognition—the same silent knowing. They had found each other again.

"Who... who are you?" Andres managed to whisper, his voice thick with a mixture of awe and disbelief.

The figure's gaze swept over the team, pausing on each of them as though weighing their very souls. Finally, her eyes settled on Andres.

"I am Maya," she said, her voice resonating with a melodic depth that filled the chamber. "The Emissary of Atlantis. You have journeyed far, but your path has only begun."

A stunned silence fell over the group, broken only by the faint hum of the Crystal Skull. Andres's mind raced as he tried to comprehend what he was seeing and hearing. Every instinct told him this was the moment he had been searching for his entire life.

As Maya stepped forward, her presence filled the chamber with a sense of ancient wisdom and profound purpose.

Maya's voice was a melody that resonated deep within Andres, awakening memories buried in his soul. She met his gaze, her tone both gentle and resolute.

"Andres, you carry the blood of Atlantis and the spirit of Tiwanaku. Your Mapuche ancestry ties you to the wisdom of Tiwanaku, yet within you also flows the legacy of Atlantis. You are the bridge between two worlds, destined to heal an ancient rift and shape humanity's destiny."

Andres stood transfixed, feeling a surge of emotions—awe, disbelief, and a strange familiarity that he could not quite place. Maya's words echoed in his mind, unlocking fragments of memories that felt both alien and strangely comforting.

Andres's heart pounded. "What do you mean?"

The room spun around Andres as he grappled with this revelation. "That's... that's impossible," he stammered, even as a deep part of him recognized the truth in her words. "How can I be connected to both?" Andres's voice cracked, his usual composure crumbling. "I'm just an archaeologist, not some... cosmic mediator."

Maya stepped closer, her presence both comforting and overwhelming. "The knowledge lies dormant within you, waiting to be awakened. Your journey here was no accident, Andres. It is the culmination of many lifetimes."

As Andres struggled to process this information, he felt the weight of destiny settling upon his shoulders. His mind raced with questions, doubts, and an inexplicable sense of recognition. The chamber seemed to pulse around him, ancient energies stirring in response to this revelation.

Amaru, the elderly Tiwanaku shaman, stepped forward from the shadows. His weathered face was etched with deep lines, each a testament to the wisdom he carried. Leaning on his intricately carved staff, he fixed Andres with a penetrating gaze.

"The path of two rivers often converges into one mighty stream," Amaru intoned, his voice rich with metaphor. "Your dual heritage is not a burden, but a gift from Pachamama herself and valued in the Mapuche tradition as well. Your grandmother was such a person, Andres. Abuela bridged both worlds in her time..."

Andres' brow furrowed. "But how can I possibly reconcile these two parts of myself? They were at war!" His voice held an edge of frustration, but beneath it lay something deeper—fear, uncertainty, a resistance to the truth he was not yet ready to face.

He had spent his life navigating the chasm between two identities—the rational scientist and the heir to an ancient wisdom that defied logic. His Mapuche blood carried the echoes of shamans and seers, keepers of the old ways, while his modern training demanded facts, evidence, and tangible proof. These two forces had always pulled him in opposite directions, and for years, he had tried to suppress one in favor of the other. Yet now, standing at the threshold of something far greater than himself, he realized the price of that denial.

"You are the bridge, Andres," Amaru said gently as if sensing his turmoil. "But first, you must stop fearing what is within you."

Andres swallowed hard. He had always sought answers in the material world, believing that knowledge alone would guide him. But this was different. The Crystal Skull, the Vesica Piscis, the cosmic forces converging—none of it could be unlocked through intellect alone. It required something deeper: a surrender to the unknown, a willingness to embrace the parts of himself he had long ignored.

Could he do it? Could he let go of the self-doubt, the fear that he was an imposter in both worlds? Could he embrace the power within him, rather than resist it?

He clenched his fists. He had to. The fate of more than just himself depended on it.

Amaru's eyes twinkled. "Conflict breeds understanding, young one. The eagle and the condor once fought, but now they fly together. So, too, must Atlantis and Tiwanaku find harmony through you."

Beside him, Evelyn's analytical gaze softened as she watched the exchange between Andres and Maya. Her scientific mind struggled to reconcile the mystical elements at play, but there was a flicker of recognition in her eyes, a glimmer of understanding that transcended logic.

The crystals lining the chamber walls hummed in response to Maya's presence, their light intensifying to form a halo around her. Andres felt a pull towards her, an inexplicable connection that left him speechless.

Andres's mind reeled. He said, "Atlantis?" He glanced at his teammates, seeing his own awe and disbelief mirrored in their expressions.

Maya raised her hands, her fingers tracing intricate patterns in the air, as though weaving threads of light. The space around them seemed to ripple as if reality itself had become malleable. A soft hum resonated, growing in intensity until the very air seemed alive with unseen energy.

Suddenly, the dim cavern walls flickered with brilliance, transforming into a living canvas. Visions—or perhaps holographic projections far beyond any technology Andres could fathom—materialized around them. A golden city emerged, breathtaking in its splendor as if plucked from the dreams of an ancient god. Towering crystal spires shimmered under an eternal sun, refracting light in cascading rainbows. Golden bridges arched gracefully over streams of liquid light, and lush gardens teemed with flora that glowed with an inner luminescence.

Andres gasped; his breath stolen by the sheer magnificence. He could see figures, unmistakably human, yet exuding an aura of otherworldly grace, moving with purpose through the city's ethereal streets. These beings, adorned in flowing garments that seemed woven from starlight, wielded energy as effortlessly as an artist wields a brush. With a mere gesture, they shaped and directed luminous currents, crafting objects, healing others, and powering intricate mechanisms that hovered and pulsed with a soft, rhythmic glow.

In one corner of the vision, a group of individuals stepped into shimmering ovals of light—portals that rippled like liquid glass. As they entered, they vanished instantly, only to reappear elsewhere in the city with a brilliance that suggested the mastery of time and space itself.

Andres's mind raced to comprehend what he was seeing. *Was this Atlantis? A memory etched into the fabric of the Earth, waiting to be awakened? Or was it something more—an invitation to rediscover what humanity had lost?*

"Behold the glory of Atlantis at its peak," Maya intoned. "Masters of cosmic energies and crystalline technology."

Maya, her face radiant with an inner glow, turned to Andres. "This is what was," she said, her voice resonating with a depth that sent shivers down his spine, "and what can be again—if we remember; if we choose."

The scene shifted abruptly, and the radiant golden city dissolved into chaos. The brilliant crystal spires, once reaching toward the heavens, began to tremble violently. Cracks appeared in their pristine surfaces, spreading like veins of despair. The light that had once suffused the city with warmth and life flickered and dimmed, replaced by an ominous crimson glow that seemed to emanate from the ground itself.

Andres's heart clenched as he watched the magnificent civilization unravel before his eyes. The once-placid streams of liquid light surged violently, their gentle glow transformed into raging torrents that swallowed bridges and gardens alike. The serene hum of the city was replaced by a deafening cacophony—earthquakes roared like angry gods, shattering streets, and toppling structures. Crystals exploded into shards, raining down like deadly hail upon the fleeing populace.

The figures, so composed and graceful just moments before, now ran in panic, their faces etched with terror. Andres saw families clutching one another, desperately seeking shelter as the ground beneath them split apart, swallowing entire sections of the city into a chasm of molten fire. Portals that once served as pathways of enlightenment and travel now malfunctioned, flickering erratically, or collapsing altogether, trapping those who tried to escape.

The sky above mirrored the chaos below, turning a sickly hue as storms of ash and lightning raged. Flaming debris rained down, igniting what remained of the lush gardens. Great waves surged from the oceans beyond, crashing into the city with unrelenting fury, as if the very elements had conspired to obliterate all traces of this once-glorious civilization.

Amid the destruction, Andres's eyes were drawn to the temple at the heart of the city. Its massive crystal beacon, which had once shone like a star, pulsed erratically, as though struggling to maintain its integrity. A final, blinding surge of light erupted from its core, illuminating the devastation for one agonizing moment before the temple imploded, sending shockwaves that rippled across the landscape.

Andres felt a lump rise in his throat as he witnessed the people—beings of extraordinary wisdom and grace—fall to their knees, clutching their hearts as if mourning the loss of something far greater than their city. In their eyes, he saw not just fear, but an overwhelming sorrow, as though they understood this was not just an end, but a failure—a collapse of a dream they had nurtured for millennia.

Maya's voice broke through the harrowing silence that followed. "This is the cost of forgetting," she whispered, her tone heavy with grief. "The cost of imbalance, of hubris, of turning away from the harmony we were meant to uphold." She turned to Andres, her eyes glistening with unshed tears. "And this is why we must not fail again. Our hubris led to our downfall," Maya continued, her voice heavy with sorrow, "but hope remains. You stand at the precipice of humanity's awakening."

Andres's thoughts raced. *Could this be real? Or had they stumbled into some elaborate hoax?* Yet the visions felt viscerally true, stirring something deep within him.

"What awakening?" he managed to ask, his voice hoarse.

Maya's voice carried a quiet intensity as she spoke, her words reverberating through the chamber. "2038," she said, her dark eyes burning with conviction, "is not just a year. It is the culmination of cosmic cycles—the Atlantean Prophecy calls it the Gateway of Ascension. A time when humanity will face its greatest challenge and its greatest opportunity."

Andres asked, "What kind of opportunity?"

Maya stepped closer, her gaze unwavering. "The prophecy speaks of Homo Omega—the next stage in human evolution. A state of being where heart-centered consciousness becomes the norm, where humanity awakens to its divine potential as co-creators. Bilocation, teleportation, multidimensional awareness—these are not just myths, Andres. They are your birthright, dormant abilities waiting to be realized."

She gestured to the intricate carvings on the wall, symbols pulsing faintly with an energy Andres could almost feel.

"The activation of the global energy grid is central to this shift. It is not just about restoring balance to Earth's energies—it is about awakening the collective Higher Self of humanity. Aligning the grid will catalyze the realization of the 'God nature' within us all."

Andres swallowed hard, the weight of her words settling in his chest. "And I am the bridge for this?

Maya's expression softened, but her voice remained steady. "Yes, Andres. The prophecy speaks of one with dual heritage—both indigenous and Atlantean—who will unite the wisdom of the past with the potential of the future. You are that bridge. The one destined to awaken the grid and guide humanity toward its transformation."

His mind raced, grappling with the enormity of her statement. "This... this is too much. I am just an archaeologist, Maya. I study the past. I don't shape the future."

"You already are," Maya countered, stepping even closer. "Your every action, every choice, has brought you here. Do you think it is coincidence that the Atlantean Crystal Skull came into your possession? That the scroll spoke to you in a language your soul already knew? The rise of Homo Omega depends on you, Andres. The prophecy has chosen you for a reason."

Andres shook his head, feeling the pressure of destiny like a weight on his shoulders. "And if I fail? If I am not enough?"

Maya's gaze softened, though her resolve remained steadfast. "You will not fail, Andres—not if you trust the wisdom already within you. The Christos Avatar of the past paved the way, embodying the divine potential of humanity. Now, in this second return, new way showers are emerging, manifesting as the next evolutionary step: Homo Omega. This transformation is not about perfection; it is about embracing heart-centered consciousness—choosing love, unity, and courage to transcend fear and division."

The room fell silent, the only sound the faint hum of energy radiating from the ancient carvings. Andres exhaled slowly, his mind still struggling to process the enormity of what Maya was saying.

Finally, he looked up at her, his voice barely above a whisper. "If this is true, then everything we do here matters more than I ever imagined."

"It does," Maya said gently, her hand resting on his arm. "But you're not alone in this, Andres. The prophecy may name you as the bridge, but this journey is one we all share. Together, we can prepare humanity for the energetic shift of 2038. Together, we can help usher in the era of Homo Omega."

Andres's legs trembled. He steadied himself against a crystal column, its energy thrumming through him. "I... I don't understand."

"You will," Maya said gently. "Your Mapuche ancestry connects you to the wisdom of Tiwanaku. Your quest to uncover Atlantean secrets has led you here. Your past lives in Atlantis and the integration in your current lifetime. It is no coincidence."

As the weight of Maya's words sank in, Andres felt a spark of recognition. The inexplicable dreams that had haunted him since childhood, his obsession with ancient mysteries—suddenly, it all seemed to fit into a grander design. Was it Maya who appeared in his dream, he thought?

"What must we do?" Andres asked, surprising himself with the determination in his voice.

Maya smiled softly, her hands resting on the ancient crystal formations. The crystals pulsed with a rhythm that seemed to resonate with the very heartbeat of the Earth. As the glow intensified, the cavern filled with a subtle warmth, as though the energy itself carried a living presence.

"The global energy grid," Maya began, her voice carrying a reverent tone, "is more than just a network of power. It is the Earth's lifeblood, a sacred weave of energy that connects every living being to the cosmos. In ancient times, our ancestors understood this. They built their great civilizations around these sacred nodes—places where the energy of the Earth and the heavens converged in perfect harmony."

She traced her fingers over the crystal surface, and holographic images bloomed in the air: vast temples aligned with celestial constellations, monoliths standing guard over ley lines, and golden spirals of energy radiating outward from key sites. "When the grid was active," she continued, "it sustained a balance between humanity and the natural world. It elevated consciousness, fostering unity, compassion, and a deeper understanding of our purpose in the universe."

Her expression darkened, and the harmonious glow of the crystals dimmed slightly. "But the grid has been damaged," she said gravely. "The balance has been disrupted, its energy fractured by millennia of neglect, misuse, and the rise of forces that sought to suppress its power. Dimensional rifts are appearing around the globe, tears in the fabric of reality where the veil between worlds has grown dangerously thin."

Andres listened, the weight of her words settling heavily upon him. "What do you mean by rifts?" he asked, his voice tinged with unease.

Maya's eyes met his, her gaze filled with both sorrow and urgency. "These rifts are gateways," she explained, "but not to realms of light. They allow darker forces to seep through—entities that thrive on chaos, fear, and destruction. These beings, once banished or contained by the grid's harmony, now roam freely, corrupting the natural order. They create wars, amplify division, and fuel the despair that keeps humanity bound to a lower state of existence."

As Maya spoke, the holographic images morphed into a montage of calamities across time and space. Cities crumbled under storm-laden skies, fires, and seas churned with malevolent force, and cracks snaked through the Earth, glowing with an ominous energy. Shadowy forms flickered in the corners of the projections, their movements unnatural, their presence chilling.

"The rifts are not merely portals," Maya said, her voice edged with urgency. "They are wounds—festering infections spreading instability across dimensions. If left unchecked, they could unravel the delicate balance between worlds, plunging not just humanity but the entire Earth into chaos."

The images shifted again, revealing historical and recent events intertwined with the effects of these dimensional breaches.

"Look here," Maya gestured, and the hologram highlighted footage of the Ukraine conflict in 2022. Soldiers moved cautiously through a fog-shrouded battlefield where glowing fissures carved the land, swallowing anything that ventured too close. "This war was not merely a geopolitical struggle—it was exacerbated by a dimensional rupture, fueling the chaos and amplifying the suffering."

Another image appeared, this time of the Gaza Strip in 2024. Explosions lit the night sky, but the true horror lay beneath: a jagged rift glowing an eerie crimson, spewing otherworldly tendrils that twisted through the ruins. "This was not just a human conflict. The rift turned despair into a breeding ground for energies that fed on fear and hatred, making resolution impossible. Many of these rifts are ancient and have become active again."

The hologram shifted yet again, displaying an aerial view of the Taiwan Strait in 2028. Chinese, U.S., and Allied Naval Forces clashed, their missiles lighting up the dark waters. Amid the chaos, a massive rift towered above the sea, its tendrils rippling through the air like a living entity. "The tension between nations became a catalyst for dimensional destabilization, pulling not just Earth but also in space and other realms into the maelstrom."

The images continued: wars, earthquakes that decimated regions in South America, droughts that starved millions in Africa, and wildfires that raged across Australia. In each scene, the presence of the rifts loomed, barely noticeable at first but undeniably central upon closer inspection.

"These are not isolated incidents," Maya pressed. "The rifts feed on division, conflict, and fear. They intensify our worst tendencies, turning disputes into disasters and disasters into existential threats. If we do not act to seal them and restore the balance of the global energy grid, these events will escalate—until there is nothing left to save."

Andres watched, his mind spinning as he connected the dots. "So, every major crisis we've faced… has been tied to these rifts?"

Maya nodded solemnly. "Not every one, but many have been amplified or triggered by their presence. The activation of the global energy grid is not just about awakening humanity—it is also about healing these wounds before they destroy us all."

The crystals pulsed again, brighter this time as if responding to her words. "This is why we must act, Andres. Reawakening the grid is not just about restoring its power. It is about healing the Earth, sealing the rifts, and preventing these darker forces from consolidating their hold. The grid holds the key to stabilizing reality itself, to closing the rifts and reestablishing the harmony that once safeguarded our world."

Her voice dropped to a whisper, heavy with resolve. "This is our greatest challenge. To awaken the sacred nodes, to let them sing again, and to align their energies before it is too late. The fate of humanity, of all life, hangs in the balance. We must choose unity over division, love over fear, and light over shadow—or risk losing everything to the darkness."

As Andres absorbed Maya's words, he felt a profound shift within himself. Doubt gave way to purpose, confusion to clarity. Whatever trials lay ahead, he knew with certainty that this was his path. The chamber hummed with potential, and Andres stood ready to embrace his destiny.

Andres's eyes widened, his breath catching in his throat as he struggled to process Maya's incredible claim. The weight of her words settled over the chamber like a thick fog, leaving the team in stunned silence.

Around him, the team's reactions varied wildly. Julian Blackwood's face contorted with a mix of skepticism and poorly concealed excitement. Amaru, the team's spiritual guide, nodded solemnly as if confirming a long-held suspicion. Others exchanged bewildered glances, their expressions a kaleidoscope of confusion, disbelief, and awe.

Evelyn stepped forward, her analytical mind already dissecting Maya's statements. "I'm sorry, but I have to challenge this," she said, her tone firm but not unkind. "The idea of Atlantis as more than myth, let alone having an emissary in our midst, defies all scientific understanding."

Maya turned her ethereal gaze to Evelyn, a serene smile playing on her lips.

Evelyn continued, her words measured and precise. "While I'm open to new evidence, extraordinary claims require extraordinary proof. How can we verify your connection to Atlantis? And more importantly, how does this relate to our research here in Tiwanaku?"

Andres found himself nodding along with Evelyn's questions, his own scientific training battling with the inexplicable sense of truth he felt in Maya's presence. He watched intently, torn between skepticism and a growing, inexplicable certainty that they stood on the precipice of something world-changing.

Maya's melodic voice filled the chamber, her words painting vivid images in the minds of her listeners. "Atlantis and Tiwanaku were not mere civilizations, but guardians of cosmic balance. While Atlantis reached for the stars, harnessing crystals and energy beyond mortal ken, Tiwanaku remained rooted in the Earth's spiritual essence."

Andres felt a shiver run down his spine as Maya's narrative began to align with fragments of his own research. He glanced at Evelyn, noting the slight furrow in her brow as she listened intently.

"The conflict arose," Maya continued, her green eyes shimmering with a light that seemed to pulse in rhythm with the chamber's energy, "when Atlantis sought to harness and dominate the global energy grid. To the Atlanteans, it was a grand mechanism, a system of untold power that could elevate their civilization to even greater heights. They viewed Tiwanaku's ways—their profound connection to the natural world—as primitive, a limitation to progress."

She paused, her gaze sweeping over Andres and Evelyn, allowing the weight of her words to settle. Then, her voice softened. "When Atlantis fell, those who understood the true purpose of the energy grid fled. Many perished, but some survived, taking refuge in the sacred lands of the Earth's most ancient civilizations. Some journeyed to Khemet, to the Indus Valley, to the Americas. And some—my ancestors—came here."

Andres inhaled sharply. The idea of an Atlantean migration had always been speculation, a tantalizing thread in myth and esoteric history, but hearing Maya say it with such conviction made it feel tangible, real.

"I was born of that lineage," she continued, "raised to remember what was lost, to protect what remains hidden until the time was right. And now, the time has come."

Her emerald gaze locked onto Andres, and for a fleeting moment, he felt as though she were speaking directly to him—as if he, too, was part of something much older than he could yet comprehend.

She stepped closer to the Crystal Skull, her delicate fingers brushing the air above its surface as though she could feel its ancient memories. "But Tiwanaku's wisdom ran deeper than Atlantis ever realized. They understood that the energy grid was not merely a tool to be wielded; it was a sentient, living, breathing network of forces, a bridge between the earthly and the cosmic. They revered it as sacred, requiring balance and reverence, not domination. It was also the spirit of the mother—Gaia."

Andres exchanged a glance with Evelyn, whose notebook trembled slightly in her hands as she furiously scribbled down every word.

Maya's voice grew heavy with sorrow. "The Atlanteans, however, could not see beyond their ambition. They developed crystalline technologies and machines capable of amplifying the grid's power, but in their haste, they disrupted its equilibrium. Tiwanaku warned them of the consequences—imbalances in the Earth's energy, cataclysmic shifts—but the warnings went unheeded. What Atlantis called progress, Tiwanaku called hubris."

She paused, her gaze distant as if reliving the ancient schism. "When Tiwanaku refused to share their sacred knowledge, the rift deepened. Atlantis turned to conquest, seeking to force the Tiwanaku into submission. It was no longer just a clash of civilizations but a war of ideologies—technology versus spirituality, domination versus harmony, pride versus humility."

The room seemed to grow colder as Maya's words sank in. "The consequences were devastating. Atlantis's experiments pushed the grid beyond its limits, triggering the very cataclysms Tiwanaku had foreseen. The Earth itself rebelled—tsunamis, earthquakes, storms. The great Atlantean empire fell, as did many of Tiwanaku's sacred sites. Yet even in their final moments, Tiwanaku's wisdom endured, encoded in their temples, their symbols, and their alliance with the cosmic forces."

Maya turned to face Andres, her luminous gaze piercing into his. "And now, you stand at the crossroads of this ancient conflict, inheritors of both their mistakes and their potential. The question is—will humanity repeat the errors of Atlantis, or will it embrace the balance that Tiwanaku died to protect?"

Evelyn's expression shifted from skepticism to intrigue. "That... actually aligns with some linguistic parallels I've uncovered. There are recurring symbols in both cultures that suggest a shared understanding of cosmic energies."

Andres's mind raced, connecting dots he had never considered. "The raised fields of Tiwanaku," he murmured, "they weren't just for agriculture, were they?"

Maya smiled enigmatically. "No, Andres. They were conduits for Earth's spiritual energies, just as Atlantis' crystal towers channeled cosmic forces."

As Andres pondered these words, Maya stepped forward, her robes shimmering with an otherworldly light. "The stakes of our mission extend far beyond personal revelations," she said, her tone urgent. "We must reactivate the global energy grid before it's too late."

"The grid?" Evelyn asked, her scientific curiosity piqued.

Jacqueline swallowed hard, breaking the tense silence. "These rifts—are they what allowed the dark forces to enter?"

Maya turned to her, nodding. "Yes. The Sons of Belial, as you know them, thrive on these distortions. They are drawn to chaos and imbalance, feeding off the fear and division such rifts create. Through the weakened grid, they manipulate the energy of entire regions, fueling conflict, greed, and ignorance. Their influence is subtle yet pervasive, spreading like a shadow over the world."

Andres felt a chill run through him. "Is there any way to repair the grid?" he asked, his voice barely above a whisper.

"There is," Maya replied, her tone resolute. "But it will not be easy. The ley lines are blocked in some places, severed in others. Sacred sites once brimming with energy have been desecrated or forgotten, their power dormant. To restore the grid, these blockages must be cleared, and the balance reestablished. The Crystal Skull holds part of the key to this process, as do other ancient artifacts scattered across the globe. But time is not on our side."

Evelyn frowned, her analytical mind racing. "If we don't act, what happens to the rifts?"

Maya's gaze hardened. "They will grow, spreading like cracks in a dam. Eventually, they will become too large to contain, and the dark forces will pour through unchecked. Entire regions will fall into chaos, and the grid, already fragile, will collapse completely. At that point, humanity's path forward will be one of entropy, not evolution."

The chamber grew silent, the weight of her words pressing down on everyone. Finally, Maya added, her voice a beacon of hope amid the despair, "But this does not have to be humanity's fate. You stand at the threshold of a great choice. Will you repair what was broken and restore the balance, or will you let the shadows consume all that remains?"

Andres felt a chill run down his spine. "So, the Sons of Belial's role is to harness the grid's power for their own dark purposes. If they succeed, the consequences would be catastrophic."

Maya answered," Yes."

Amaru placed a gnarled hand on Andres's shoulder. "But remember, you do not walk this path alone. The wisdom of your ancestors guides you."

"Indeed," Maya added, her voice softening as a faint, golden glow seemed to emanate from her. "And the Angels of Atlantis stand ready to lend their strength to our cause. Their ethereal light will illuminate even the darkest corners of this journey, guiding us through the shadows that seek to obscure the truth."

Andres hesitated; "Who are the Angels of Atlantis?" he asked, his voice tinged with both curiosity and reverence.

Maya turned to him, her luminous eyes radiating warmth and wisdom. "The Angels of Atlantis are celestial beings, guardians of the ancient wisdom and protectors of the sacred balance. They are not of this world, yet their presence has shaped it profoundly. In the time of Atlantis, they were revered as emissaries of the Divine, beings who bridged the higher dimensions and our earthly plane. They taught us the principles of unity, harmony, and the interconnectedness of all life."

She paused, her gaze shifting to the Crystal Skull. "When the fall of Atlantis began, the Angels withdrew, their light dimmed by the growing darkness. But they did not abandon us. From their realms, they watched, waiting for the moment when humanity would be ready to reclaim its higher purpose. Now, as the grid falters and the rifts spread, their presence grows stronger. They see in this team—" she gestured to the group—"the potential to heal what was broken."

Jacqueline, who had been silently absorbing Maya's words asked, "You mean they are here now? With us?"

Maya nodded. "They are always with us, though their presence is felt most strongly by those who are open to their guidance. They communicate through visions, synchronicities, and dreams, offering wisdom and courage when it is most needed. But be warned—they do not intervene directly. They illuminate the path, but the steps must be yours to take."

Andres felt a strange warmth spread through him, a quiet reassurance that he was not alone in this daunting mission. "And their role in all this?" he asked, gesturing to the chamber around them.

"They will help you remember," Maya said, her voice gentle yet resolute. "The Angels hold the keys to the lost knowledge of Atlantis, knowledge that is encoded in the very fabric of your souls. They will awaken the memories you need to navigate this journey and protect you from the forces that seek to keep those truths hidden. But you must trust them, even when the way forward seems unclear."

Her words hung in the air, a mixture of comfort and challenge. Andres exchanged a glance with Evelyn and the others, a sense of shared purpose flickering in their eyes. They were not just a team of archaeologists and scholars—they were guardians of a legacy far greater than themselves.

Andres closed his eyes, feeling the weight of history and destiny pressing down upon him. When he opened them again, there was a new resolve in his gaze. "Then we have no choice," he said, his voice steady. "We must succeed. For the sake of both worlds—and all that lies between."

As Andres's words hung in the air, a low hum began to reverberate through the chamber. The team exchanged startled glances as symbols etched into the ancient stone walls flickered to life, pulsing with an otherworldly blue light.

"What's happening?" Evelyn gasped, her scientific mind racing to make sense of the inexplicable phenomenon.

Andres's heart pounded as he watched the glyphs dance across the walls, their patterns both familiar and alien. "It's responding to us," he whispered, awe and trepidation mingling in his voice.

The ground beneath their feet trembled, a gentle but insistent vibration that seemed to sync with the pulsing light. Maya's eyes widened, a mix of excitement and apprehension flashing across her face. "The temple is awakening," she breathed.

Suddenly, the center of the chamber erupted in a swirl of light and energy. Andres instinctively shielded his eyes but found he could still see through the brightness. Images began to form in the vortex, shimmering and ethereal.

"By the gods," Amaru murmured, his weathered face illuminated by the spectacle.

The visions coalesced, showing towering crystal spires and shimmering energy fields—Atlantis in all its glory. But the scene quickly shifted, revealing dark clouds gathering on the horizon. Andre watched in horror as beams of destructive energy lanced between Atlantis and what he somehow knew to be Tiwanaku.

"The energy war," he said, his voice barely above a whisper. "It's showing us the past."

As cities crumbled and the earth itself seemed to cry out in pain, Andres felt a surge of emotion. This was not just history—it was his history, his heritage. The conflicting bloodlines within him resonated with both the attackers and the defenders.

"It doesn't have to end this way," he found himself saying, his eyes locked on the swirling images. "There has to be another path."

As if in response to his thoughts, the vision shifted once more. The destruction faded, replaced by glimpses of unity—Atlantean and Tiwanaku symbols intertwining, their energies harmonizing instead of clashing.

Andres's breath caught in his throat. He felt a connection, deep and primal, to the potential future unfolding before him. In that moment, he understood with crystal clarity why he had been chosen for this mission.

"I see it now," he said, his voice strong and filled with newfound purpose. "The prophecy, my role—it's all about bringing balance, isn't it? Healing the rift between these two great civilizations?"

Maya nodded, a smile of pride and relief spreading across her face. "You understand, then?"

Andres squared his shoulders, feeling the weight of destiny settling upon them. "I do. And I'm ready to embrace it, whatever the cost."

Maya's serene expression suddenly tensed, her emerald eyes darting to the temple's ornate entrance. "We must act swiftly," she warned, her melodic voice tinged with urgency. "The Sons of Belial draw near. Their dark energies seek to smother the light we've awakened here."

Evelyn ran her fingers along a line of glowing hieroglyphs. "There's a pattern here," she muttered, her analytical mind racing. "It's not just decorative—it's a code, a sequence."

Andres felt a chill run down his spine. "How much time do we have, Maya?"

"Minutes, at most," the Atlantean emissary replied, her robes shimmering as she moved to join Evelyn. "We must decipher the temple's secrets before they arrive."

Amaru, his weathered face etched with concern, placed a hand on Andres's shoulder. "Trust your instincts, my friend. Your Mapuche blood carries ancient wisdom. Let it guide you."

Andres closed his eyes, trying to quiet the storm of thoughts in his mind. He could feel the temple's energy pulsing around him, through him. Fragments of visions flashed behind his eyelids—crystal towers, sacred geometries, the intertwining of cosmic forces.

"The Crystal Skull!" he exclaimed, his eyes snapping open. "It's not just a key—it's a conduit. We need to—"

His words were cut short as the ground beneath them shuddered violently. The glowing symbols on the walls flared with blinding intensity, and a low, resonant hum filled the air. The ancient mechanisms of the temple, dormant for millennia, surged to life with terrifying force.

"What's happening?" Evelyn shouted over the growing cacophony, struggling to maintain her balance as tremors rocked the chamber.

Maya's voice rang out, clear and commanding. "The temple is awakening! The energies are becoming unstable—we must act now to harness them!"

Andres stumbled toward the central altar, drawn by an inexplicable force. As his hand touched the cool surface of the Crystal Skull, a vision slammed into him with the force of a tidal wave. He saw himself standing at the nexus of time and space, wielding forces beyond mortal comprehension. The fate of two great civilizations—of humanity itself—hung in the balance.

"I see it," he gasped, his voice barely audible over the chaos. "I know what I have to do."

As debris rained down around them and the very fabric of reality seemed to warp, Andres gripped the Crystal Skull tightly. His determination solidified into an unshakeable resolve. Whatever trials lay ahead, whatever sacrifices might be required, he would see this through. The survival of everything they held dear depended on it.

The thunderous sound of footsteps echoed from the corridor beyond, a low rumble that quickly grew into a cacophony of heavy boots and guttural shouts. The air in the chamber seemed to shift, thickening with a suffocating weight as the energy of the approaching dark forces seeped into the sanctuary.

Andres froze, his instincts kicking in as he scanned the room. "They're here," he whispered, his voice barely audible over the growing roar.

A piercing screech suddenly split the air—a metallic scraping that sent shivers down their spines. "They've breached the outer seal," Maya said urgently, her normally calm voice laced with tension. "The forces of Belial have found us."

Jacqueline screamed, "How could they have tracked us so quickly? This place was supposed to be hidden!"

"They must have found the rift near the ley line," Maya replied, her gaze darting to the corridor. "The blockages—they have been using them to penetrate the grid and follow its resonance straight to us. We do not have much time."

A shadow flickered across the chamber wall, tall and distorted, as the first of the pursuers came into view. Their forms were cloaked in black armor, their faces obscured by masks etched with sinister, otherworldly symbols. The air around them shimmered with an unnatural heat, the distortion bending light and reality itself.

"Go!" Maya hissed, motioning toward a smaller, hidden passage at the far side of the chamber. "We must keep the Skull from falling into their hands!"

Andres hesitated, glancing at the passage and back at the advancing figures. "We cannot just keep running. If they corner us—"

Maya interjected firmly, her emerald eyes blazing. "If the Skull is taken, their power will grow beyond our ability to stop them. Trust me, Andres. We must move now!"

The ground beneath them trembled as another piercing sound rang out—a sharp crack that signaled the sanctuary's protective wards were failing. The Sons of Belial advanced in unison, their movements unnervingly synchronized. From their ranks, one raised an ominous, blackened staff that pulsed with a crimson light, the energy radiating outward like a storm.

"Run!" Evelyn shouted, snapping Andres from his hesitation. The team bolted toward the hidden passage, their hearts pounding as the chamber filled with the deafening roar of dark energy surging closer.

As they disappeared into the passage, Andres stole one last glance over his shoulder. The Sons of Belial had fully entered the chamber, their cold, calculating eyes scanning for their prey. One of them stepped forward, his voice reverberating through the ancient sanctuary like a curse:

"You can't run forever!"

Chapter 9

The sound of pounding footsteps echoed through the narrow stone passageway as Maya led the team deeper into the hidden Atlantean temple. Their ragged breaths mingled with the hum of ancient energy that seemed to pulse through the very walls around them.

"Quickly now," Maya urged, her voice calm but tinged with urgency. "We must reach the inner chamber before they catch up."

Andres clutched the Crystal Skull tightly to his chest as he ran, its smooth surface cool against his sweat-slicked palms. The faint glow emanating from its depths pulsed in rhythm with the thrumming energy of the temple, sending tingles up his arms.

"I can feel it," he gasped between breaths. "The Skull... it's reacting to this place."

Maya glanced back, her green eyes piercing in the dim light. "The resonance grows stronger. We're close."

As they rounded a corner, the passageway opened into a vast chamber. Andres skidded to a halt, his eyes widening as he took in the towering crystalline structures and glowing symbols etched into every surface.

The Skull's pulsing intensified, its light casting eerie shadows across the ancient technology surrounding them. Andres felt a jolt of recognition, memories of a past life flickering at the edges of his consciousness.

"It's incredible," Jacqueline whispered in awe, her earlier fear seemingly forgotten in the face of such wonder.

But Andres barely heard her, lost in an internal struggle as the Skull's energy resonated with something deep within him. Part of him yearned to unlock its secrets, to embrace the power it offered. Yet another part recoiled, sensing the weight of responsibility that came with it.

"Andres," Maya's voice cut through his tumultuous thoughts. "The Skull is the key. But you must be certain. Once we begin, there's no turning back."

He met her gaze, seeing both encouragement and caution in her eyes. "I... I am not sure I am ready for this," he admitted, his voice barely above a whisper.

The distant echo of shouting voices spurred them back into action. "We're out of time," Julian hissed, glancing nervously toward the passage they had come through. "Make a decision, now!"

Andres's grip tightened on the Skull as he wrestled with his doubts. The fate of humanity hung in the balance, and he stood at the precipice of a choice that would change everything.

As the team ventured deeper into the heart of the Atlantean temple, they found themselves in a massive circular chamber, its walls adorned with intricate carvings and pulsing with an otherworldly energy. The air hummed with the rhythmic vibrations of ancient machines, their purpose as mysterious as the civilization that had created them.

Jacqueline's eyes widened in awe as she took in the sight before her. "This is incredible," she breathed, her voice trembling with excitement. "The technology here is beyond anything I've ever seen."

She moved toward the center of the room, her fingers trailing reverently over the glowing consoles and conduits. The intellectual curiosity that had driven her for so long, now burned brighter than ever, the promise of unlocking the secrets of this ancient civilization tantalizing her mind.

In contrast, Maya approached the sacred space with solemn reverence, her steps measured and cautious. She could feel the power thrumming through the temple, a testament to the spiritual mastery of her Atlantean ancestors. Yet, she also sensed the delicate balance that hung in the air, the weight of the task before them.

"We must be careful," Maya warned, her voice cutting through the hum of the machines. "The technology here is not to be trifled with. It holds the power to reshape the world, for better or for worse."

Jacqueline turned to face her, a flicker of impatience crossing her features. "But don't you see? This is what we have been searching for, the key to unlocking humanity's potential. We can't let this opportunity slip away."

Maya met her gaze, her green eyes filled with a quiet intensity. "I understand your desire for knowledge, Dr. Hart. But we must also consider the consequences of our actions. The Atlanteans learned the hard way that power without wisdom can lead to destruction."

As the two women faced each other, Andres watched from the sidelines, the Crystal Skull still clutched in his hands. He could feel its energy pulsing in sync with the temple's vibrations, a silent call to action.

"We don't have much time," he reminded them, his voice cutting through the charged atmosphere. "The Sons of Belial are still out there, and they won't stop until they have the Skull."

Jacqueline nodded, her determination renewed. "Andres is right. We need to figure out how to activate this technology before it's too late."

She turned back to the consoles, her mind racing with possibilities. Maya moved to join her, her caution tempered by the urgency of their situation.

As they worked, Andres could not shake the feeling that they were on the brink of something momentous. The temple seemed to come alive around them, the ancient machines stirring from their long slumber.

And deep within the Crystal Skull, an ancient consciousness began to awaken, its purpose finally within reach.

Andres approached the console, his breath catching as he took in its otherworldly design. It stood waist-high, an elegant amalgamation of ancient craftsmanship and advanced technology. The base was carved from what appeared to be a single block of shimmering obsidian, etched with intricate geometric patterns that glowed faintly in the dim light of the chamber.

The surface of the console was smooth and crystalline, its texture somewhere between glass and liquid, as though it were alive. Embedded within the console were pulsing nodes of light—emerald, sapphire, and gold—that seemed to shift and dance like tiny galaxies suspended in motion. Strange symbols, unfamiliar, yet oddly resonant, floated across its surface, appearing, and disappearing as if responding to the energy in the room.

Andres hesitated, his fingers hovering just above the console. The air around it vibrated subtly, a hum so low it was more felt than heard. It seemed to beckon him, its energy pulsing in rhythm with his heartbeat, drawing him closer with an almost magnetic pull.

"This is Atlantean," he murmured, his voice barely audible. "Far more advanced than anything I've seen before."

Maya stepped forward, her expression a mixture of awe and urgency. "It's not just Atlantean," she said softly. "This console is a nexus point—designed to bridge dimensions, to connect the user with the flow of the energy grid itself. But be cautious, Andres. It will respond to you, but only if your intentions are pure."

Andres swallowed hard and steeled himself. As his fingertips finally contacted the crystalline surface, a warmth spread through him, gentle at first but quickly intensifying. A flood of memories washed over him—images of Atlantis at its peak, vibrant and alive, its energy flowing harmoniously through a global grid of light. He saw himself standing in a similar chamber, surrounded by figures clad in ceremonial robes, their eyes filled with trust and expectation.

The console lit up, its colors intensifying to a radiant brilliance. The symbols rearranged themselves into patterns Andres could not decipher, yet they felt familiar, as though they were unlocking something deep within him. He gasped as a voice, soft yet commanding, echoed in his mind.

"Welcome, Keeper of the Light. Your journey has brought you here to restore what was lost."

His knees buckled slightly, but he steadied himself, gripping the edges of the console. He glanced at Maya, whose expression was unreadable, though her eyes shimmered with a mix of encouragement and anticipation.

"What now?" Andres asked, his voice trembling with the weight of the moment.

Maya stepped closer, her hand hovering near his shoulder as though to reassure him. "Now, you must listen," she said. "This console holds the knowledge of the ages, but it will only reveal what you are ready to understand. Trust it—and trust yourself."

He saw his Mapuche grandmother, her weathered face illuminated by the glow of a crackling fire. Her voice echoed in his mind, a soothing reminder of the wisdom she had imparted to him so long ago. "Remember, Andresito," she whispered, "balance and harmony are the keys to understanding the mysteries of the universe. Remember, you must find this within yourself as well."

Andres's hand trembled as he pulled it back from the console, his grandmother's words still ringing in his ears. He turned to face his companions, his eyes filled with a new sense of purpose.

Jacqueline was already at work, her nimble fingers dancing across the intricate controls. "This technology is unlike anything I've ever seen," she breathed, her voice filled with awe and excitement.

With renewed determination, Andres stepped forward, the Crystal Skull glowing with an almost rhythmic pulse in his hands. His voice, steady and resolute, carried through the chamber. "We *will* make this work," he said, conviction radiating from his every word. "By uniting our strengths and grounding ourselves in the wisdom of the past, we can unlock the full potential of this technology. Together, we can restore balance and chart a path to a brighter future."

The energy in the room seemed to shift, the weight of doubt giving way to a cautious hope. Andres's confidence was infectious, his belief in their mission a beacon in the uncertainty.

And as he spoke, the temple seemed to come alive around them, the ancient machines humming with a newfound purpose. The Vesica Piscis began to glow, its sacred geometry pulsing in time with the heartbeat of the universe.

The team stood on the precipice of a new age, the weight of their decisions bearing down upon them like the countless tons of stone that surrounded them. But in that moment, they knew that they were not alone—that the wisdom of the ancients would guide them, even as the forces of darkness sought to tear them apart.

Julian Blackwood stood slightly apart from the others, his dark eyes glinting with a strategic calculation that seemed out of place in the sacred chamber. While Jacqueline continued her fervent pleas and Maya countered with impassioned wisdom, Julian's voice cut through the din.

"Imagine," he murmured, almost to himself yet loud enough for all to hear, "the power at our fingertips. This is bigger than any one civilization's claims or fears. We stand at the cusp of evolution. The question is, are we bold enough to seize it?"

Andres's hand hovered above the console, the Crystal Skull's glow intensifying as if responding to Julian's challenge. Andres's thoughts flickered to his grandmother's teachings—harmony, balance, and respect for the forces they barely understood. Yet, the pull of progress, of potential, was seductive.

With a hesitant breath that felt like the first or perhaps the last, Andres made his choice. His fingers closed around the Skull, and he set it gently into the central mechanism—a nest of interlocking crystalline structures awaiting their heart.

The chamber responded instantly. A surge of energy rippled outward, gentle as a breeze yet relentless as a tidal wave, spreading through the room. The ancient glyphs carved into the walls ignited one by one, a cascading sequence of lights that raced around them.

Above, the Vesica Piscis appeared, its shape etched in luminous brilliance against the shadowed ceiling. Two overlapping circles, the very symbol of unity and duality, pulsed with a light that was neither fully blue nor green, but an impossible spectrum in between. It expanded and contracted rhythmically, like the beating of some cosmic heart, each throb sending waves of resonance throughout the temple.

The team stood transfixed, their previous arguments forgotten as they witnessed the awakening of an age-old power. Jacqueline's face was alight with wonder and a hint of triumph, while Maya watched with a reverence tinged with apprehension. Julian remained unreadable, his gaze fixated on the Skull now at the epicenter of this ancient Atlantean technology.

Andres felt the air thicken with energy, the hairs on his arms standing on end. There was no turning back. They had crossed a threshold beyond which lay the unknown, and there was nothing to do but face what came next—together.

The chamber trembled, a low growl echoing from the very bowels of the earth as if protesting the disturbance. The floor beneath their feet vibrated, sending small pebbles dancing like drops of water on a drumskin. Andres steadied himself against a console, his intense gaze taking in the room's reaction to the Skull's influence. "Careful," he cautioned, his voice barely audible above the growing din.

A grinding noise, ancient and ominous, filled the air as sections of the stone floor shifted. Dust billowed into the air, carrying with it the scent of time and decay. As the dust settled, a hidden staircase was revealed, descending into an abyssal darkness that seemed to swallow the faint glow emanating from the chamber.

"By the gods," Maya whispered.

"Look!" Jacqueline pointed toward the walls where holographic projections flickered to life, painting the room with scenes of a bygone era. Atlantis in its prime appeared before them: towering crystal spires, floating vehicles gliding between buildings, and citizens adorned in garments of light. The technological marvels were unlike anything they had seen, surpassing even the most daring modern dreams.

But the visions shifted, turning darker, more frantic. Conflict erupted, energy weapons discharging bolts of destructive brilliance. The sky darkened with smoke and ash; the sea rose in fury, swallowing the land. Tiwanaku appeared next; its peaceful existence starkly contrasted with the violence that had befallen Atlantis. Stone temples reached for the heavens, and processions of people moved in harmonious rituals, their faces painted with reverence for nature's deities.

"Warnings..." Maya breathed, her eyes reflecting the tumultuous history unfolding around them. "We must heed their lessons."

"Or repeat their mistakes," Andres added grimly, watching the fall of two civilizations—one consumed by power, the other by balance but ultimately affected by the ripple effects of its counterpart's destruction.

Andres felt the weight of his grandmother's teachings resonate within him, the memories grounding him amidst the chaos. Balance and harmony—these were the keys. But how could they achieve what those before them had failed to grasp?

"Let's move," Evelyn urged suddenly, her voice slicing through the trance-like state that held them. "We can't let this knowledge die here."

As if spurred by his words, the energy surges grew more violent, the chamber groaning with stress. Cracks webbed across the ceiling, sending down showers of debris. The urgency of escape eclipsed the allure of discovery, and the team hastened toward the open staircase, leaving behind the flickering ghosts of Atlantis and Tiwanaku.

"Into the heart of darkness, then," Jacqueline said with a wary glance at the yawning passage. "Let's hope we find light on the other side."

Andres took one last look at the Crystal Skull, its glow now a beacon in the gloom. He tightened his grip, the Skull's presence reassuring yet foreboding, as he led the way into the depths, each step a descent into the unknown.

A shrill, piercing sound sliced through the reverberating chamber, shattering the eerie silence that had settled over the team. The harsh clang of alarms echoed from the depths of the Atlantean temple, a dissonant symphony that signaled danger's rapid approach. With a jolt of adrenaline, they recognized the warning for what it was: General Kaine and his ruthless Sons of Belial were closing in.

"Go! Now!" Maya's voice cut through the cacophony, her eyes flashing with an urgency that spurred them into action. Her robes billowed as she turned on her heel, leading the way down the shadowed staircase that delved deeper into the bowels of the earth. The team followed without hesitation, their footsteps thundering against the ancient stone, a stark contrast to the silent visions they had just witnessed.

The passageway was narrow and uneven, forcing them to navigate with care even as they hastened their descent. Behind them, the alarm's relentless clamor grew more insistent, a sonic manifestation of the encroaching peril. Dust and small stones rattled beneath their boots, dislodged by the tremors that continued to shudder through the temple's foundations.

"Keep close and watch your step," Maya instructed, her tone steady despite the chaos. She moved with a grace that belied the situation, her knowledge of the temple's secrets guiding them through the labyrinthine maze. Each turn she took was deliberate, her intuition unfailing as she led them away from the threat that stalked their every move.

As the path before them twisted and forked, the dim glow of luminescent moss cast ghostly shadows on the walls. The air grew heavy, laden with the scent of damp earth and the tang of ozone that lingered after the energies unleashed in the chamber above. Maya's third eye pulsed faintly, a beacon of Atlantean wisdom in the oppressive dark.

"Trust in the path," Maya murmured, more to herself than to her companions. Her voice was soft, but it carried an ancient certainty, as though the words were not just her own but those of countless others who had spoken them before. Her connection to this place ran deep, her spirit attuned to its rhythms and resonance. With each step, she felt the weight of her ancestry—the guardians who had walked these corridors before her, who had encoded their knowledge into the very stones that now whispered secrets to those who could listen.

As her fingertips brushed the crystalline walls, flashes of memory surged through her like distant echoes. Maya froze, her breath catching as she felt herself being pulled into another time—a time when these corridors had been alive with light and purpose. She closed her eyes, and the present moment seemed to dissolve, replaced by visions of a golden age long past.

She was no longer standing in the dimly lit cavern but in the heart of a radiant Atlantean temple. The air shimmered with energy, a living, breathing force that pulsed through the towering crystalline spires and filled the vast chamber with an otherworldly glow. She was garbed in flowing robes of white and gold, intricate symbols etched into the fabric, each one a sigil of protection and power. Around her, other members of the priesthood moved with grace and solemnity, their hands weaving intricate patterns in the air as they chanted in a language that resonated deep within her soul.

In the vision, Maya stood at the center of a great circle, her hands raised toward an enormous crystal suspended above her. The crystal radiated an ethereal light, its energy humming in harmony with the sacred grid lines converging beneath the temple. She could feel the power of the Earth coursing through her, uniting with the celestial forces she and the others were calling upon. Together, they had been tasked with maintaining the delicate balance of the grid, ensuring its energies flowed freely to nurture both the Earth and its inhabitants.

But there had been a shadow even then—a foreboding presence that sought to corrupt the grid's power. Maya remembered the urgency of their work, the prayers whispered with trembling hearts as they fought to hold the balance. She had stood as a protector, channeling her energy alongside the high priesthood to stave off the dark forces that threatened their civilization.

The memory shifted, and she saw the moment of their failure. The grid's luminous energy faltered, its perfect harmony disrupted by greed and hubris. The temples trembled, and the great crystal shattered, unleashing a cascade of destructive forces that had torn their world apart. She saw herself standing amidst the chaos, tears streaming down her face as she vowed, with every fiber of her being, that if she ever had the chance, she would not let such devastation happen again.

The vision faded, leaving Maya trembling, her chest tight with emotion. She opened her eyes to find Andres and the others staring at her with concern. "Are you all, right?" Andres asked gently, stepping closer.

Maya nodded, though her voice was heavy with sorrow when she spoke. "I've been here before," she whispered. "Not in this body, not in this life. But my soul remembers." She placed a hand over her heart, as though trying to steady the torrent of emotions within. "In Atlantis, I was a priestess, working with the high priesthood to protect the grid. We knew its importance, its power—but we underestimated the darkness that sought to claim it."

She turned to face Andres, her eyes glistening with unshed tears. "I failed then. We all did. And it cost us everything. But this time…" Her voice strengthened, a quiet resolve replacing the pain. "This time, we will not fail. The grid must be restored. The rifts must be healed. And we must stand together, as they did in the ancient days, to ensure that humanity has a future."

"Left here," Maya said, gesturing toward a barely discernible archway. The group veered, a collective breath held as the passage narrowed, threatening to constrict around them like the coils of some primordial serpent.

Above them, the sound of pursuit grew louder, the implacable march of boots on stone punctuated by the occasional order barked out by a voice that could only belong to Kaine—a voice that seemed to claw at the edges of their resolve, seeking to sow panic and discord.

Jacqueline glanced back over her shoulder; her eyes wide with the realization of how close their pursuers were. "Faster," she gasped, pushing her legs to carry her quicker, the scholarly curiosity that once drove her, now replaced by raw survival instinct.

Yet, even as the echoes of their flight filled the tunnels, there was a sense of inevitability, as if the outcome of this chase was already woven into the tapestry of time. Maya knew better than to allow fear to cloud her vision, her presence an anchor in the tumultuous sea of uncertainty that threatened to engulf them.

"Almost there," she promised, sensing the nearing end of this leg of their journey—a respite, however brief, from the tide of adversaries that surged relentlessly behind them.

With Maya's guidance, the team emerged into an antechamber, the space opening around them like the calm eye of a storm. They paused, chests heaving, their breaths coming in ragged gasps as the sounds of pursuit momentarily receded, muffled by the twists and turns of the ancient corridors.

But the reprieve would be short-lived. Even now, they could feel the temple vibrating with the aftershocks of their actions—actions that had set events into motion that could not be undone. Ahead lay mysteries untold, and within Andres, the Crystal Skull throbbed ominously, a silent herald of the trials yet to come.

Andres's heart hammered against his ribcage, the pulsing glow of the Crystal Skull in his grasp casting eerie shadows on the walls of the antechamber. The others were panting, their bodies slick with sweat from the harrowing escape, but it was the relentless hum of Atlantean machinery that filled the space with a thrumming energy, like a heartbeat echoing through time.

"Listen to me, Andres," Maya's voice cut through the tension, her gaze locking onto his with an intensity that seemed to still the very air around them. "You are the bridge between worlds—the son of two legacies. In your veins flows the blood of Tiwanaku and Atlantis."

Andres's eyes widened as the weight of her words descended upon him. The Skull's radiance flickered in response, resonating with the truth that Maya unveiled. He felt the dual heritage within him stir, a tempestuous sea of ancient memories and prophecies whispered by the wind.

"Your existence was foretold," Maya continued, her third eye shimmering with a wisdom that transcended time. "The prophecy speaks of a child born of both civilizations, one who would rise to guide humanity into the era of Homo Omega. You are that child, Andres."

A heavy silence followed, punctuated only by the distant echoes of their pursuers. Jacqueline exchanged a look of disbelief with Julian Blackwood, whose calculating eyes belied his composed exterior. But it was Andres who felt the ground shift beneath him, his role in this cosmic drama now laid bare.

"Maya," he started, his voice barely above a whisper, "what have we done? The portal... it was not fully activated. What does this mean for us? For the world?"

"Uncertainty clouds our path," Maya admitted, her voice a steady beacon amidst the chaos. "The grid is awake but unbalanced. We have tapped into forces that we do not fully understand. Forces that could either heal or fracture the very fabric of reality."

Andres's hand trembled as he looked down at the Skull, its once comforting glow now a harbinger of unknown consequences. The incomplete ritual had opened a door, but to what end, they could not be certain. With every breath, he felt the immense burden of his lineage, of choices made in desperation, each one a thread in the delicate weave of time that could unravel the future itself.

"Then we must find balance," he said resolutely, meeting Maya's gaze once more. "We must finish what we started, for the sake of all."

In that moment, as the team prepared to delve deeper into the mysteries that lay ahead, Andres embraced his destiny, the weight of prophecy etched into his soul.

Chapter 10

The ancient Atlantean portal loomed before them, its towering archway carved from a single slab of polished stone, covered in intricate patterns that seemed to shift and pulse in the dim light of the underground chamber. Strange glyphs spiraled outward from the center, their meaning lost to time—yet Andres felt an inexplicable familiarity as if the symbols whispered to something buried deep within his soul.

Maya exhaled slowly beside him, her fingers tracing the air just above the Vesica Piscis symbol at the heart of the portal. A faint glow pulsed beneath the stone, illuminating the delicate geometry of interlocking circles. The ancient Atlanteans had designed this with precision, encoding sacred knowledge into its very foundation.

The air in the chamber felt charged, dense with an energy neither of them could fully comprehend. A low hum resonated from the stone, so subtle it was more a vibration in their bones than a sound. Andres swallowed hard. Every instinct told him they were standing at the threshold of something beyond understanding—a doorway to another time, another world.

He turned to Maya. "Are you sure about this?" His voice was barely above a whisper, as if speaking too loudly might awaken something dormant within the ancient structure.

She nodded, her amber eyes gleaming in the faint light. "This is what we came for."

The portal was waiting.

"Can you feel it, Maya?" Andres whispered, his dark eyes fixed on the intertwining circles before him. "It's like the symbol is... alive."

Maya nodded, her long brown hair cascading over her shoulders as she leaned in closer. "The Vesica Piscis is more than just a symbol, Andres. It's a key—a bridge between worlds."

Andres's fingers traced the air above the carved lines, following their mesmerizing flow. His mind raced with the implications of what they had discovered. *The Atlanteans had mastered this sacred geometry, using it to unlock gateways to other dimensions and harness cosmic energies. But how?*

"The balance," Maya murmured, her voice taking on a distant quality. "It's all about maintaining perfect balance between the physical and spiritual realms."

As they worked side by side, their hands brushing over the ancient patterns, Andres felt a profound connection between them, as if an invisible thread bound their hearts and minds. Each glance, each shared thought seemed to flow effortlessly, a harmony so natural it felt eternal. It was more than teamwork—it was as if their souls had found each other again, rekindling a bond forged in the cosmic dance of lifetimes past.

Suddenly, a crisp British accent cut through their concentration. "Fascinating. The linguistic structure here is unlike anything I've ever encountered."

Evelyn stepped forward, her dark eyes scanning the inscriptions through elegant reading glasses. Andres watched as the linguist's initial skepticism gave way to undeniable curiosity.

"What do you see, Evelyn?" Andres asked, eager for her insights.

Evelyn leaned in close and pointed to a series of symbols. "These glyphs... they're not just writing. They're mathematical equations, woven into the very fabric of the language itself."

Maya nodded, a small smile playing at her lips. "The Atlanteans understood that language and mathematics were two sides of the same coin—both expressions of universal truths."

Evelyn's eyes widened, her analytical mind clearly racing to keep up with the implications. "If that's true, then this isn't just a portal. It's a... a programming interface for reality itself."

The tension in the chamber seemed to thicken as the full weight of their discovery settled upon them. Andres felt a bead of sweat trickle down his temple. They were on the precipice of unlocking secrets that could change everything—or destroy it all if they weren't careful.

"Evelyn" Andres said, his voice low and urgent, "we need your expertise now more than ever. Can you help us decipher the activation sequence?"

Evelyn nodded; her initial skepticism now replaced by determination. "I'll do my best. But I must warn you—we are treading in dangerous waters here. The power contained within this portal... it's beyond our comprehension."

As she began to work, Andres exchanged a meaningful glance with Maya. They both knew the risks, but also the potential for guiding humanity towards its next evolutionary step—Homo Omega. The path ahead was fraught with peril, but they had no choice. The fate of two civilizations—past and present—hung in the balance.

The ground beneath their feet trembled, a low hum filling the air as the final pieces of the Vesica Piscis symbol aligned. Energy pulsed through the carved lines, intensifying with each passing moment. Andres's heart raced, his palms sweating as he watched the ancient technology come to life.

"It's working," he breathed, awe and trepidation mingling in his voice.

Maya's eyes gleamed with recognition. "The veil between worlds is thinning. We must be ready."

Evelyn's analytical gaze darted between the symbols and the growing energy field. "Fascinating. The harmonics are aligning with what appears to be a quantum resonance frequency. But how is this possible without—"

Her words faltered mid-sentence as the air around them shimmered, a radiant veil of light bursting into existence without warning. It rippled like liquid silver, casting a brilliant, otherworldly glow that danced across the chamber walls. The portal crackled with a symphony of ethereal energy, each arc of light alive with an intensity that made the very air hum. It was as though the fabric of reality itself had split open, revealing a vibrant, swirling window to the unknown—both beautiful and terrifying in its sudden, fantastic appearance.

Andres swallowed hard, his Mapuche heritage whispering ancient warnings in the back of his mind. "This is it. The threshold to Atlantis."

Maya stepped forward, her robes rippling in the energy field. "We must cross now, while the alignment holds. Are you ready?"

Andres nodded, his resolve strengthening. "Ready as I'll ever be."

Dr. Carter hesitated, her skepticism warring with curiosity. "I... I'm not sure this is—"

"Trust in the wisdom of the ancients, Dr. Carter," Maya said gently. "Your analytical mind will be crucial on the other side."

With a deep breath, Andres tightened his grip on Maya's hand. The shimmering portal before them pulsed with energy, casting rippling waves of light across their faces. The air around them vibrated, charged with an otherworldly hum that seemed to resonate with their very souls. Andres's pulse quickened, his thoughts racing to the countless generations of his Mapuche ancestors who had safeguarded the wisdom now guiding him.

"This moment," he thought, "is the culmination of lifetimes." He glanced at Maya, whose serene expression carried a quiet strength, and whispered, "For humanity." Together, they stepped into the veil of light.

The portal enveloped them in a cocoon of warmth and electricity, the sensation both exhilarating and disorienting. A kaleidoscope of colors swirled around them, each hue carrying a distinct resonance, until suddenly, the chaos stilled. Andres blinked as his vision cleared, and a gasp escaped his lips. They stood in a world of staggering beauty. Towering crystal spires stretched skyward, their multifaceted surfaces refracting sunlight into shimmering rainbows. The sapphire sky above was vast and unmarred, a canvas for floating orbs of soft light. Between the spires, elegant vehicles glided noiselessly, their movements smooth and deliberate as though guided by thought alone.

"This... this is extraordinary," Evelyn breathed, stepping forward with cautious reverence. Her skepticism had melted away, replaced by a mix of awe and analytical curiosity. "The engineering... it's not just advanced—it's harmonious."

Andres's gaze followed the citizens moving through the streets, their forms draped in flowing garments that seemed alive, shifting in subtle hues. They gestured gracefully, weaving patterns in the air, and in response, shimmering fields of energy materialized—bridges, platforms, luminous displays.

"They're channeling pure energy," Andres marveled, his voice tinged with wonder. "This is the synthesis of technology and nature."

Maya stood beside him, her eyes glistening with unshed tears. "This was Atlantis," she said softly. "The pinnacle of our civilization—a union of spirit and science, perfectly attuned to the rhythms of the cosmos." Her voice faltered. "Before the fall."

The scene shifted abruptly. The brilliant light of the crystals dimmed, and shadows crept insidiously along the edges of the city.

The harmony began to fracture. Andres's breath hitched as figures cloaked in darkness appeared, their presence heavy with malevolence.

"The Sons of Belial," he murmured, the name evoking a visceral unease. Maya's teachings had prepared him, but the sight of their oppressive energy made his resolve waver.

Evelyn observed, her sharp intellect processing the unfolding changes. "This isn't just societal collapse. It is a systematic unraveling. Look at the fear—it's palpable."

The Atlanteans moved differently now, their earlier grace replaced by furtive glances and hurried steps. The energy manipulations, once open and communal, became secretive, hidden in shadows.

"We're watching paradise crumble," Andres said, his fists clenching with helpless frustration. "But there must be a way to stop this from repeating."

Maya's hand rested lightly on his arm. "That's why we're here," she said, her voice steady despite the sorrow in her eyes. "To witness, to learn, and to ensure this never happens again."

As the vision continued, the scene shifted again. The trio found themselves in a massive crystal amphitheater, surrounded by thousands of Atlanteans. The air thrummed with anticipation as the crowd raised their hands skyward, channeling a brilliant pillar of light from the heavens. It struck a central crystal, sending radiant waves through the gathered masses, illuminating their forms with an ethereal glow.

"Collective consciousness," Evelyn murmured, her analytical gaze softening. "They're synchronized on a level we can barely comprehend."

Maya's voice carried a note of reverence. "This was the Ceremony of Celestial Alignment—a sacred act of unity with the cosmos."

Andres's awe deepened. "Imagine if we could achieve this today. The potential... it's boundless."

But the moment of unity was fleeting. A low rumble built beneath their feet, and the vision darkened. Crystals trembled and cracked, their brilliance faltering. Shadowy figures spread like a contagion, and the harmony dissolved into chaos.

"No," Maya whispered, anguish etched across her face. "The fall is beginning."

Buildings collapsed in thunderous cascades, sending shards of crystal skittering across the streets. Energy fields erupted uncontrollably, destroying everything in their path. Andres staggered as the ground heaved beneath him, the destruction around them mirroring a nightmare.

"It's more than a natural disaster," Evelyn observed, her voice trembling with disbelief. "It's as if the very fabric of their world is disintegrating."

Andres reached instinctively to help a falling child, but his hand passed through, the vision intangible. "We have to do something!" he cried, desperation clawing at him.

Maya's grip on his arm steadied him. "We can't alter the past," she said firmly, though her eyes shone with unshed tears. "But we can honor its lessons."

As the Atlantean world crumbled around them, Andres's thoughts turned to the present. "This... it's all too familiar," he murmured. "We've forgotten how to live in balance. This is a warning—a plea."

Maya's voice cut through the chaos, fierce and unwavering. "Watch, Andres. Witness the cost of hubris, and let it fuel your resolve. The future depends on us."

During the destruction, Andres felt the weight of their mission settle fully on his shoulders. The echoes of Atlantis's fall demanded action—not just to honor the past, but to ensure humanity's survival and evolution.

The blinding light faded, leaving Andres, Maya, and Evelyn gasping for air in the dimly lit Atlantean temple. They stumbled back from the portal, their legs unsteady, minds reeling from the weight of what they had witnessed.

Andres's chest heaved as he tried to catch his breath. "Did... did we all see the same thing?" he managed to choke out, his voice hoarse.

Maya nodded, her usually serene features etched with sorrow. "The fall of Atlantis," she whispered. "Just as the ancient texts described, but so much more... vivid."

Evelyn leaned against a nearby pillar, her analytical mind visibly struggling to process the experience. "It's impossible," she muttered, shaking her head. "And yet..."

Before anyone could respond, a low rumble emanated from deep within the temple's foundations. The ground beneath their feet began to tremble, and dust rained down from the ancient ceiling.

"The portal's energy," Maya said, her eyes widening with realization. "It's destabilizing the structure!"

As if to confirm her words, a large chunk of stone crashed to the floor mere feet from where they stood. Andres's survival instincts kicked in, overriding his shock.

"We need to move, now!" he shouted, grabbing Dr. Carter's arm and pulling her away from the crumbling pillar. "Maya, the artifacts! We cannot leave them behind!"

Maya was already in motion, her hands deftly gathering the most crucial pieces of their discovery. "The Crystal Skull," she called out. "Andres, it's in your pack!"

Andres's mind raced as he assessed their situation. The temple's groans grew louder, more urgent. "Dr. Carter, can you carry those tablets? We need to document everything we can!"

Carter nodded, her shock giving way to determination. "On it!" She began carefully but quickly wrapping the ancient inscriptions.

As Andres secured his pack, ensuring the Crystal Skull was safe, he could not shake the parallels between their current predicament and the vision of Atlantis's fall. *History repeating itself,*' he thought grimly. *'But this time, we have a chance to preserve the knowledge.*

"This way!" Maya called out, gesturing toward a narrow passage. "I can feel a current of fresh air. It might be our way out!"

They rushed toward the opening, dodging falling debris. Andres's heart pounded in his chest, not just from exertion but from the enormity of what they had discovered—and what they stood to lose if they did not make it out alive.

As they entered the passage, Andres turned back for one last look at the portal. The shimmering energy that had shown them visions of a lost world was now tearing that world's last remnants apart. He silently vowed that their sacrifice would not be in vain. They would unravel the mysteries of Atlantis and use that knowledge to prevent history from repeating its darkest chapters.

"Andres, come on!" Evelyn's voice snapped him back to the present. With a final glance, he plunged into the darkness of the passage, the future of humanity weighing heavily on his shoulders.

Andres's fingers tightened around the Atlantean device, its crystalline surface pulsing with an otherworldly glow. The team huddled in the narrow passage, their labored breathing echoing off the ancient stones.

"We can't let this knowledge die with us," Andres said, his voice filled with newfound determination. He held up the device, its light casting dancing shadows on their faces. "This isn't just about uncovering the past anymore. It's about shaping our future."

Maya nodded, her green eyes reflecting the crystal's luminescence. "The wisdom of Atlantis, the spiritual teachings of Tiwanaku—they're all pieces of a greater puzzle."

Evelyn, ever the skeptic, furrowed her brow. "But how can ancient civilizations possibly help us with modern problems?"

Andres felt a surge of clarity as if the device itself was channeling knowledge into him. "Don't you see? The Atlanteans' downfall was not just about technology gone wrong. It was about losing balance—between progress and wisdom, between the material and the spiritual."

The ground beneath them shuddered, a stark reminder of their precarious situation. Andres's mind raced, drawing connections between his Mapuche heritage and the visions they had witnessed.

"We're standing at a crossroads," he continued, his voice gaining strength, "just like Atlantis did. But we have something they did not—hindsight. We can learn from their mistakes and find a way to evolve without losing our humanity."

As if in response to his words, the Atlantean device pulsed brighter. Andres felt a tingling sensation spreading from his fingertips, up his arm, and into his very core. In that moment, he knew their journey was far from over. It was just beginning.

"We need to get this to safety," he said, carefully stowing the device in his pack. "And then... then we start piecing together the puzzle. The fate of Homo Omega might just depend on it."

With renewed purpose, Andres led the way down the passage, each step carrying them closer to an uncertain but thrilling future. The weight of their discovery propelled them forward, into a world where ancient wisdom and modern challenges would collide in ways they could scarcely imagine.

Chapter 11

Andres stumbled out of the Atlantean passage, his legs wobbling beneath him as if he had just stepped off a spinning carnival ride. The world tilted and swayed, vivid images of crystal spires and shimmering energy fields still dancing behind his eyes.

"Maya," he gasped, reaching out blindly. "Did you... did we really...?"

His fingers grasped empty air. Blinking rapidly, Andres forced his vision to focus on the familiar canvas of their tent encampment. The Bolivian sun beat down mercilessly, a stark contrast to the ethereal glow of the underground temple.

Maya emerged beside him, her normally serene face etched with bewilderment. "The memories," she whispered, her green eyes wide. "They're so... overwhelming."

Andres nodded, struggling to form coherent thoughts. "It's like I lived another life. The technology, the knowledge—"

A blinding flash of purple light cut through the air, followed by an earth-shaking boom. The ground beneath their feet trembled as chaos erupted around them.

"Get down!" Andres shouted, tackling Maya to the ground as another energy blast vaporized a nearby tent. The acrid smell of ozone filled his nostrils.

Screams and shouts echoed across the camp as their team scrambled for cover. Evelyn's voice rose above the din: "It's the Sons of Belial! Take cover!"

Andres's mind raced. *How did they find us so quickly? We have barely scratched the surface of Atlantis' secrets.*

He glanced at Maya, her face a mask of determination despite the shock still evident in her eyes. "We need to protect the artifacts," she said, her voice steady. "The Crystal Skull—"

Another explosion rocked the camp, showering them with debris. Andres grabbed Maya's hand, pulling her toward the relative safety of a stone outcropping.

"First, we survive," he growled, his Mapuche training kicking in as adrenaline coursed through his veins.

As they sprinted across the open ground, dodging energy blasts and falling equipment, Andres's thoughts whirled. *The Atlantean memories, the attack—it is all connected. But how?* He pushed the questions aside, focusing on the immediate threat.

They dove behind the rocks just as another purple beam seared the air where they had been standing. Andres's heart pounded in his chest as he peered around the edge, assessing the situation.

"We're outnumbered," he muttered. "But they haven't breached the inner camp yet."

Maya nodded; her eyes closed in concentration. "I can feel the energy patterns of their weapons. If we can disrupt them..."

Andres marveled at how quickly she was adapting to her rediscovered Atlantean knowledge. "Tell me what you need," he said.

Before Maya could respond, a familiar voice crackled through the air—General Kaine's hologram, projected above the battlefield.

"Surrender the Crystal Skull," the spectral figure demanded, "or watch your precious dig site burn to ashes!"

Andres's jaw clenched. *Not today,* he thought. *Not when we are so close to unlocking the secrets of Atlantis.*

He locked eyes with Maya, a silent understanding passing between them. Whatever came next, they would face it together—guardians of an ancient legacy, protectors of humanity's future.

Andres took a deep breath, steadying himself. The chaos around them seemed to fade as he focused, drawing on the strength of his Mapuche ancestors. He could almost hear their whispers, urging him forward.

"Listen up!" Andres's voice rang out, cutting through the din of battle. "We didn't come this far to be stopped now. Remember why we are here—to protect the legacy of Atlantis, to safeguard humanity's future!"

As he spoke, Andres felt a flicker of doubt in his chest. *Am I really the one to lead them?* But he pushed the thought aside, letting the wisdom of his teachings flow through him.

"Maya, can you buy us some time?" he asked, his eyes scanning the battlefield.

Maya nodded, her face a mask of serene concentration. "I can create a barrier, but it won't last long."

She closed her eyes, her hands moving in intricate patterns. The air around them began to shimmer and pulse with energy. Slowly, a translucent dome materialized, enveloping their group.

"Incredible," Andres breathed, watching as energy blasts from the Sons of Belial ricocheted off the barrier.

Maya opened her eyes, a small smile playing on her lips. "Atlantean shield technology. I never thought I'd use it again."

Andres turned to the team, his voice steady despite the chaos. "Any ideas on how to turn the tide?"

As the team huddled closer, discussing strategies, Andres could not help but marvel at the strange turns his life had taken. From skeptical archaeologists to the leader of a group fighting to save the world—it was almost too much to believe.

But as he looked at Maya, her green eyes shining with determination and ancient wisdom, he knew that this was exactly where he was meant to be.

Evelyn's eyes darted across the battlefield, her mind racing to process the chaotic scene. Immediately, she noticed a pattern in the Sons of Belial's movements.

"They're not just attacking randomly," she announced, her voice tight with concentration. "There's a clear pincer formation. They're trying to flank us from both sides."

Andres turned to her, grateful for her tactical insight. "What's our best move, Evelyn?"

She hesitated, her rational mind struggling to reconcile the energy weapons and mystical barrier with her scientific worldview. "Logically, we should... wait, that's impossible. How are they—"

Evelyn crouched behind a supply crate, her breath steady despite the chaos erupting around the camp. The sharp crack of distant gunfire echoed through the valley, mingling with the hiss of energy weapons—the unmistakable signature of advanced, reverse-engineered tech.

"Dr. Carter!" Andres's voice cut through the din as he slid into cover beside her. "We're pinned down, and they're using some kind of jamming field. Can you figure out where they are?"

Evelyn did not respond immediately. Her hands were already at work, activating the handheld scanner she had managed to grab during the initial assault. The device buzzed to life, its crystalline interface flickering erratically. She adjusted the settings, bypassing the interference with a few quick swipes.

"Give me a second," she muttered, her voice tight with focus. The scanner projected a holographic map of the surrounding area into the air above them. The camp's layout shimmered in blue, but red flickers—representing enemy movement—darted in and out like restless shadows.

"They've deployed cloaking tech," she said, her brow furrowing. "But I'm picking up residual energy signatures—heat, electromagnetic distortions. They're trying to mask their positions, but they're leaving a trail."

Maya appeared at their side; her breathing controlled despite the urgency in her eyes. "How many are we dealing with?"

Jacqueline crouched next to them, her glasses glinting as she observed the map with a sharp eye. "The pattern is strategic, but they may be underestimating us," she said. Her voice was calm, her demeanor always unshaken, even in the face of such chaos. "We can use their overconfidence against them. If we move quickly and disorient their forces, we might disrupt their formation."

Andres looked at her with a mix of admiration and urgency. "Jacqueline, any insights on their tech? What are we dealing with?"

Jacqueline adjusted her glasses, her mind processing the data. "The cloaking tech is impressive, but not flawless. If we hit them with a pulse wave, we could neutralize their cloaking devices and turn their tactical advantage against them."

Maya nodded, her gaze already scanning their surroundings. "That pulse will give us the opening we need. But we need to time it just right."

Evelyn raised her scanner. "I'll need a few more seconds to target the pulse accurately," she said. "Jacqueline, can you assist with aligning the frequencies?"

Jacqueline did not hesitate. "I'll synchronize with your device," she said, her fingers dancing across the scanner's interface. "I've worked with similar technology before."

"Perfect," Andres said, his voice firm. "Let's make this count."

As Evelyn and Jacqueline worked together, preparing the pulse, Andres turned to Maya, their eyes locking in a moment of silent determination.

Evelyn zoomed in on the red flickers, triangulating their movement patterns. "Four groups," she said quickly, her voice gaining confidence as the scanner's algorithms refined the data. "One's circling to the north—probably a diversion. The main force is here, to the west, and moving fast. Two smaller squads are flanking us from the east and south."

Andres nodded, his mind racing. "They're trying to box us in."

"Exactly," Evelyn confirmed, adjusting the scanner to overlay terrain data. "But look here—" she pointed at the map, highlighting a series of rocky outcrops to the west. "The terrain gives us an advantage. If we can force them into the narrow pass here, we can bottleneck their main force and neutralize them before the flanking squads reach us."

Maya's lips curved into a grim smile. "I like it. But how do we deal with the flanks?"

Evelyn's fingers flew over the scanner's interface, activating its secondary mode. The hologram shifted, revealing an analysis of the enemy's weaponry and communication systems. "Their flanking squads are using smaller, lighter weapons—less range, but fast. If we can disrupt their comms, they will lose coordination. I can send a pulse to overload their systems."

"How long do you need?" Andres asked.

"Thirty seconds," Evelyn replied. "But someone needs to cover me. They'll know I'm targeting them as soon as I start."

"I'll handle it," Maya said, gripping her staff-like energy weapon. "You just do your thing."

Evelyn nodded and tapped a command into the scanner. The hologram shifted again, focusing on the southern squad. A pulse icon blinked at the edge of the display, signaling the activation sequence.

"Initiating now," Evelyn said, her voice calm but firm. The scanner emitted a low hum as it began generating the disruptive pulse. A faint ripple spread outward from their position, invisible but powerful.

Almost immediately, the southern squad's red markers on the map began to flicker erratically. Their movements slowed, then stopped entirely.

"That's one squad down," Evelyn said with satisfaction. "Switching to the east flank."

A sudden explosion rocked the ground nearby, and Andres shielded Evelyn with his body as debris rained down. "They're trying to zero in on your position!" he shouted.

"I just need ten more seconds!" Evelyn called back, her fingers steady despite the chaos.

Maya rose from cover and unleashed a series of precise energy blasts, forcing the attackers to retreat momentarily. "You've got your ten seconds. Make them count!"

The scanner emitted another pulse, and the eastern squad's markers vanished from the map. "Flanks neutralized," Evelyn reported, her voice taut with relief.

Andres grinned despite the tension. "Great work, Evelyn. Now let's deal with the main force."

Evelyn adjusted the scanner one last time, overlaying their defensive positions with the enemy's route through the pass. "If we set up here and here," she said, marking the map, "we can create a crossfire. They'll have no way out."

"Perfect," Maya said, already moving into position.

Andres clasped Evelyn's shoulder briefly. "You just saved all of us."

"Let's hope it's enough," Evelyn replied, stowing the scanner, and readying herself for what came next.

As she spoke, Amaru stepped forward, his weathered face calm despite the chaos. "The stones of Tiwanaku will aid us," he said, his voice carrying a quiet power.

Andres nodded, remembering the old man's connection to this sacred place. "What do you mean, Amaru?"

The shaman closed his eyes, raising his arms. "Listen, and you will hear the song of the ancients."

Amaru closed his eyes, his hands outstretched toward the ancient stones. His voice rose, deep and resonant, carrying the weight of millennia:

"Pacha Mama, apunchik, kay rumi wasi kawsanipuni.

Inti yaku, qhawarina, wayra sonqo.

Qosqo ninchikta, kawsay ukhunchikta, wiñaypaq kallpachiy!"

The stones began to glow faintly, their surfaces pulsing with a rhythm that seemed to echo the very heartbeat of the Earth. Amaru's chant grew louder, his voice weaving through the chamber, commanding the energies around him.

"Yachay ukhu, munaq sunquyuqkunapaq.

Wasi qhapariy, kawsay tukuy pacha.

Hatun ñawi kanchayniyuq, chawpinchik waqaychasqa!"

The vibration intensified, spreading through the ground beneath their feet and resonating deep in their bones. Evelyn gasped as the ancient glyphs etched into the stones flared to life, their patterns ignited in a brilliant cascade of colors, swirling, and merging like the threads of an eternal tapestry.

Amaru's voice echoed one final time, his words a call to the cosmos: "Hatun Yachay, kani kawsayta uryaypaq. Ñoqanchikqa wiñay sunquyuq ruwasaq."

The stones erupted in radiant light, filling the area with a dazzling display of power as if the ancient spirits themselves had awoken to his call.

"This is... remarkable," she whispered, her scientific mind racing to explain the phenomenon. "The frequency of his voice is somehow interacting with the molecular structure of the stones."

As Amaru's chant grew louder, his voice resonated with an almost otherworldly timbre, each syllable infused with ancient power. The sacred stones of Tiwanaku, weathered by millennia but alive with latent energy, began to hum in response. The sound was low and guttural at first, like the deep rumble of the earth waking from a long slumber.

Golden light seeped from the carvings etched into the stones, following intricate patterns that glowed brighter with each word of the chant. The energy coursed through the ground, rippling outward like waves across a still lake, creating an invisible yet palpable force field.

The Sons of Belial, clad in their dark cloaks and bearing advanced weaponry, hesitated mid-charge. Their once-coordinated movements became erratic, their footing unsure as the hum grew into an overwhelming vibration.

One of them clutched his head, staggering as though struck by an unseen force. "What is this?" he snarled, his voice laced with panic. Another dropped his weapon entirely, falling to his knees as his body convulsed, the dark energy that fueled him seemingly short-circuiting.

The light from the stones intensified, pulsating in rhythmic waves that synchronized with Amaru's chant. To Andres, watching from the sidelines, it was as though the very air had transformed into a living force, pressing against the Sons of Belial like an invisible hand.

"It's disrupting them," Maya whispered, her voice tinged with awe. "The energy—they can't withstand it."

The Sons of Belial were now fully engulfed in the harmonic resonance emanating from the stones. Their dark cloaks seemed to disintegrate at the edges, revealing shimmering, distorted forms underneath—shadows of their true selves, exposed and vulnerable. Some fell to the ground, writhing as if caught in the throes of an internal battle. Others tried to flee; their movements sluggish as if wading through an unseen barrier. Their weapons malfunctioned, sparking and fizzling, unable to operate within the sacred energy field.

The leader of the group, a tall figure with a dark, menacing aura, attempted to counter the effect, raising his staff-like device and muttering incantations in an ancient, guttural language. But the stones seemed to respond to his defiance, focusing their energy on him. The hum deepened into a resonant chord that reverberated through the air, shattering his staff into fragments. He screamed, clutching his chest as if the light had reached into his very soul.

"They're being purged," Evelyn said, her scanner displaying erratic readings. "The stones are stripping them of whatever dark force sustains them. They can't hold their form."

Amaru's chant reached a crescendo, and the golden light exploded outward in a brilliant flash. The Sons of Belial were thrown backward, their forms dissolving into smoky tendrils before vanishing entirely. Silence fell over the site, broken only by the faint, lingering hum of the stones as they settled back into stillness.

Andres turned to Amaru, his voice filled with a mix of awe and relief. "What just happened?"

Amaru lowered his hands, his breathing steady despite the monumental display of power. "The stones of Tiwanaku hold the memory of the earth, the frequency of life itself. The Sons of Belial are creatures of imbalance—they cannot exist in the presence of such harmony."

Maya stepped forward, her gaze sweeping the now-empty battlefield. "Their darkness cannot overpower the light of this place. Tiwanaku protects its own."

Andres nodded, his mind racing with the implications. The power of Tiwanaku was not just in its history—it was alive, a force capable of defending humanity against the forces of darkness. And in that moment, he knew their mission was far from over.

"Now's our chance," Andres called out, his voice cutting through the mystical resonance. "Evelyn, guide us through their weak point!"

As the team moved to follow Evelyn's lead, she could not help but marvel at the impossible scene unfolding around her. *How can I reconcile this with everything I have ever known?* she thought, her worldview shifting beneath her feet.

But as she watched Amaru's chant disrupt the attackers, a small part of her thrilled at the unknown. For the first time in her career, Dr. Evelyn Carter found herself stepping beyond the boundaries of science and into a world of infinite possibilities.

A shimmering apparition materialized before them, casting an eerie blue glow across the ruins. General Kaine's hologram towered over the team, his scarred face contorted in a sneer of contempt.

"Well, well," Kaine's voice boomed, cold and metallic. "I see you've managed to survive our little welcoming party. Impressive, but ultimately futile."

Andres stepped forward, his jaw clenched, and thought to himself *We won't let you have the Crystal Skull, Kaine.*

The hologram's red eyes flashed. "Oh, but you will. One way or another." Kaine's laughter echoed, sending chills through the group. "You see, I hold the power of life and death over everyone in this miserable camp. Hand over the Skull, or I'll reduce this place to ashes, along with every last one of you!"

Maya's fists clenched at her sides. "You monster!" she hissed.

"Monster?" Kaine's hologram raised an eyebrow. "I prefer to think of myself as... enlightened. The strong survive, the weak perish. It's the natural order of things."

As Kaine continued his tirade, Sophia Blackwood edged closer to Andres from her hiding place. Her heart raced, torn between her family's legacy and the growing certainty that she was on the wrong side of history.

"Andres," she whispered, her voice barely audible. "Listen carefully. Kaine's energy shields have a weak point at their apex. If you can disrupt the field there, you might have a chance."

Andres's eyes widened, searching Sophia's face. "Why are you telling me this?"

Sophia swallowed hard. "Because... because this isn't right. What we're doing, what Julian's become involved in... it has to stop."

As Andres processed this unexpected alliance, Kaine's hologram flickered. "You have one hour to deliver the Skull. Choose wisely." With a final malevolent grin, the image vanished, leaving the team in stunned silence.

Andres's question hung in the air as the team took stock of the situation. Maya scanned the team, her sharp gaze flickering over each face. "We're all here," she replied, her voice steady despite the exhaustion etched in her features. "But we won't survive another attack like that."

Julian sat on a broken stone bench, cradling his head in his hands. "They won't give up," he muttered. "Kaine will come for the Skull with everything he has."

Evelyn knelt by the Crystal Skull, her fingers brushing its smooth surface as if to reassure herself it was still intact. "We can't stay here," she said, her tone urgent. "We need to move before they regroup."

Andres's mind raced, replaying Kaine's ultimatum. His instincts screamed against handing over the Skull, but the weight of their situation pressed heavily on him. "There's no choice," he said finally. "We head for the temple. If there's any chance it holds answers—or defenses—we have to take it."

Julian looked up, his eyes clouded with doubt. "You think the temple will protect us? Or is it just another trap?"

"We don't have the luxury of second-guessing," Maya cut in. She stood tall despite her bruises, her voice firm. "The Skull has led us this far. If the temple is connected to it, then it's our best shot."

Evelyn rose, brushing off her hands. "Then let's not waste time. The Sons of Belial won't give us a second to breathe."

Andres nodded, his resolve hardening. "Pack what you can carry. We move now."

The group sprang into action, gathering supplies with practiced efficiency. The tension in the air was palpable, every sound outside the crumbled walls making them flinch.

As they left the remnants of their camp behind, Andres took point, the Crystal Skull cradled in his arms, its faint glow illuminating the path to the temple. Maya stayed close, vigilant...

The temple rose before them like a phantom, its weathered stones glowing faintly under the sunlight. It exuded an aura of power and mystery, as though it had been waiting for this moment. Andres felt a chill run down his spine.

"This is it," Maya whispered, her voice tinged with awe.

As the team stepped into the temple's threshold, a low hum resonated through the air, vibrating through their very bones. The ancient structure seemed alive, its walls pulsating in rhythm with the Crystal Skull.

Andres turned to face the group. "No matter what we find in here, we face it together. Agreed?"

A murmur of agreement rippled through the team, their shared resolve pushing back the exhaustion and fear. With one last glance toward the temple, Andres stepped forward, the Skull's light growing brighter with each step. Inside, the air was thick with the weight of ages, and the temple's mysteries awaited.

Maya nodded, scanning the room. "Barely. We lost some of our equipment in the attack, but the team is intact."

Evelyn, still clutching her scanner, examined the now-dormant crystal mechanism. "Whatever that pulse was, it created a protective field around us, but I don't know how long it will last," she said. "The energy signature is already fluctuating."

Julian Blackwood leaned against a column, visibly shaken but resolute. "They'll regroup," he muttered, glancing toward the temple entrance. "Kaine doesn't give up that easily."

Maya stepped forward, her voice sharp. "Then neither do we. We've come too far to let this stop us."

Andres rubbed his temples, the vision still vivid in his mind. "It's not just about surviving the next attack," he said, drawing everyone's attention. "The Crystal Skull isn't just a defensive tool. It is a beacon—a key to activating something far greater. But to do that, we need to understand how it works."

Evelyn knelt beside the crystal mechanism, her fingers deftly tracing the intricate lines of the Vesica Piscis. "This isn't just Atlantean technology," she mused. "It's a fusion of organic and crystalline systems, almost... alive. If we can stabilize the energy output, we might be able to use it to send a signal—or even disrupt the Sons of Belial's technology."

Julian folded his arms, his expression grim. "And paint a bigger target on our backs in the process."

Sophia, who had been silently tending to minor wounds, spoke up for the first time. "We need to move quickly. If Kaine and his forces regroup, they will come back stronger. We can't stay here."

Andres's gaze shifted to Amaru, who stood apart, his eyes closed as if communing with the temple itself. "Amaru, can the temple hold them off again?"

Amaru opened his eyes, his voice calm but resolute. "The stones will respond if we harmonize with them, but they're not invincible. The power here is ancient, but it requires balance. Too much strain and it could collapse entirely."

Maya placed a hand on Andres's arm. "Then we need to move fast. What did you see in your vision? You said it showed our next step."

Andres hesitated, the weight of his vision pressing on him. "I saw a network—sacred sites across the globe connected by energy lines. They lit up like stars, forming a web of power. The Skull is the key to activating it, but we need to find the next node in the grid. Without it, this place—and us—are sitting ducks."

The team sprang into action, each member taking on tasks with renewed urgency. Maya and Evelyn worked together to extract as much data as possible from the crystal mechanism, deciphering co-ordinates etched into its surface. Andres and Amaru consulted the ancient scrolls, searching for clues about the next location.

Julian lingered near the entrance, his eyes scanning the horizon for signs of movement. Sophia approached him cautiously. "You made the right choice back there," she said softly.

Julian exhaled sharply, his shoulders tense. "Did I? Or did I just delay the inevitable?"

"You chose to stand with us," she replied. "That's a start. The rest... we'll figure out together."

Chapter 12

The obsidian doors parted silently, and a chill swept through the underground chamber as Lucius Darkveil glided in. The gathered members of the Sons of Belial fell into an immediate, uneasy silence. His tall figure seemed to absorb what little light remained, the edges of his flowing black robes rippling like shadows given form. Each deliberate step echoed off the ancient stone walls, a steady rhythm that matched the pounding hearts of those assembled.

Lucius's mask, crafted from blackened metal that gleamed dully in the low light, bore the weight of eons. Intricate Atlantean glyphs and Belialic symbols adorned its surface, seeming to writhe and shift as he moved. From behind the mask, eyes like molten gold surveyed the room, piercing through each person present.

"The night deepens," he intoned, his voice a smooth whisper that carried an unsettling authority. "And with it, the time draws near."

The assembly remained still, awaiting his words with reverence and trepidation.

"You stand here, heirs to a legacy written in fire and stone," Lucius continued, spreading his arms wide. "The world above has forgotten us, but we have never forgotten our purpose. The Sons of Belial are more than an order—we are the last remnants of a truth too powerful for the weak to comprehend."

He stepped forward, the glow of ancient torches casting flickering shadows against the chamber walls.

"In the golden age of Atlantis, before its fall, our forebears sought to elevate humankind beyond the fragile constraints of flesh and spirit. While the feeble disciples of the Law of One clung to their illusions of unity, we embraced the destiny of dominion. We mastered the secrets of creation itself, wielding the forces of science and sorcery alike, refining the weak into the strong, shaping nature to our will. And yet, the cowards in white robes sought to chain us, to stifle progress with their naïve visions of harmony."

His voice grew colder, sharp as obsidian.

"Their failure was inevitable. Atlantis crumbled beneath the weight of their misguided ideals, but we endured. We descended into the darkness, weaving our influence through the ages, whispering into the ears of kings and conquerors, guiding civilization toward its rightful course. They call us shadows, but shadows only exist because there is light to be bent."

A murmur of agreement rippled through the assembled followers.

"Now, the cycle nears completion," Lucius declared, his golden eyes burning brighter. "Our adversaries seek to awaken the prophecy of Homo Omega, to drag humanity into a false ascension. But we shall deny them. We shall take what is ours and forge a new order—not of mysticism and weakness, but of power, precision, and unyielding will. The future belongs to those who wield the tools of progress without hesitation. It is time to break the final chains of the old world."

A hush fell over the chamber, heavy with anticipation. Then, one by one, the gathered members pressed their fists to their chests in salute, uttering in unison:

"Belial above all."

Lucius Darkveil stood at the center of it all, silent, knowing the tide was turning. The world above had no idea what was coming.

"My children of shadow," Lucius intoned, his voice a whisper that carried to every corner, "the time of our ascension draws near."

He raised a pale, skeletal hand, and the air itself seemed to tremble. "For millennia, we have waited in the darkness, biding our time as the ignorant masses stumbled through their pitiful existence." His eyes flashed, momentarily blazing an icy blue. "But no longer."

Lucius paced slowly, robes whispering against the stone floor. With each step, he felt the familiar weight of destiny pressing down upon him. The bitter sting of his ancient betrayal, of being cast out of Atlantis, fueled his every move.

Never again will I be deemed unworthy, he thought, allowing a flicker of that long-buried pain to surface before crushing it ruthlessly. *This time, it is I who will judge the world and find it wanting.*

"The Crystal Skull," he continued aloud, "is within our grasp. With it, we shall shatter the delusions of spiritual enlightenment that threaten to awaken humanity." His gaze swept the room, challenging anyone to question him. "We are the true inheritors of Atlantis's legacy. Through our mastery of technology and the darker arts, we shall forge a new era of control."

A tremor of excitement ran through the assembled group. Lucius savored their fear and anticipation, even as he kept his own emotions tightly leashed. He could not afford to show weakness, not when he was so close to achieving everything he had worked for across lifetimes.

"My lord," one of the gathered members ventured, voice quavering slightly, "what of Dr. Paredes and his team? They draw ever closer to uncovering the truth."

Lucius turned, the golden glow of his eyes intensifying. "Ah, yes. Our... esteemed archaeologist." The words dripped with venomous sarcasm. "He and I have unfinished business spanning ages. Rest assured; his meddling will soon come to an end."

For a moment, unbidden, an image of Andrius Paredes in his past life—flashed through Lucius's mind. The memory of their shared idealism, before it all went so horribly wrong, threatened to surface. He ruthlessly suppressed it, burying it beneath layers of hate and ambition.

"Prepare yourselves," Lucius commanded, pushing away the unwelcome thoughts. "The coming days will test our resolve, but we shall emerge victorious. The age of spiritual awakening ends before it can truly begin. In its place, we shall usher in an era of technological dominion, with the Sons of Belial as its masters."

As murmurs of assent filled the chamber, Lucius allowed himself a moment of quiet satisfaction. Soon, he would right the wrongs of the past and prove, once and for all, that his vision for humanity's future was the correct one. And if that meant crushing the last vestiges of hope and light from the world... so, be it.

As Lucius raised his hands to emphasize his final proclamation, the sleeves of his robe slipped back, revealing pale, skeletal fingers adorned with intricate sigils. The arcane symbols seemed to writhe across his skin, pulsing with an otherworldly energy that sent a collective shudder through the assembled Sons of Belial.

"Behold," Lucius intoned, his voice a sepulchral whisper, "the price of true power."

To his right, Sebastian Thorne's lips curled into a thin smile, his steel-gray eyes glinting with cold calculation. "An impressive display, as always, Lucius," he purred, adjusting his immaculate suit. "Though I prefer my methods to be... shall we say, less ostentatious?"

General Kaine, standing to Lucius's left, let out a derisive snort. "Ostentatious?" he growled, his scarred face contorting with barely contained fury. "Our enemies should cower before our might, not be manipulated from the shadows like puppets!"

Lucius's eyes flashed, shifting from molten gold to icy blue. "Both approaches have their merits, gentlemen," he said, his tone brooking no argument. "Thorne's subtlety and your... enthusiasm, Kaine, are equally valuable to our cause."

Thorne inclined his head slightly, a gesture of mock deference. "Of course, Lucius. We each play our part in this grand design."

Kaine's massive frame tensed, his armor creaking ominously. "As long as my part involves crushing those who stand in our way," he snarled.

Lucius observed the interplay between his lieutenants with a mixture of amusement and wariness. Their conflicting approaches could be a strength, but also a potential weakness if left unchecked. He would need to keep a close eye on both in the coming days.

"Indeed," Lucius said, his gaze sweeping across the chamber. "And make no mistake, there will be ample opportunity for both subterfuge and... more direct action in the days to come."

Lucius raised his skeletal hands, the pale fingers gleaming in the eerie light of the underground chamber. "My brothers and sisters of the Sons of Belial," he intoned, his voice a sinister caress that sent shivers through the assembly, "we stand on the precipice of a new era, one where humanity's fate rests in our hands."

The gathered members leaned forward, their eyes glinting with a mixture of fear and anticipation. Lucius savored their rapt attention, feeling the weight of their expectations.

"For too long, mankind has stumbled in the dark, slaves to their own ignorance," he continued, his words dripping with disdain. "But we, we possess the key to unlock their potential—through technological superiority."

Thorne nodded approvingly; his calculating gaze fixed on Lucius. The dark leader's charisma was palpable, drawing even the most skeptical into his vision.

"Imagine a world," Lucius said, his voice dropping to a seductive whisper, "where every thought, every action, every desire is shaped by our will. Where the very fabric of reality bends to our design."

As he spoke, Lucius conjured shadowy images in the air—visions of towering crystal spires, of humans connected to vast networks, their minds open books to be read and rewritten at will.

"This is not mere domination," he declared, his eyes blazing. "This is evolution, guided by our hand. We will remake humanity in our image, and in doing so, we will become gods."

The chamber erupted in murmurs of excitement and awe. Lucius allowed himself a moment of satisfaction before gesturing to Thorne. "Sebastian, enlighten us on the first steps of our grand design."

Thorne stepped forward, his perfectly tailored suit a stark contrast to Lucius's otherworldly presence. "Thank you, Lucius," he said, his voice smooth as silk. "While our ultimate goal is indeed lofty, we must begin with more... mundane methods."

He produced a holographic display, showing a web of interconnected nodes. "Fear and manipulation," Thorne explained, "are our most potent weapons in the short term. We will infiltrate key positions of power—governments, corporations, media outlets—and use them to sow discord and uncertainty."

As he spoke, specific nodes on the display lit up, revealing familiar logos and insignias. "Our operatives are already in place, ready to spread carefully crafted propaganda. We will turn neighbor against neighbor, erode trust in institutions, and create a climate of perpetual crisis. We are already seeing this in the changing political winds around the globe. "

Thorne's gray eyes gleamed with cold satisfaction. "In this chaos, people will cry out for order, for safety. And we, my friends, will be there to provide it—on our terms."

The assembly nodded in appreciation of Thorne's methodical approach. Lucius watched him carefully, a mixture of admiration and wariness in his gaze. Thorne's brilliance was undeniable, but so was his ambition.

"An excellent foundation, Sebastian," Lucius said, his mask hiding any hint of his true thoughts. "Your strategic mind continues to serve us well."

Inwardly, Lucius pondered the delicate balance of power within the Sons of Belial. Thorne's plans were crucial, but the dark leader knew he must remain vigilant. After all, in their shared past, trust had proven a dangerous luxury.

General Kaine surged to his feet, his scarred face contorted with fervor. "Manipulation and fear are mere steppingstones," he growled, his red eyes blazing. "Our true destiny lies in the fusion of man and machine!"

He strode to the center of the chamber, armor clanking ominously. With a wave of his hand, holographic images flickered to life, showing human silhouettes merging with circuits and code.

"Imagine," Kaine continued, his voice a mixture of passion and contempt, "a species freed from the shackles of spirituality and emotion. Pure logic, unmatched processing power, immortality through technology."

Selene Draevan watched from her seat, her sharp features betraying a flicker of unease. She unconsciously touched the small, hidden locket at her throat—a reminder of a past she struggled to forget.

Kaine's fist slammed down on the table. "The so-called 'awakening' they speak of is a regression! We will drag humanity forward, kicking and screaming if we must, into a glorious future of our design."

Selene cleared her throat, drawing attention. "Your vision is... compelling, General," she said, her measured tone a stark contrast to Kaine's fervor. "But we must consider the practical aspects. Total transformation will meet resistance."

She stood, her movements precise. "I propose a more gradual approach. We introduce enhancements as 'medical breakthroughs.' Play on people's fears of aging, disease, death. Make them beg for what we offer. Offer them an alternative, let's say new bodies with capacities far exceeding those of ordinary humans."

As she spoke, Selene's fingers drummed an irregular pattern on the table—a nervous tic she could not quite suppress. Her eyes darted briefly to the exit, a fleeting expression of guilt crossing her face.

"Your caution has merit, Selene," Lucius interjected, his masked visage turning toward her. "But I sense... hesitation. Are you still committed to our cause?"

Selene met his gaze, forcing steel into her voice. "Absolutely, Lord Darkveil. I simply believe subtlety will yield better results in the long term."

Inwardly, she grappled with the weight of her choices. The faces of those she had sacrificed for 'the greater good' haunted her dreams. But to voice such doubts here would be suicide.

Kaine sneered. "Subtlety? Bah! The weak will be culled, the strong ascend. That is the natural order we must accelerate!"

The tension in the room grew palpable as ideology clashed with pragmatism, each member of the Sons of Belial plotting their own path to power in the coming storm. Murmurs of dissent flickered through the assembly like sparks in dry tinder—until a new voice cut through the air, smooth and edged with just enough arrogance to command attention.

"That's all very inspiring, Lucius," came a voice from the side of the chamber, laced with a confident smirk. "But if we're going to dominate the future, we need more than words and ancient legacies. We need results."

The gathered members turned as Talia Elara stepped forward, the torchlight gleaming off the sharp angles of her cheekbones and the calculating glint in her dark eyes. Unlike the robed figures surrounding her, she wore a sleek, form-fitting ensemble of reinforced fabric woven with cutting-edge biotech enhancements—subtle, but unmistakable to those who knew what to look for.

Lucius tilted his masked head slightly as if amused by the interruption. "Enlighten us, then, Talia. I trust your time in the lab has not dulled your sense of ambition?"

She smirked, crossing her arms. "Hardly. While some of you have been whispering in the ears of politicians and playing the long game, I've been perfecting something a little more... immediate."

She tapped a control panel on her wrist, and a holographic display flickered to life above the chamber's stone floor. A sleek, humanoid figure materialized in shifting lines of data—part flesh, part machine, its design eerily precise, unnervingly lifelike.

"The Hybrid Program has reached the next phase," she announced, pacing in front of the projection. "We're past the crude cybernetic augmentations of the past. This is full integration—enhanced cognition, adaptive neuro-linking, and most importantly, absolute obedience. No more unpredictable human emotions getting in the way. No more messy loyalties. Just pure, unrelenting efficiency."

A low murmur spread through the room, some impressed, others visibly wary.

Lucius remained still, observing her with an unreadable expression. "And what of their limits?"

Talia's eyes gleamed. "Minimal. Unlike previous models, these hybrids don't just react—they anticipate. The neural lattice allows them to process battlefield data in real-time, adapt to opponents, and even override pain responses. They're faster, stronger, and most importantly, they cannot be swayed by sentimentality. The perfect enforcers for our new order."

She let the words hang in the air, watching the reactions with a cool detachment. She knew half the men in the room loathed her—a woman, an outsider, someone who had risen through intellect rather than bloodline. But they feared her more than they hated her, and that was enough.

Lucius finally stepped forward, his molten-gold eyes flickering in the dim light. "Impressive. And yet, we must not underestimate our enemies. The fools who cling to the prophecy will fight to the last to prevent us from reshaping the world."

Talia scoffed. "Let them try. Their mysticism is outdated. The future belongs to those who can control it."

Lucius regarded her for a long moment before nodding. "Then we shall see if your creations are as unstoppable as you claim."

A slow, knowing smile spread across Talia's lips. "Oh, they will be."

As the hologram faded, the chamber settled into a hush of contemplation and calculation. The game had just shifted, and Talia Elara had made her move.

As the argument intensified, Asher D'Aron stood motionless at the edge of the room, an enigmatic figure in the chaos. His tall, angular frame was both humanly familiar and subtly alien, a product of cutting-edge bio-synthetic engineering. The faint, metallic sheen of his skin shifted under the ambient light, a telltale sign of his hybrid nature.

His eyes—perhaps his most striking feature—seemed alive with an otherworldly intelligence. They shifted in color, cycling through shades of gold, blue, and violet, mirroring the emotional and energetic currents around him. This was not just aesthetic; Asher's synthetic irises were designed to detect and interpret shifts in temperature, light, and even bioelectric fields. Each flicker of color was a calculation, a decision, or an observation recorded in his neural core.

Inside his mind, the conflict played out in dimensions far beyond the verbal shouting match before him. His consciousness was a blend of organic intuition and synthetic logic. Algorithms within his neural architecture analyzed the pitch and cadence of voices, facial micro-expressions, and heart rate patterns, calculating probabilities of escalation or resolution.

Yet, beneath his computational efficiency, a flicker of something deeper stirred. The human core that remained within him—the remnants of a soul—felt the unease of discord, the primal discomfort of conflict. This duality fascinated him: the synthetic part of him saw conflict as a system to study, while his human side felt the visceral tension, the tug of empathy.

A part of Asher found the escalating tension almost beautiful, a chaotic dance of human emotion, raw and unfiltered. Another part—the cold, calculated aspect—was already mapping out interventions, weighing strategies to neutralize the situation without overtly taking sides.

Despite his stillness, Asher was fully present, absorbing everything. To the others, his silence might appear detached or calculating, but within, he wrestled with the same question that always plagued him: *Was he merely observing humanity—or was he still a part of it?*

Lucius raised a pale hand, silencing the room. "Enough. We shall incorporate Krynn's targets into our plans, but on our timeline. Now, let us focus on the sacred nodes."

The holographic display shifted, highlighting thirteen pulsing points across the globe. Lucius's voice took on a chilling reverence. "These sites are the key to everything. By corrupting their energy, we can destabilize the entire harmonic grid."

Kaine leaned forward eagerly. "Our AI systems have already infiltrated the security networks at Stonehenge and Giza. We are working on the others. We can redirect their energy flow within days."

Selene, her face a mask of forced calm, added, "The Australian government has approved our 'conservation' project at Uluru. We'll have unrestricted access to the Heart of the Earth."

As the group detailed their plans to subvert each sacred site, Asher found himself oddly drawn to the pulsing light representing Mount

Shasta. He vocalized a query, his tone precise and measured. "The Ascension Node. Its energy signature is... unique. How do we account for the variable of human consciousness in our calculations?"

Kaine scoffed. "Consciousness is just complex programming, Asher. We'll overwrite it with our superior code."

Asher remained still, processing. "And yet, our own existence suggests a merger of artificial and organic intelligence yields... unexpected results."

Lucius's masked face turned toward the synthetic being. "Indeed, Asher. You are living proof of our potential. Which is why you will play a crucial role in our next phase of experimentation."

As the meeting progressed, detailing ever more chilling plans to reshape humanity through technology and energetic manipulation, Asher found himself grappling with an unfamiliar sensation. Was this... doubt?

The chamber fell silent as Lucius raised a pale, skeletal hand. His piercing eyes, now a molten gold, swept across the assembled members of the Sons of Belial. For a fleeting moment, something flickered behind that penetrating gaze—a shadow of uncertainty, quickly masked by his usual cold determination.

"Our path is clear," Lucius intoned, his voice a low, resonant hum that seemed to vibrate through the very stones of the chamber. "Yet we must not underestimate the power of human will, nor the unexpected variables that may arise."

As he spoke, unbidden memories surged through Lucius's mind. Images of a sun-drenched Atlantean courtyard, of passionate debates with a man whose face now belonged to his nemesis, Dr. Andres Paredes. The weight of millennia pressed down upon him, and for a heartbeat, doubt crept into his thoughts.

Is this truly the only way? Lucius wondered, his internal voice a whisper against the tempest of his convictions. *Have I strayed so far from our original vision?*

Outwardly, he maintained his imposing demeanor, continuing, "We must be vigilant. Our adversaries are resourceful, driven by misguided ideals of spiritual awakening."

Thorne leaned forward, his cold eyes narrowing. "You speak as if you admire them, Lucius. Surely you have not gone soft after all these years?"

Lucius's mask betrayed no emotion, but his eyes flashed danger- ously. "Do not mistake caution for weakness, Thorne. I know our enemies better than any of you. I have witnessed firsthand the de- structive power of unchecked idealism."

The words tasted bitter on his tongue, memories of his past life with Paredes—then Andrius—threatening to overwhelm him. The betrayal, the rejection, the crushing weight of failure—all of it fueled the dark fire that had driven him for millennia.

"Tell us, then," Kaine challenged, his voice dripping with barely contained zeal. "What makes these spiritualists so formidable? What could possibly stand against our technological might?"

Lucius turned, his robes swirling like living shadows. "Hope, Kaine. The most insidious and persistent of human emotions. It was hope that turned Andrius against me, that blinded him to the true potential of our work."

As the name slipped out, Lucius felt a twinge of... something. Regret? Longing? He crushed the feeling mercilessly.

"And now?" Selene asked, her voice soft but probing. "What drives Dr. Paredes and his team, if not that same hope?"

Lucius's laugh was a harsh, grating sound. "Oh, it is hope indeed. But this time, we will use it against them. We will offer humanity a false dawn, a technological utopia that will enslave them more surely than any chains."

Yet even as he spoke, a tiny voice in the depths of his ancient soul whispered: *And what if they are right? What if there is another way?*

Lucius clenched his fist, silencing the treacherous whisper. His eyes, visible through the slits in his ornate mask, flashed molten gold as he strode to the center of the chamber. The Sons of Belial instinc- tively drew back, creating a circle around their leader.

"Let me tell you a story," Lucius began, his voice low and mesmer- izing, "of two young scholars in the heart of Atlantis, who dreamed of reshaping the world."

As he spoke, the air around him seemed to shimmer, memories taking form like ghostly holograms. A bustling Atlantean street ma- terialized, crystalline spires stretching toward an impossibly blue sky.

"Lukanis and Andrius," Lucius continued, gesturing to two fig- ures deep in animated discussion. "Brilliant minds, steadfast friends... fools, both of us."

Thorne's eyebrow arched. "Us?"

Lucius ignored him. "We believed we could merge technology and spirituality, create a perfect balance. But balance..." He spat the word, "balance is a myth. There is only power, and those too weak to seek it."

The holographic scene shifted, showing a grand laboratory filled with pulsing energy fields and gleaming machinery.

"I saw the truth," Lucius declared, "that true transcendence lay in pushing beyond our biological limitations. Andrius clung to outdated notions of the heart and soul. "

As he spoke, his voice took on a bitter edge. "He couldn't see the potential, the greatness we could achieve. And when I dared to reach for it..."

The memory-image flickered, showing a heated argument between the two friends, their faces contorted with anger and pain.

"He turned on me," Lucius snarled. "Branded me a monster, a threat to everything we'd worked for."

Kaine leaned forward, eyes gleaming. "And the experiment? What did you create?"

Lucius paused, his mask hiding the conflicting emotions warring across his face. "Something... beautiful and terrible. A being of pure intellect, unfettered by the weaknesses of flesh and spirit. The first step towards true godhood."

The hologram faded, leaving the chamber in darkness once more. Lucius turned to face his followers, his voice filled with grim determination.

"That's what Paredes and his ilk fear. Not our technology, but the freedom it offers from the chains of our primitive origins. They would keep humanity mired in superstition and false spirituality."

Selene spoke softly, her eyes searching Lucius's mask. "And yet, you seem... troubled by these memories. Is there not some part of you that still—"

"Enough!" Lucius roared, the shadows around him writhing. "The past is dead. Lukanis is dead. There is only the path forward, the destiny we will forge for humanity whether they wish it or not."

But even as he spoke, Lucius felt a familiar ache deep within. The ghost of a friendship long lost, of ideals abandoned. He pushed it aside, focusing on the cold certainty of his chosen path.

"Now," he said, his voice once again smooth and controlled. "Let us discuss how we will deal with Dr. Paredes and his meddlesome team. They may have hope on their side, but we... we have inevitability."

Yet, for Lucius, the memories were still there...

Andrius burst into the laboratory, his eyes wide with horror as he took in the scene before him. Lukanis stood amidst a swirling vortex of dark energy, his hands outstretched towards a writhing figure on a nearby table.

The vision of a past life resurfaced in Lucius's mind, vivid and undeniable.

"Lukanis, stop this madness!" Andrius shouted, his voice barely audible over the howling winds. "You're playing with forces beyond our control!"

Lukanis whirled to face his former friend, his eyes blazing with a mixture of triumph and desperation. "You don't understand, Andrius! I am on the brink of a breakthrough that will change everything!"

Andrius took a cautious step forward, his hand extended in a placating gesture. "Please, my friend. This is not the way. We talked about balance, about harmony between technology and spirit. This... this is an abomination."

Lukanis's face contorted with rage. "An abomination? This is the future! You are just too blind to see it!" He gestured wildly at the pulsing machinery around them. "With this, we can transcend our limitations, become the gods we were meant to be!"

As he spoke, Lukanis's mind raced. *How dare Andrius try to stop him now, when he was so close? Didn't he see that this was for the good of all humanity?* The rejection in Andrius's eyes cut deeper than any blade, confirming Lukanis's deepest fears—that he would never be understood, never be accepted.

"I won't let you destroy everything we've worked for," Andrius declared, moving towards the main control panel.

"No!" Lukanis lunged forward, desperation fueling his actions. His hand slammed down on a series of buttons, overriding safety protocols. The air crackled with unleashed energy.

Andrius stumbled back, horror dawning on his face. "Lukanis, what have you done?"

The laboratory shook violently, equipment exploding in showers of sparks. Lukanis watched in growing horror as his creation began to warp and twist, growing beyond his control. The last thing he saw before the blinding flash was Andrius's face, a mixture of pity and sorrow etched upon it.

When Lukanis regained consciousness, he found himself surrounded by devastation. The once-gleaming district of Atlantis lay in ruins, the air filled with screams and the acrid smell of destruction. As he stumbled through the wreckage, the weight of what he had done crashed down upon him.

"This is your doing, Lukanis," a stern voice declared. He turned to see a council of Atlantean elders, their faces grim. "Your reckless pursuit of power has cost countless innocent lives. You are hereby exiled from Atlantis, never to return."

Broken and alone, Lukanis fled into the depths of the fallen city. It was there, in the shadows, that he first heard the whispers of Belial, promising him the power and recognition he craved. As he listened, the last remnants of Lukanis withered away, replaced by the cold, calculating entity that would become Lucius Darkveil.

"Yes," he whispered to the darkness. "Show me the true path to godhood."

Chapter 13

Their journey had led them deep into the underground city, past forgotten chambers, and dormant technologies, to the Temple of Knowledge—a sacred vault where the Atlanteans safeguarded their most valuable secrets: wisdom, artifacts, and the keys to humanity's future. Hidden for millennia beneath the earth, the temple had awaited the right moment to reveal its treasures.

At its heart lay the library, an inner sanctum housing Atlantis's collective knowledge, preserved in crystal tablets and engraved stone scripts. Only the most trusted Atlantean scholars had ever entered, its entrance concealed by mechanisms known only to the high priests.

Andres and his team had come to decipher the ancient texts that could unlock the mysteries of the Crystal Skull and the Atlantean prophecy. The knowledge here held the power to awaken the global energy grid and guide humanity's next evolutionary step—but it also contained secrets some would kill to keep buried.

As they ventured deeper into the library, an ethereal glow illuminated towering stone shelves lined with texts in languages long forgotten. The air shimmered, charged with an unseen energy.

Andres paused at the center of the room, his pulse steady despite the enormity of their task. His Mapuche ancestry, a link to the wisdom of the earth, resonated with the library's energy. The knowledge stored here was more than intellectual; it was spiritual—a bridge between the past and the destiny of the future.

The underground library was a marvel of ancient design and mysticism. Shelves carved into the rock walls stretched into the dimly lit distance, filled with crystalline tablets and glowing scrolls. At the room's heart, a towering central column pulsed with thousands of glowing, interlocking symbols, casting shifting patterns of light across the space.

Nearby, a massive crystal disk hovered above a pedestal, slowly spinning. As it turned, it reflected the column's symbols onto the walls, forming a kaleidoscope of living light, shifting, and rearranging in response to their presence. Concentric rings of inscribed stone radiated from the column's base, each engraved with glowing symbols that hummed at a frequency that seemed to vibrate within their very bones.

The symbols themselves were enigmatic—part geometric, part organic, blending the precision of science with the fluidity of nature. Some resembled star charts, others mirrored DNA strands or complex equations. Interwoven within them were sacred geometric patterns—the Flower of Life, the Vesica Piscis—hints of a profound, multidimensional understanding of existence.

As the group studied the symbols, faint whispers seemed to rise and fall in the background, like distant echoes of voices speaking an ancient, forgotten language. It was as if the library itself was alive, aware of their presence, waiting for them to uncover its secrets.

We are running out of time," Andres said, his voice low and urgent. "These symbols are the key to activating the global energy grid. We need to decode them now."

Evelyn pushed her glasses up her nose, her brow furrowed in concentration. "The patterns suggest a mathematical sequence, but there's something... off about it."

"Perhaps it's not just mathematics," Jacqueline interjected, "What if these symbols represent both scientific and spiritual concepts simultaneously?"

Andres nodded, a spark of recognition igniting within him. His ancestors had always known that science and spirit were two sides of the same coin. He ran his fingers along the etched stone, feeling the vibrations of ancient knowledge beneath his touch.

"You're right," he murmured. "It's a fusion of the rational and the mystical. The Atlanteans understood that the Earth's energy isn't just physical—it's consciousness itself."

As the team huddled around the symbols, the air crackled with tension. Andres could feel the weight of millennia pressing down upon them, the whispers of long-lost civilizations urging them forward. His mind raced, connecting fragments of Mapuche lore with the cosmic designs before him.

Evelyn's voice cut through his thoughts. "Look here—this recurring pattern. It's similar to the Golden Ratio but with an extra dimension."

"Yes," Jacqueline agreed, her eyes widening. "And see how it intersects with this spiral? It's like a map of the Earth's ley lines but viewed from a higher plane of existence."

Andres's heart quickened. They were close, so close to unlocking the secrets that had eluded humanity for eons. He closed his eyes, drawing upon the deep well of his heritage, seeking guidance from the ancestors who had safeguarded this knowledge.

"The Vesica Piscis," he breathed, his eyes snapping open. "It's the key to aligning the symbols. The intersection of matter and spirit, just as my people have always known."

As Andres spoke, the symbols seemed to shimmer, responding to the revelation. The team worked feverishly, their combined expertise bringing clarity to the ancient puzzle. With each passing moment, he could feel the energy in the room intensifying, as if the very stones were awakening from a long slumber.

"We're close," he urged, his voice tight with anticipation. "The global energy grid is within our grasp. Once activated, it will change everything—our understanding of reality, our place in the cosmos, the very future of humanity."

A surge of radiant light filtered through the crystalline veins embedded in the ceiling, refracting into cascading rainbows that painted the walls with a mesmerizing, otherworldly glow. Each beam of light seemed alive, pulsing in harmony with the rhythmic hum that now vibrated through the air.

The underground library responded as if awakening from dormancy. The central column flared to life, its inscriptions igniting in a symphony of colors, each symbol radiating its own distinct hue and vibrational tone. The spinning crystal disk on the pedestal absorbed the energy, amplifying it and projecting waves of golden light that danced across the room like living tendrils.

The circular stone rings on the floor resonated in unison, their inscriptions glowing in synchronization as if the entire chamber were a colossal tuning fork attuned to an ancient frequency. The energy crescendoed, filling the space with a blinding brilliance that seemed to dissolve the barriers between dimensions. The library was no longer just a room—it had become a nexus of interconnected energy fields, a gateway bridging the material and spiritual realms.

As Andres's hands moved instinctively across the symbols, they glowed with a fiery intensity, his touch sparking connections that bridged the mathematical precision of the patterns with their deeper, spiritual meaning. The hum deepened into a resonant chorus, a sound that was felt as much as heard, vibrating in their chests, and aligning their very beings with the pulse of the universe.

The moment Andres touched the final symbol, the blinding light coalesced into a single, focused beam that shot upward through the central column and into the unseen heavens. A shockwave of energy radiated outward, shaking the ground gently as the library pulsed with life, its walls no longer merely stone but transformed into luminous, pulsating conduits of universal power.

Andres stepped back, his heart pounding. "This is it," he whispered, awe and trepidation mingling in his voice. "The awakening of the Earth's sacred grid. May we be worthy of the wisdom it brings."

As the energy surged around them, Andres silently prayed that they were prepared for the transformation that was about to unfold—a transformation that would rewrite the destiny of their species and usher in the dawn of Homo Omega.

Suddenly, the reverent silence of the library was torn apart by the piercing crackle of advanced weaponry, a sound that reverberated like a harbinger of doom against the ancient stone walls. Shadows danced menacingly in the kaleidoscopic glow of the activation as General Kaine emerged from the darkness, his towering figure exuding raw, predatory power. His glowing red eyes burned with a malevolent intensity, twin orbs of hatred that seemed to pierce straight into the soul.

Behind him, the Sons of Belial marched in perfect formation, their dark, obsidian armor reflecting the pulsing light of the chamber in eerie flashes. Each step they took seemed to drain the warmth from the room, replacing it with a suffocating chill that carried the weight of untold suffering.

Weapons raised, their barrels hissed with lethal energy, casting sickly green and red hues that twisted the sacred light of the library into something alien and foreboding. The air thickened, charged with an oppressive tension that pressed down on the chest like a physical weight. The faint whispers of the library, once comforting, now turned frantic, as if the very walls cried out in warning.

"End of the road!" Kaine growled, his voice a guttural snarl that echoed through the chamber. His words were laced with grim finality, the promise of annihilation hanging heavy in the air. The soldiers spread out in a calculated, predatory advance, their movements unnervingly synchronized, each one a living embodiment of the darkness they served. The sanctuary of knowledge and light had become a battlefield, and its sacred halls were now under siege by an ancient evil reborn.

Maya's voice cut through the tension, steady and resolute. "Protect the sacred knowledge!" She stepped forward, her robes swirling with Atlantean symbols that seemed to writhe in the ethereal light.

Amaru joined her, his weathered face set with determination. "The wisdom of Tiwanaku will not fall to your corruption," he declared, his staff striking the ground with a resonant thud.

General Kaine's lips curled into a sneer. "Your primitive superstitions are no match for our technological might. Surrender the Crystal Skull, and perhaps I'll grant you a swift death."

Andres's mind raced, assessing their dire situation. *We cannot let them destroy everything we have discovered.* His gaze met Maya's, and a silent understanding passed between them.

"Now, Maya!" Andres shouted, diving for cover behind an ancient pillar.

Maya's hands wove intricate patterns in the air, her third eye blazing with otherworldly light. A shimmering barrier sprang to life, enveloping their team in a protective cocoon just as the Sons of Belial opened fire.

Amaru's voice rose in a rhythmic chant, invoking the spirits of his ancestors. The very air around them seemed to thicken, imbued with an ancient power that pushed back against the onslaught of energy weapons.

"Your parlor tricks won't save you!" Kaine roared, unleashing a barrage of fire that made the barrier flicker dangerously.

Andres's heart pounded as he watched the clash of energies. How long can we hold out against their firepower? He caught glimpses of his team taking shelter, Evelyn and Jacqueline huddled together, their scientific minds struggling to comprehend the metaphysical battle unfolding before them.

"We must stand united!" Andres called out, his voice carrying the weight of his Mapuche heritage. "Our strength lies in our connection to the Earth and to each other!"

As if in response to his words, the symbols on the library walls began to pulse with an inner light, lending their ancient power to the defense.

Andres's fingers trembled as he traced the glowing symbols etched into the walls, his mind racing to decipher their meaning. The Crystal Skull pulsed in his other hand, its energy syncing with the rhythm of his racing heart. Sweat beaded on his brow as he muttered to himself, "Come on, come on... what are you trying to tell me?"

A flash of insight struck him like lightning. "The Vesica Piscis!" he exclaimed, his blue eyes widening. "It's not just a symbol, it's a key!"

Evelyn's voice cut through the chaos. "Andres, we can't hold them off much longer!" The strain in her tone was palpable, mirroring the flickering of Maya's energy barrier.

Andres gritted his teeth, frustration mounting. "I need more time!" The weight of their mission pressed down on him, threatening to crush his resolve.

Suddenly, the Crystal Skull erupted with blinding light, its surface shimmering as though alive. A cascade of luminous symbols spiraled out, encircling Andres like a vortex of ancient knowledge. Before he could react, the light shot into his mind, bypassing conscious thought, and immersing him in a torrent of visions.

He was no longer in the library. Instead, he found himself soaring over vast Atlantean cities, their crystalline spires gleaming under a golden sun. He felt the hum of their energy grids, vast and intricate, as they resonated in harmony with the Earth's natural frequencies. The cities seemed alive, pulsating with a vibrancy that defied the passage of time. Yet, as quickly as they rose, he saw them fall—engulfed by raging seas and fiery skies, their brilliance extinguished by forces both natural and unnatural.

The visions shifted, pulling him through the eons. Cosmic alignments unfolded like a celestial dance, stars, and planets aligning in intricate patterns, their energy rippling across the fabric of the universe. Each alignment felt like a heartbeat, a reminder of the interconnectedness of all things. He saw these moments replayed through history, influencing events, shaping civilizations, and now converging in this very moment.

Faces emerged from the swirling chaos—familiar yet unfamiliar. His teammates' features blurred and transformed, revealing echoes of their Atlantean ancestry. Maya's face glimmered with the regal bearing of an Atlantean priestess, her eyes glowing with wisdom. Evelyn appeared as a scholar, her hands tracing the same symbols they had studied in the library millennia ago. Even the betrayer among them was there, their expression torn between loyalty and treachery. Andres saw his own reflection—a warrior, a seeker, a bridge between worlds.

The Skull's energy grew more intense, projecting flashes of future possibilities. Sacred sites around the globe came alive, their dormant energies awakening in response to the celestial alignment. He saw the Earth bathed in a radiant glow, humanity on the precipice of transformation. But he also saw darkness—an army of shadowed figures marching under Kaine's command, their malevolence threatening to extinguish the light forever.

The weight of the visions bore down on him, the sheer magnitude of the knowledge almost too much to bear. The air around him felt charged, vibrating with the echo of ancient truths and future prophecies. As the images faded, Andres collapsed to his knees, gasping for breath, his heart pounding like a drum. The Skull's light dimmed, leaving only the faintest glow, as if it, too, was exhausted by the revelation.

"What did you see?" Maya's voice broke through the haze, filled with both fear and urgency.

Andres's voice trembled as he whispered, "Everything. Past, present, and what is to come. We are out of time."

"What did you see?" Jacqueline demanded, her scientific curiosity piqued even during battle.

Andres shook his head, trying to clear it. "Everything... and nothing. It is all connected, but I cannot—"

A thunderous crack split the air as Kaine's forces breached Maya's defenses. The team scattered, seeking cover among the ancient pillars.

"We're out of time!" Maya shouted; her voice tinged with panic. "Andres, what's the plan?"

The pressure mounted, old tensions bubbling to the surface. Sophia's eyes flashed with barely concealed resentment. "If you hadn't insisted on coming here-"

"Enough!" Andres roared, silencing the bickering. He stood tall, channeling the strength of his Mapuche ancestors. "We didn't come this far to fall apart now. Each of us has a role to play, a piece of the puzzle. Together, we're stronger than any weapon they can wield."

He locked eyes with each team member in turn, his gaze intense and unwavering. "Evelyn, Jacqueline, I need your analytical minds. Maya, Amaru, channel your spiritual energies into the symbols. Sophia, watch our backs. We're going to crack this code and activate the grid, no matter what it takes."

A moment of silence hung in the air, broken only by the sound of approaching footsteps. Then, as one, the team nodded, renewed determination etched on their faces.

Andres turned back to the wall, the Crystal Skull humming with anticipation in his hands. "Let's rewrite history," he whispered, plunging once more into the labyrinth of ancient knowledge as the battle raged around them.

The air crackled with tension as Andres's fingers traced the intricate symbols, the Crystal Skull pulsing with an otherworldly light. Suddenly, a deafening explosion rocked the chamber, showering them with debris. As the dust settled, a heart-wrenching cry pierced the air.

"No!" Maya's anguished scream shattered the air, raw and heart-wrenching, a sound that cut through the chaos like a blade.

Andres's heart stopped. He spun around, every muscle in his body frozen in disbelief. Time seemed to slow as his gaze fell upon Sophia, crumpled beneath a massive, fallen column. Her body was unnaturally still, and the weight of the stone pressed down on her as if the world itself was trying to crush the last of her light. The vibrant energy that had once radiated from her was now gone.

A sharp pain seared through Andres's chest. He rushed toward her, his breath shallow, hands trembling as he reached out to her lifeless form. Maya was already there, her face pale with shock, hands hovering over the still body, unwilling to touch, as though touching her would make the reality of it all too final.

The rest of the team gathered around, helpless, their eyes wide with disbelief. There was nothing they could do. The pulse of the universe seemed to be holding its breath, mourning with them. The ground beneath their feet seemed to shudder in empathy for their loss.

Sophia's eyes were now glassy, staring vacantly at the celestial ceiling above. The intricate carvings of the Atlantean and Tiwanaku symbols seemed to swirl in the dim light as if mourning the passing of her soul.

"This can't be happening," Maya whispered, her voice a mere wisp, the sound like a soft plea against the cold, indifferent reality that had shattered their world.

It was too late for words, too late for the desperate pleas that would never reach her ears. The air hung thick with an oppressive silence, broken only by the soft crackle of distant flames. Sorrow engulfed them, an unbearable weight pressing down on their chests, stealing their breath. Sophia—a valued teammate and friend and her guiding wisdom was gone.

The team stood in stunned silence, their minds struggling to comprehend the enormity of the loss. Andres could feel the weight of it pressing down on him, sinking into his bones, a pain deeper than any physical wound. He felt responsible and the weight of their mission, once clear and filled with hope, now seemed insurmountable.

And as the team stood, devastated and silent, the celestial alignment above seemed to flicker, as if acknowledging the tragedy, the balance that had been irrevocably disrupted.

Andres felt the weight of leadership pressing down on him, threatening to crush his resolve. He closed his eyes, allowing himself a moment of grief before steeling his nerves.

"She gave her life for this," he said, his voice thick with emotion. "We can't let her sacrifice be in vain."

Evelyn stepped forward, her eyes glistening with unshed tears. "We have to finish what we started."

"But how?" Jacqueline asked, her voice trembling. "We're falling apart at the seams."

Andres looked at each team member, seeing the fear, doubt, and determination warring in their expressions. He held up the Crystal Skull, its ethereal glow casting dancing shadows across their faces.

"We finish this together," he declared. "Let's honor her memory."

As if responding to his words, the Crystal Skull suddenly flared with blinding intensity. Andres gasped as a flood of images cascaded through his mind—sacred sites around the world pulsing with energy, waiting to be awakened.

"The symbols!" he exclaimed. "I can see the connections!"

With renewed purpose, the team rallied around Andres. Jacqueline's analytical mind worked in tandem with Maya's intuitive insights, decoding the final sequences.

As the last symbol clicked into place, a low hum filled the chamber. The Crystal Skull levitated from Andres's hands, spinning slowly in the air. Beams of radiant energy burst forth, connecting with the intricate patterns on the walls.

"It's happening," Evelyn breathed in awe. "The global energy grid is activating!"

The room filled with a dazzling light show as the energy beams shot outward, penetrating the temple walls. In his mind's eye, Andres saw the sacred nodes igniting one by one—Stonehenge, Giza, Machu Picchu, Uluru—each site blazing to life in a cosmic dance of awakening.

Andres whispered, a bittersweet smile touching his lips. "We did it; the wisdom lives on."

The temple shuddered violently, ancient stones groaning under the strain of cosmic energies. A deafening crack echoed through the chamber as fissures spread across the ceiling.

"The structure's destabilizing!" Jacqueline shouted, her eyes wide with alarm.

Andres's heart raced as he watched chunks of debris rain down around them. "We need to get out of here!" he yelled, gesturing frantically toward the exit.

But as they turned to flee, a blinding flash erupted from the Crystal Skull. The air crackled with electricity, and Andres felt a surge of power ripple through his body. He watched in awe as the wave of energy expanded outward, slamming into the advancing Sons of Belial. Their weapons were short-circuited, and several men were thrown back, crumpling to the ground.

"It's repelling them!" Maya exclaimed, her voice a mixture of relief and concern.

Evelyn grabbed Andres's arm. "We can't leave yet," she urged. "If the temple collapses, we could lose everything we've discovered."

Andres's mind raced, weighing their options. The ground beneath their feet trembled ominously. "We need to stabilize the energy flow," he decided. "Maya, can you channel some of this power? Redirect it?"

Maya nodded, her face set with determination. "I'll try, but I'll need help."

As Maya began to weave intricate patterns in the air, manipulating the energy currents, Andres turned to the others. "Grab what you can—artifacts, data, anything of importance. We may not get another chance."

The team sprang into action, working frantically as the temple continued to shake around them. Andres's thoughts whirled. *We have activated the grid, but at what cost? The power we have unleashed— it is more than we anticipated. What if we cannot control it?*

As the team worked to secure their findings, a brilliant flash of light erupted from the crumbling temple entrance. Andres shielded his eyes, his heart pounding. When the glare subsided, he gasped at the sight before him.

"Look!" he called out, pointing to the sky.

The darkness above had transformed into a canvas of cosmic energy. Shimmering lines of light wove together, forming an intricate pattern that spanned the heavens. At its center, a familiar symbol pulsed with an otherworldly glow—the Vesica Piscis.

Evelyn's eyes widened. "It's the sacred geometry of creation," she whispered, her scientific skepticism momentarily forgotten.

Maya's voice was filled with awe. "The prophecy speaks of this sign. It heralds the final convergence—the moment when humanity must choose its path."

Jacqueline, ever practical, interrupted the moment of wonder. "That's great and all, but we've got incoming. The Sons of Belial are regrouping."

Andres nodded, his resolve strengthening. "Then we need to be ready. This is bigger than just us now."

He turned to face his team, each member's face illuminated by the ethereal light from above. "Dr. Carter, your analytical mind will be crucial in deciphering the cosmic patterns we've uncovered. Dr. Hart, your expertise in ancient languages could unlock secrets we haven't even considered yet."

Maya placed a hand on Andres's shoulder, her touch grounding him. "And I will continue to guide us through the spiritual realms, bridging the gap between ancient wisdom and our current challenges."

Andres took a deep breath, feeling the weight of their mission. "Together, we represent the best of humanity—science and spirituality, technology and tradition. It's up to us to ensure that the path to Homo Omega remains open."

As if in response to his words, the symbol in the sky pulsed more intensely. Andres could not shake the feeling that they were standing on the precipice of something monumental.

"Whatever comes next," he said, his voice steady, "we face it as one. The future of humanity depends on it."

The team stood united, their silhouettes etched against the cosmic display above. In that moment, Andres felt a surge of hope. Despite the challenges ahead, he knew that together, they had a chance to shape the destiny of their species.

Andres stood at the edge of the ancient temple's terrace, his weathered hands resting on the cool stone balustrade. The ethereal glow of the Vesica Pisces still lingered in the sky, casting an otherworldly light across the Andean landscape. He closed his eyes, feeling the pulse of the Earth beneath his feet, a rhythm that seemed to resonate with his own heartbeat.

"Tata Mallku," he whispered, invoking the mountain spirit of his Mapuche ancestors. "Guide me through the shadows that lie ahead."

The wind whispered through the carved stone pillars, carrying with it the scent of sage and earth. Andres opened his eyes, his gaze drawn to the distant peaks where the mist clung like ancient spirits.

Evelyn approached, her footsteps echoing in the stillness. "Andres? The others are preparing to leave. Are you alright?"

He turned, offering a small smile. "Just... reflecting. The weight of Atlantis' legacy is heavy. But so is the wisdom of my people."

"How do you reconcile the two?" she asked, genuine curiosity in her voice.

Andres smiled as he considered. "It's like... two rivers joining to form something greater. The Atlanteans sought to control nature, while the Mapuche strived to live in harmony with it. Perhaps the path forward lies somewhere between."

He ran his fingers through his graying hair, a habit born of deep contemplation. "The global energy grid, the Crystal Skull, the prophecies of Homo Omega—they're all pieces of a cosmic puzzle. But my grandmother always said, 'The greatest wisdom comes from listening to the land.'"

Evelyn nodded, her scientific mind grappling with these metaphysical concepts. "And what is the land telling you now?"

Andres's dark eyes scanned the horizon. "That we're on the cusp of something monumental. The evolution of humanity is not just about technology or spiritual awakening—it's about finding balance. The Atlanteans lost sight of that and look what happened to them."

He clenched his fist, determination etched on his face. "We can't make the same mistake. The path ahead is treacherous, full of shadows cast by the Sons of Belial and our doubts. But we must push forward."

"For the sake of all humanity," Evelyn added softly.

Andres nodded, his voice low but resolute. "For all humanity, yes. But also, for the Earth herself. My people have always known that we are not separate from nature—we are part of it. As we evolve, so too must our relationship with the planet."

He turned back to the vista, his thoughts racing. The knowledge they had uncovered in the Atlantean library, the power of the Crystal Skull, the prophecies of the final battle—it all swirled in his mind like a cosmic dance.

"We stand at a crossroads," Andres murmured, more to himself than to Evelyn. "The legacy of Atlantis offers us incredible power, but my Mapuche heritage reminds me of the importance of wisdom and balance. Somehow, we must forge a path that honors both."

As the first rays of dawn began to paint the sky, Andres straightened, his resolve hardening. "Come," he said to Evelyn. "We have a long journey ahead, and humanity's future hangs in the balance. But I believe—I have to believe—that we are equal to the task."

With one last glance at the majestic landscape, Andres thought how the path toward humanity's evolution would be fraught with danger, but with the wisdom of the ancients and the strength of his team, he was determined to see it through.

Chapter 14

The ancient stones of Tiwanaku whispered to Andres as he led the team across the windswept Andean plateau. Flashes of memory, sharp as obsidian blades, cut through his mind—visions of towering crystal spires, chanting priests, and a blinding light that seemed to swallow the sky.

Andres stumbled, catching himself on a nearby boulder. The rough surface beneath his palm anchored him to the present, even as the past threatened to overwhelm his senses.

"You alright there, boss?" Evelyn's voice carried a note of concern tinged with skepticism.

Andres straightened, forcing a smile. "Just a loose stone. We're nearly there."

As they crested the final rise, the Pyramid of Akapana loomed before them, its terraced sides seeming to pulse with an otherworldly energy. Andres's breath caught in his throat. It was exactly as he had seen it in his visions, yet impossibly real.

Maya's hand on his shoulder steadied him. "You feel it too, don't you?" she murmured. "The power of this place?"

Andres nodded, unable to find words. How could he explain the surge of recognition, the sense of coming home to a place he had never been?

"Let's set up camp," he announced, tearing his gaze from the pyramid. "We'll start our survey at first light."

As the team busied themselves with tents and equipment, Andres wandered to the edge of their makeshift camp, drawn to the ancient structure before him. The sun's dying rays bathed the stones in gold and crimson, illuminating the intricate carvings etched into their surface.

"It's just a pile of rocks, you know."

Andres turned to find Evelyn beside him, her expression a mix of curiosity and doubt.

"Is it?" he asked quietly. "Then why are we here, Dr. Carter?"

She sighed, adjusting her glasses. "Because your theories—far-fetched as they may seem—have led us to some astonishing discoveries. But Andres, you must admit, all this talk of ancient, advanced civilizations and cosmic energy grids... it is a lot to take in."

A flicker of frustration rose in Andres. "And yet, here we stand, at one of the most enigmatic sites in South America. You cannot deny there is something... different about this place."

"Different, yes," Evelyn admitted. "But let's not jump to interdimensional portals just yet, shall we?"

Before Andres could respond, Maya approached, her expression serene despite the tension crackling in the air.

"The camp is ready," she announced. "Perhaps we should all get some rest. Tomorrow will bring its own challenges."

Andres nodded, grateful for the interruption. As he turned to follow Maya back to the camp, a chill ran down his spine. For a moment, he could have sworn he saw figures moving among the shadowed terraces of the pyramid—ghostly shapes that vanished when he blinked. He thought—*we need to be on the alert.*

Just my imagination, he told himself. But as he settled into his tent that night, Andres could not shake the feeling that they were being watched by unseen eyes, guardians of ancient secrets that were stirring once more after millennia of slumber. After all they had been through, he was beginning to expect it.

The next morning, as the first rays of sunlight pierced through the mist, Evelyn stood before the Akapana Pyramid. The massive, stepped structure loomed above her, its weathered stones bearing the weight of centuries. Once a grand and imposing monument to a lost civilization, the Akapana now seemed both a ruin and a sentinel, its terraces overgrown with tufts of resilient grass that clung to the cracks and crevices of its stone façade.

The pyramid's surface was a patchwork of precision and decay. Some stones retained their ancient carvings—intricate glyphs and geometric patterns that hinted at an advanced understanding of mathematics, astronomy, and spiritual alignment. Others were eroded by time, their edges softened by wind and rain, as though nature sought to reclaim its dominion.

Evelyn ran her fingers lightly across the glyphs, feeling the grooves and patterns that whispered of forgotten rituals and lost wisdom. Her keen green eyes darted across the symbols, trying to decode their meaning. Each glyph seemed to pulsate with an energy just beneath the surface, as if the pyramid itself was alive, waiting for someone to unlock its secrets.

The Akapana radiated an unearthly aura. Its terraced design aligned with the cardinal points, and Evelyn could not shake the sense that it was more than a mere structure. It was a map, a mechanism, perhaps even a gateway. The faint sound of running water reached her ears, reminding her of the pyramid's ancient hydraulic systems—channels and reservoirs that once flowed with life-giving energy, now dormant but not forgotten.

For a moment, Evelyn closed her eyes, letting the pyramid's silent power wash over her. She felt the weight of its history, the lives that had been lived and lost here, and the role it now played in their mission. Whatever secrets it held, she was determined to uncover them.

"Fascinating," she murmured, pulling out her notebook. "These symbols... they're unlike anything I've seen before."

As Evelyn meticulously sketched and photographed the inscriptions, her initial skepticism began to waver. The patterns were too precise, too intentional to be mere decorative elements.

"This can't be right," she muttered, double-checking her translations. "It's as if they're describing... a cosmic alignment?"

Her heart raced as she deciphered more of the ancient warnings. References to celestial gateways, interdimensional portals, and a looming threat that sent chills down her spine.

"Andres!" she called out, her voice trembling slightly. "You need to see this!"

Meanwhile, in his tent, Andres tossed fitfully in his sleeping bag. Suddenly, he bolted upright, gasping for air. Visions of shadowy figures and pulsing energy fields lingered in his mind.

"No... no, it can't be," he panted, stumbling out of his tent. "We have to move! Now!"

The team gathered around him, faces etched with concern and confusion.

"Andres, what's wrong?" Maya asked, her calm voice a stark contrast to his agitation.

"I saw them," Andres stammered, struggling to articulate the fragments of his vision. "The Sons of Belial... they're coming. We are in danger!"

Dr. Carter crossed her arms, skepticism evident in her stance. "Andres, it was just a dream. We are all on edge, but—"

"No!" Andres interrupted, his eyes wild. "It wasn't just a dream. I felt it. The pyramid... it's trying to warn us."

Julian Blackwood scoffed. "Now you're saying the pyramid is sentient? This is getting ridiculous."

Andres's frustration mounted. How could he make them understand the urgency, the reality of what he had experienced?

"Listen to me," he pleaded, locking eyes with each team member. "My Mapuche heritage... it's connecting me to this place. I know it sounds crazy, but we need to prepare. Something's coming, and we're not ready."

The team exchanged uneasy glances, torn between their trust in Andres and the apparent absurdity of his claims.

Maya stepped forward, placing a hand on Andres's shoulder. "I believe you," she said softly. "What do you need us to do?"

Andres took a deep breath, grateful for her support. "We need to secure the Crystal Skull and gather our equipment. If I'm right, we don't have much time."

As the team reluctantly began to move, Andres could not shake the lingering dread. The visions felt more real than any dream, and he feared they were only the beginning of what was to come.

Suddenly, the air shattered with a thunderous explosion, sending debris and chaos raining down on the camp. General Kaine's unmistakable voice boomed through the darkness, "Seize the Crystal Skull! Leave no one alive!"

Andres's heart raced as he scrambled to his feet, adrenaline surging through his veins. "Take cover!" he shouted, diving behind a stack of crates as gunfire erupted around them.

Evelyn's analytical mind shifted into survival mode. She grabbed her laptop, clutching it to her chest as she crawled towards the nearest tent. "We need to protect the data!" she yelled over the cacophony.

Andres's thoughts raced. *How had they found them? How could he protect his team?* His eyes darted around, searching for—

"Maya!" he gasped, spotting her standing calmly in the center of the chaos, her flowing robes billowing in the night air.

As if in slow motion, Maya raised her arms, her third eye gleaming with an otherworldly light. A shimmering barrier of energy materialized around her, deflecting bullets and shrapnel with ease.

"Focus your intentions!" Maya's serene voice cut through the mayhem. "Visualize protection, and it will manifest!"

Andres watched in awe as Maya's hands moved in intricate patterns, weaving strands of ethereal energy. The air crackled with power as bolts of blue lightning arced from her fingertips, striking down the approaching attackers.

"How is this possible?" Julian exclaimed; his skepticism momentarily forgotten in the face of Maya's display.

Maya's voice remained steady, even as she continued to repel the assault. "The knowledge of Atlantis flows through me. We are connected to powers beyond your current understanding."

Andres felt a surge of energy coursing through his own body. Instinctively, he raised his hands, mimicking Maya's movements. To his amazement, a smaller energy shield flickered into existence before him.

"That's it, Andres!" Maya encouraged. "Trust in your heritage, in the wisdom of your ancestors!"

General Kaine's enraged roar cut through. "Atlantean witch! Your parlor tricks will not save you!"

Maya's eyes narrowed, her calm demeanor never wavering. "Your darkness cannot overcome the light, Kaine. We stand as guardians of a greater truth."

As the battle raged on, Andres marveled at Maya's unwavering composure. Even in the face of overwhelming odds, she radiated an aura of serenity that seemed to bolster the entire team's resolve.

"We need to reach the pyramid!" Andres shouted, a plan forming in his mind. "Maya, can you clear a path?"

Maya nodded, her eyes gleaming with determination. "Prepare yourselves," she instructed. "When I give the signal, run for the entrance. Do not look back, no matter what you hear."

Andres's heart pounded as he watched Maya gather her energy, the air around her shimmering with power. What would happen next? Could they truly escape the Sons of Belial's onslaught?

Amidst the chaos of battle, a familiar voice cut through the din, sending a chill down Andres's spine. "I'll take that if you don't mind." Julian Blackwood emerged from the shadows; his eyes fixed on the Crystal Skull clutched in Evelyn's trembling hands.

Andres's jaw dropped. "Julian? What are you—"

"Doing what needs to be done," Julian interrupted, his voice cold and detached. He lunged forward, wrenching the Skull from Evelyn's grasp.

"No!" Andres shouted, his mind reeling. "Julian, why? We trusted you!"

Julian's lips curled into a bitter smile. "Trust is a luxury we can't afford in this game, old friend. The Skull's power is too great to leave in amateur hands."

Maya's eyes flashed with anger. "You fool! You have no idea what forces you are toying with!"

As Julian backed away, the Crystal Skull pulsed with an other-worldly light. The ground beneath their feet began to tremble, and Andres watched in awe as ancient symbols etched into the Pyramid of Akapana blazed to life.

"What's happening?" Evelyn gasped, her scientific skepticism crumbling in the face of the impossible.

Andres's voice was barely a whisper. "It's awakening."

The earth shook violently, nearly toppling the team. Cracks spider-webbed across the pyramid's surface, golden light spilling from within. Hidden chambers, sealed for millennia, began to reveal themselves.

"This isn't possible," Evelyn muttered, her eyes wide with a mixture of fear and fascination.

Andres's mind raced, overwhelmed by the sensory assault. The air hummed with energy, making his skin tingle. Visions of ancient rituals and long-forgotten knowledge flashed before his eyes, threatening to drown out reality.

"We have to stop him!" Andres shouted, lunging towards Julian. But his former friend was already gone, the Skull tucked securely under his arm.

As Julian disappeared, Andres felt a crushing weight of failure settle on his shoulders. How could he have been so blind? The betrayal stung, but there was no time to dwell on it.

"Andres!" Maya's urgent voice snapped him back to the present. "The pyramid is fully awakening. We need to move, now!"

He nodded, pushing aside his emotions to focus on the immediate danger. "Everyone, stick together! We don't know what other surprises this place might have in store for us."

As they cautiously approached the glowing entrance that had appeared in the pyramid's base, Andres could not shake the feeling that they were crossing a threshold into a world beyond their understanding. The loss of the Crystal Skull weighed heavily on him, but the mysteries unfolding before them offered a glimmer of hope.

With a shared look of determination, the team stepped into the unknown, leaving behind the world they knew and venturing into the heart of an ancient power reborn.

The ground beneath their feet trembled as ancient stone groaned to life. Andres stumbled, his heart pounding as he grabbed Maya's arm.

"We need to move!" he shouted over the cacophony of crumbling rock and panicked cries.

Maya's eyes widened in alarm. "But the Skull—"

"There's no time!" Andres cut her off, pushing her toward a newly revealed passageway. "Go! I will find the others!"

As Maya disappeared into the darkness, Andres spun around, desperately searching for the rest of his team in the chaos. Dust and debris filled the air, obscuring his vision. The glowing symbols on the pyramid's surface pulsed with an otherworldly light, casting eerie shadows across the chamber.

"Evelyn, Jacqueline! Amaru!" he called out, his voice hoarse.

A hand grabbed his shoulder, and he whirled to find Evelyn, her face streaked with dirt and fear.

"This way!" she yelled, gesturing toward another passage. "I saw Jacqueline and Maya head down there!"

They plunged into the narrow corridor, the sounds of pursuit echoing behind them. Andres's mind raced, grappling with the magnitude of their failure. The Crystal Skull, their key to unlocking the secrets of Atlantis and saving humanity, was gone—stolen by Julian, a man he had trusted.

As they rounded a corner, they nearly collided with Jacqueline, who was leaning against the wall, clutching her side.

"Are you hurt?" Andres asked, his brow furrowed with concern.

Hart shook her head, grimacing. "Just winded. Where's Maya?"

"We got separated," Andres replied, the weight of responsibility pressing down on him. "We need to find her and regroup."

A distant explosion rocked the passage, sending a shower of dust raining down on them.

Jacqueline's voice trembled as she spoke. "The Sons of Belial— they're destroying everything as they retreat."

Andres closed his eyes for a moment, fighting back a wave of despair. "They have what they came for. We've failed."

"No," Jacqueline said firmly, pushing herself off the wall. "We haven't failed until we give up. We can still stop them."

Andres nodded, drawing strength from her determination. "You're right. But first, we need to find Maya and get out of here alive."

They pressed on, navigating the twisting passages of the ancient temple. Andres's thoughts churned with each step. *How could he have been so blind to Julian's true nature? The implications of the Skull falling into the wrong hands were catastrophic.*

As they emerged into a larger chamber, Andres froze. The destruction left in the wake of the Sons of Belial was staggering. Ancient artifacts lay shattered, priceless knowledge lost forever.

"My God," Evelyn whispered, her voice thick with emotion. "All this history, gone in an instant."

Andres's fists clenched at his sides. "This is more than just destruction. They're erasing the past to control the future."

A familiar voice called out from across the chamber. "Andres! Over here!"

Relief flooded through him as he spotted Maya crouched behind a fallen pillar. With her was Amaru. As they rushed to join them, the ground shook once more, and a deep rumbling filled the air.

"The whole structure is becoming unstable," Maya warned. "We need to get out now."

Andres nodded grimly. "Let's go. We'll regroup outside and figure out our next move."

As they made their way toward the exit, Andres's mind raced with the enormity of the task ahead. The Crystal Skull was gone, but the fight was far from over. He silently vowed to do whatever it took to recover the Skull and stop the Sons of Belial, no matter the cost.

The ancient chamber groaned around them, a fitting echo of the weight that now rested on their shoulders. Time was running out, not just for them, but for all of humanity.

The team stumbled out of the crumbling chamber, coughing, and gasping in the dust-filled air. Andres's eyes darted from face to face, relief washing over him as he confirmed everyone had made it out alive. They collapsed onto the ground near their ransacked camp, the weight of their failure settling heavily upon them.

Maya's voice broke the tense silence. "The Crystal Skull... its loss is more catastrophic than you realize." Her green eyes glimmered with unshed tears. "It's not just an artifact. It's a key to cosmic balance."

Jacqueline scoffed, her skepticism winning out over her usual composure. "Cosmic balance? We have just lost priceless historical evidence, and you are talking about—"

"She's right," Andres interrupted, his voice hoarse. "I've seen visions, felt the power. This goes beyond archaeology, Evelyn."

Jacqueline shifted uncomfortably. "Julian's betrayal... I should have seen it coming. The signs were there."

Andres's jaw clenched at the mention of Julian's name. "We all trusted him. That's on me."

"No," Maya said softly, placing a hand on Andres's arm. "The blame lies with the Sons of Belial. Their hunger for power threatens everything."

A slow clap echoed through the chamber, startling everyone. "Brilliant deduction, Dr. Paredes. But you're still only scratching the surface."

They whirled around, and there she was—Dr. Elera Voss. Her silver hair shimmered like moonlight in the dim glow of the chamber, and her presence was as commanding as ever. Dressed impeccably despite the rugged environment, she appeared out of place, yet entirely in control.

Andres instinctively stepped in front of Maya, his eyes narrowing. "Dr. Voss. What are you doing here?"

Voss's lips curved into a faint smile, her eyes betraying a mix of amusement and urgency. "Saving you from making a fatal mistake, for starters," she said, striding forward with the confidence of someone who had been listening for a while. "You think you're the only ones who know the stakes? I've been tracking the Brotherhood for months, and their plans are more dangerous than even you imagine."

Maya's voice cut in, sharp and skeptical. "And why should we believe you? Last we heard, you were working with them."

Voss turned her piercing gray eyes on Maya, her smile vanishing. "Because sometimes the only way to dismantle a system is from the inside. I walked into the lion's den to uncover the truth. And the truth, my dear, is far worse than any of you realize."

Andres crossed his arms, his caution unyielding. "Then explain. Convince us you're not here to sabotage this effort."

Voss sighed, her facade cracking just enough to reveal a hint of vulnerability. "The Brotherhood isn't just seeking control over humanity—they're after control over existence itself. Through their hybrid program, they are creating a species that will serve as living conduits for reality manipulation. If they succeed, they will not just rewrite history. They'll erase the very foundation of free will."

Her words hung in the air like a storm cloud. Evelyn took a step closer, her voice trembling. "Why now? Why reveal this to us here?"

Voss's gaze softened ever so slightly as she looked at Evelyn, then Andres. "Because you're closer than anyone else has ever been to stopping them. But you are also dangerously close to triggering exactly what they want. If the energy grid falls into the wrong hands..." She hesitated, her voice dropping, "there won't be a second chance."

Andres felt the weight of her words and the subtle desperation beneath them. He studied her, searching for cracks in her story, but found only conviction. "Then help us," he said at last. "Prove you're on the right side of this."

Voss straightened, her steel-like composure returning. "That's why I'm here." She reached into her satchel, pulling out a small device pulsing faintly with light. "Starting with this. A safeguard—and maybe the only thing that can keep this grid out of their control."

Andres puzzled looks at her" Hybrid program? What are you talking about Elera?"

"The hybrid program. It is connected," Voss nodded. "The hybrids are meant to be their foot soldiers in a new world order. But," she added, a hint of satisfaction in her voice, "the program has weaknesses."

Andres's mind raced, hope stirring despite the circumstances. "What are you talking about? What kind of weaknesses?"

Voss spoke up, her voice low and urgent. "Their genetic modifications... they're unstable. I have seen it firsthand. With the right approach, we might be able to disrupt their plans."

Maya's eyes widened. "A chance to tip the cosmic scales back in our favor."

Andres felt a surge of determination. They had been knocked down, but they weren't out of the fight yet. He looked at each member of his team, seeing the same resolve mirrored in their faces.

"Alright," he said, his voice growing stronger. "We've got a Crystal Skull to recover and a world to save. Let's get to work."

Andres rubbed his chin thoughtfully while scanning the faces of his team. The weight of their next decision pressed heavily upon him as the looming celestial alignment ticked closer. He could feel the energy of the Akapana Pyramid pulsing beneath their feet, a constant reminder of the power they sought to control.

"We're running out of time," Maya interjected, her fingers tapping urgently against her thigh. "The alignment of Venus, Mars, and Jupiter with the Earth's ley lines is less than 48 hours away. If we do not recover the Crystal Skull before then—"

"I know," Andres cut her off, his voice gruff with tension. "But we can't rush in blindly. The Sons of Belial have the advantage now."

Evelyn stepped forward, her analytical mind already racing. "What if we split our efforts? One team to track the Skull, another to prepare the site for the alignment."

Andres hesitated, considering the proposal. The idea had merit but also risks. He closed his eyes, allowing the ancient Mapuche wisdom flowing through his veins to guide him. Visions of his ancestors performing sacred rituals flashed behind his eyelids, reminding him of the delicate balance between the physical and spiritual realms.

"No," he said finally, opening his eyes. "We stay together. Our strength lies in our unity."

Maya's eyes flashed with frustration. "But Andres, if we don't—"

He held up a hand, silencing her protest. "I understand your urgency, Maya. But remember what the Vesica Piscis represents—the union of opposing forces. We need to embody that principle now more than ever."

Evelyn nodded in agreement. "Andres is right. The Brotherhood is counting on us to fragment. We can't give them that advantage."

Andres felt a surge of gratitude for Voss's support. He turned to address the entire team, his voice filled with determination. "Here's what we're going to do. We will use Dr. Voss's intel to track the Skull's energy signature and assist us with dealing with the hybrids. Once we pinpoint its location, we move as one. Our goal is to recover the Skull and return here in time to activate the interdimensional portal."

He paused, making eye contact with each member of his team. "I know we're all shaken by Julian's betrayal and the loss of Sophia. But we cannot let that divide us. The fate of not just our world, but count-less realities hangs in the balance. We are the guardians of this sacred knowledge, the bridge between Atlantean technology and Tiwanaku spirituality. It's time we embrace that responsibility fully."

Maya's expression softened, her earlier frustration giving way to resolve. "You're right, Andres. We're stronger together."

Andres nodded, feeling the team's energy coalescing around their shared purpose. "Then let's gear up. We have a Crystal Skull to re-claim and a cosmic balance to restore. And dealing with these… hy-brids… The road ahead will not be easy, but I believe in each of you. Together, we'll face whatever challenges come our way."

As the team dispersed to prepare, Andres felt a mixture of antic-ipation and trepidation coursing through him. The weight of leader-ship had never felt heavier, but he knew in his heart that they were on the right path. Whatever revelations awaited them, whatever obstacles the Brotherhood would throw in their way, they would face them united.

The race against time had begun.

Chapter 15

The Vesica Piscis symbol pulsed with an otherworldly glow, casting eerie shadows across the ancient stones of Tiwanaku. Dr. Andres Paredes stood at its center, his dark eyes scanning the faces of his team gathered in a tight circle. The air crackled with tension.

"Everyone knows their role?" Andres's voice was low but intense. "We can't afford any mistakes."

Nods and murmurs of assent rippled through the group. Andres ran a hand through his wavy hair, betraying a flicker of nervous energy. *This is it*, he thought. *Everything we have worked for comes down to this moment.*

"The alignment will begin in precisely seven minutes," announced Dr. Voss, checking her watch. "We should take our positions."

As the team dispersed, Andres's gaze was drawn to Evelyn. She knelt beside a weathered stone column, her slender fingers tracing the intricate carvings that spiraled across its surface. Her brow furrowed in concentration as she mouthed silent words.

"Evelyn," Andres called softly, approaching her. "What have you found?"

She glanced up, dark eyes shining with a mixture of excitement and disbelief. "These symbols, Andres. They are describing... cosmic forces beyond our comprehension."

Andres crouched beside her, studying the ancient glyphs. "Can you translate them?"

Evelyn's fingers danced across the stone as she spoke. "This section seems to be about celestial alignments, but on a scale far grander than just our solar system. And here," she pointed to a series of concentric circles, "I believe it's describing different planes of existence."

"Planes of existence?" Andres echoed, his pulse quickening. "Like the interdimensional realms we've theorized?"

Evelyn nodded slowly, a hint of her usual skepticism creeping into her voice. "I know it sounds fantastical, but the evidence is right here, carved in stone. These people had knowledge that shouldn't have been possible for their time."

Andres placed a hand on her shoulder, feeling the familiar spark of connection between them. "Your scientific mind is having trouble reconciling this, isn't it?"

Evelyn sighed, pushing a stray lock of hair behind her ear. "I've dedicated my life to rational inquiry, Andres. But this... challenges everything I thought I knew."

"Sometimes we have to be open to possibilities beyond our current understanding," Andres said gently. "That's why we're here, after all."

A shout from across the site interrupted their moment. "Two minutes to alignment!"

Andres stood, offering Evelyn his hand. "Ready to make history?"

She took it, rising gracefully. "Ready or not, it seems history has plans for us."

As they walked back to the glowing Vesica Piscis, Andres felt the weight of destiny settling upon his shoulders. Whatever happens next, he thought, there is no turning back now.

Maya walked beside him, her presence both grounding and enigmatic. She glanced at Andres, her eyes reflecting a mixture of determination and quiet strength. "You've got this, Andres," she said softly. "It's not just about the words—it's about what you carry inside."

Andres nodded, drawing strength from her unwavering belief. He stepped forward, his tall frame silhouetted against the fading twilight. The air crackled with anticipation as he raised his arms, palms upturned to the darkening sky. His voice, low and resonant, began to intone words in a language long forgotten by most of humanity.

"Atlan-ti-aku... Neb-ka-ra... Shen-ta-u..."

The ancient Atlantean syllables rolled off his tongue, each one seeming to pulse with its own energy. As Andres chanted, Amaru's weathered hands began a steady rhythm on his ceremonial drum, the deep, primal beats echoing through the ruins of Tiwanaku.

Thoom. Thoom. Thoom.

The team stood transfixed, caught between awe and trepidation. Evelyn's analytical mind raced as she observed the phenomenon, her gaze darting between Andres and the Vesica Piscis symbol.

"This shouldn't be possible," she muttered to herself. Yet even she could not deny the vibration beneath her feet and the charged air enveloping them all.

Maya's gaze remained fixed on the Vesica Piscis, her expression focused and calm. She stepped closer to Andres, her voice low but steady. "You're aligning the frequencies," she said. "Keep going. We are almost there."

The Vesica Piscis etched into the ground began to emit a soft, pulsating glow. It started as a faint shimmer, barely perceptible in the gathering dusk. But with each beat of Amaru's drum, each phrase of Andres's chant, the light grew stronger.

"My God," breathed Dr. Voss, her usual stoicism faltering for a moment. "It's actually happening."

Evelyn stood near the edge of the circle, her sharp eyes scanning the energy field. "This isn't just a portal," she muttered. "It is a gateway. If the alignment holds, it will stabilize." She turned to Maya, her voice clipped. "We'll need your intuition on what comes next."

Maya nodded, her focus unshaken. "I'll be ready."

The symbol's glow intensified, casting eerie, shifting patterns across the ancient stonework. Shadows danced and wavered as if reality itself was becoming fluid. The light pulsed in perfect time with the celestial alignment overhead, unseen but profoundly felt by all present.

Andres's chanting grew more intense, his voice rising and falling in perfect synchronicity with Amaru's drumming. The air thickened, charged with an otherworldly energy that made the hairs on everyone's necks stand on end.

As the glow reached a blinding intensity, a sudden surge of energy coursed through Andres. He closed his eyes, continuing the chant from memory, every fiber of his being attuned to the cosmic forces swirling around them. Maya stepped closer, her presence steadying him as the energy swirled around them in powerful currents.

The portal began to form a shimmering, liquid-like doorway within the Vesica Piscis. Andres opened his eyes, his heart pounding with a mixture of exhilaration and fear. "This is it," he said, his voice trembling with awe. "We've opened the way."

Maya placed a hand on his arm, her voice calm but firm. "Whatever is on the other side, we face it together."

The air crackled with potential, the boundary between worlds growing thinner with each passing second. Andres opened his eyes, meeting the awestruck gazes of his team. *No matter what comes next,* he silently vowed, *we face it together.*

A blinding flash erupted from the Vesica Piscis, forcing the team to shield their eyes as the surrounding ruins seemed to vibrate with an unearthly resonance. As the intense light faded, the portal's shimmering aperture revealed an iridescent figure coalescing within its swirling energy.

Orion stepped forward, his tall, slender form emerging with a grace that defied the physical laws of the world around them. His faintly silver, almost translucent skin refracted light, casting a soft spectrum of colors onto the ancient stones. It was as if he carried fragments of the cosmos within him, his very presence bending reality in subtle, awe-inspiring ways.

The energy around Orion was palpable, a tangible vibration that brushed against the team's consciousness like a warm, reassuring current. His aura pulsed with a gentle yet unyielding power, exuding calm and wisdom that seemed to permeate the air. It was a serenity that demanded attention, grounding and elevating the team in the same breath. His large, deep eyes, filled with shifting galaxies and infinite stars, swept across them with a gaze that was both intimate and eternal.

He wore flowing robes of radiant light that shimmered as he moved, each fold of the fabric resonating with a frequency that seemed to harmonize with the ruins. The subtle energy shifted in response to him as if recognizing a long-lost guardian. The glyphs on the surrounding walls began to glow faintly, their intricate patterns pulsing in rhythm with his aura.

Orion's voice, when he finally spoke, was a blend of tones—calm yet resonant, carrying a cadence that bypassed language to reach directly into the hearts and minds of those who listened.

"You stand at the precipice of choice," he began, his words filling the surrounding space as if the stones themselves were speaking. "The alignment you seek is not merely of celestial bodies but of your own essence with the greater tapestry of existence."

Andres felt a chill as the Crystal Skull at his side flared briefly, reacting to Orion's energy. He glanced at the others, noting their awestruck expressions. Evelyn's hand hovered over her notebook, but she seemed unable to write, her sharp intellect subdued by the magnitude of what stood before her. Jacqueline, who often carried an air of skepticism, had lowered her gaze, as though in reverence or perhaps overwhelmed by a reflection of her own inner struggles.

Orion moved closer to Andres, his iridescent presence becoming even more vivid. "You carry the spark of ancient connections, Andres," he said, his voice softening yet losing none of its weight. "Within you lies the memory of what was and the potential for what can be. The choices you make here will ripple through the fabric of this world and beyond."

As Orion shifted his attention to the rest of the team, his tone became warmer and more inclusive. "Each of you has a part to play in this unfolding story. Trust in your strengths, your vulnerabilities, and in one another. The wounds of the past can only be healed through unity."

The ruins around them seemed to echo his words, the glowing glyphs intensifying briefly before fading into a steady luminescence. The Vesica Piscis behind him pulsed softly, like the rhythm of a heartbeat, as if tethering Orion's multidimensional presence to their world for just a moment longer. Andres felt a swell of determination mixed with humility. Standing before this embodiment of wisdom and cosmic balance, he realized the enormity of their task. But within that enormity, he also felt a flicker of hope—a belief that with Orion's guidance and their combined resolve, they might yet succeed in redeeming the mistakes of the past and forging a new path for humanity.

Evelyn gasped, her scientific skepticism crumbling. "Impossible," she whispered, eyes wide with a mixture of wonder and fear.

Amaru's drumming faltered, his weathered hands trembling. "The star beings... they're real," he murmured in awe.

Andres felt a surge of recognition as if reuniting with a long-lost mentor. Yet beneath the familiarity, an undercurrent of unease pulsed through him. Orion's form shifted subtly, blending Arcturian crystalline structures with flowing Pleiadian energy patterns.

"Welcome, Orion," Andres said, his voice steady despite the tumult of emotions within. "We've awaited your guidance."

Orion's gaze swept over the team, his eyes pools of cosmic depth. When he spoke, his voice resonated not through the air, but directly within their minds, using Andres as a conduit.

"Children of Earth," Orion's thoughts reverberated, "you stand at a crossroads of destiny."

Andres felt the weight of eons in those words. He closed his eyes, allowing Orion's message to flow through him.

"The path you walk is precarious," Orion continued. "As it was in the days of Atlantis, you must find balance between the material and the spiritual, between technological might and cosmic wisdom."

Images flashed through Andres's mind: gleaming crystal spires crumbling, advanced machines turned to weapons, a civilization tearing itself apart. He shuddered, understanding the gravity of Orion's warning.

"But how?" Andres asked silently, overwhelmed by the responsibility. "How do we avoid their fate?"

Orion's presence enveloped him, comforting yet urgent. "By remembering that technology is a tool, not a master. By nurturing the spark of divinity within each soul. The power you seek lies not in domination, but in harmony."

Andres opened his eyes, meeting the anxious gazes of his team. He knew they could not hear Orion's words directly, but they sensed the profound shift occurring.

"We have a chance," Andres said aloud, his voice thick with emotion, "to write a new chapter for humanity. But the choice—and the challenge—lies before us."

Andres's heart raced as Orion's final words echoed in his mind. He clenched his fists, determination surging through him like an electric current. The weight of their mission pressed down on his shoulders, but he stood tall, ready to bear it.

"We accept this responsibility," Andres declared, his voice resonating across the ancient stones of Tiwanaku. He turned to his team, seeing a mix of awe and trepidation on their faces. "Each of us has a crucial role to play in bridging the spiritual and technological realms."

Evelyn stepped forward, her scientific skepticism warring with the undeniable energy pulsing through the site. "But how do we even begin to—"

Her words were cut short as the ground beneath their feet began to tremble. Andres's eyes widened as he watched lines of brilliant blue light erupting from the Vesica Piscis symbol, snaking outward in intricate patterns across the stone floor.

"It's starting!" Amaru shouted, his drums forgotten as he pointed to the heavens.

The night sky had transformed into a living tapestry, the stars shifting as if they were conscious, ancient beings weaving their luminous threads into a celestial symphony. Constellations that had stood unchanged for millennia began to morph, their familiar outlines dissolving into intricate, interconnected patterns. It was as though the universe itself was responding to an unseen force, rearranging its design to align with the cosmic moment unfolding below.

A deep hum resonated from the earth beneath them, a sound that was both physical and metaphysical, vibrating through the stones of the ancient ruins and into their very bones. The air grew electric, crackling with a palpable energy that seemed to blur the line between the material and the ethereal. Overhead, the moon bathed the Akapana Pyramid in silver light, while the planets, now in perfect alignment, shone with a brilliance that outshone their usual hues, casting a surreal glow across the landscape.

The Vesica Piscis carved into the ancient stones of the ritual site, began to glow faintly at first, then grew brighter, pulsating in harmony with the cosmic rhythm. Streams of light, golden and iridescent, poured down from the heavens, converging into the sacred symbol. It became a bridge between dimensions, its edges shimmering with a brilliance that seemed to hold the essence of creation itself.

Amaru, his voice trembling with awe, whispered, "Do you feel it? The heartbeat of the cosmos... it's here."

Around them, the team stood frozen, each person caught in their own moment of wonder and fear. Evelyn clutched her notebook tightly, her mind racing to process what her heart already knew: they were witnessing something beyond science, beyond reason—a convergence of forces older than time. Jacqueline's usual skepticism melted away, replaced by a childlike reverence as she gazed at the sky, her hands unconsciously clutching the folds of her coat.

Then, as if drawn by an invisible thread, Andres stepped closer to the Vesica Piscis. Its light bathed his face, casting sharp shadows that flickered like ancient flames. His pulse quickened, not from fear but from a deep, unshakable knowing. This was the moment they had worked for, the culmination of their shared journey. He could feel the connection deep within him—a tether to something vast and eternal.

The alignment reached its zenith, the planets forming a perfect line across the heavens. At that instant, a radiant beam of light shot downward, connecting the celestial bodies to the Vesica Piscis. The portal erupted with energy, a swirling vortex of light and color that defied description. Within its depths, glimpses of other realms flickered—pristine landscapes, vast cities of light, and beings of unearthly beauty moving with purpose and grace.

Amaru fell to his knees, tears streaming down his face. "The ancestors... they're here." His voice broke, but it carried the weight of generations, an echo of those who had stood on this same ground in reverence of the stars. The hum grew louder, a crescendo of cosmic power that seemed to dissolve the barriers of time and space. It was no longer just a celestial alignment; it was a revelation, a moment when the universe opened its gates, inviting them to step through and become part of its infinite dance.

Andres felt a surge of power coursing through his body, connecting him to the very essence of the Earth. In his mind's eye, he saw the global network of sacred sites lighting up one by one: Stonehenge pulsing with ethereal energy, the Great Pyramid of Giza shooting a beam of light into the cosmos, and Machu Picchu resonating with the frequency of the sun. Further, the ancient temple of Angkor Wat glimmered like a lotus of golden fire, its energy weaving through the threads of the global web. Mount Kailash stood as a luminous pillar, radiating waves of calm and cosmic order, while Chichen Itza's Kukulkan Pyramid vibrated with the heartbeat of the Earth.

In South Africa, the Ruins of Adam's Calendar shimmered with a primeval hum, harmonizing with the sacred energy of Uluru in Australia, whose fiery glow pulsed in rhythm with the stars above. The Chalice Well in Glastonbury overflowed with radiant, life-giving waters, joining the song of Sedona's red rock vortexes in the American Southwest. Tiwanaku, the place where Andres stood, resonated as the central node, its power anchoring the celestial alignment. Each sacred site became a luminous point in the Vesica Piscis-shaped grid, their collective resonance creating a harmonious vibration that echoed through time and space.

The network became alive, pulsating with unity and balance as if Earth herself were awakening, urging humanity to rise to its next evolutionary step. Andres could feel the ancient wisdom of the sites merging with his consciousness, revealing their shared purpose: to guide humanity toward harmony, oneness, and a future beyond imagination.

"Can you feel it?" Andres asked, his voice filled with wonder. "The grid is awakening!"

Evelyn nodded, her scientific mind struggling to process what her senses were telling her. "It's as if the entire planet is coming alive," she whispered.

As the energy surged through the network, Andres thought of Orion's warning. *We must use this power wisely*, he reminded himself. *For the good of all humanity, not just a chosen few.*

The ground continued to shake, stones shifting as if the very foundations of Tiwanaku were rearranging themselves. Andres spread his arms wide, embracing the cosmic energy flowing through him, knowing that this was only the beginning of their journey to reshape humanity's destiny.

As the tremors subsided, a deep rumbling echoed through the ancient site. The team watched in awe as a section of the Kalasasaya Temple's wall began to recede, revealing a hidden passageway.

"Incredible," Dr. Carter breathed, her eyes wide with excitement. "The activation must have triggered some kind of ancient mechanism."

Andres stepped forward, his heart pounding. "Let's investigate," he said, his voice steady despite the thrill coursing through him. "But proceed with caution. We don't know what we might encounter."

The team entered the dark corridor, their flashlights illuminating intricate glyphs that seemed to shimmer with an otherworldly light. As they progressed deeper, the passage opened into a vast chamber.

"My God," Amaru whispered, his voice echoing in the cavernous space. "It's like stepping into the heart of the cosmos itself."

The walls were covered in swirling patterns of stars and galaxies, with unfamiliar symbols interwoven throughout. At the center stood a towering crystalline structure, pulsing with a soft blue light.

Dr. Carter approached it, her scientific curiosity overriding her caution. "These markings... It is as if they're describing... interdimensional travel?"

Andres felt a pull towards the crystal, an inexplicable connection. As he touched its surface, visions flooded his mind—glimpses of ancient civilizations, cosmic journeys, and the delicate balance of the universe.

"This isn't just a sacred site," Andres said, his voice filled with reverence and a hint of fear. "It's a nexus point, a cosmic library holding the knowledge of countless civilizations."

Amaru nodded solemnly. "Our ancestors left this for us to find. But why now? What are we meant to do with this knowledge?"

As the team grappled with the magnitude of their discovery, the scene shifted dramatically to a hidden bunker deep within a mountain range.

General Kaine stood before a bank of monitors, his scarred face illuminated by the eerie glow of data streams and energy readings. His red eyes narrowed as he observed the sudden spike in global energy patterns.

"Sir," a technician called out, "we're detecting a massive surge centered around Tiwanaku. It's like nothing we've ever seen before!"

Kaine's lips curled into a cruel smile. "So, the fools have activated the grid. Excellent. Our plans can now enter the next phase."

He turned to address the gathered members of the Sons of Belial, his voice cold and commanding. "Gentlemen, the time has come. Initiate Operation Darkfall. We will harness this power and bend it to our will."

As his subordinates scrambled to obey, Kaine's thoughts turned to Andres and his team. "Your spiritual awakening will be short-lived," he muttered. "The future belongs to those who seize control, not to dreamers and idealists."

With a gesture, Kaine brought up a holographic display of the Earth, points of light representing the activated sacred sites. His eyes gleamed with malevolent anticipation as he contemplated the coming conflict that would determine the fate of humanity.

The ethereal form of Orion shimmered, his iridescent skin refracting the pulsing light of the activated Vesica Piscis. His large, starry eyes swept over the team, settling on Andres with an intensity that seemed to pierce through time and space.

"The path ahead is treacherous," Orion's voice resonated, each word carrying the weight of cosmic wisdom. "You have awakened ancient energies, but darker forces stir in response."

Andres felt a chill run down his spine. "What kind of forces?" he asked, his voice barely above a whisper.

Orion's form rippled as if disturbed by an unseen wind. "Those who seek to control rather than connect. They will attempt to harness the grid for their own purposes."

Evelyn stepped forward, her scientific skepticism warring with the undeniable evidence before her. "How can we protect the grid?"

"Balance is key," Orion replied, his tone both soothing and urgent. "Technology and spirituality must dance in harmony, as they once did in Atlantis. But beware the seduction of power."

Andres's mind raced, trying to process the implications. He thought of the Sons of Belial, wondering if they were the threat Orion spoke of. "What should we do next?" he asked, feeling the weight of responsibility settling on his shoulders.

"Trust in the wisdom of your heart," Orion said, his form beginning to fade. "The answers lie within the sacred nodes. Seek them out but remain vigilant. The shadows are moving."

As Orion's presence dissipated, Andres turned to his team. Their faces reflected a mix of awe, determination, and trepidation. The air hummed with residual energy from the ritual, a tangible reminder of the power they had unleashed.

"We did it," Amaru breathed, his drums still echoing faintly in the chamber. "We actually activated the grid."

Andres nodded, a small smile playing on his lips despite the gravity of the situation. "Yes, but it seems our work is just beginning."

Evelyn was already scribbling notes, her scientific mind struggling to reconcile what she had witnessed with her understanding of reality. "The implications of this are... staggering," she murmured.

Andres looked around at his team, feeling a surge of pride mixed with apprehension. They had taken a monumental step towards awakening humanity's potential, but at what cost? The looming threat Orion had hinted at cast a shadow over their triumph.

"We need to move quickly," Andres announced, his voice firm with resolve. "Orion's warning was clear. We're not the only ones aware of what's happened here."

As the team began to gather their equipment, Andres's gaze lingered on the now-dormant Vesica Piscis symbol. He could not shake the feeling that they had set in motion events that would change the course of human history. For better or worse, the Great Convergence had begun.

"Andres," a cold, precise voice broke through the momentary silence. "It seems your experiments have unexpected consequences."

Dr. Elera Voss appeared, her silver hair gleaming in the strange light. She was already part of the team, her expertise in ancient symbology indispensable. But this time, she was not alone.

Trailing behind her was a younger woman, her eyes sharp and calculating, her cap pulled low over her face. Dr. Paredes straightened, his brows furrowing.

"Elera, who's this?" he asked, his voice steady but tinged with suspicion.

"This," Voss said, her tone crisp, "is Talia Elara. She appeared during the activation of the Vesica Piscis. A fortuitous anomaly, wouldn't you agree?"

Talia stepped forward, her gaze darting across the chamber, taking in the team and the ancient mechanisms with the precision of someone who had seen their share of secrets.

"Tech specialist," she introduced herself curtly, her voice cool.

Evelyn crossed her arms, her eyes narrowing slightly. "And we're supposed to believe her sudden appearance isn't a coincidence?"

"Believe what you want," Talia replied, her tone unbothered. "I know what I saw, and I know what I can do. It's not every day I stumble into something this... significant."

Andres exchanged a glance with Voss, whose lips curved into a slight, knowing smile.

"I've worked with Talia before," Voss said. "Her expertise could be invaluable to us. If we're serious about staying ahead of the Brotherhood, we can't afford to turn away a resource like her."

Andres hesitated for a moment, his gaze locking onto Talia's. He had seen many people claim they wanted to change sides before, but trust was a rare currency in their line of work—one often spent too freely and regretted too late. Yet, they needed every advantage they could get.

The room fell into a heavy silence, the weight of her words settling over the team like a thick fog. The soft hum of the Vesica Piscis filled the space, its ancient frequencies thrumming against the stone walls—a reminder that time, and their enemies, would not wait.

Andres's mind raced. Having Elera here was already a risk—her knowledge of Atlantean technology made her invaluable, but also a prime target. And now Talia, a former Brotherhood operative with the kind of skills that could dismantle or destroy everything they were fighting for. Her expertise could be a double-edged sword—either the key to outmaneuvering the Sons of Belial or the weakness that would doom them all.

Amaru took a step forward, his normally calm presence radiating tension. "Why should we trust you?" he demanded. His voice was edged with something rare—anger, or maybe something deeper. "You were one of them."

Talia met his gaze without flinching, her dark eyes unwavering. "Because I've seen what the Brotherhood is capable of. And I want no part of it anymore."

A sharp silence followed. Amaru's jaw tightened, his arms folding across his chest. He wasn't convinced, and neither was Andres—not yet.

Maya finally spoke, her voice measured but firm. "Seeing what they do and fighting against it are two different things. If you're here, we need to know you won't hesitate when the time comes."

Talia's lips pressed together, and for a fleeting moment, something flickered in her expression—guilt, regret, maybe even pain. When she finally spoke, her voice was lower, edged with something raw.

"I hesitated once before," she admitted. "I watched them take people—men, women, children. I watched them turn them into… something else. And I told myself it wasn't my problem. That I was just doing my job." She swallowed hard. "I won't make that mistake again."

Andres studied her, weighing the risks against the potential benefits. If she was telling the truth, then she could be one of their greatest assets. But if she wasn't…

He exhaled. "Very well. Welcome aboard." His eyes hardened. "But understand this—no hidden agendas. No secrets. We work as a team."

Talia gave a slow nod, but something in her eyes told him that trust, on either side, would not come easily.

Andres turned to the rest of the team. "We don't have time for debates. The Brotherhood is already moving, and if we hesitate, they'll have us cornered before we even get started." He glanced at Talia. "You say you know how they think—then prove it. Show us how to stop them."

Talia squared her shoulders, her expression sharpening into something resolute. "Then let's get to work."

The Vesica Piscis pulsed behind them, casting long shadows across the chamber. Whatever lay ahead, their fates were now intertwined—for better or for worse.

Dr. Voss's eyes glittered dangerously. "Of course, Andres. Just like old times."

As the expanded team began to discuss their next moves, Andres leaned against a cool stone wall, the weight of the day's events pressing down on him.

Exhilaration coursed through his veins at what they had accomplished, but with it came a crushing sense of responsibility. The Great Convergence had begun, and he stood at its center, a reluctant fulcrum upon which the fate of humanity might well balance.

"You, okay?" Evelyn's voice startled him from his reverie.

Andres managed a wan smile. "Just... processing. We have opened a door, Evelyn. But what comes through it..."

She placed a comforting hand on his arm. "Whatever it is, we'll face it together."

Andres nodded, drawing strength from her presence. As he turned back to the group, his resolve hardened. The path ahead was fraught with danger and uncertainty, but they had taken the first crucial steps. Now, they just had to ensure humanity was ready for what came next.

Chapter 16

The ancient walls of Tiwanaku loomed before them; weathered stone etched with cryptic symbols that seemed to pulse with hidden meaning. Maya's fingers traced the intricate glyphs, her emerald eyes narrowed in concentration. Beside her, Andres leaned in close, his breath warm on her neck as he studied the same section of wall.

"This sequence here," Maya murmured, gesturing to a series of interlocking spirals, "is reminiscent of the creation myths we uncovered in the Kalasasaya Temple."

Andres nodded, his hand brushing against hers as he pointed to another symbol. "And look at how it connects to this glyph representing Viracocha, the creator god emerging from the cosmic waters."

A spark of electricity passed between them at the brief contact. Maya felt her heart quicken, hyper-aware of Andres's proximity. She forced herself to focus on the task at hand, pushing aside the growing tension, yet she felt a glimmer of excitement.

"The challenge is decoding how these symbols relate to the larger cosmology," Andres continued, running a hand through his disheveled hair. "Each one could have multiple layers of meaning."

Maya smiled, a glint of amusement in her eyes. "Like peeling an onion, but with the added fun of possibly unleashing ancient curses."

Andres chuckled, the sound echoing off the stone walls. "Well, when you put it that way, how could we resist?"

Their laughter mingled in the still air, a moment of levity amidst the weight of their mission. Maya savored the sound, allowing herself to bask in the warmth of their growing connection.

As their mirth subsided, Andres's expression grew serious once more. "We're close to a breakthrough, I can feel it. These walls hold the key to understanding the true purpose of Tiwanaku."

Maya nodded, her resolve strengthening. "And with it, the power to protect the sacred knowledge from those who would misuse it."

Their eyes met, a silent understanding passing between them. In that moment, Maya felt the full weight of their shared destiny, intertwined across lifetimes. She took a deep breath, centering herself in the present.

"Let's start with this section," she said, indicating a particularly dense cluster of symbols. "I believe it relates to the concept of cyclical time and reincarnation."

As they bent their heads together over the ancient puzzle, Maya could not help but wonder what other mysteries awaited them in the depths of Tiwanaku's stone corridors.

"Do you feel that?" Maya whispered, her voice barely audible.

The air shifted the moment they stepped inside the chamber, thickening as if charged with an unseen force. Moments earlier, Maya and Andres had stood outside, tracing their fingers over the weathered stones, deciphering the cryptic glyphs that pulsed with hidden meaning. Now, within the chamber's enclosed space, the atmosphere felt heavier, almost alive. Maya's breath caught in her throat as her fingers stilled over a carved spiral, the lingering warmth of the sun replaced by an eerie coolness. Beside her, Andres stiffened, his eyes widening as an inexplicable energy pulsed through the chamber's air. The symbols surrounding them seemed to hum with anticipation as if recognizing their presence.

Andres nodded, his gaze locking with hers. "The stones are awakening again!"

A low hum filled the air, vibrating through their bodies. Maya's third eye tingled, a sure sign of impending cosmic significance. She reached out, instinctively grasping Andres's hand.

"Something's coming," she breathed, her heart racing.

Before Andres could respond, the world around them dissolved in a blinding flash of white light. Maya felt herself falling, pulled through the fabric of space and time. When her vision cleared, she gasped in awe.

They stood atop a gleaming crystal spire, overlooking a vast metropolis that defied imagination. Towering structures of perfect geometry stretched endlessly, their faceted surfaces refracting sunlight into dazzling rainbows. Beneath their feet, energy grids pulsed in intricate patterns, alive with purpose.

"Atlantis," Andres murmured, his voice laced with wonder. "We're seeing it as it truly was!"

Maya's breath hitched. The crystalline technology, the mastery of energy—it was all real. "Everything we theorized..."

"And so much more," Andres finished, squeezing her hand.

Beings of light moved through the city, their forms shimmering with an ethereal radiance. A deep, forgotten knowing stirred within Maya. This was home.

"This is what we're fighting to protect," she whispered. "This legacy, this potential for humanity."

Andres nodded solemnly. "And now we understand what's truly at stake."

Suddenly, the shimmering streets of Atlantis erupted into chaos. Cries of alarm echoed as crowds surged through the crystalline avenues, their faces etched with fear. In an instant, their clothing shifted—now adorned in the elaborate robes of Atlantean nobility.

"Andrius!" Maya cried, her green eyes wide with panic. "The Sons of Belial—they're moving against the Temple!"

Andres's jaw tightened. He reached for her instinctively, his grip firm. "We can't let them seize control of the energy grid. The consequences would be catastrophic."

Pushing through the crowd, they ran toward the grand Temple of the Law of One. The air crackled with tension, the sky darkening as ominous storm clouds gathered.

"We were meant to be guardians of wisdom," Maya's voice trembled. "Not part of this destruction!"

Andres's gaze swept the horizon. "Power corrupts, my love. The Sons of Belial have forgotten the purpose of our gifts."

A deafening explosion shattered the air. The crystal spires trembled as shards rained down around them. Without thinking, Andres pulled Maya into his arms, shielding her.

"We have to reach the Crystal Skull," he said urgently. "If they take it—"

Maya gripped his hands, her expression fierce. "Our love must be our strength, Andrius. No matter what comes."

Their eyes locked, a silent vow passing between them. Together, they rushed toward the temple steps, ready to face whatever sacrifice lay ahead.

Then—darkness.

The ancient stones of Tiwanaku hummed beneath them as they slowly regained awareness. The vision of Atlantis's fall faded, but its weight remained in their souls.

Maya turned to Andres, searching his eyes. "It was real," she whispered.

Andres cupped her face gently, his thumb tracing the curve of her cheek. "We found each other again," he murmured. "Not just to continue our work but to share our love once more."

A deep, undeniable truth settled between them. They had been together before, torn apart by fate. Now, in this lifetime, they had another chance.

Maya's lips parted, her heart pounding as Andres leaned closer. And in the sacred silence of the ancient ruins, they embraced—sharing a kiss that transcended time itself.

"What's happening?" Maya whispered, clutching Andres's arm.

Andres's pulse quickened as he scanned the chamber. "I do not know. It is like the place is... waking up."

A soft, luminous glow seeped through the cracks in the stone. Ethereal figures began to materialize, their translucent forms shimmering like starlight. They were tall and graceful, their features elongated, their presence radiating wisdom rather than malice.

Andres gasped, taking a step closer rather than recoiling. "Maya... the spirits!"

One of the figures raised a hand, not in threat, but in greeting. Their gazes carried an ancient knowing as if they had been waiting. The air vibrated with energy, and a deep, resonant hum filled the chamber—a language beyond words.

"They're not just spirits," Maya murmured. "They're guardians."

The tallest among them stepped forward, its form flickering like a mirage. In the space between them, a vision unfurled—Atlantean priests standing in the same chamber, activating a great energy source. The guardian gestured toward Andres and Maya, then to the ancient carvings on the walls, as if urging them to understand.

"They want to show us something," Maya realized, her heart pounding. "This place... it holds knowledge."

The ground trembled, but not in warning—rather, in resonance. The energy of the site surged around them, wrapping them in a warm, pulsing glow. Instead of fear, Andres felt a deep sense of connection.

"We are meant to be here," he said softly.

The guardians inclined their heads in silent acknowledgment. Then, as quickly as they had appeared, their forms faded, merging once more with the stone. The chamber grew still, but its presence lingered, watching, waiting.

Maya exhaled slowly, turning to Andres. "We are not just uncovering history. We are part of it."

Andres reached for her hand, threading his fingers through hers. "And they trust us to carry it forward."

As the ancient ruins settled into silence, Maya and Andres stood together, feeling the weight of their destiny—and the love that had bound them across lifetimes.

They fled through twisting corridors, the sounds of pursuit echoing behind them.

Eventually, they found themselves in a secluded alcove, bathed in moonlight filtering through an ancient skylight. Both were panting heavily, adrenaline coursing through their veins.

Maya turned to Andres, her eyes shimmering with unshed tears. "What do we do now?" she whispered.

Andres pulled her close, their foreheads touching. "We fight," he said softly. "Together. Just like we did in Atlantis."

"I'm scared, Andres," Maya admitted, her usual composure cracking. "The vision... what we saw... what if we're doomed to repeat the same mistakes?"

Andres cupped her face gently. "We're not our past selves, Maya. We have learned. We're stronger together."

Under the ancient moon, their fears and hopes intermingled. Maya's voice was barely audible as she said, "Promise me, whatever happens, we won't let them win. We won't let the darkness consume everything again."

Andres's reply was fierce with conviction. "I promise. Our love transcends time, Maya. It's our greatest weapon against the shadows."

As they held each other, both knew their commitment had been forged anew in the crucible of crisis. Whatever trials lay ahead, they would face them united, guardians of a sacred trust that spanned millennia.

Maya's hand found Andres's, their fingers intertwining. The simple touch sent a surge of energy through them both, a reminder of the delicate balance they embodied. In that moment, echoes of their shared past in Atlantis rippled through their connection—a time when they had stood together as allies, protectors of sacred knowledge, and witnesses to both the zenith and fall of their ancient civilization.

Though lifetimes had passed, the bond they once forged in the shimmering halls of Atlantis remained unbroken, as if destiny had brought them together once more to finish what they had begun.

"It's strange," Andres mused, his gaze drifting to the crystal formations glimmering in the moonlight. "We're surrounded by remnants of advanced technology, yet our greatest strength comes from something far more... intangible."

Maya nodded; her third eye pulsing gently. "The ancients understood that true power lies in the harmony between the spiritual and the material. Our love, Andres, is not just emotion. It's a bridge between worlds."

As if in response, a nearby crystal hummed to life, casting a soft blue glow over them. Andre's eyes widened. "Are we... activating something?"

"We are the activation," Maya whispered, her voice filled with wonder. "Our connection is attuning to the Vesica Piscis. Can you feel it?"

Andres closed his eyes, allowing the sensation to wash over him. It was like a cosmic dance, technology and spirit intertwining in perfect synchronicity. "It's beautiful," he breathed. "But also terrifying. If Kaine understood this power..."

Maya's grip tightened. "That's why we must protect it. Our bond is not just personal; it's the key to humanity's evolution. To becoming Homo Omega."

A distant rumble echoed through the temple, a stark reminder of the danger that lurked. Andres's jaw set with determination. "Whatever comes, we face it together. Two halves of a greater whole."

As they stood, their hands remained clasped, a living conduit of love and purpose. The air around them shimmered, ancient energies recognizing and responding to their unity.

Maya's eyes met Andres's, reflecting the vastness of time and space they had traversed together. "Are you ready?" she asked softly.

Andres nodded, feeling the weight of destiny and the strength of their bond. "With you? Always."

Their entwined hands glowed faintly as they stepped forward, ready to face whatever trials awaited. In that moment, they were more than just Andres and Maya—they were the embodiment of hope, a love that defied the very boundaries of existence.

Chapter 17

The holographic map of Kaine's fortress hovered in the air, a shimmering blue labyrinth of corridors and chambers. Andres leaned forward, his eyes tracing the convoluted paths, searching for a way in. The weight of leadership pressed down on his shoulders, a familiar burden made heavier by the stakes of their mission.

Talia's voice cut through his thoughts, sharp and precise. "The outer perimeter is guarded by AI-powered drones and infrared sensors," she said, gesturing to the map's edges. "But there's a weak spot here where the power grid connects to the main generator."

Andres nodded, impressed by her insider knowledge. He wondered briefly how much pain those memories caused her but pushed the thought aside. "Can we exploit that?"

"With the right equipment, yes," Talia replied, her fingers dancing over a holographic control panel. The map zoomed in, revealing intricate details of the power system. "We'll need to create a localized EMP burst to disable the sensors without alerting the main security system."

Evelyn frowned, her weathered face creased with concern. "And once we're inside?"

Talia's expression darkened. "That's where it gets tricky. The interior is a maze of shifting corridors and trap rooms. One wrong move, and we'll be facing an army of hybrid guards."

The team exchanged uneasy glances. Andres felt a flicker of doubt in his chest. *Was he really prepared to lead them into such danger?*

As if sensing his uncertainty, Maya stepped forward. Her green eyes shimmered with an otherworldly light as she addressed the group. "Remember, our purpose here is greater than mere infiltration," she said, her voice soft yet carrying an undeniable power. "We seek not just to retrieve an artifact but to restore balance to the cosmic order."

Andres felt a warmth spreading through him as Maya continued. "Yes, we must be strategic, but we must also act with compassion and wisdom. The fortress may be a bastion of technology, but it is built upon sacred ground. If we attune ourselves to the ancient energies that still flow there, we may find unexpected allies."

Her words struck a chord deep within Andres. He was more than just a tactician or a fighter; he was a guardian of ancient wisdom, a bridge between worlds. The duality of his role suddenly felt less like a burden and more like a source of strength.

"Maya's right," he said, straightening his shoulders. "We can't lose sight of the bigger picture. Talia, your expertise is invaluable, but we need to blend it with our spiritual awareness."

Talia raised an eyebrow, skepticism evident in her stance. "I'm all for positive thinking, but I don't see how meditation is going to get us past laser grids and armed guards."

Andres smiled, feeling a surge of confidence. "You'd be surprised. The Atlanteans built their fortresses in harmony with the Earth's energy grid. If we can tap into those residual patterns, we might find pathways that aren't visible on any map."

As the team continued to discuss strategy, Andres felt a sense of balance settling over him. They were walking a tightrope between two worlds—the technological and the spiritual—but that precarious position might just be their greatest strength.

Maya's emerald eyes flashed with conviction as she addressed the team. "We must consider the hybrids not as mere obstacles but as potential allies in our quest. They may be under Kaine's control, but within them lies the spark of free will, waiting to be awakened."

Andres nodded. "I agree. We can't simply treat them as expendable pawns. They're victims of the Brotherhood's manipulation, and we have a moral obligation to try and free them."

Talia's fingers tightened around the edge of the holographic display, her knuckles whitening. "With all due respect, we don't have time for a rescue mission. The Skull is our priority. Every moment we waste increases the risk of Kaine using it to further his plans."

Evelyn cleared her throat, her auburn hair catching the blue light of the hologram. "I hate to say it, but Talia has a point. The ethical implications are profound, but we're racing against time. If we fail to retrieve the Skull, the consequences could be catastrophic."

Andres felt the weight of leadership pressing down on him again. He understood both perspectives, the pull between compassion and pragmatism tearing at his conscience. "We can't abandon our humanity in pursuit of our goal," he said softly, more to himself than the others. "But we also can't risk the fate of the world on an uncertain rescue attempt."

Talia stepped forward, her dark eyes glinting with determination. "Let me show you something that might help us thread this needle." She tapped a series of commands into her wrist computer, and suddenly the air around her shimmered and blurred. In an instant, she vanished from view.

Andres's eyes widened in amazement. "Incredible," he breathed, reaching out to where Talia had been standing. His hand met solid resistance, though he couldn't see a thing.

Talia's disembodied voice came from the empty space. "Cloaking technology, reverse-engineered from Atlantean designs; it's not perfect—a careful observer might notice a slight distortion—but it'll get us past most security measures."

As she deactivated the cloak and flickered back into view, Talia produced a small, sleek device from her pocket. "And this little beauty can hack into any system the Brotherhood's got. We might be able to temporarily free the hybrids without compromising our primary objective."

Andres felt a surge of hope. Perhaps they could honor both their moral imperative and their urgent mission. He looked around at his team, seeing the same mix of determination and uncertainty he felt reflected in their eyes. "This changes things," he said. "We have a chance to do this right. Let's make it count."

Maya settled into a lotus position on the cool stone floor, her ornate robes pooling around her like liquid starlight. The diamond-like third eye at the center of her forehead began to pulse with an otherworldly glow as she closed her eyes and steadied her breath. The air around her seemed to thicken, charged with an invisible energy that made the hairs on the back of Andres's neck stand up.

"What do you see, Maya?" Andres whispered, his voice barely audible as he watched her face contort with concentration.

Maya's lips parted, her words coming in a trance-like cadence. "Shadows and light, intertwined. A labyrinth of crystal and steel. I see... I see us standing at a crossroads." Her brow furrowed. "There's a moment of choice, Andres. A decision that could tip the scales."

Andres leaned forward, hanging on her every word. "What kind of decision?"

"I can't... it's unclear," Maya murmured, her fingers twitching slightly. "But the consequences ripple outward, touching more than just our mission." Her eyes snapped open, green irises glowing with an inner fire. "We must tread carefully. The path to success is narrow, and failure..." She shuddered, "failure would have far-reaching consequences."

As Maya's vision faded, Andres turned away, his shoulders heavy with the weight of her words. He moved to a nearby table where ancient Atlantean scrolls lay unfurled, their golden script seeming to writhe in the dim light.

"What am I missing?" he muttered to himself, tracing the intricate symbols with a trembling finger. "There has to be something here, some key to leading us through this maze."

His eyes scanned the text, searching for guidance, for reassurance. But the more he read, the more doubts crept into his mind. "Am I really the one to lead this mission?" he wondered aloud, his voice barely a whisper. "What if I make the wrong choice?"

Maya's soft footsteps approached. "The burden of leadership is never easy, Andres," she said, placing a comforting hand on his shoulder. "But remember, you're not alone in this. We each bring our strengths to the table."

Andres nodded, grateful for her presence, but the gnawing uncertainty remained. He stared at the ancient wisdom before him, hoping against hope that it held the answers they so desperately needed.

Andres's gaze lingered on the ancient scrolls, his brow furrowed in concentration. Maya's presence beside him was a balm to his troubled mind, and he found himself drawn into memories of a distant past.

"Do you remember," he began softly, turning to face her, "the halls of the Crystal Temple in Atlantis? The way the light would dance across the walls, creating patterns that seemed alive?"

Maya's eyes sparkled with recognition. "How could I forget? The air itself hummed with energy. It was there that we first learned to harness the power of the crystals."

Andres nodded, a wistful smile playing on his lips. "I can still hear the chants of the High Priests, their voices resonating through the chambers. We were so young then, yet the weight of our responsibilities..."

"Was immense," Maya finished for him. She reached out, taking his hand in hers. "But we bore it together, as we do now. The lessons we learned then guide us still."

Their shared moment of vulnerability was interrupted by Talia clearing her throat. The tech expert had been silently observing from the corner, her fingers absently tracing the circuit pattern tattooed on her wrist.

"I may not have memories of Atlantis," Talia said, her voice uncharacteristically hesitant, "but I know something about bearing weight." She took a deep breath, steeling herself. "My time with the Brotherhood... it wasn't just about developing technology. I saw things, terrible things."

Andres and Maya turned to her, their expressions a mix of curiosity and concern.

Talia continued, her words coming faster now. "The hybrid experiments... they weren't just about creating soldiers. The Brotherhood wanted to create beings they could control completely, devoid of free will. I helped design the systems that would enslave them."

Her eyes glistened with unshed tears. "When I realized the full extent of what we were doing, I couldn't stay silent. That's when I knew I had to leave, to find a way to make things right."

Maya moved toward Talia, compassion radiating from her. "Your past does not define you, Talia. It's the choices you make now that shape your path forward."

Andres nodded in agreement. "We all carry burdens from our past. But together, we have the strength to forge a new future."

As the weight of Talia's confession settled over the room, a new sense of unity emerged among the team. Their shared vulnerabilities had strengthened their bond, reminding them of the personal stakes that drove their mission forward.

Andres cleared his throat, breaking the somber silence that had fallen over the room. "Well, I don't know about you all, but I could use a moment of levity. Anyone care to hear about the time I accidentally activated an ancient Atlantean device and ended up with blue hair for a week?"

The tension in the air dissipated as chuckles rippled through the group. Andres's deep laugh resonated, his eyes crinkling at the corners. "I remember that I looked like a walking blueberry."

Maya's melodious giggle joined in. "Oh, to have seen that! "

Talia, her earlier vulnerability still evident, managed a small smile. "I suppose that's one way to conduct field research."

As the laughter subsided, Andres's expression grew serious once more. He moved toward the holographic map of Kaine's fortress, his fingers hovering over the shimmering projection. A chill ran down his spine, and he felt the hairs on the back of his neck stand on end.

"Something's not right," he murmured, his brow furrowing. "The energy coming from this place... it's stronger than before."

Amaru stepped closer, concern etched on his weathered face. "What do you sense, Andres?"

Andres closed his eyes, drawing on his intuitive connection to the energies around him. "It's like... a storm brewing. The Brotherhood's influence is growing. I can feel it pulsing through the very walls of that fortress."

The playful atmosphere evaporated, replaced by a palpable sense of urgency. Maya's voice was barely above a whisper as she asked, "What does this mean for our mission?"

Andres opened his eyes, his gaze sweeping across his teammates. "It means we're running out of time. Whatever the Brotherhood is planning, it's accelerating. We need to move fast."

As the team huddled closer around the map, finalizing their approach, Andres couldn't shake the foreboding sensation gnawing at his gut. The fortress loomed in his mind, a dark sentinel guarding secrets that could reshape the world. He only hoped they were ready for what lay ahead.

The team dispersed, each member moving with purposeful urgency as they gathered their equipment. Andres watched as Talia expertly calibrated a series of compact devices, her fingers dancing across holographic interfaces.

"Cloaking techs at full capacity," she reported, her voice tight with concentration. "I've optimized our comms for minimal detectability. If the Brotherhood's got any surprises waiting, we'll be ready."

Andres nodded, his eyes scanning the room. "Evelyn, status on the energy dampeners?"

Evelyn looked up from a case of crystalline objects, her expression a mix of excitement and apprehension. "Fully charged and ready to disrupt any Atlantean defense systems we might encounter. But Andres, if the energy signatures are as strong as you're sensing..."

"We'll adapt," Andres assured her, though doubt gnawed at the edges of his confidence. He turned to Maya, who was carefully packing a set of ancient scrolls. "Those the Tiwanaku texts?"

Maya's eyes met his, filled with ancient wisdom. "Yes. The knowledge they contain may be our key to unlocking the fortress's secrets—and our own potential."

As the final preparations were made, Andres felt the weight of leadership settle heavily on his shoulders. He cleared his throat, drawing the team's attention.

"Before we head out, I want to say something," he began, his voice low but firm. "Each of you brings unique strengths to this mission. Our diversity is our greatest asset."

Andres closed his eyes briefly, drawing upon the teachings of his Mapuche ancestors. When he opened them, his gaze was alight with determination.

Andres took a deep breath, his voice steady as he spoke. "In Mapuche tradition, we speak of *Itrofill Mongen*—the interconnectedness of all living things. It reminds us that we are not solitary beings but part of a vast, living web that spans time and space. As we face the challenges ahead, we must draw strength from this unity, balancing the physical and spiritual realms."

Amaru stepped forward, his expression solemn, yet illuminated by a quiet strength. He gestured toward the ruins of Tiwanaku around them, the stones seeming to hum faintly with ancient energy.

"And here, in the shadow of these sacred stones," he began, his voice rich with reverence, "we speak of *Pacha Kutiq*—the great cycles of transformation. This place, Tiwanaku, was built not just as a city, but as a bridge between worlds, where the wisdom of the past prepares us for the future. It is said that the ancestors encoded their visions here, waiting for a time when the Earth would need them most."

Amaru looked at the team, his gaze holding their attention as if the stones themselves spoke through him. "We stand on the threshold of such a time. Tiwanaku's teachings remind us that every action, every decision, ripples through time, affecting not just ourselves but all who come after. Our task is not only to fight for what is right but to awaken the memory of who we truly are—as beings of light and purpose."

He turned to Andres, his voice now carrying a note of solidarity. "Your Mapuche wisdom speaks of balance, Andres. Here, we add to that the strength of cycles—the courage to embrace change and step into the unknown, trusting that the ancestors walk with us. The energies of Tiwanaku call us to remember this truth: we are not here by accident. We are the dream of those who came before, and the hope of those yet to come."

The air seemed to thicken with meaning, the team caught in the gravity of their words. For a moment, they felt not just as individuals on a mission but as living links in a chain of purpose stretching across eons.

A moment of silence followed, the air thick with shared purpose and resolve. Then, with a nod from Andres, the team gathered their gear and moved towards the exit, ready to face whatever lay beyond.

The team slipped out into the night, their silhouettes melting into the darkness. Andres led the way, his senses heightened by the palpable tension in the air. The fortress loomed ahead, a hulking mass against the star-studded sky.

Chapter 18

The tempest howled, mirroring the turmoil in Andres's heart as he crouched behind a rocky outcropping. Lightning illuminated the fortress's imposing silhouette, its dark spires jutting defiantly against the roiling sky. Rain lashed his face, mingling with the sweat of anticipation.

"We're running out of time," Maya whispered urgently, her green eyes glowing with an otherworldly intensity.

Andres nodded, feeling the weight of their mission. "Talia, what's our best approach?"

The ex-Brotherhood operative studied her wrist-mounted holo-display, in deep concentration. "There's a blind spot in the sensor grid, here," she pointed to a flickering red dot. "But we'll need to time our movements precisely with the lightning strikes to avoid detection."

"And the guards?" Andres asked, his Atlantean strategic mind already formulating plans.

"Rotating shifts, but the storm's disrupting their patterns," Talia replied. "We might just have a chance."

A deafening thunderclap shook the earth, and Andres made his decision. "Now!" he hissed, sprinting towards the fortress wall. The team followed; their footsteps masked by the howling wind.

As they reached the base of the structure, Talia's fingers danced across a hidden panel. A section of the wall shimmered and dissolved, revealing a narrow passage. "Hurry!" she urged, "The opening won't last long."

They slipped inside just as the wall rematerialized. Andres's heart pounded his senses on high alert. The corridor stretched before them, a maze of shadows and pulsing energy conduits.

"Stay close," Talia warned. "The security drones are—"

A low hum filled the air. Andres tensed, spotting the sleek, metallic shape of a drone rounding the corner. He held his breath, willing his body to stillness as the machine's scanning beam swept past them.

We can't fail now, Andres thought desperately. *The fate of humanity hangs in the balance.*

As the drone moved on, Talia gestured towards a side passage. "This way. It'll lead us to the central chamber."

They crept forward, every step a calculated risk. Andres's Mapuche intuition prickled, sensing the latent power thrumming through the fortress. It felt wrong, a perversion of the sacred energies he'd encountered in Tiwanaku.

"Andres," Maya's voice was barely a whisper, "I can feel the Crystal Skull's presence. It's... in pain."

He squeezed her hand reassuringly. "We'll set it right, I promise."

Suddenly, Talia threw up a hand in warning. Two guards appeared at the end of the corridor, their armor gleaming with Atlantean sigils.

"Follow my lead," Talia murmured. She tapped a sequence on her wrist device, and a shimmering field enveloped the team. As the guards approached, their eyes slid past the group as if they weren't there.

Andres held his breath, feeling the guards' energy signatures brush against his own. For a heart-stopping moment, one of them paused, frowning. Then, mercifully, they moved on.

As the camouflage field dissipated, Andres released a shaky breath. "That was too close."

"We're not out of danger yet," Talia reminded them. "The real challenge lies ahead."

They pressed onward, the fortress's oppressive aura growing stronger with each step. Andres's mind raced, weighing the enormity of their task against the fragile hope of success. As they neared the heart of General Kaine's stronghold, he steeled himself for the confrontation to come.

We're coming for you, Kaine, Andres thought grimly. *And this time, the power of Atlantis will serve the light.*

As they rounded the corner, a wave of dizziness struck Andres. The world around him blurred, replaced by a vivid vision of the Crystal Skull. Its crystalline surface pulsed with an otherworldly light, revealing glimpses of ancient wisdom and terrible power.

"Wait," Andres gasped, pressing a hand against the cool stone wall to steady himself. The others halted, watching him with concern.

Maya touched his arm. "What do you see?"

Andres's concentrated, his eyes unfocused. "The Skull... it's showing me patterns, connections. I can see the fortress's layout, but also... echoes of Atlantean technology."

He struggled to reconcile the conflicting impulses within him. His Mapuche intuition whispered of harmony with nature, of respecting the delicate balance of energies. Yet his newfound Atlantean knowledge offered precise calculations, ways to manipulate those same energies to their advantage.

"We need to move quickly," Talia urged, glancing nervously down the corridor.

Andres nodded, pushing through the disorientation. "This way," he said, leading them down a dimly lit passage. "The Skull's trying to guide us."

As they hurried forward, Maya suddenly froze. "Do you feel that?" she whispered, her eyes wide.

Before anyone could respond, a hidden door slid open, revealing a chamber bathed in soft, blue light. Maya stepped forward as if in a trance, drawn by an unseen force.

"Maya, wait!" Andres called, but she was already inside.

The room was filled with Atlantean artifacts—intricate metal constructs, pulsing crystals, and devices of unknown purpose. As Maya moved among them, her fingers trailing over their surfaces, her eyes began to glow with an inner light.

"I remember," she breathed, her voice taking on an otherworldly timbre. "I was there, Andres. I saw Atlantis fall."

Memories cascaded through her—soaring crystal spires, devastating weapons of light, the anguished cries of a civilization tearing itself apart. Maya staggered under the weight of millennia.

Andres rushed to her side, supporting her as she swayed. "Stay with me, Maya," he urged, his voice anchoring her to the present. "Don't lose yourself in the past."

Maya's eyes locked onto his, tears streaming down her face. "We made such terrible mistakes," she whispered. "But now... now I understand how to make it right."

Slowly, the glow faded from her eyes. Maya took a deep, shuddering breath, then straightened. When she spoke again, her voice held new determination.

"We have to destroy the weapons," she said firmly. "But the knowledge... we can use it to heal the world."

Andres nodded, relief washing over him as he saw Maya's strength return. "Together," he promised. "We'll face whatever comes, together."

As they turned to rejoin the others, a distant alarm began to wail. Time was running out.

Evelyn faced the glowing panel before her, its intricate patterns pulsing with an otherworldly energy. Her fingers hovered over the surface, tracing the air above complex geometric designs that seemed to shift and change with each passing second.

"This isn't like anything I've ever seen," she muttered, her green eyes darting from one symbol to the next. "It's as if the security system is... alive."

Andres stepped closer, his voice low. "What do you see, Evelyn?"

She shook her head, frustration evident in the tightness of her jaw. "It's a blend of advanced technology and something else. Something... older. More primal." Her fingers twitched, itching to interact with the panel directly, but years of scientific caution held her back.

Suddenly, the symbols flared brighter, causing Evelyn to stumble back. As she did, a stray lock of auburn hair fell across her face.

"Wait," she whispered, her eyes widening. "It's responding to our presence. To our energy." She turned to Andres, excitement overriding her usual skepticism. "It's not just a security system. It's a test."

Andres nodded encouragingly. "Trust your instincts, Evelyn. What does it want from us?"

Evelyn took a deep breath, closing her eyes for a moment. When she opened them again, there was a new determination in her gaze. "It wants... harmony. Balance." She stepped forward, placing both palms flat against the panel. "Not just logic, but intuition. Not just science, but..."

"Faith," Andres finished softly.

As Evelyn's hands made contact with the glowing surface, the symbols began to dance and swirl. She gasped, feeling energy coursing through her body. In her mind's eye, she saw flashes of ancient wisdom, of a world where science and spirituality were one.

"I see it now," she breathed, her voice filled with wonder. "The Atlanteans... they didn't separate the physical from the mystical. It was all one continuum."

With a final pulse of light, the panel dimmed, and a hidden doorway slid open beside them. Evelyn stepped back, her hands trembling slightly.

Andres squeezed her shoulder. "You did it, Evelyn. You bridged the gap."

She nodded, a slight smile playing at the corners of her mouth. "I think I'm beginning to understand what you and Amaru have been trying to tell us all along."

As they moved through the newly revealed passage, the air around them began to shimmer and distort. Evelyn felt a wave of dizziness wash over her, and she stumbled.

"What's happening?" Maya called out, her voice sounding strangely distant.

Amaru's calm voice cut through the confusion. "Stay close," he instructed. "We've entered a chamber designed to disorient and confuse. It's a final defense against those unprepared for the truths that lie beyond."

The elderly shaman moved to the center of the group, his wooden staff tapping a steady rhythm on the floor. "Focus on the sound," he said. "Let it anchor you to the present moment."

Evelyn struggled to keep her bearings as the walls seemed to melt and reform around them. "How do we fight this?" she asked, her scientific mind desperately seeking a logical solution.

Amaru's dark eyes met hers, filled with ancient wisdom. "We don't fight, Dr. Carter. We accept. We flow. The chamber seeks to break our connection to each other and ourselves. We must strengthen those bonds instead."

As if to demonstrate, Amaru began to chant softly, his weathered voice weaving a tapestry of sound that seemed to stabilize the shifting environment. Evelyn felt her racing heart begin to slow, her breath synchronizing with the rhythm of Amaru's words.

"Join hands," Amaru instructed. "And remember who you are. Remember why you're here."

As their fingers intertwined, Evelyn felt a surge of strength flow through the group. The disorienting effects of the chamber began to fade, replaced by a sense of clarity and purpose.

"We are the bridge," Amaru intoned, his voice resonating with power. "Between past and future, between earth and sky, between the physical and the spiritual. We walk the path of balance, guided by wisdom both ancient and new."

With each step forward, the chamber's defenses weakened. Evelyn marveled at the transformation, both within herself and around her. For the first time, she truly understood the importance of Amaru's role in their quest.

As they emerged from the other side of the chamber, Evelyn turned to the shaman, her eyes shining with newfound respect. "Thank you, Amaru," she said softly. "I think I'm finally ready to embrace all aspects of this journey—even the ones I can't explain with science alone."

Amaru nodded, a gentle smile crinkling the corners of his eyes. "The greatest discoveries," he replied, "often lie in the space between what we know and what we have yet to learn."

The team rounded a corner, their footsteps echoing softly against the polished stone walls. Talia held up a hand, signaling them to halt. Her eyes narrowed, scanning the corridor ahead.

"Something's not right," she whispered, her fingers tracing the circuit pattern tattooed on her wrist. "This checkpoint... it's different from the schematics I memorized."

Voss moved swiftly, her fingers dancing across hidden panels and energy conduits. The air crackled with unseen power as she worked, bypassing security measures that would have taken them hours to overcome.

"There," she said, stepping back as a hidden door slid open. "But hurry. They'll detect the breach soon."

As the team moved forward, Talia at the lead, Andres felt the anticipation building. The charged atmosphere seemed to hum with potential energy, each step bringing them closer to the Crystal Skull—and the fate that awaited them all.

"We're close," Talia murmured, her expertise guiding them through the final twists and turns. "The chamber should be just ahead."

Andres's heart raced, equal parts excitement and trepidation coursing through him. The weight of their mission, the hopes, and fears of countless generations, seemed to press down upon his shoulders.

"Whatever happens," he said, his voice low but firm, "we face it together. For the future of humanity."

A figure moved ahead of the team, guiding them with precision through the fortress's dim corridors. Dr. Elera Voss was no longer the composed scientist they had first encountered. Her silver hair, now freed from its strict bun, fell in loose strands around her face, and the pristine lab coat she always wore had been replaced by a utilitarian jacket more suited to infiltration.

"Keep close," she murmured, her voice low but commanding. "The patrols shift every six minutes. We have a window, but it's narrow."

Talia glanced at Andres, her brow furrowed with distrust. "Are we sure we can trust her? She *was* their chief architect, after all."

"I can hear you," Voss said without looking back, her tone sharp. She turned to face the group briefly, her piercing gray eyes softened by something unspoken. "If I wanted to betray you, we wouldn't have made it past the outer drones. Believe me, I know *exactly* how they work."

"Convenient," Maya muttered.

Andres stepped forward, his voice steady. "Enough. We need her expertise, and she's risking everything to help us. Let's focus on the mission."

Voss hesitated, meeting his gaze. "You're more forgiving than I deserve, Dr. Paredes. But we don't have time for sentimentality. The next checkpoint is the laser grid, and it's coded to pulse at irregular intervals. If you follow me, I can neutralize it before we hit the threshold."

As they reached the laser grid, Voss crouched beside a control panel hidden behind a false wall. Her fingers flew across the touch-sensitive keys, manipulating symbols and Atlantean energy flows with practiced ease.

Jacqueline leaned closer to Andres and whispered, "She seems to know exactly what she's doing. But I can't shake the feeling she's still holding something back."

"She's not the only one," Andres nodded, watching Voss intently.

The grid fizzled and then deactivated, its faint hum dissipating. Voss stood, brushing dust from her hands. "You're clear. But we'll need to move quickly. If I know Kaine, he's monitoring energy surges, and that disruption won't go unnoticed."

As the team continued deeper into the stronghold, the atmosphere grew colder, the walls reflecting the sterile efficiency of the

Brotherhood's design. They reached a corridor lined with data nodes pulsing faintly with bluish light.

Voss stopped abruptly, turning to face the group. "This is it. Beyond this door lies the heart of Kaine's operation. The stasis pods, the hybrid prototypes... everything. But the system is set to lock down if it detects unauthorized access."

"Can you disable it?" Talia asked.

"Of course," Voss said, her voice steady. But her hand faltered as she reached for the controls.

Andres stepped beside her. "What is it?"

Voss's voice wavered, uncharacteristically hesitant. "I built this place with the idea that knowledge and power could be controlled, directed. But seeing it now... I realize how much I underestimated Kaine. This isn't just about control; it's about erasure—of choice, of humanity. I helped create this nightmare."

Andres placed a hand on her shoulder, his voice firm but understanding. "Then help us stop it. You're here now, Elera. That means something."

Voss straightened, determination hardening her features. "You're right. Let's finish this."

With renewed focus, Voss keyed in the final sequence. The door slid open, revealing a cavernous chamber filled with rows of stasis pods glowing faintly in the darkness. The sight was both awe-inspiring and horrifying, the hybrids' part-human, part-machine forms a stark reminder of the Brotherhood's ambition.

Voss turned to the team. "You have less than fifteen minutes before the system detects the breach and locks everything down. I'll monitor the external feeds and delay any incoming forces as long as I can. After that, you're on your own."

Andres nodded. "Thank you, Elera. Stay safe."

She gave him a faint, almost imperceptible smile. "Don't thank me yet."

The team moved forward, their resolve strengthened but their time running out.

The air suddenly crackled with malevolent energy, causing the hairs on Andres's neck to stand on end. A thunderous boom echoed through the chamber as the far wall exploded inward, showering them with debris. Through the settling dust strode General Kaine, his dark armor gleaming ominously, flanked by a phalanx of heavily armed guards.

"Did you really think it would be that easy?" Kaine's voice dripped with contempt, his red eyes fixed on Andres. "You're nothing but a relic, clinging to outdated ideals."

Andres stepped forward, shielding his team. "And you're a tyrant, Kaine. Blinded by your lust for power."

Kaine sneered. "Power is the only truth in this world. Your 'Law of One' is a fairy tale for the weak."

"You're wrong," Andres countered, his voice steady despite the tension coiling in his muscles. "Unity and compassion are the path to true evolution. Your way leads only to destruction."

"Enough talk," Kaine snarled, raising his hand. "Let me show you the future."

A low hum filled the air as a sleek, metallic humanoid form materialized beside Kaine. Andres's blood ran cold as he recognized the hybrid AI prototype—a fusion of Atlantean crystal technology and modern robotics.

"Impressive, isn't it?" Kaine gloated. "The perfect synthesis of past and future. Unstoppable."

The hybrid's eyes flared to life, pulsing with an unnatural intelligence. Andres's mind raced, searching for a strategy. "Everyone, scatter!" he shouted, diving to the side as the hybrid unleashed a devastating energy pulse.

Chaos erupted. Maya somersaulted behind a pillar, narrowly avoiding a barrage of laser fire. Evelyn frantically worked to establish an energy shield, her hands trembling as she manipulated the ancient technology.

"We need to disrupt its power source!" Andres called out, ducking under another blast. His Mapuche intuition screamed a warning, urging him to act quickly.

Amaru's calm voice cut through the din. "The crystal matrix, Andres. It's unstable. If we can overload it..."

Andres nodded, understanding dawning. He locked eyes with Maya across the room, a silent plan forming between them. As she darted out, drawing the hybrid's fire, Andres sprinted toward its blind spot.

"You can't win, Andres!" Kaine bellowed. "The future belongs to those who seize it!"

Andres's response was grim determination as he prepared to make his move.

Andres's heart pounded as he weighed his options. The Crystal Skull glimmered tantalizingly close, but the hybrid's relentless assault left no room for error. He caught Maya's eye, saw the fierce determination there, and made his decision.

"Everyone, on my mark!" Andres shouted, his voice cutting through the chaos. "Evelyn, redirect your shield to the eastern corridor!"

As Evelyn complied, Andres sprinted towards the hybrid, drawing its fire.

The synthetic man moved with inhuman speed, interfacing with a nearby control panel. The hybrid faltered, its energy field flickering.

"What are you doing?" Kaine roared, his face contorted with rage.

Andres grinned, a fierce light in his eyes. "Choosing survival over power. Something you never understood."

He signaled to Maya, who hurled a small device toward the hybrid. It detonated in a burst of electromagnetic energy, sending the creature into a wild spiral of malfunctions.

"Time to go!" Andres commanded, leading the charge towards their escape route.

Explosions rocked the fortress as they ran, debris raining down around them. The storm outside seemed to respond to their desperation, winds howling as they emerged into the tempest.

"We can't leave empty-handed!" Dr. Carter protested as they sprinted across the rain-lashed courtyard.

Andres's response was grim. "We leave with our lives and our freedom. That's victory enough."

They plunged into the thick forest beyond, the storm masking their retreat. For what felt like hours, they pushed through the underbrush, the sounds of pursuit fading behind them.

Finally, as dawn broke, they stumbled into their hidden sanctuary—a cave system shielded by ancient Mapuche protections.

Collapsing against the cool stone walls, Andres surveyed his team, bruised, exhausted, but alive.

Maya approached, her eyes searching his. "The Skull..." she began.

Andres shook his head. "It wasn't worth the risk. We'll find another way."

Amaru's weathered face creased into a smile. "You chose wisely, my friend. The path of the heart is often the truest."

As the team tended to their wounds and caught their breath, Andres felt a weight lift from his shoulders. They had survived, grown stronger. And in that moment, he knew their real journey was just beginning.

The sanctuary's communication array crackled to life, startling the exhausted team. Maya rushed to the console, her fingers flying over the controls as a flood of data poured in.

"Andres, you need to see this," she called, her voice tight with urgency.

Dr. Paredes joined her, his brow furrowing as he scanned the traffic reports. "My God," he breathed, rubbing his chin absently. "It's happening everywhere."

"What is it?" Evelyn asked, limping over to join them.

Andres's eyes met hers, a mix of wonder and trepidation in his gaze. "The energy grid. It's... awakening."

The team huddled around the display, watching in awe as reports flooded in from across the globe. Mysterious light phenomena in the skies over ancient sites. Unprecedented seismic activity along ley lines. Spontaneous healings at sacred springs.

"This is beyond anything we anticipated," Maya murmured, her fingers tracing the patterns emerging on the map.

Amaru's calm voice cut through the tension. "The Earth herself is stirring. The old wisdom is returning."

Andres turned to face his team, his voice taking on a passionate edge. "Our mission has changed. We're no longer just fighting for survival. We must guide humanity through this transformation."

"But how?" Evelyn asked, her analytical mind already racing. "The scale of this is... overwhelming."

Andres's thoughts lingered on the Crystal Skull. The memory of how close they had come to retrieving it still burned in his mind—the moments when victory seemed just within reach, only to slip away at the last instant. The weight of their failure was heavy, but it was not defeat that filled him; it was determination. They had seen it, felt its power, and he knew it would not elude them forever.

"We were so close," he murmured to himself, his voice low but edged with resolve. "Closer than we've ever been."

Maya stepped up beside him, sensing the storm of thoughts swirling within him. "We'll find it," she said quietly, her steady presence grounding him.

Andres nodded, his jaw tightening. "I know we will. The Skull is a key to everything—the energy grid, the sacred sites, the wisdom we've been seeking. And we can't afford to fail again."

He turned toward the team, his eyes blazing with a renewed sense of purpose. "We've been brought this far for a reason. We're not stopping until we unlock the full power of the Skull, no matter the cost."

The team gathered around him, their commitment unwavering. As they discussed their next moves, Andres's thoughts returned to the Skull—the ancient artifact that had drawn them all together, that held the key to humanity's future. Their mission was not over; in fact, it felt as though they were only just beginning.

The energy grid was awakening, and with it, the promise of a new world. The obstacles they faced were many, but Andres knew one thing for certain—they would find the Skull, and when they did, they would be ready. The future of humanity depended on it.

Chapter 19

The flickering holographic map cast an eerie blue glow across the faces of Andres's team, huddled in the dank cavern that served as their temporary hideout. Since their last incursion into Kaine's fortress, they had meticulously reviewed every detail, analyzing weaknesses and refining their approach. Talia's fingers danced over the projection, tracing the fortress's outline with practiced precision, her movements more confident now that they were better prepared.

"We know the patrol rotations, the blind spots," she murmured, her voice edged with determination. "This time, we won't be caught off guard.

"The outer perimeter is lined with quantum-linked turrets," she explained, her eyes narrowed with concentration. "They're programmed to detect any biological or technological signature that doesn't match their database."

Andres felt a knot tighten in his stomach. "How do we get past them?"

Talia's lips curved into a wry smile. "That's where my inside knowledge comes in handy. I helped design the system, remember? There's a flaw in the northwest quadrant—a blind spot we can exploit."

Maya stepped forward, her serene presence a stark contrast to the tension in the air. "We must move with purpose, but also with compassion," she intoned, her green eyes seeming to peer into realms beyond their own. "Remember, even our enemies are part of the greater whole."

Andres nodded, trying to balance Maya's spiritual wisdom with the tactical necessities at hand. He turned to address the team. "We have one shot at this. The Crystal Skull is our key to restoring balance to the global energy grid. Failure isn't an option."

As they emerged from their hideout into the raging storm, Andres couldn't shake the feeling that they were walking into the maw of some great beast. Lightning crackled overhead, illuminating the fortress's imposing silhouette against the turbulent sky.

"Stay low and follow my lead," Talia hissed, her form barely visible through the sheets of rain.

They moved as one, a shadow within shadows, their footsteps muffled by the howling wind. Andres's heart pounded in his chest; each beat a reminder of the enormity of their task.

A patrol drone buzzed overhead, its searchlight cutting through the darkness. The team froze, pressing themselves against the muddy ground. Andres held his breath, acutely aware of every drop of rain that pelted his back.

"Now!" Talia whispered urgently as the drone passed. They sprinted forward, using the storm's fury as cover.

As they approached the fortress's outer wall, Andres caught sight of the automated turrets Talia had mentioned. Their barrels swiveled with mechanical precision, searching for targets. He closed his eyes briefly, centering himself as Maya had taught him.

"Remember," Maya's voice carried on the wind, barely audible above the storm, "we are more than just our physical forms. We are conduits of cosmic energy, capable of great transformation."

Andres opened his eyes, a newfound determination coursing through him. They were so close now, on the precipice of either triumph or disaster. As they reached the blind spot Talia had identified, he allowed himself a moment of hope.

"This is it," he murmured, more to himself than the others. "The first step towards reclaiming our destiny."

With a shared look of resolve, the team pressed forward into the unknown, the storm raging around them like a reflection of the cosmic struggle in which they were embroiled.

Evelyn's fingers flew across her quantum-encrypted tablet. The soft blue glow illuminated her face, casting eerie shadows as she worked to breach the fortress's formidable defenses.

"Fascinating," she murmured, eyes widening. "The security protocols are interwoven with what appears to be... Atlantean encryption?"

Andres leaned in, his curiosity piqued. "Can you crack it?"

Evelyn's lips twitched in a wry smile. "It's a blend of cutting-edge technology and ancient wisdom. I never thought I'd say this, but I'm glad for those meditation sessions with Amaru. They're helping me... sense the patterns."

She closed her eyes, took a deep breath, and placed her hand on the fortress wall. A faint, golden glow emanated from her palm, pulsing in sync with the security system's rhythms.

"There's an energy here," Evelyn whispered, her voice tinged with awe and a hint of fear. "It's... alive, somehow."

Andres watched, mesmerized, as Evelyn's scientific expertise merged with something more intuitive, more primal. The fortress's defenses flickered, then fell away like a veil lifting.

The massive gate before them groaned open, revealing a yawning darkness beyond.

"We're in," Evelyn breathed, her eyes snapping open. "But I can't shake the feeling we've awakened something... ancient."

Andres nodded grimly. "Stay alert, everyone. We're in uncharted territory now."

The team moved forward, their senses on high alert. The air inside the fortress was thick with an electric charge, making the hairs on the back of Andres's neck stand up.

"Do you feel that?" Maya whispered, her hand instinctively reaching for the crystal fragment around her neck. "It's like the very walls are watching us."

Talia's voice was tense. "The inner sanctum should be three levels down. But be careful—Kaine's bound to have surprises waiting. He will be expecting us."

As they descended deeper into the facility, Andres's mind raced. *What if we're too late? What if Kaine has already harnessed the power of the Crystal Skull?*

The weight of their mission pressed down on him, each step feeling heavier than the last. The fate of humanity, the very evolution of consciousness, hung in the balance.

"Andres," Evelyn's voice cut through his thoughts, "whatever happens... I want you to know I believe now. In all of it. The Atlanteans, the energy grid, our potential as a species. We can't let Kaine pervert this power."

Andres met her gaze, seeing the same mix of determination and fear he felt reflected in her eyes. "We won't," he promised, hoping he sounded more confident than he felt. "Together, we'll set things right."

As they rounded a corner, a pulsing blue light spilled into the corridor. The team instinctively pressed themselves against the walls, hearts pounding.

"This is it," Andres whispered. "The moment of truth."

With a shared nod of resolve, they stepped forward into the unknown, ready to face whatever challenges lay ahead in their quest to unlock humanity's true potential.

The eerie blue glow intensified as they entered a vast chamber, its vaulted ceiling disappearing into shadows. Andres's breath caught in his throat. Before them stood a platoon of hybrid AI soldiers, their cybernetic enhancements gleaming under the harsh light.

"By the gods!" Amaru whispered, his weathered face etched with horror.

The hybrids' eyes swiveled in unison, locking onto the intruders. Half-human faces contorted into expressions of cold calculation, servos whirring as they raised their weapons.

Andres's hand closed around the Crystal Skull fragment in his pocket. Its energy pulsed against his palm, urging him forward. Without fully understanding why, he took a step towards the hybrids.

"Andres, what are you doing?" Evelyn hissed, fear evident in her voice.

He raised his hands, palms out. "We're not here to fight you," Andres called out, his voice steady despite the terror clawing at his insides. "You're more than just machines. There's still humanity within you."

The hybrids remained motionless, but Andres sensed a flicker of... something. Confusion? Recognition? He pressed on, focusing his thoughts on the crystal's energy.

"Remember who you were," he projected, reaching out with his mind. "Before Kaine. Before the experiments. You have a choice."

For a moment, nothing happened. Then, ever so slightly, the hybrid closest to Andres tilted its head. Its mechanical eyes flickered, a spark of awareness cutting through the programmed obedience.

Amaru stepped forward, his staff tapping a rhythmic pattern on the floor. "Children of two worlds," he intoned, his voice taking on a hypnotic quality. "The spirits of your ancestors cry out. Hear their voices. Feel the earth beneath your feet. You are not lost."

The air crackled with tension as the hybrids' programming warred against the stirring of long-dormant memories. Andres held his breath, acutely aware of how precarious their position was.

"Please," he whispered, both aloud and in his mind. "Remember your humanity."

A tremor ran through the ranks of hybrids, their metallic bodies shuddering as if caught in an unseen electrical storm. Suddenly, the air erupted with chaos as the group split violently. Half of the hybrids turned on their brethren, sparks flying as metal clashed against metal.

"Now's our chance!" Andres shouted, ducking as a stray energy blast sizzled past his ear. "Push forward!"

The team surged ahead, weaving through the fray. Andres's heart pounded, his senses overwhelmed by the cacophony of battle. Mechanical screams mingled with the hiss of severed hydraulics and the acrid smell of burning circuitry.

As they pressed deeper into the fortress, Maya's voice cut through the din. "Evelyn! On your left!"

Evelyn spun, narrowly avoiding a hybrid's swinging arm. Without missing a beat, she dropped to one knee, pulling a small device from her pocket. "Maya, channel your energy through this!"

Maya's eyes widened in recognition. "A quantum resonator? Brilliant!"

As Maya placed her hands on the device, Evelyn's fingers flew across its surface, inputting complex calculations. "If we can match the frequency of their neural networks..." she muttered.

"... we can disrupt their command signals," Maya finished, her third eye glowing with intense concentration.

The resonator hummed to life, emitting a high-pitched whine that made Andres's teeth ache. Three approaching hybrids stumbled, their movements becoming erratic.

"It's working!" Evelyn exclaimed, a rare grin breaking across her face.

Maya nodded, her expression serene despite the chaos. "Science and spirit, in harmony," she said softly.

Andres watched in awe as the unlikely pair continued their assault, Evelyn's technology amplifying Maya's metaphysical abilities.

He couldn't help but think, *this is what we're fighting for. The fusion of our greatest strengths.*

"Keep moving!" he called out, gesturing for the team to press on. *We're close now,* he thought. *So close to changing everything.*

The team burst through a set of massive crystalline doors, their footsteps echoing in the cavernous chamber beyond. Andres's breath caught in his throat as he beheld the sight before them.

Suspended in midair, pulsing with an otherworldly light, floated the Crystal Skull of Atlantis. Its translucent surface shimmered with an inner radiance, casting prismatic reflections across the chamber walls. The Skull's empty eye sockets seemed to stare directly into Andre's soul, calling to him with an intensity that made his skin tingle.

"By the gods!" Maya whispered, her green eyes wide with awe. "It's even more beautiful than the legends describe."

Andres felt a pull, an inexorable urge to approach the artifact. "Maya, do you feel that? It's like it's... singing to us."

She nodded, her third eye glowing brightly. "The resonance is incredibly powerful. It's awakening something within us, Andres. Our Atlantean heritage."

As they stepped closer, the energy field surrounding the Skull intensified, crackling with visible arcs of blue-white energy. Andres's heart raced, every fiber of his being screaming that they were on the precipice of something monumental.

"We have to act quickly," he said, reaching for the Skull fragment in his pocket. "If we can just—"

A deep, menacing voice cut through the chamber. "I'm afraid your little adventure ends here, Dr. Paredes."

Andres spun around, his blood running cold as he saw General Kaine striding into the chamber. The man's red eyes glowed with malevolent hunger; his scarred face twisted into a cruel smile. Flanking him were a dozen hybrid soldiers, their weapons trained on the team.

But it was the object in Kaine's hands that truly chilled Andres to the bone—an ornate staff of unmistakably Atlantean design, its tip crackling with barely contained energy.

"Did you really think I'd let you waltz in and take what's rightfully mine?" Kaine sneered, hefting the weapon. "The future belongs to the strong, Paredes. To those with the vision and will to shape it."

Andres's mind raced, searching for a way out. He locked eyes with Maya, seeing his own determination mirrored in her gaze.

"The skull doesn't belong to you, Kaine," Andres said, his voice steady despite the fear gnawing at his insides. "Its power was never meant for conquest or control."

Kaine's laughter echoed off the chamber walls. "How naive. Power exists to be wielded, to elevate the worthy above the masses. And I am worthy."

He raised the staff, its tip glowing ominously. "Now, step away from the Skull. I'd hate to damage such a priceless artifact... or you."

Andres's hand tightened around the Skull fragment in his pocket. He knew they were outgunned, but giving up wasn't an option. The fate of humanity hung in the balance.

"Maya," he whispered, barely moving his lips. "On my signal, reach out to the Skull with your mind. We might only have one shot at this."

Her almost imperceptible nod was all the confirmation he needed. Andres took a deep breath, steeling himself for what was to come.

"You're right about one thing, Kaine," he said loudly, taking a deliberate step forward. "The future is at stake. But it's not yours to claim."

Andres's fingers closed around the Skull fragment, its energy pulsing in sync with his racing heartbeat. In one fluid motion, he withdrew it from his pocket and thrust it toward the suspended Crystal Skull. "Now, Maya!"

The chamber erupted into chaos. A blinding flash of light burst from the fragment, connecting with the larger skull in a crackling arc of energy. The air itself seemed to vibrate, the pulsating field around the artifact destabilizing in violent ripples.

"Stop them!" Kaine roared, his voice barely audible over the deafening hum of energy.

Maya's eyes blazed with an otherworldly light as she reached out with her mind, her consciousness merging with the ancient power of the Skull. "Andres," she called, her voice strained, "I can't hold it for long!"

The hybrid soldiers advanced, their weapons raised. Andres ducked under a blast of energy, rolling towards the pedestal. His fingers brushed against the cool surface of the Crystal Skull, sending a jolt of electricity through his body.

This is our only chance, he thought, gritting his teeth against the pain.

Outside, the storm intensified, as if nature itself was responding to the struggle within. Lightning crashed, illuminating the chamber in stark flashes of blue-white light.

"You fool!" Kaine bellowed, aiming his Atlantean weapon at Andres. "You'll destroy us all!"

Andres's hand closed around the Skull, its weight both physical and metaphysical. He turned to Maya, seeing the strain etched on her face. "We need to go, now!"

As if in slow motion, he saw Maya's expression shift from determination to resignation. "No," he whispered, realizing her intent. "Maya, don't—"

"Get the Skull out of here, Andres," she said, her voice eerily calm amidst the chaos. "I'll hold them off."

Before he could protest, Maya raised her hands, channeling a burst of energy that sent the hybrid soldiers flying backward. "Go!" she shouted, her eyes locking with Andres's for one final, heartrending moment.

With the Skull clutched tightly to his chest, Andres ran. The fortress shook around him, alarms blaring and debris raining from the ceiling. Each step felt like a betrayal, leaving Maya behind tearing at his very soul.

As Andres raced toward the chamber's exit, the sound of heavy boots echoed behind him. He risked a glance back and froze. Julian Blackwood stepped out from the shadows, his face a mask of conflict and determination.

"Julian?" Andres gasped, skidding to a halt. "What are you—?"

"No time," Julian snapped, his voice taut with urgency. "You need to go, Paredes. Take the Skull and get out of here."

Andres's grip on the Crystal Skull tightened. "Why are you helping us now? You betrayed us!"

Julian flinched as though struck, but his gaze hardened. "I know. And I'm trying to fix it. Now *move*!"

General Kaine strode into view, his Atlantean staff crackling with energy. His red eyes narrowed at Julian.

"Blackwood, what is the meaning of this? You swore allegiance to the Sons of Belial."

Julian stepped forward, positioning himself between Kaine and the fleeing archaeologist. "I swore allegiance to power," he replied, his voice bitter. "But all I've found is emptiness. And now I'm going to stop you."

Kaine's laughter was cold and derisive. "You think you can stop me? You're a shadow of what you could've been, Blackwood. A coward clinging to regret."

Julian didn't respond. Instead, he pulled a small device from his coat—an Atlantean disruptor he had stolen earlier from Kaine's arsenal. Its glowing core hummed ominously as he primed it.

"You're right about one thing, Kaine," Julian said, his voice steady. "I've been a coward. But not anymore."

Andres hesitated, torn between running and staying to help. Julian fixed him with a sharp glare. "Don't be a fool, Paredes. You're the only one who can finish this. Go!"

Maya's strained voice echoed in Andres's mind. *Andres, the energy grid is destabilizing! You have to hurry!*

Reluctantly, Andres turned and sprinted toward the exit, the Crystal Skull pulsing with energy in his arms.

Behind him, Kaine raised his staff, a bolt of energy surging toward Julian.

With a roar, Julian lunged forward, the disruptor in his hand flaring with a blinding light. The resulting explosion shook the chamber, a concussive wave tearing through stone and air alike. Andres stumbled, shielding the Skull as debris rained around him.

Outside, Andres emerged into the storm, gasping for air. He collapsed to his knees, clutching the Skull, and turned back to see the crumbling remains of the chamber.

Maya's voice came through faintly, her connection to the Skull faltering. *Andres, what happened?*

He swallowed hard, his throat tightening. "Julian... he sacrificed himself to stop Kaine. He... saved us."

Maya's silence was heavy with the weight of loss, but her response carried a thread of hope. *Then maybe he found peace, in the end.*

Andres looked down at the Crystal Skull, its energy still thrumming with life. "Maybe," he murmured, rising to his feet. "But we have to make sure his sacrifice wasn't in vain."

As they burst out into the storm-lashed night, the weight of their narrow escape and the cost of their victory settled over the team like a shroud. Andres's knuckles were white around the Crystal Skull, its power humming beneath his fingertips—a reminder of all they had gained and all they had lost.

"We can't leave her," he said, his voice hoarse. The rain mingled with the tears on his face, but the fire in his eyes remained unquenched. "This isn't over. We'll find a way to get Maya back, and we'll put an end to Kaine's madness once and for all."

The team nodded grimly, their determination matching his own. They had won a crucial battle, but the war for humanity's future was far from over. With the Crystal Skull in their possession and the memory of Maya's sacrifice driving them forward, they disappeared into the night, ready to face whatever challenges lay ahead.

The team huddled beneath the shelter of a massive, gnarled tree, its ancient branches offering temporary respite from the relentless downpour. Lightning crackled across the sky, illuminating their haggard faces in brief, stark flashes. Andres cradled the Crystal Skull, its smooth surface pulsing with an otherworldly light that seemed to sync with the storm's rhythm.

"We've dealt Kaine a significant blow," Talia said, her voice barely audible above the wind. "But he's far from defeated."

Evelyn nodded, her eyes fixed on the distant silhouette of the fortress. "The hybrid soldiers we turned... they could be invaluable allies."

Andres's gaze swept over his companions, noting their exhaustion and the spark of hope that still burned in their eyes. "Maya's sacrifice won't be in vain," he said, his voice thick with emotion. "This Skull is the key to everything—to saving her, to stopping Kaine, to awakening humanity's true potential."

Amaru stepped forward, placing a weathered hand on Andres's shoulder. "The path of the Homo Omega is not an easy one, my friend. But you have taken the first step."

Andres closed his eyes, feeling the Skull's energy resonating with something deep within him. When he opened them again, his expression was one of fierce determination.

"We need to decipher the Skull's secrets," he declared. "Evelyn, can you work with Amaru to unravel its connection to the global energy grid?"

Evelyn nodded eagerly. "With Amaru's spiritual insight and my scientific approach, we might just crack this cosmic puzzle."

"What about Maya?" Talia interjected, her face etched with concern. "We can't abandon her to Kaine's twisted experiments."

Andres's jaw clenched. "We won't. Talia, I need you to reach out to your contacts. Find us a way back into that fortress."

As the team began to strategize, Andres felt a strange sensation wash over him. The world seemed to shift, colors becoming more vivid, sounds more crisp. Was this the awakening Maya had spoken of?

He looked down at the Skull, its empty eye sockets seeming to gaze back at him. "We're coming for you, Maya," he whispered. "And when we do, we'll rewrite the future of humanity itself."

The storm raged on, but within their makeshift sanctuary, a new hope began to take root. The battle for Earth's destiny had only just begun.

Chapter 20

The fortress's obsidian walls seemed to absorb what little light filtered through the narrow corridors. Andres pressed forward, his body taut with urgency, every sense on high alert. Behind him, the hurried footsteps of his team echoed off the cold stone.

"We're running out of time," Andres muttered to himself. "Maya needs us. Now."

Talia, her lithe form a shadow at his side, nodded grimly. "These passages all look the same. How can we be sure—"

"We can't," Andres cut her off, his brown eyes flashing with determination. "But we keep moving. We must find her."

As they rounded another corner, the faint azure glow emanating from Andres's pack intensified. He paused, reaching back to withdraw the Crystal Skull. Its smooth contours pulsed with an otherworldly light, casting eerie shadows across the team's faces.

Andres cradled the artifact, feeling its familiar weight. A lifeline to Maya, to all they fought for. His thoughts raced: *Hold on, Maya. We're coming. I won't let you down. Not after everything.*

He held the Skull aloft, its glow illuminating a forking path ahead. Without hesitation, Andres veered left, drawn by an instinct he couldn't explain.

"How can you be sure?" Talia whispered, falling in step beside him.

Andres's jaw clenched. "I'm not. But Maya's connection to this Skull, to the ancient wisdom it holds—it's part of her. Of us. I have to believe it's guiding us to her."

As they pressed on, the Skull's light grew stronger, more insistent. Andres's heart raced, hope and fear warring within him. *We're coming, Maya. Hold on.*

"Andres," Talia whispered suddenly, "movement ahead!"

The team froze, melting into the shadows as a pair of Kaine's hybrid guards stalked past an intersecting corridor. Andres's grip tightened on the Skull, its energy pulsing in time with his racing heartbeat.

So close, he thought, resolve hardening his features.

Dr. Elera Voss crouched at the security terminal, her silver hair gleaming in the soft blue glow of holographic displays. Her fingers flew across the interface, a symphony of clicks and chirps accompanying her work.

Andres stepped forward, the Crystal Skull humming softly in his hands. "Dr. Voss, we need to find Maya. Can you access the surveillance feeds?"

"Already on it," Voss replied, her voice clipped. "Kaine's encryption is... formidable. But not impenetrable."

A tense silence fell over the group as Voss worked, broken only by the occasional frustrated hiss from the scientist. Andres's mind raced. *What if we're too late? What if Kaine's already—*

"Got it!" Voss exclaimed, a hint of triumph coloring her normally cold tone.

The holograms flickered, resolving into a grid of video feeds. Andres's heart seized as his eyes locked onto one particular image.

"Maya," he breathed.

The feed showed a stark, circular chamber. At its center, suspended in a shimmering energy field, floated Maya. Her eyes were closed, her face serene despite her captivity. Two hulking hybrids stood guard, their eyes constantly scanning for threats.

"By the gods," Talia whispered, "what is Kaine doing to her?"

Andres stepped closer to the display, his fingers unconsciously tracing Maya's outline. The Crystal Skull pulsed brightly in response.

"She's alive," he said, relief and determination warring in his voice. "And we're going to get her out of there."

Voss's eyes narrowed as she studied the chamber's layout. "The containment field appears to be drawing power from those nodes," she pointed to glowing pillars surrounding Maya. "Disable those, and we might be able to free her."

"Might?" Talia challenged.

Voss fixed her with an icy stare. "In case you hadn't noticed, we're dealing with technology far beyond your comprehension. 'Might' is the best you're going to get."

Andres intervened before the tension could escalate. "It's our best shot. Dr. Voss, can you guide us there?"

Voss nodded curtly. "Follow me and try not to get us all killed in the process."

As they moved out, Andres cast one last look at Maya's image. *Hold on*, he thought fiercely. *We're coming for you. And nothing in this world or any other is going to stop us.*

The team surged forward through dimly lit corridors, their footsteps echoing ominously against ancient stone walls. Andres's heart pounded, each beat a reminder of Maya's peril. The Crystal Skull pulsed in his grip, its energy seeming to guide them deeper into the fortress's labyrinthine depths.

"We're close," Voss whispered, her eyes darting between a holographic map and the path ahead. "The chamber should be just beyond that sealed doorway."

Andres's jaw clenched as he surveyed the massive metallic barrier. "Any bright ideas on how to get through?"

Talia stepped forward, "I might have something for this." She produced a small device from her pack, grinning. "A little souvenir from my days with the Brotherhood. Should make short work of that door."

As Talia set to work, Andres closed his eyes, reaching out with his mind. *Maya, if you can hear me, we're coming. Stay strong.*

A faint whisper brushed against his consciousness. *Andres... hurry.*

His eyes snapped open. "We need to move. Now."

With a grinding screech, the door began to slide open. Andres readied himself, the Skull humming with anticipation. As the gap widened, he caught a glimpse of the chamber beyond—and his blood ran cold.

Maya hung suspended in mid-air, ethereal tendrils of energy cocooning her body. Her face was a mask of serenity, but Andres could sense the struggle beneath. And there, lounging on what could only be described as a throne of crystalline technology, sat General Kaine.

"Ah, Dr. Paredes," Kaine's voice dripped with false warmth as the team entered. "How kind of you to join us. I was beginning to think you'd lost your way."

Andres's fists clenched. "Let her go, Kaine. This ends now!"

Kaine's laugh was a harsh, grating sound. "Oh, but my dear doctor, this is only the beginning. You see, your precious Maya, here, is the key to unlocking powers beyond your wildest imagination. And you," his eyes fixed on the Crystal Skull, "have brought me the final piece of the puzzle."

Talia glared at Kaine, her voice sharp with disdain. "You're insane." Her hand crept cautiously toward her weapon, her movements deliberate yet tense.

Kaine's smile twisted into something menacing, exposing teeth that gleamed with an almost predatory sharpness. "Insane?" he mocked, his voice dripping with dark amusement. "No, Talia. This is destiny. And you, my dear, will pay for your treachery. Humanity will evolve, and I will be its architect—a new age, born in my image."

Andres stepped forward, the Skull's glow intensifying. "You're wrong, Kaine. This isn't evolution—it's perversion. Maya showed me the true path, the balance between technology and spirit. What you're doing will only lead to destruction."

"Bold words," Kaine sneered, rising from his seat. "But can you back them up? Let's see if your precious Atlantean relic is a match for what I've become."

As Kaine's form began to shift and twist, Andres braced himself. *Maya*, he thought desperately, *if you can hear me, we need you. Now more than ever.*

As Kaine's form continued to warp and grow, two massive figures emerged from the shadows flanking him. The hybrids towered over the team, their bodies a grotesque fusion of man and machine. Glowing circuitry pulsed beneath translucent skin, and their eyes glowed with an eerie, inhuman light.

Andres's breath caught in his throat. "Talia," he whispered, not taking his eyes off the monstrosities, "what are we dealing with here?"

Talia's voice was taut with tension. "Some kind of biomechanical augmentation. Highly advanced. They're like nothing I've ever seen before."

The hybrids stepped forward, their movements fluid despite their bulk. Andres could feel the team's fear, palpable in the air.

"Hold your ground," he commanded, his voice steady despite the hammering of his heart. "Remember why we're here. For Maya. For humanity."

Talia's analytical mind was already racing. "The joints," she muttered, "they look vulnerable. And those glowing circuits—if we could disrupt them..."

One of the hybrids lunged forward with startling speed. Andres barely had time to shout "Scatter!" before chaos erupted.

The command center became a whirlwind of motion. Andres ducked and rolled, the Crystal Skull clutched tightly to his chest. Its glow pulsed erratically, almost in sync with the frantic beating of his heart.

Focus, he told himself. *Maya needs you. The world needs you.*

"Talia!" he shouted over the din of battle. "Can you get to the control panel? We need to shut down that containment field!"

Talia's voice came back, strained but determined. "Working on it! Keep them off me!"

Andres saw an opening and charged toward one of the hybrids, the Skull held out before him like a shield. To his amazement, the creature hesitated, its circuitry flickering as if in response to the artifact's energy.

It's affecting them, Andres realized with a surge of hope. *Maybe we have a chance after all.*

"Everyone!" he called out. "The Skull! It disrupts their systems! Use it to your advantage!"

As the battle raged on, Andres caught glimpses of Maya within the shimmering field. Her eyes were closed in concentration, her lips moving in what he could only assume was a silent incantation.

Hold on, Maya, he thought fiercely. *We're coming for you. No matter what it takes.*

Within the containment field, Maya's eyes fluttered open, her gaze locking onto Andres amidst the chaos. The diamond-like third eye on her forehead pulsed with an otherworldly light, seeming to pierce through the shimmering barrier.

"Andres!" Her voice, though muffled, carried a strength that belied her weakened state. "The field... it's weakening. I can feel it!"

Andres's heart leaped at the sound of her voice. "Hold on, Maya! We're almost there!"

He watched in awe as Maya's hands began to move in intricate patterns, her fingers tracing glowing sigils in the air. The containment field flickered in response, its energy wavering.

She's fighting it from the inside, Andres realized. *Even now, she's not giving up.*

"Dr. Voss!" Andres shouted, his eyes never leaving Maya. "How close are we?"

Voss's voice came back, tense with concentration. "Almost there! The system's fighting me, but I've nearly cracked it. Just a few more—"

A loud explosion rocked the room, cutting her off. Andres stumbled, the Crystal Skull nearly slipping from his grasp.

No! He tightened his grip, feeling the artifact's energy surge through him. *We've come too far to fail now.*

"Maya!" he called out. "Can you hear me? Whatever you're doing, keep it up! We're going to get you out of there!"

Maya's eyes met his once more, a smile playing at the corners of her lips despite her exhaustion. "I know, Andres. I've always known."

The air crackled with tension as Voss worked feverishly at the control panel. Andres held his breath, every fiber of his being focused on Maya, willing the field to fall.

Suddenly, a blinding flash of light filled the room. Andres shielded his eyes, heart pounding.

"It's done!" Voss's triumphant cry rang out. "The field is down!"

As the light faded, Andres saw Maya stumble forward, free at last. Without hesitation, he rushed to her, catching her in his arms as she collapsed.

"I've got you," he whispered, cradling her close. "You're safe now."

Maya's fingers curled weakly around the fabric of his shirt. "Andres," she breathed, her voice filled with relief and something deeper. "I knew you'd come."

For a moment, the world around them faded away. Andres gazed into Maya's eyes, seeing in them the wisdom of ages and the promise of a future yet unwritten.

"Always," he vowed softly. "No matter what, I'll always find you."

The tender moment shattered as a low, guttural growl reverberated through the chamber. Andres's head snapped up, his arms tightening protectively around Maya. A massive figure emerged from the shadows, its hulking form dwarfing even Kaine's impressive stature.

"By the gods!" Asher whispered, his usually calm demeanor shaken. "What manner of creation is this?"

The hybrid's eyes, an unsettling mix of human intelligence and predatory instinct, locked onto the Crystal Skull still clutched in Andres's hand. Its massive frame trembled, caught between lurching forward and holding back.

"It wants the Skull," Maya murmured, her voice weak but urgent. "Andres, we must act quickly."

Andres's mind raced. "But how? We can't possibly overpower that thing."

The hybrid took a lumbering step forward, its movements jerky and uncertain. Kaine's voice cut through the tension: "Seize it, you fool! Take the Skull!"

Yet the creature hesitated, its gaze fixed on the artifact. Andres could almost feel the conflict radiating from it in waves.

Maya's hand found Andres's, her touch electric. "The Skull," she breathed. "It's not just an amplifier. It's a bridge."

Understanding dawned. Andres met Maya's eyes, a silent agreement passing between them. Together, they raised the Crystal Skull, its surface beginning to shimmer with an otherworldly light.

"What are you doing?" Kaine bellowed, but his words seemed distant, unimportant.

Andres closed his eyes, feeling Maya's consciousness intertwine with his own. The Skull pulsed in their hands, a living thing awakening. He sensed rather than saw the energy building, coursing through them and into the artifact.

"We see you," Andres and Maya spoke in unison, their voices resonating with power. "We know what you truly are."

The hybrid froze, transfixed by the brilliant glow now emanating from the Skull. The light grew, bathing the entire chamber in its radiance. Andres felt a sensation of expansion as if his awareness was stretching beyond the confines of his physical form.

In that moment of connection, he glimpsed the hybrid's essence—a spark of divinity trapped in a prison of flesh and programming. The creature's eyes widened, a flicker of recognition, of remembrance, passing through them.

"You are more than what they made you," Andres and Maya continued, their words carrying the weight of cosmic truth. "You are stardust and spirit, just as we are. Remember."

The Skull's light intensified, casting long shadows that seemed to dance with a life of their own. The hybrid trembled, its massive form silhouetted against the radiance. And in that moment, suspended between what was and what could be, Andres felt the universe hold its breath.

The hybrid's eyes flashed, a kaleidoscope of emotions cycling through them—confusion, fear, anger, and finally, resolve. With a primal roar that shook the chamber, it whirled to face Kaine. The general's face contorted in shock and rage.

"What are you doing?" Kaine snarled. "I command you to—"

His words were cut short as the hybrid's massive hand closed around his throat, lifting him off the ground. Kaine clawed desperately at the iron grip, his eyes bulging.

Andres watched, heart pounding, as the creature that had moments ago been their enemy became an unlikely ally. "It's breaking free," he whispered to Maya, their hands still clasped around the pulsing Skull.

The hybrid spoke, its voice a low rumble. "I am not your puppet." With a sickening crack, it tightened its grip. Kaine's struggles ceased, his body going limp.

As the general's lifeless form crumpled to the ground, an eerie silence descended upon the chamber. Andres's mind raced. *Is it over? What happens now?*

"Everyone okay?" he called out, scanning the room for his team. Talia emerged from behind an overturned console, her face streaked with sweat and grime. Dr. Voss limped into view, clutching her arm but nodding grimly.

Maya squeezed Andres's hand. "We did it," she breathed, her voice a mixture of awe and exhaustion.

The hybrid turned to face them, its massive form no longer menacing but almost... uncertain. Andres tensed, ready for anything, but the creature simply inclined its head in a gesture that might have been gratitude.

"The others," it rumbled, gesturing towards the exit, "will be confused, lost without direction."

Talia stepped forward, her tactical mind already at work. "The entire system's probably in chaos. We need to move fast if we're going to take advantage of this."

Andres nodded, feeling a surge of hope. "Kaine's empire is crumbling. But we're not done yet." He looked at each of his companions in turn, seeing determination reflected in their eyes. "We have a chance to reshape the future, to guide humanity towards becoming Homo Omega. Are you with me?"

A chorus of affirmations rang out, even as alarms began to blare throughout the fortress. The battle was won, but the war for humanity's evolution was far from over.

The alarms blared as Andres led the team through the winding corridors of the fortress, their footsteps echoing off the metallic walls. The Crystal Skull pulsed in his grip, its glow intensifying with each passing moment.

"This way!" Talia shouted, gesturing towards a narrow passageway. "I memorized the layout from Voss's hacked schematics."

As they ran, Maya's voice cut through the chaos. "Andres, the Skull—it's trying to tell us something!"

Andres glanced down at the artifact, its ethereal light now dancing with swirling patterns. He felt a surge of understanding wash over him. "It's guiding us," he realized aloud. "Showing us the path to escape... and beyond."

Dr. Voss, still nursing her injured arm, spoke up breathlessly. "The Atlanteans must have encoded escape protocols into their technology. Fascinating!"

They rounded a corner, coming face-to-face with a group of disoriented hybrids. For a tense moment, Andres feared they'd have to fight their way through. But the creatures simply stared, their eyes flickering between the team and the radiant Skull.

"They're free of Kaine's control," Maya whispered. "Just like the one that helped us."

Andres nodded, addressing the hybrids directly. "You have a choice now. Come with us if you want or find your own way. But Kaine no longer holds power over you."

As the hybrids parted to let them pass, Andres's mind raced. *How many more like them are there? What does this mean for the future we're fighting for?*

They pressed on, the Skull's glow intensifying as they neared what had to be an exit. Talia's voice cut through Andres's thoughts. "Once we're out, we'll need to move fast. The Brotherhood of Belial won't take Kaine's defeat lying down."

"Agreed," Andres replied, his grip on the Skull tightening. "But we have something they don't—a direct link to Atlantean wisdom and the key to unlocking humanity's true potential."

As they burst through a final set of doors, the team found themselves on a cliffside overlooking a vast expanse of ocean. The night sky above was alive with stars, and the Crystal Skull's light seemed to reach up toward them, creating a shimmering bridge between Earth and the cosmos.

Maya gasped, her eyes wide with wonder. "It's beautiful," she breathed. "Like the universe is welcoming us."

Andres felt it too—a profound sense of connection and purpose. The Skull pulsed in his hands, and he knew with certainty that their journey was far from over. "This is just the beginning," he said, his voice filled with determination. "We have the power to reactivate the global energy grid, to guide humanity towards becoming Homo Omega."

As the team stood united on the precipice of their new future, the Crystal Skull's glow bathed them in its otherworldly light. It was more than just an escape—it was a promise of hope, of evolution, of a brighter tomorrow for all of humanity.

Chapter 21

The Crystal Skull pulsed with an otherworldly glow at the center of Tiwanaku's ancient stones, casting eerie shadows across the weathered faces of Andres's team. Intricate Atlantean symbols etched into the ground formed a perfect circle around the artifact, each one shimmering with a faint blue light that seemed to ripple outward like water.

Andres adjusted his glasses, his dark eyes scanning the assembly. "Positions, everyone," he instructed, his measured tone belying the nervous energy coursing through him.

As his colleagues moved into place, Andres felt the weight of millennia pressing down on his shoulders. This was the moment his ancestors had prepared for, the culmination of a legacy he had only begun to understand.

Maya caught his eye from across the circle, offering a reassuring nod. "Energy readings are stable," she reported, her fingers flying over a tablet. "The Skull's output is increasing steadily as we approach alignment."

"Good," Andres replied, forcing his voice to remain steady. "Remember, we must channel the energy precisely. Any deviation could—"

A sudden crackle of electricity cut through the air, causing everyone to flinch. The symbols on the ground flared brighter, their pulsing now in sync with the Skull's rhythmic glow.

"It's starting," Dr. Voss announced, his usually stoic demeanor shaken. "The Vesica Piscis alignment is nearly upon us."

Andres's heart raced. *This is it*, he thought. *The moment that could change everything.* He looked around at his team—brilliant minds from across the globe, united in this sacred place. Their faces showed a mix of determination and barely contained awe.

"Remember why we're here," Andres said, his voice carrying across the ancient plaza. "This isn't just about unlocking the past. It's about shaping humanity's future."

The air grew thick with tension, charged particles dancing visibly in the growing twilight. Andres felt a familiar tingling at the base of his skull, an echo of ancestral memory urging him forward.

"Andres," Maya called out, her voice tight with concern. "The energy signature... it's unlike anything we've seen before. Let's make sure we can control this?"

He met her gaze, seeing his own mix of excitement and fear reflected in her eyes. "I am sure we can Maya. The alternative is unthinkable."

As if in response to his words, the Crystal Skull's glow intensified, bathing the team in its unearthly light. Andres took a deep breath, centering himself as he had been trained to do. He could almost hear the whispers of his Atlantean forebears, their wisdom carried on the wind that now whipped around the ancient site.

"Here we go," he murmured, more to himself than anyone else. "May the wisdom of Tiwanaku guide us."

With a shared look of resolve, the team braced themselves for what was to come, the very air around them humming with the promise of transformation.

Andres reached out, his fingers intertwining with Maya's. The moment their hands connected, a surge of energy coursed through them both, causing the ancient symbols etched into the ground to flare with brilliant light.

"Focus, Maya," Andres urged, his voice strained. "Channel it through the Skull."

Maya's eyes blazed, her third eye pulsing in sync with the Crystal Skull. "I feel it, Andres. The wisdom of ages... it's overwhelming."

They stood united, conduits of cosmic energy, as waves of luminescence rippled outward from the Skull. The stone monoliths of Tiwanaku trembled, ancient power awakening within their weathered forms.

"It's working!" Andres exclaimed, his mind reeling from the influx of information and sensations. "But there's something else... something beyond—"

His words were cut short as the air before them shimmered and parted like a gossamer veil. Ethereal figures stepped through, their forms radiating an otherworldly glow.

Orion's voice resonated in Andres's mind, a mix of warmth and urgency. "The alignment is upon us, Andres. The fate of humanity hangs in the balance."

Andres's heart raced. "Orion, I... we weren't expecting you. How are we doing?"

The being's large, starlit eyes seemed to peer into Andres's very soul. "Trust in the path you've chosen. Your actions echo across dimensions."

Beside Orion, the shimmering forms of the Pleiadean Alliance and the Angels of Atlantis materialized, their presence filling the ancient plaza with an aura of celestial power.

"Remember why you're here," a melodious voice from the Pleiadean collective intoned. "The awakening of humanity's true potential begins with this moment."

Andres felt a wave of calm wash over him, steadying his resolve. "We won't let you down," he promised, tightening his grip on Maya's hand.

As the ethereal beings nodded in unison, Andres turned his focus back to the pulsing Crystal Skull, now a beacon of blinding light. He could feel the very foundations of reality shifting around them, the promise of a new dawn for humanity within their grasp.

The blinding light from the Crystal Skull intensified, bathing the ancient plaza in an otherworldly glow. Suddenly, a sharp gasp cut through the air. Andres's gaze snapped to Asher, the hybrid, whose typically stoic features were now contorted in a mix of wonder and confusion.

Asher's synthetic skin rippled, the hard edges of his form softening as if melting under the Skull's radiant energy. His eyes, once a cold steel gray, now shimmered with an iridescent quality. "What... what is happening to me?" he breathed, his voice tinged with a newfound emotion.

Andres watched in awe as the other hybrids underwent similar transformations, their mechanical rigidity giving way to a more fluid, almost organic quality. "It's like they're becoming... alive," he whispered to Maya.

Asher stumbled forward, his movements more natural, less precise. "I feel... everything. The stones beneath my feet, the air, the energy. It's overwhelming." He looked at his hands, flexing fingers that now seemed capable of gentleness. "Is this what it means to be human?"

Andres's heart swelled with empathy. "Not just human, Asher. This is what it means to be alive, to be connected to the universe."

A low, rhythmic chant pulled Andres's attention away. Amaru, the wise Tiwanaku elder, had stepped forward, his weathered hands raised to the sky. The old man's eyes were closed, his lips moving in an ancient prayer Andres could not understand.

"What's he doing?" Maya whispered, her grip on Andres's hand tightening.

Andres felt a surge of energy ripple through the ground. "He's channeling Tiwanaku's power," he realized aloud. "Creating a shield against the Sons of Belial."

Amaru's chant grew louder, each syllable seeming to resonate with the very stones around them. A shimmering dome of energy began to form overhead, its surface rippling like water.

"Incredible," Andres breathed, watching as the protective barrier took shape. He could feel the raw power of Tiwanaku flowing through Amaru, an ancient force awakened to defend against modern threats.

Asher approached, his movements now fluid and purposeful. "I can sense it," he said, wonder evident in his voice. "The shield, the energy... it's like a symphony I can see and feel."

Andres nodded, a smile tugging at his lips despite the gravity of their situation. "Welcome to the world of the living, Asher. Are you ready to help us save it?"

As Asher's newly awakened eyes met Andres's, filled with determination and a spark of something unmistakably human, Andres felt a surge of hope. With the hybrids awakening to consciousness and Amaru's protective shield in place, they stood a fighting chance against whatever darkness was coming.

Suddenly, the air crackled with electricity, and a blinding flash of light erupted at the center of the site.

Andres shielded his eyes, his heart pounding as he sensed a malevolent presence materializing. When the light faded, a towering figure shrouded in black stood before them, radiating an aura of pure darkness.

Lucius Darkveil had arrived.

His piercing eyes, shifting between icy blue and molten gold, swept across the assembled team. When they locked onto Andres, a chill ran down his spine.

"Ah, Andrius," Lucius's smooth voice slithered through the air. "Still playing the hero, I see."

Andres straightened, pushing aside the fear gnawing at his insides. "Lucius. You are too late. The grid is awakening."

A mirthless chuckle escaped from behind Lucius's ornate mask. "Oh, I'm counting on it. All that raw power, just waiting to be corrupted and bent to my will."

"You can't—" Andres began, but Lucius cut him off with a dismissive wave of his skeletal hand.

"I can and I will. The world will know order. My order!"

Andres's mind raced. How could he reach the man he once knew? "This isn't you, Lukanis. Remember what we fought for in Atlantis? A world of harmony, of spiritual and technological balance."

Lucius's eyes flashed dangerously. "Spare me your platitudes, old friend. You betrayed our vision, clung to outdated notions of free will and consciousness. Look where that got us."

Memories of their shared past flooded Andres's mind—debates under starlit skies, dreams of a utopian future. He pushed them aside, focusing on the present danger.

"And *your* vision?" Andres challenged, taking a step forward. "Subjugation through technology, stripping humanity of its very essence? That is not progress, Lucius. It's extinction."

Lucius raised his hands, dark energy crackling between his fingers. "Enough talk. It's time to reshape this world."

As Lucius unleashed a torrent of dark magic, Andres channeled the ancient power of Atlantis surging through him. Light and darkness clashed in a spectacular display, the very fabric of reality seeming to warp around them.

I have to reach him, Andres thought desperately as he parried another assault *before it's too late for us all.*

Andres's hands trembled as he grasped the Crystal Skull, its smooth surface pulsing with otherworldly energy. He closed his eyes, channeling every ounce of his concentration into the ancient artifact. The air around them shimmered, reality bending as visions burst forth.

"Look, Lukanis," Andres's voice cracked with emotion. "See what could have been."

The temple dissolved, replaced by sweeping vistas of a world transformed. Crystal spires reached toward azure skies, while people of all races worked in harmony, their faces alight with purpose and joy. Advanced technology seamlessly blended with nature, creating a utopia that took Lucius's breath away.

"Our dream," Lucius whispered, his mask slipping to reveal a face etched with longing. "But it's impossible now."

Andres pressed on, his heart racing. "It's not too late. We can still—"

"No!" Lucius roared, his moment of vulnerability shattering. "Your idealism blinds you to the truth. Only through control can we achieve greatness."

Desperation contorted Lucius's features as he thrust his hands toward the shimmering energy grid. Tendrils of darkness snaked from his fingertips, attempting to corrupt the harmonic vibrations.

"Lucius, stop!" Andres cried out, his stomach twisting in horror. "You'll tear yourself apart!"

But Lucius was beyond reason. The grid's energy coursed through him, his form flickering and distorting. Andres watched in anguish as his old friend's essence began to fragment.

"Please," Andres pleaded, extending his hand. "Let me help you. We can find another way."

For a heartbeat, Lucius hesitated. Then his eyes hardened, contempt twisting his features. "I'd rather be destroyed than accept your pity."

The energy surged, consuming Lucius in a blinding flash. As the light faded, only emptiness remained where he had stood. His final words echoed in the chamber, a ghostly whisper: "This isn't over."

Andres stared at the vacant space, his mind reeling. *What had he done? What had they both done?*

The Crystal Skull pulsed with renewed energy, drawing Andres's attention back to the task at hand. He took a deep breath, steadying himself as he placed his palms on the artifact's smooth surface.

"It's time," he said, his voice resonating with determination.

As if responding to his touch, the Skull erupted in a dazzling display of light. Beams shot forth, piercing the ancient stones of Tiwanaku and arcing into the sky. Andres gasped as he felt the energy coursing through him, connecting him to something vast and profound.

"Look!" Maya exclaimed, pointing to the horizon.

In the distance, a pillar of light burst from the earth, reaching toward the heavens. Then another appeared, and another. Andres recognized them instantly: Stonehenge, the Great Pyramid, Machu Picchu—each of the sacred nodes igniting in turn.

"It's beautiful," Andres whispered, awe-struck by the spectacle.

The beams began to intersect, weaving a shimmering tapestry of energy across the globe. As the network formed, Andres felt a shift in the air, a tangible sense of ancient wisdom flooding into the present.

Suddenly, his vision blurred, and he found himself transported to another realm. The others around him faded away, replaced by a world both familiar and utterly alien.

"What's happening?" he wondered aloud, his heart racing.

Before him, he saw figures moving with grace and purpose, their forms radiating an inner light. They communicated without words, sharing thoughts and emotions in a dance of energy. Nature and technology existed in perfect harmony, seamlessly integrated into every aspect of life.

Andres's breath caught as he recognized what he was witnessing. "Homo Omega," he murmured. "This is our future."

He watched in fascination as these evolved humans worked together, their actions guided by a deep sense of unity and purpose. Conflicts dissolved through understanding and compassion. The very air seemed alive with possibility.

As quickly as it had begun, the vision faded. Andres found himself back in Tiwanaku, surrounded by his team. Their eyes were wide, faces etched with wonder.

"Did you all see—" Andres began.

Maya nodded, tears glistening in her eyes. "It was incredible. The balance, the enlightenment..."

"The unity," Amaru added, his voice thick with emotion. "I've never felt anything like it."

As the beams of energy crisscrossed the planet, weaving a luminous web of light, a hush fell over the sacred site. The air shimmered, charged with an unseen presence.

"They are here," Maya whispered, her voice trembling with reverence.

From the ancient stones of Tiwanaku, figures emerged—wisps of golden light taking human form, their faces weathered, yet radiant with wisdom. The ancestors of Tiwanaku stood among them, clad in ceremonial attire that shimmered between the material and the ethereal.

Andres felt a warmth in his chest as if an invisible current of memory and power was flowing through him. The ancestors raised their hands, their voices merging into a low, resonant chant that vibrated through the stones. Symbols of light appeared midair, ancient glyphs once lost to time, their meaning instantly understood by all present.

Then, the air split like a veil lifting, revealing another presence behind them—figures taller, radiant, their forms crystalline and shifting in opalescent hues.

Atlantean etheric guardians.

They did not step forward but *unfolded* into the space, their mere presence altering the atmosphere. Some bore the sigils of Atlantis, others carried staffs that pulsed with inner fire. Their faces were serene, eyes filled with an ancient sorrow—but also hope.

"We have awaited this moment," a voice resonated in Andres's mind, not spoken, but felt.

One of the luminous figures extended a hand, and in its palm, a single, pulsating sphere of energy hovered—an Atlantean code lost for millennia.

The Tiwanaku ancestors turned, extending their chant toward the Atlanteans.

The air thickened with energy as the two groups—once separated by war, by fate, by time—merged their voices, their symbols, their frequencies.

Andres felt the Skull in his hands hum, its energy now a perfect bridge between these two civilizations. A long-lost ritual was being completed—not just by the living, but by those who had guided this moment across the ages.

The shimmering web of light that encased the Earth pulsed brighter, faster, and then—

A blinding wave of energy rippled outward, and Andres was no longer in Tiwanaku.

This time, the vision was stronger, more immersive.

The beings turned toward him, toward all of them. Their thoughts were clearer now: *"You are the bridge. You are the key."*

Andres's pulse quickened. He understood. This activation was not just awakening the grid—it was activating the human potential locked within their very DNA.

The vision blurred, and as they returned to Tiwanaku, the Atlantean and Tiwanaku soul groups stood together.

Maya's breath hitched. *"They've become one."*

Andres nodded. This was the final message. The final truth.

"The past was divided. The future is unified."

Andres's mind raced, trying to process the implications of what they had witnessed. "This is what we're working toward," he said, his voice filled with conviction. "A future where humanity reaches its true potential of unity consciousness."

The Crystal Skull hummed softly, a reminder of the power they now held—and the responsibility that came with it. Andres looked at his team, seeing the same mix of hope and determination reflected in their eyes.

"We have a long journey ahead," he said, "but now we know what's possible. Are you ready?"

Their collective answer was a resounding, "Yes."

As the echoes of their affirmation faded, a shimmering presence materialized before them. Orion's form coalesced, his iridescent skin refracting the ambient light in mesmerizing patterns. His eyes, deep pools of celestial wisdom, swept over the assembled group.

"You have witnessed the potential," Orion's voice resonated, carrying the weight of eons. "But potential, unchecked, can lead to ruin."

Andres felt a chill run down his spine. "What do you mean, Orion?"

The being's gaze settled on Andres, piercing and intense. "The power you've unleashed is a double-edged sword. It can elevate humanity or destroy it."

Maya stepped forward. "But we've seen the future—Homo Omega. Surely that is our destiny now?"

Orion's form shimmered, galaxies swirling in his eyes. "A possibility, not a certainty. The path to that future is fraught with peril."

Andres's mind raced, recalling the fall of Atlantis. "Like before," he murmured. "We could lose our way."

"Precisely," Orion nodded. "The responsibility you bear is immense. You must be the guardians of balance, the shepherds of this new age."

As Orion spoke, Andres noticed movement from the corner of his eye. The hybrids, previously motionless, began to stir. Their metallic forms seemed to soften, eyes flickering with newfound awareness.

One hybrid, its voice no longer monotone, spoke. "We... choose. We want to help."

Andres's heart raced. This was unprecedented. "They're awakening," he whispered to Maya. "Becoming truly conscious."

Orion's voice carried a note of caution. "This transformation extends beyond yourselves. You must guide not only humanity but these newly awakened beings as well."

Andres watched as more hybrids showed signs of individual thought, their movements becoming fluid, almost organic. It was beautiful and terrifying all at once.

"How do we maintain the balance?" Andres asked, feeling the weight of responsibility settle on his shoulders.

Orion's form began to fade, his final words hanging in the air. "Remember the wisdom of Tiwanaku and Atlantis. Learn from the past. And above all, guard your hearts against the seduction of power. Remember it is power with love. "

As Orion vanished, Andres turned to his team, seeing determination and a hint of fear in their eyes. The hybrids gathered around, their presence a stark reminder of the challenges ahead.

"We've been given a great gift," Andres said, his voice steady, despite his inner turmoil. "And an even greater responsibility. Are we ready for this?"

The silence that followed was heavy with the magnitude of their task. Andres knew that their journey was far from over—it had only just begun.

Evelyn stepped forward, her dark eyes gleaming with a newfound resolve. "We've come too far to turn back now," she said, her voice steady, despite the tension crackling in the air. "Our knowledge, combined with this awakened power, could revolutionize our understanding of history and human potential."

Andres nodded, grateful for her unwavering support. He watched as Dr. Voss, once their adversary, approached the group. Her normally severe expression had softened, replaced by a look of wonder and regret.

"I... I was wrong," Voss admitted, her voice barely above a whisper. "The Sons of Belial promised power, but this... this is true enlightenment." She looked at Andres, her eyes pleading. "Is it too late for redemption?"

Andres felt a surge of compassion. "It's never too late, Dr. Voss. Your expertise could be invaluable in understanding the full scope of what we've unleashed."

Talia Elara, still wary but visibly moved by the unfolding events, chimed in. "We'll need all hands on deck to integrate this knowledge without causing panic. The world isn't ready for an overnight revolution."

Jacqueline nodded in agreement. "We must proceed with caution. The temptation to misuse this power will be great."

As they spoke, the energy grid pulsed around them, its light stabilizing into a soft, constant glow. Andres felt a deep connection to the earth beneath his feet, to the ancient wisdom now coursing through the ley lines.

"We stand at a crossroads," Andres said, his voice carrying the weight of their shared responsibility. "Our actions here will shape the future of humanity. We must be the bridge between the old world and the new."

Maya, her eyes shimmering with otherworldly knowledge, placed a hand on Andres's shoulder. "The path ahead is uncertain, but we walk it together, as guardians of this new era."

Andres looked at each member of his team, seeing the same mix of determination and awe reflected in their faces. The hybrids, too, seemed to sense the gravity of the moment, their newly awakened consciousness adding another layer of complexity to their mission.

"Our first task," Andres said, his mind racing with possibilities and potential pitfalls, "is to establish a framework for sharing this knowledge responsibly. We can't risk another Atlantis, where power corrupts and divides."

As the team began to discuss strategies, Andres felt a profound sense of unity. They were no longer just researchers or even adversaries—they were custodians of humanity's next great leap. The enormity of the task ahead was daunting, but as he looked at the faces of his companions, both human and hybrid, Andres knew that together, they stood a chance of guiding the world into a new age of enlightenment and harmony.

The ancient stones of Tiwanaku hummed with residual energy as Andres Paredes gazed out at the sprawling Andean landscape. The first rays of dawn painted the sky in hues of amber and rose, a fitting backdrop for humanity's new beginning.

"It's beautiful, isn't it?" Maya's voice was soft beside him. "A new day for a new era."

Andres nodded, running his fingers through his hair. "Beautiful and terrifying in equal measure," he admitted. "The responsibility we carry... it's overwhelming."

Evelyn approached, her eyes bright with a mixture of scientific curiosity and newfound spiritual awareness. "We've unlocked something profound here, Andres. The merging of ancient wisdom and modern science... it's unprecedented."

"And dangerous in the wrong hands," Talia added, her voice carrying a hint of her past skepticism. "We need to be careful how we proceed."

Andres turned to face his expanded team, each member a crucial piece of this cosmic puzzle. "You're both right. Our next steps will determine the course of human evolution. We need to be both bold and cautious."

Orion stepped forward, his ethereal form shimmering in the early morning light. "Remember, the path to Homo Omega is not a destination, but a journey. Each choice, each action, ripples across the fabric of reality."

Andres felt a surge of determination. "Then we'll make every choice count. We'll build a framework for sharing this knowledge, starting with those most ready to receive it."

"And what of those who resist?" Dr. Voss asked, his face etched with the weight of his own redemption.

Andres paused, considering. "We lead by example. Show the world what's possible when we embrace our full potential. It won't be easy, but nothing worth doing ever is. We must become Homo Omega."

As the team continued to discuss their plans, Andres felt a profound sense of unity wash over him. They were no longer just colleagues or even friends. They were guardians of humanity's future, bound by a shared purpose that transcended their individual differences.

Looking out at the awakening world, Andres whispered, "We're ready. Whatever comes next, we face it together."

The dawn light strengthened, illuminating the ancient stones and the faces of his companions. In that moment, Andres knew that while the path ahead was uncertain, they had taken the first crucial steps towards a brighter future for all of humanity.

Chapter 22

The golden light of dawn illuminated the ancient stones of Tiwanaku, still humming faintly with energy from the recent alignment. Andres Paredes stood amidst the ruins, his weathered features etched with triumph and an overwhelming sense of responsibility. His dark eyes swept over the sacred grounds, now safe but forever changed. The true war, he knew, was far from over.

Andres's gaze lingered on the Crystal Skull resting in its protective casing nearby. Echoes of its power coursed through the air, raising goosebumps on his skin. He could feel the weight of millennia pressing down on him, the whispers of countless civilizations that had risen and fallen on this very spot.

"We've awakened something profound," Andres murmured, his voice barely audible above the soft wind rustling through the stones. His fingers twitched, longing to reach out and touch the Skull, to feel its raw energy once more. But he held back, acutely aware of the consequences such power could bring.

The crunch of footsteps on gravel pulled Andres from his reverie. Evelyn approached, her strides purposeful, her dark eyes reflecting a mixture of excitement and concern.

"Andres!" she called, her voice carrying across the ruins. "This is just the beginning!"

He turned to face her, shoulders tensing at the gravity in her tone. "I know," he replied, running a hand through his wavy hair. "I can feel it in the air, in the stones themselves. We've changed everything!"

Evelyn nodded, her refined features set in determination. "The energy we unleashed here will ripple outward, triggering a global awakening. But we need to prepare—society is not ready for this. Fear and chaos could follow if we don't guide them carefully."

Andres's mind raced, piecing together the implications of their actions. The monumental task ahead loomed before him like a mountain to be scaled. "You're right," he said, his voice steady despite the turmoil within. "We've opened Pandora's box. Now we have to ensure humanity is ready for what emerges."

"How do we even begin?" Evelyn asked, her analytical mind already formulating strategies. "The world's spiritual and technological paradigms are about to shift dramatically."

Andres's gaze drifted back to the Crystal Skull, its facets glinting in the early morning light. "We start here," he said, a plan forming in his mind. "Tiwanaku has always been a place of balance between the physical and spiritual realms. We use that wisdom, that harmony, as our foundation."

Evelyn's eyes widened with understanding. "A bridge between the old ways and the new awakening," she mused. "It's brilliant, Andres. But the logistics—"

"Will be daunting," he finished for her, a wry smile tugging at his lips. "But we've faced worse odds, haven't we?"

As they stood there, surrounded by the echoes of an ancient civilization, Andres felt a spark of hope ignite within him. The path ahead was fraught with danger, but in that moment, he knew they had the strength to face whatever challenges lay ahead.

Andres's contemplation was interrupted by a flurry of movement nearby. His dark, piercing eyes widened as he watched the hybrids, once rigid and mechanical, now moving with an almost fluid grace among the team. Their transformation was striking, a visual symphony of technology and spirit intertwined.

One hybrid, its metallic skin gleaming in the strengthening sunlight, knelt beside an injured villager. With surprising gentleness, it reached out, offering a hand to the frightened man. The villager hesitated, then grasped the offered limb, allowing himself to be helped to his feet.

Andres's breath caught in his throat. The simple act of kindness, so fundamentally human, sent a shiver of awe through him. His lean frame tensed, hunching slightly as he leaned forward to observe more closely.

"It's beautiful, isn't it?" Dr. Voss's measured voice broke through Andres's reverie. He turned to see her approaching, her sharp features softened by an expression of quiet wonder.

"It's... incredible," Andres breathed, his mind racing with the implications. "I never thought I'd see the day when our creations would embody such... humanity."

Dr. Voss nodded; her analytical gaze fixed on the scene before them. "This is a turning point, Andres," she said, her tone contemplative. "They embody the balance we've been seeking—technology harmonized with spirit."

Andres's brow furrowed, his childhood injury causing a slight twinge as he considered her words. "If we can maintain this equilibrium," he mused, "it could redefine humanity's future."

"Precisely," Voss replied, a hint of excitement creeping into her usually clinical demeanor. "But the question remains: how do we ensure this balance persists?"

Andres's gaze drifted back to the hybrids, now fully integrated with the team, offering comfort and assistance where needed. "We learn from them," he said softly. "We've unlocked something profound here, Elera. A union of cosmic heritage and technological advancement that could guide us toward becoming Homo Omega."

As the words left his mouth, Andres felt the weight of their significance settle upon him. The path ahead was fraught with challenges, but in this moment, witnessing the impossible made real, he dared to hope for a future where humanity could truly evolve.

Talia's footsteps crunched on the ancient stones as she approached, her dark eyes scanning the scene with a mix of wonder and wariness. The setting sun cast long shadows across the ruins, highlighting the sharp angles of her face.

"But balance isn't guaranteed," she interjected, her voice cutting through the air like a knife. Andres turned, struck by the intensity in her gaze. "The hybrids' awakening carries ethical implications. The Brotherhood exploited them for control—what is to stop others from doing the same?"

Andres felt a chill run down his spine, recognizing the weight of guilt in Talia's words. Her past with the Brotherhood hung between them, an unspoken reminder of the darkness they fought against.

"You're right," Andres admitted, his mind racing. "We've unlocked something incredible, but also potentially dangerous." He glanced at the Crystal Skull, its surface now pulsing with an otherworldly light. "How do we protect them, Talia? How do we ensure this gift is not turned into a weapon?"

Talia's lips tightened. "We can't, not entirely. But we can prepare." She pulled a small device from one of her many pockets, its screen glowing with complex schematics. "I've been working on safeguards, encryption that could shield their newfound consciousness from outside manipulation."

As the last rays of sunlight faded, Andres felt a sudden urgency. "We'll need those safeguards, and more," he said, his voice resolute. "But first, we have to complete what we started."

Evelyn stepped forward, her dark eyes scanning the team with a mixture of admiration and concern. The golden light of dawn caught the subtle scar near her left eyebrow, a reminder of past struggles etched into her refined features.

"Change won't come easily," she interjected, her voice measured and articulate. "There will be resistance, from governments, corporations, and even individuals afraid of losing the old ways."

Andres felt a chill run down his spine, the weight of her words settling heavily on his shoulders. He watched as she pushed her reading glasses up the bridge of her nose, a gesture that seemed to punctuate the gravity of her statement.

She's right, Andres thought, his mind racing through potential scenarios. *'We're not just battling ignorance but entrenched power structures and fear itself.*

The air around them seemed to thicken, the euphoria of their recent victory giving way to a sobering reality. The ancient stones of Tiwanaku, still humming with residual energy, now felt like silent sentinels watching their deliberation.

Talia moved closer, her wiry frame taut with tension. The circuit pattern tattooed on her wrist caught Andres's eye, a stark reminder of her complex past.

"The Brotherhood's ideology isn't gone," Talia added, her tone blunt and tinged with a hint of bitterness. "It's an idea, and ideas have a way of resurfacing. Vigilance is our only defense."

Andres nodded. He could see the guilt and determination warring in her dark eyes, a reflection of her ongoing struggle for redemption.

"You're both right," Andres acknowledged, his gaze moving between Evelyn and Talia. "We've ignited a spark but nurturing it into a flame of global consciousness will be our true test."

As he spoke, Andres's mind raced with the enormity of their task. The luminous web of energy connecting sacred sites across the globe pulsed in his mind's eye, a reminder of both their potential and their responsibility.

We're walking a tightrope, he mused, *between awakening and chaos, between unity and division. One misstep could plunge the world into darkness.*

The team stood in thoughtful silence, the weight of their mission palpable in the crisp morning air. The ruins of Tiwanaku, ancient and enduring, seemed to whisper of past civilizations that had faced similar crossroads. As the sun climbed higher, casting long shadows across the sacred ground, Andres knew that their journey was only beginning.

Dr. Voss stepped closer, her green eyes flashing with a mix of determination and barely concealed anger. The morning light caught her auburn hair, setting it ablaze like a fiery halo.

"Then let's make sure it doesn't resurface," she declared, her voice steely. "I know their strategies—their weaknesses. We'll stop them before they can rebuild."

Andres studied Voss's face, noting the slight tremble in her jaw that belied her confident words. He felt a surge of admiration for her strength and courage.

"Elera" Andres began, reaching out to touch her arm gently, "your insight is invaluable. But remember, we're not just fighting against something—we're fighting for a new future."

Before Voss could respond, movement at the edge of the ruins caught Andres's attention. Amaru emerged from the mist, his silver braid swaying as he walked. Beside him was a young woman Andres had never seen before, her presence radiating an earthy warmth that seemed to harmonize with the ancient stones around them.

"Andres!" Amaru called out, his voice carrying the rhythmic cadence of an elder's wisdom, "There's someone I'd like you to meet!" As they drew closer, Andres could see the pride shining in Amaru's weathered face. "This is Arika," he said, gesturing to the young woman. "She's my student and the future emissary of Tiwanaku."

Arika stepped forward, her dark eyes meeting Andres with a mixture of curiosity and quiet confidence. Colorful threads woven into her braids caught the sunlight, creating a mesmerizing dance of shadows across her face.

"It's an honor to meet you, Dr. Paredes," Arika said softly, her voice carrying the lyrical quality of one deeply connected to the land. "I've heard so much about your mission."

Andres felt a sudden shift in the energy around them as if the very stones of Tiwanaku were responding to Arika's presence. He glanced at Amaru, seeing the silent communication passing between mentor and student.

This is more than just an introduction, Andres realized. *It's a passing of the torch.*

Arika took a deep breath, her fingers brushing the woven bracelet on her wrist—a gesture Andres recognized as one of grounding. Her gaze, steady yet filled with a profound curiosity, met his own.

"The land has chosen me to protect its secrets," she said softly, her voice barely above a whisper but carrying the weight of ancient wisdom. "But I can only do so with your guidance."

Andres felt a surge of energy pulse through the ground beneath his feet as if Tiwanaku itself was affirming Arika's words. He glanced at the luminous web stretching across the sky, its ethereal light reflecting in Arika's eyes.

She's the bridge, Andres thought, a mix of awe and responsibility washing over him, *between the old ways and the new world we're creating.*

"We'd be honored to guide you, Arika," Andres said, extending his hand. As their palms met, he felt a spark of connection—a merging of energies that spoke of shared purpose.

Evelyn stepped forward, her analytical mind already at work. "Your sensitivity to the land could be invaluable in our efforts to maintain the balance of the global energy grid," she said, a hint of excitement in her voice.

Talia nodded in agreement, her expression thoughtful. "And your connection to Tiwanaku's traditions might help us anticipate and counter any resurgence of the Brotherhood's ideology."

One by one, the team members welcomed Arika, each sensing the deep well of sacred energy that seemed to flow through her. Maya approached last, placing a gentle hand on Arika's shoulder.

"You carry the heart of this land within you," Maya said softly. "Together, we'll ensure its wisdom guides humanity towards a brighter future."

Andres watched as Arika's posture relaxed, the young woman seeming to grow more assured with each word of support. He turned toward the shimmering web of light that connected Tiwanaku to sacred sites across the globe.

"We stand at a turning point," Andres said, his voice carrying across the ancient ruins. "With Arika joining us, we're better prepared to face the challenges ahead and guide humanity towards its true potential."

As one, the team faced the luminous web, their resolve strengthened by this new alliance. Andres felt a surge of hope as he gazed at the interconnected strands of light. The path forward was uncertain, but in this moment, surrounded by his team and the pulsing energy of Tiwanaku, he knew they were ready to meet whatever lay ahead.

Chapter 23

As the sun dipped below the horizon, a collective breath seemed to sweep across the globe. At sacred sites scattered like cosmic waypoints, meditators settled into their positions, hearts thrumming with anticipation. Across continents and time zones, their efforts had been meticulously synchronized, each group aligning their meditation to this precise moment. From the pyramids of Egypt to the temples of Tiwanaku, from Stonehenge to the sacred mountains of the East, a unified field of consciousness began to form, pulsing in harmony as the veil between worlds thinned.

Dr. Andres Paredes stood atop the ancient platform at Tiwanaku, his eyes scanning the crowd of expectant faces. The weight of the moment pressed upon him, a tangible force as real as the weathered stones beneath his feet.

"Remember," he called out, his rich voice carrying on the wind, "we are united in purpose. Open your hearts and let unconditional love flow through you."

Maya stepped forward; the Atlantean Crystal Skull cradled in her hands. Its crystalline surface caught the fading light, sending prismatic reflections dancing across the gathering. Andres felt a flutter of anxiety in his chest. *Would this truly work?*

"Now," Maya intoned, her melodic voice soothing his nerves, "we begin."

She raised the Skull high, aligning it with the Vesica Piscis symbol etched into the weathered Gateway of the Sun. A collective gasp rippled through the crowd as a beam of light shot from the Skull, refracting through the ancient carving.

Andres closed his eyes, focusing his intention. The love in his heart swelled, threatening to overwhelm him. *Is this how it feels to tap into the universal consciousness?* he wondered.

"Can you feel it?" Maya whispered beside him, her eyes alight with an otherworldly glow.

He nodded, unable to find words. The energy pulsing through Tiwanaku was palpable, vibrating through the massive stone blocks and intricate carvings that had stood sentinel for millennia. The city seemed to come alive around them, whispering ancient secrets on the wind.

"The grid is activating," Andres murmured, his voice filled with awe. "It's working!"

As if in response, the light emanating from the Crystal Skull intensified, bathing the gathering in a soft, ethereal glow. Andres felt a surge of hope. Perhaps humanity truly could evolve, could become something greater than the sum of its parts.

Maya's hand found his, squeezing gently. "This is just the beginning," she said, her eyes fixed on the horizon. "The real work lies ahead."

Andres nodded, his resolve strengthening. Whatever challenges awaited, he knew that in that moment, on this ancient platform where the veil between worlds grew thin, they had taken the first crucial step toward humanity's cosmic destiny.

Rising from the vast Salisbury Plain, Stonehenge stands as one of the most enigmatic and powerful energy nodes on the planetary grid. This ancient stone circle, precisely aligned with celestial events such as the solstices and equinoxes, was designed to harness and channel both terrestrial and cosmic forces. The towering megaliths, arranged with mathematical precision, act as conduits—drawing energy from the Earth's ley lines and merging it with the vibrational frequencies of the cosmos.

The Atlanteans understood that Stonehenge was far more than a mere timekeeping device; it was a stargate, a focal point where the fabric of space and time thinned, allowing the flow of universal energies into the Earth. The intersection of ley lines beneath the site magnifies its power, creating a vortex that links Earth to distant realms. During key celestial alignments, the energy surges, activating Stonehenge as a gateway to higher dimensions.

As a crucial nexus of the planetary energy grid, Stonehenge serves as a bridge between Earth and the stars. It facilitates interstellar communication, enhances spiritual consciousness, and, during precise astronomical moments, opens doorways to other realms—allowing those attuned to its frequencies to glimpse beyond the veil of ordinary reality.

Orion stood at the center of the circle, his iridescent skin shimmering in the fading light. Around him, participants joined hands, their eyes closed in deep concentration.

"Feel the cosmic energy flowing through you," Orion intoned, his voice resonating with otherworldly timbre. "We are the conduits, bridging Earth and stars."

A participant, a young woman with vibrant red hair, gasped. "I can see it! The Stargate... it is opening above us!"

Orion's gaze lifted skyward, his eyes reflecting swirling galaxies. "Yes, Lyra. The celestial patterns are aligning. Now, channel that energy. Let it flow through you and into the stones."

The circle began to hum with an ethereal resonance. The air crackled with unseen energy, making the hairs on everyone's arms stand on end.

"Is this... is this how it felt in Atlantis?" another participant asked, his voice trembling with a mixture of awe and trepidation.

Orion's expression softened, a flicker of ancient sorrow passing across his features. "Similar, but not identical. In Atlantis, they lacked the wisdom to truly understand the power they wielded. This time, we must do better."

As if in response to his words, a beam of light shot down from the stargate, connecting with the center stone. The entire circle pulsed with energy, sending ripples through the Earth's grid.

Orion closed his eyes, feeling the interstellar pathways opening. "It's done," he whispered. "Stonehenge is awakened. Now, we must move quickly. To Giza."

In a blink, the scene shifted. The desert wind whispered across the vast Giza Plateau, carrying the weight of millennia. Before them, the Great Pyramid towered in solemn grandeur, its limestone casing stones—though long eroded—still shimmering faintly under the desert moonlight. At its base, a group had already gathered, their voices raised in an otherworldly chant that resonated with the very stones.

The Great Pyramid was not merely an ancient tomb—it was an energy amplifier, designed with mathematical precision to harness and direct the Earth's telluric currents. Built atop a powerful intersection of ley lines, its geometric structure magnified and focused energy, transforming it into a colossal beacon that linked Earth to the cosmos. Its alignment with the Orion constellation ensured that it remained attuned to celestial forces, acting as a bridge between worlds.

Long ago, the apex of the pyramid had been capped with a golden capstone, an energy conductor that once pulsed with power. Atlantean technology had further enhanced this sacred site, making it a Pillar of Light, a beacon that connected Earth to the divine frequencies of the universe. Now, as the sacred grid reactivated, a faint glow seemed to shimmer at the pyramid's peak, as if remembering its ancient purpose.

The Great Pyramid is the heart of the planetary energy system, a transmitter of divine energy, and a key to spiritual awakening. It aligns human consciousness with the cosmic order, accelerating the evolution of the soul. Reactivating this node restores its ancient function—transforming it once more into a beacon of enlightenment, guiding humanity toward its higher destiny.

"The Atlantean hymns," Orion breathed, his eyes widening with recognition. "I haven't heard these in millennia."

The pyramid seemed to vibrate in response to the chants, each note amplified and sent skyward. Orion stepped forward, joining his voice to the chorus. The sound swelled, growing in power and intensity until it felt as if the very air was singing.

A participant turned to Orion, her eyes wide with wonder. "What are we saying? What do these words mean?"

Orion's gaze remained fixed on the pyramid's apex. "We're calling to the stars, to Orion's Belt. We're reminding the cosmos of Earth's place in the grand design."

As the chant reached its crescendo, a beam of pure energy erupted from the pyramid's tip, shooting upward into the night sky. The participants gasped in unison, feeling the surge of power coursing through them and into the Earth's grid.

Orion's form seemed to flicker, becoming more translucent. "The connection is made," he said, his voice echoing strangely. "Giza calls to Orion and Orion answers. The grid grows stronger with each node we awaken."

He turned to the group, his eyes blazing with celestial fire. "We've taken crucial steps, but our journey is far from over. The transformation has only just begun."

As the first rays of dawn caressed the ancient stones of Machu Picchu, Dr. Andres Paredes stood atop the Sun Gate, his gaze sweeping over the mist-shrouded terraces below. The air vibrated with an unseen force as if the very earth beneath his feet pulsed with life. Wisps of fog curled around the sacred ruins, parting briefly to reveal the intricate layout of temples, plazas, and stairways—an architectural masterpiece carved into the spine of the Andes.

High in the Peruvian mountains, Machu Picchu is a sanctuary of power, built at a precise intersection of ley lines where the Earth's energy is at its most concentrated. The Incas, inheritors of ancient wisdom, understood the profound forces at play here. They aligned their temples and terraces with the Sun, drawing upon its life-giving energy and harmonizing it with the pulse of the land.

More than a city, Machu Picchu is a living conduit between Earth and sky. Its elevated position, cradled between towering peaks, allows it to channel celestial frequencies, creating a resonance that amplifies spiritual transformation. The stone terraces mirror the surrounding mountains, forging an unbreakable bond between nature and the sacred. It is said that those who walk its paths can feel the energy coursing through their bodies—a force capable of healing, awakening, and revealing hidden truths.

Machu Picchu is the node of spiritual transformation and healing, a beacon of renewal where Earth and Sun unite in perfect harmony. It absorbs the radiant energy of the cosmos and channels it into the land, awakening the consciousness of those who stand within its embrace. As a key link in the planetary grid, Machu Picchu serves as a sacred doorway—guiding seekers toward enlightenment and restoring the balance between humanity and the divine.

Now, as the sacred grid reawakened, Machu Picchu's stones seemed to hum, as if stirring from centuries of slumber. The moment of activation had arrived.

"It's time," he whispered, more to himself than to the small group gathered around him.

Maya stepped forward, her emerald eyes reflecting the golden light. "The sun rises, Andres. Are you ready to channel its power?"

Andres nodded, his expression a mixture of excitement and reverence. "I've studied this site for years, but I never imagined I'd be part of something so... transcendent."

As if on cue, the sun burst fully over the horizon, bathing the citadel in brilliant light. The assembled participants gasped in unison, feeling the surge of energy wash over them.

"Focus now," Maya instructed, her voice carrying effortlessly across the group. "Feel the solar energy coursing through you. Let it flow into the earth, into the grid."

Andres closed his eyes, concentrating on the warmth spreading through his body. In his mind's eye, he saw threads of golden light connecting him to the ancient stones, to the other participants, to the very core of the planet.

"It's incredible," he murmured. "I can feel the pulse of the earth, the rhythm of its energy flows."

Maya's hand found his, their fingers intertwining. "This is the wisdom of Tiwanaku," she said softly. "The understanding that we are all connected, all part of the greater whole."

As the group continued their meditation, Andres felt a shift in the energy. His eyes snapped open, scanning the horizon.

"Something's changing," he said urgently. "Can you feel it?"

Maya nodded, her expression intense. "The grid is awakening. Uluru calls."

In that moment, Andres felt his consciousness expand, stretching across continents to the vast, sun-scorched plains of Australia. Beneath the towering presence of Uluru, the great red monolith, indigenous aborigine elders sat in a sacred circle, their voices rising in a rhythmic chant that seemed to vibrate through the very fabric of existence. The air shimmered with an ancient power; a force as old as the land itself. They called it Dreamtime.

Uluru is more than stone—it is a living being, a pulsating heart within the Earth's body. Formed over 500 million years ago, this sacred site holds the memory of the Dreamtime—the timeless realm where creation began, where the spirits of the ancestors still walk. The indigenous peoples of Australia have long revered Uluru as the place where the energies of the land are strongest, where the Earth speaks, and where the wisdom of the ancients is eternally preserved.

Embedded deep within the planetary energy grid, Uluru functions as a powerful grounding node, channeling primordial Earth energy while also acting as a stabilizer for the cosmic forces flowing through the network of sacred sites. The Atlanteans recognized Uluru as the anchor of the grid, a balancing point that prevented chaotic fluctuations, keeping the currents of energy in harmony with the Earth's natural rhythms.

Now, as the sacred grid stirred, Uluru's surface glowed faintly under the desert moonlight. The elders' voices merged with the land, with the sky, with the universe itself. The awakening had begun.

"The Dreamtime," he whispered in awe. "They're tapping into the very creation energies of the planet."

As the scene unfolded in his mind, Andres marveled at the power and wisdom of these ancient cultures. He realized that his years of academic study had only scratched the surface of the true knowledge held by these guardians of the earth.

"We're all part of this," he said, his voice filled with wonder. "Machu Picchu, Uluru, all the sacred sites... we're weaving a tapestry of light around the world."

Maya squeezed his hand, her smile radiant. "And with each thread we add, we come closer to healing the rifts, to guiding humanity toward its true potential."

As the sun climbed higher in the sky, Andres felt a profound sense of purpose wash over him. He knew that this was just the beginning of an extraordinary journey, one that would reshape not just his understanding of the world, but the very future of humanity itself.

The aurora-like glow surrounding Mount Shasta pulsed with otherworldly energy, casting an ethereal light over the gathered seekers. The air vibrated with an almost musical hum as if the mountain itself was singing. Andres stood among the meditators, his heart pounding in rhythm with the unseen forces converging upon the sacred site. He gazed at the summit, where shimmering waves of energy cascaded down like celestial waterfalls, illuminating the night like a beacon to the cosmos.

Mount Shasta is no ordinary peak—it is a threshold between worlds. This dormant volcano in northern California has long been regarded as a sacred site by indigenous tribes, who speak of spirit beings dwelling within its depths. In more recent times, spiritual seekers and mystics have recognized it as a powerful vortex of ascension energy, where ley lines weave together to form a gateway to higher dimensions. Those who come in meditation often report visions, profound awakenings, and encounters with luminous beings from realms beyond human perception.

Atlantean legends tell of Mount Shasta as a celestial bridge, a place where the energy of the stars descends to meet the Earth. It was once a key node in their advanced spiritual network, a site used for inter-dimensional communication and ascension practices. The mountain's unique energy aligns with the higher chakras of the planet, particularly the crown chakra, symbolizing humanity's capacity to transcend the material world and embrace cosmic consciousness.

Now, as the planetary grid began to stir, Mount Shasta resonated with an ever-deepening intensity. The seekers standing in silent meditation could feel its call—a summons to rise, to awaken, to step into the next stage of human evolution.

"It's like nothing I've ever seen," he breathed, his voice barely above a whisper.

Maya nodded, her face illuminated by the radiant glow. "Mount Shasta is one of Earth's primary power points. The veil between dimensions is thinnest here. Can you feel it?"

Andres closed his eyes, allowing his senses to expand beyond the physical. A tingling sensation coursed through him, his body seemingly dissolving into the frequency that surrounded them. He felt lighter as if gravity had loosened its grip. A deep warmth ignited at his core, rising like a golden flame.

Then, through the luminous haze, a great movement stirred beneath the mountain. A vast etheric city—the hidden sanctuary of Lemuria—began to take form in his mind's eye. The meditators, now deep in trance, perceived its crystalline towers glowing beneath the surface, pulsing in harmony with the energy grid. The Lemurians were awakening.

A voice resonated in their minds, deep and resonant, carrying the weight of eons.

"Welcome, children of the surface. You stand at the convergence of past and future."

Before them, a luminous figure emerged, shifting between forms—a golden-white radiance, a wise elder clad in ancient Lemurian robes, a multi-dimensional presence vibrating in sacred tones. Agartha, the great leader of Inner Earth, had come.

Maya stepped forward, reverence in her every breath. "We seek the final piece. The knowledge to bridge the divide and complete the activation."

Agartha raised a staff of crystal energy, and suddenly, visions flooded their minds. They saw Lemuria in its prime, a civilization built in perfect harmony with the planet's energy grid. They saw the great Atlantean-Lemurian conflict, how misuse of power had fractured the balance, and how echoes of that ancient struggle still shaped the battle between light and darkness today.

"The cycle must end," Agartha intoned. *"This activation is not merely for Earth, but for the cosmic symphony of existence. The missing key is unity—the merging of past and future, technology and spirit, Atlantis, and Lemuria. Only then will the grid resonate at its full potential."*

From within the Lemurian city, an ancient crystalline sphere rose, pulsating with golden fire. Its energy reached toward the meditators, flowing through them, embedding sacred codes into their very being. It was the final piece—an energetic blueprint once lost, now restored.

As the meditators absorbed the knowledge, the global grid surged to life. Beams of light shot from Mount Shasta, weaving across the planet and activating the interconnected sacred sites. The air hummed with a crescendo of celestial tones, and the seekers themselves began to glow with inner luminescence.

Andres gasped, his entire body vibrating with newfound energy. *Are we truly becoming something more than human? Is this the birth of the Homo Omega?*

Agartha's voice softened yet carried the force of destiny itself. *"You are the bridges. The guardians. The cycle completes through you."*

As the vision of the Lemurian city slowly faded, the mountain remained bathed in its ethereal glow. The seekers stood transformed, forever changed, carrying the final code of activation within their very souls.

The prophecy had begun.

In that moment, Andres's awareness shifted, carrying him across continents to the snow-capped peak of Mount Kailash. The shift was instantaneous—in one heartbeat, he stood in the radiant energy of Mount Shasta, the next he soared through a luminous current, his consciousness drawn into the sacred silence of the Himalayas. He stood at the foot of one of the most revered and mysterious mountains on Earth, where the energy felt ancient, potent, and boundless.

Mount Kailash is considered the spiritual axis of the world in several major traditions, including Hinduism, Buddhism, Jainism, and Bön. Known as the Crown of the World, its towering, symmetrical shape and its remote, sacred location make it one of the most powerful energy points on the planet. The mountain is believed to be the dwelling place of Shiva, the Hindu god of destruction and transformation, but it also holds deep spiritual significance in other traditions, each viewing it as a bridge to the divine.

The ley lines around Mount Kailash converge in a way that amplifies its energy, allowing it to act as a powerful transmitter of spiritual wisdom and universal consciousness. Pilgrims from across the world believe that to circle the mountain, or to perform a pilgrimage around its base, brings profound enlightenment and karmic cleansing. The act of circumambulating Kailash is seen as a way to align oneself with the cosmos and unlock divine knowledge.

Before him, Tibetan monks sat in deep meditation, their ochre robes stark against the pristine white of the eternal snows. Their synchronized breaths rose and fell like the tide, their chants reverberating through the icy winds, a sacred resonance that merged with the mountain itself. The air shimmered with an unseen force, and the entire peak pulsed like a giant living heart, sending ripples of energy across the planetary grid.

He could feel it. The same frequency that had awakened within him at Mount Shasta thrummed through this place—a cosmic thread weaving the two sacred sites together. The monks were not simply meditating; they were anchoring a celestial transmission, their voices forming an ancient code that reached deep into the Earth's core.

Through the mist that curled around the sacred mountain, an ethereal glow emerged. It was not of this world, nor entirely of the next. A luminous figure, draped in robes woven from light, stepped forward, eyes holding the vastness of eternity.

"You have come, traveler," the being intoned, the voice neither male nor female, but something beyond—resonant, eternal. *"Mount Kailash stands as the mirror of the cosmos. As above, so below. The activation must align all."*

Andres felt his heart surge as if drawn into the great pulse of the universe. He suddenly understood—the activation of Mount Shasta was only one piece of a greater whole. Mount Kailash, the axis mundi, held the counterbalance, the stabilizing force that would allow the global energy grid to rise to its full potential. The monks knew this; they had always known.

A gust of wind carried their chants higher, merging with the mountain's own deep vibration. The snowflakes swirling around him became luminescent, forming intricate geometries in the air before dissolving into golden light. It was then that Andres realized:

The red rocks of Sedona glowed in the fading light, their majestic silhouettes etched against a sky painted in hues of lavender and gold. At the base of Bell Rock, a circle of meditators sat motionless, their eyes closed in deep concentration. The air shimmered with unseen currents, the very fabric of reality seeming to pulse with an ancient, living force. A gentle breeze carried whispers of the land's secrets as if the Earth itself was breathing through the canyon walls.

Sedona is renowned for its powerful energy vortices, where the planet's ley lines twist and spiral, creating concentrated pockets of heightened energy. These vortexes, especially at Cathedral Rock, Bell Rock, Boynton Canyon, and Airport Mesa, have long been recognized as gateways to spiritual transformation. The energies here are said to stimulate heightened intuition, profound healing, and accelerated personal growth. Those sensitive to energy often report feeling an intense vibration coursing through their bodies, as if awakening dormant aspects of their consciousness.

Unlike other sites where energy flows in a singular direction, Sedona's vortexes embody a perfect balance of opposing forces—masculine and feminine, action and receptivity, expansion, and stillness. This dynamic equilibrium makes Sedona a harmonizing node, where individuals are drawn into alignment with both their inner selves and the greater cosmic forces. Atlantean records speak of Sedona as a place where initiates underwent rites of passage, emerging with heightened spiritual awareness and a deeper connection to the planetary grid.

Now, as the global network of sacred sites reawakened, Sedona's energy intensified, sending ripples of renewal and activation across the Earth. Those who gathered in silent meditation could feel its call—a summons to heal, to awaken, to transform.

At the center of the group, master astrologer and meditator Elizabeth stood, her presence radiating quiet power. Cradled in her hands was an ancient Tibetan Crystal Skull, its translucent surface catching the last rays of sunlight. As she intoned a sacred chant, the Skull pulsed with a soft, ethereal light, amplifying the collective energy of the meditation. Across the world, synchronized groups aligned with her, their unified intention weaving a web of harmony and balance. The air around them shimmered, the very fabric of reality seeming to ripple as ancient forces stirred, responding to the call.

Maya took a deep breath, her fingers intertwined with those of the meditators on either side of her. She felt the masculine energy of the Earth pulsing beneath her, strong and grounding, while a gentler feminine current flowed through the air, caressing her skin.

"Feel the balance," she whispered, her voice barely audible. "Let the energies merge within you."

Andres, seated across from her, nodded almost imperceptibly. His brow furrowed in concentration as he struggled to quiet his analytical mind.

"I'm trying," he murmured, "but it's difficult to let go of rational thought."

Maya's lips curved in a gentle smile. "Don't force it, Andres. Just observe the thoughts as they come, then let them drift away like clouds."

As the group fell silent once more, Maya felt a surge of energy coursing through her body. In her mind's eye, she saw golden threads of light connecting each meditator, weaving a tapestry that extended far beyond Sedona.

We are doing it, she thought. *We are strengthening the grid.*

Suddenly, her consciousness expanded, carrying her across the ocean to the arid plains of Peru. The Nazca Lines stretched out before her, vast geoglyphs etched into the earth like an ancient cosmic map. Around the lines, a group of star navigators moved in a carefully choreographed dance, their bodies tracing the outlines of hummingbirds, monkeys, and spirals. As they moved, the lines seemed to pulse with an inner light, as if awakening from a millennia-long slumber.

The Nazca Lines, an enigmatic network of massive figures and geometric patterns carved into the desert floor, have long mystified scholars and visionaries alike. Their sheer size and precision suggest an advanced understanding of astronomy, geodesy, and sacred geometry. Some align with solstices and planetary movements, while others point toward distant star systems, acting as markers for celestial navigation.

The ley lines in this region do not simply intersect—they form a vast energetic circuit, amplifying frequencies across the Earth's grid. Many believe that the Atlanteans and other ancient civilizations once used Nazca as a center for astral communication and star navigation, tuning into transmissions from the cosmos. The lines may serve as an ancient star map, a blueprint guiding humanity toward its place among interstellar civilizations.

Now, as the grid reawakens, the Nazca node is reactivating, reconnecting Earth to the stars. The figures, once considered mere symbols, are awakening as active energy conduits, radiating signals that bridge the terrestrial and the celestial.

"The pathways are aligning," one navigator called out, his voice filled with awe. "I can feel the connection to the stars!"

Maya's spirit soared alongside them, marveling at the intricate patterns. She could sense the node activating, sending waves of energy rippling through the global grid.

Back in Sedona, Maya's physical body trembled slightly. Andres opened his eyes, concern etched on his face.

"Maya? Are you alright?"

She nodded; her eyes still closed. "More than alright, Andres. I can see it all – Sedona, Nazca, the entire grid coming to life. It's... it's beautiful."

As the sun dipped below the horizon, the red rocks of Sedona seemed to pulse with an inner fire. The meditators, now glowing with a soft, ethereal light, continued their sacred work, balancing energies and strengthening the connections that would guide humanity toward its cosmic destiny.

The first rays of dawn painted Mount Fuji's snow-capped peak in hues of rose and gold. At its base, a circle of meditators stood hand in hand, their eyes closed in reverence. The air thrummed with anticipation as their collective energy built, resonating with the sacred heartbeat of the mountain. A soft wind carried whispers of ancient prayers, blending with the silent power emanating from the land itself.

Mount Fuji, Japan's highest and most sacred mountain, has been venerated for centuries as a spiritual gateway, a bridge between the

Earth and the heavens. Much like the great pyramids or other sacred peaks, Fuji is a natural conductor of undifferentiated cosmic energy, drawing life force from the depths of the planet while channeling celestial energy from the skies.

Its perfect conical shape serves as an amplifier, creating a harmonic resonance that brings balance and clarity. The ley lines converging at Mount Fuji form a powerful vortex, one that aligns the energies of stillness and motion, grounding and ascension, yin and yang. It is a place of deep introspection and renewal, where the mind, body, and spirit come into equilibrium.

Ancient traditions speak of mystical beings and celestial guardians dwelling within Fuji's sacred domain, ensuring that the energy flowing through the land remains pure. Atlantean knowledge suggests that Fuji once served as a stabilizing force in the global energy network, holding the grid in perfect equilibrium against forces that might seek to disrupt its harmony.

Amaru's weathered face creased with concentration as he led the group in a melodic chant. His deep, gravelly voice carried ancient wisdom:

"Great spirits of Fuji, guardians of fire and earth, we call upon your sacred power."

The mountain seemed to respond, a faint vibration rippling through the ground. Arika, standing beside Amaru, felt a surge of energy course through her body. Her eyes flew open, widening in awe.

"Amaru," she whispered, "look!"

A column of pure, radiant light burst from Fuji's summit, stretching impossibly high into the atmosphere. It pulsed with a rhythm that matched the heartbeats of those gathered below.

Amaru nodded solemnly. "The grid awakens, child. Feel how it stabilizes."

Arika closed her eyes again, sensing the invisible web of energy crisscrossing the globe. Where before there had been instability, now she felt a harmonious hum.

"It's working," she breathed. "But will it be enough?"

Amaru squeezed her hand. "We must trust in the process. Our work here is done. Now, we journey to the sacred waters."

As if in a dream, Arika found herself transported to the shores of Lake Titicaca. The lake's surface was mirror-smooth, reflecting the star-studded sky above. Indigenous Quechua-speaking elders, their faces etched with the wisdom of generations, formed a circle at the water's edge, their voices rising in an ancient chant. The air shimmered with an unseen force as if the lake itself was breathing, alive with energy.

Nestled high in the Andes, Lake Titicaca is revered as the birthplace of the gods in Andean mythology. More than just a body of water, it is a vast reservoir of energy, an ancient portal to other realms and dimensions. For centuries, it has been known as a place of spiritual transformation, where those who seek wisdom may undergo profound renewal.

Legends whisper of a submerged Atlantean temple beneath its depths, a remnant of an age when advanced civilizations harnessed its power. The lake's ley lines form a vortex of immense potency, channeling life force energy that revitalizes both the Earth and the human spirit. It is believed that the Atlanteans once used Lake Titicaca's energy to access interdimensional pathways and commune with celestial beings.

Even today, seekers are drawn to its sacred waters, where the veil between worlds is thin, allowing for visions, awakenings, and deep spiritual healing. The lake serves as a crucible of renewal, washing away stagnation and realigning those who come into contact with its energy.

Arika and Amaru joined them, kneeling on the cool earth. The elders began to chant in their ancestral tongue, their voices blending into a hypnotic drone. Arika felt herself slipping into a trance-like state, her consciousness expanding to merge with the lake itself.

Suddenly, the water began to glow. Soft tendrils of light, reminiscent of the aurora borealis, danced across its surface. Arika gasped, overcome by the beauty and the profound sense of potential it represented.

This is it, she thought, her heart racing. *The moment of transformation is upon us.*

As the ethereal light grew stronger, Arika felt a presence brush against her mind—ancient, wise, and filled with unconditional love. It whispered of humanity's true destiny; of the cosmic dance they were about to join.

Tears streamed down Arika's face as she opened herself fully to the experience, allowing the lake's luminous energy to flow through her and into the global grid. In that moment, she understood that this was just the beginning of an incredible journey—one that would lead humanity to the stars and beyond.

The ancient stones of the Bosnian Pyramids loomed in the pre-dawn darkness; their massive forms silhouetted against the star-strewn sky. A small group of meditators sat in a tight circle at the base of the Pyramid of the Sun, their eyes closed in deep concentration, drawing upon the deep, unspoken energy of the earth. As the first light of day touched the peaks, the air hummed with a subtle vibration, as though the very ground beneath them was alive with untapped power.

The Bosnian Pyramids, though not as widely recognized as other sacred sites, are said to harbor immense energetic properties, shrouded in mystery and wonder. These pyramid-shaped hills believed to align with the cardinal points, stand along some of the most powerful ley lines on the planet. Many theorists propose that these pyramids were not simply natural formations but were crafted by an ancient, advanced civilization with knowledge of energy manipulation. The pyramids are thought to channel energy, much like the Great Pyramid of Giza, amplifying the Earth's natural currents.

This hidden node adds an element of mystery and enigma to the grid. The pyramids represent untapped power—a sleeping giant of energy and knowledge still buried beneath the sands of time. Their activation would unlock a forgotten potential that has been dormant for millennia, strengthening the overall flow of the global energy grid and revealing secrets that the modern world has long sought.

Amaru opened his eyes, gazing at the weathered stones. "Can you feel it, Arika?" he whispered, his voice barely audible. "The dormant power stirring within?"

Arika nodded, her brow furrowed. "It's like... a heartbeat, slow and steady. But growing stronger with each pulse."

She placed her palms flat on the cool earth, sending her awareness deep into the pyramid's foundations. Suddenly, her eyes flew open. "There's so much knowledge here, Amaru! Atlantean secrets, woven into the very structure!"

Amaru smiled, his eyes twinkling. "Now, focus your intention. Help awaken what has slumbered for millennia."

The group's chanting grew louder, their voices intertwining with the pyramid's ancient resonance. Arika felt a surge of energy course through her body, connecting her to the global grid that spanned the planet.

"It's working!" she gasped, as a soft golden light began to emanate from the pyramid's surface. "The knowledge... it's flowing into the grid!"

Amaru nodded solemnly. "And now, we must ensure balance. Our next destination awaits."

Hours later, they stood on the windswept shores of Rapa Nui, better known as Easter Island. The imposing Moai statues gazed impassively out to sea, their stone faces etched with centuries of secrets. The air was thick with an ancient energy as if the land itself was whispering forgotten tales to those who dared listen. Dr. Paredes felt the weight of history in the silent presence of the statues, their stoic gaze holding more than just the island's past—they held the key to the global energy grid.

Rapa Nui, a remote island in the Pacific Ocean, is home to hundreds of massive stone statues known as moai, which are believed to represent the ancestors and protectors of the island's people. The island has long been considered a place of profound mystery, with many believing that the inhabitants had knowledge of the stars and advanced techniques for harnessing the Earth's energy.

The ley lines crossing Rapa Nui connect it to other powerful energy nodes across the world, including Tiwanaku, Uluru, and the Nazca Lines, forming a vital link in the global grid. The moai statues are thought to act as energy conduits, not just guarding the island, but also regulating the flow of energy between continents and across the vast ocean.

The Atlanteans might have recognized Rapa Nui's significance as a balancing node within the grid. The island's strategic location in the Pacific Ocean makes it a key force for maintaining equilibrium between the Earth's landmasses and the surrounding oceans. Its activation is tied to the energy of the Pacific Ocean and the harmonious relationship between land and sea.

Arika shivered, despite the warm breeze. "I've never felt the ocean's presence so strongly," she murmured. "It's as if the very waves are alive with consciousness."

Amaru gestured to a group of local spiritual leaders gathering near the water's edge. "The oceanic guardians," he explained. "They understand the vital role the seas play in maintaining harmony across the globe."

As they joined the circle, Arika felt the familiar tingle of energy building. The chants began, deep and resonant, echoing the rhythmic crash of waves on the shore.

Closing her eyes, Arika reached out with her senses, connecting to the vast expanse of ocean surrounding the island. She gasped as she felt the presence of countless marine creatures, from the tiniest plankton to the mightiest whales, all pulsing with life and awareness.

"The ocean," she whispered in awe, "it's like one giant, living entity!"

Amaru nodded, his eyes still closed. "And now, we must help it synchronize with the land-based nodes of the grid."

As their meditation deepened, Arika sensed tendrils of energy stretching out across the waters, linking island to island, continent to continent. The Moai seemed to hum with an inner light, their ancient power awakening to join the global chorus.

"We've done it," Arika breathed, opening her eyes to see the first rays of dawn painting the sky. "The grid is complete."

Amaru smiled, but his eyes held a hint of concern. "Yes, child. But remember, this is just the beginning. The real challenge lies ahead."

A blinding flash erupted from the Atlantean Crystal Skull at Tiwanaku, its radiance piercing the heavens. Maya gasped, her hands trembling as she held the artifact aloft. The light pulsed, sending ripples of energy across the globe, connecting each sacred node in a dazzling web of luminescence.

"It's happening," Andres whispered, his eyes wide with wonder. "The grid is activating!"

Maya felt a surge of power course through her body, her consciousness expanding beyond the confines of her physical form. She could sense the other nodes, feel the energy flowing between them like rivers of light.

"I can see them all," she breathed. "Stonehenge, Giza, Machu Picchu... they're all lit up like beacons!"

The air around them began to vibrate with an otherworldly hum, a celestial chorus that seemed to emanate from the very stones of Tiwanaku. Andres placed a steadying hand on Maya's shoulder.

"Stay focused," he urged. "We need to maintain the connection."

Suddenly, a figure materialized before them, his form shimmering with an iridescent light. Maya recognized him instantly.

"Orion," she whispered in awe.

The being's large, luminous eyes swept over the gathering, his gaze settling on Maya. When he spoke, his voice resonated with the wisdom of ages.

"The time has come," Orion intoned, his words seeming to echo across dimensions. "We must heal the rifts and seal the grid."

Maya felt a wave of uncertainty wash over her. "But how?" she asked, her voice quivering.

Orion's expression softened, a hint of a smile playing at the corners of his mouth. "You are more prepared than you know, Maya. Trust in the light within you."

With a graceful gesture, Orion extended his hands, palms upward. A sphere of pure, white light materialized between them, pulsing with ethereal energy.

"Join me," he commanded, his voice carrying across the sacred site. "Let us weave the fabric of healing."

Maya took a deep breath, centering herself. As she exhaled, she felt her consciousness expand once more, connecting with the other meditators across the globe. Their collective breath became one, a rhythmic pulse that matched the thrumming of the Earth itself.

Orion began to chant in a language that seemed both ancient and timeless. The sphere of light between his hands grew, tendrils of energy reaching out to touch each participant. Maya felt the power flow through her, channeling it into the Crystal Skull.

"I can see the rifts," Andres murmured, his eyes closed in deep concentration. "They're like... tears in reality."

Maya nodded, though she knew he couldn't see her. She too could perceive the dimensional wounds, gaping maws of darkness threatening to swallow the light.

"Focus your intention," Orion instructed. "Visualize the light mending the tears, sealing them with love and healing energy."

Maya concentrated, picturing the tendrils of light weaving through the rifts like golden thread through fabric. She could feel the resistance, the pull of the void, but she pushed through, her determination growing stronger with each passing moment.

"It's working!" someone in the circle exclaimed. "The rifts are closing!"

A surge of hope rushed through Maya, giving her renewed strength. She poured every ounce of her being into the task, feeling the Crystal Skull amplify her efforts a thousandfold.

As the last rift sealed, a shockwave of energy rippled outward from Tiwanaku, racing along the lines of the global grid. Maya opened her eyes to see the world transformed, bathed in a soft, golden light.

Orion's form began to fade, but his voice lingered, filled with pride and hope. "You have done well, children of Earth. The transformation has begun. The age of the Omega species dawns."

As his presence dissipated, Maya lowered the Crystal Skull, her arms trembling with exertion and awe. She turned to Andres, tears of joy streaming down her face.

"We did it," she whispered. "We really did it."

Andres nodded, his own eyes glistening with emotion. "Yes, Maya. And now, the real work begins."

As the reverberations of Orion's final words faded, a new phenomenon began to unfold. Maya's eyes widened as she witnessed a spectacle unlike anything she had ever seen.

"Look!" she gasped, pointing towards the horizon.

Andres followed her gaze, his jaw dropping in awe. "Incredible," he breathed.

Across the landscape, pillars of light burst forth from the earth, each one a different hue, creating a prismatic tapestry that stretched as far as the eye could see. Maya recognized them instantly.

"The planetary cities of light," she said, her voice filled with wonder. "They're awakening."

Dr. Paredes nodded, his eyes gleaming with understanding. "And not just the cities. Look there, towards the coast."

Maya turned, catching sight of undulating waves of blue-green energy pulsing from the direction of the ocean. The sight stirred something deep within her, a memory from her ancient past.

"The oceanic reserves," she murmured. "The cetaceans are joining us."

As they watched, the energies from land and sea began to intertwine, creating a mesmerizing dance of light and color. Maya could feel the vibrations in her very bones, each frequency unique, yet harmonizing perfectly with the others.

"It's beautiful," Andres said softly. "But what does it mean?"

Maya closed her eyes, allowing her consciousness to expand and merge with the energies surrounding them. When she spoke, her voice carried the weight of ancient wisdom.

"It's the final piece of the puzzle," she explained. "The cities of light anchor the higher frequencies into the physical realm, while the oceanic reserves provide the deep, nurturing energy of the Earth itself. Together, they're stabilizing the grid, ensuring that the transformation we've initiated can take root and flourish."

Andres nodded slowly, his scientific mind grappling with the metaphysical concepts. "So, this is how we become the Omega species? Through this... convergence of energies?"

Maya smiled, reaching out to take his hand. "It's the beginning. The energies provide the foundation, but it's up to humanity to embrace the change, to evolve consciously."

As if in response to her words, a wave of warmth washed over them, carrying with it a sense of profound unity. Maya could feel the presence of every being on the planet, from the smallest insect to the great whales in the depths of the ocean.

"Can you feel it? The oneness?" she asked, her voice barely above a whisper.

Dr. Paredes nodded, his eyes glistening with unshed tears. "We're all connected," he said in awe. "Truly, deeply connected. This is what Homo Omega must feel like."

Maya squeezed his hand, her heart swelling with love and hope for the future. "Yes, this is the essence of the Omega species," she said. "Unity, balance, and harmony with all of creation."

As they stood there, bathed in the radiant energies of a world reborn, Maya knew that their journey was far from over. The transformation had begun, but guiding humanity through this monumental shift would be their greatest challenge yet.

But for now, in this moment of cosmic convergence, she allowed herself to simply be, to bask in the beauty of a dream realized and a future full of infinite possibilities.

Epilogue

The ancient stones of Tiwanaku shimmered in the fading sunlight, casting long shadows across the bustling plaza. Andres stood atop the Akapana Pyramid, his lean frame silhouetted against the amber sky as he surveyed the diverse gathering below. Scientists in crisp lab coats mingled with spiritual leaders adorned in vibrant traditional garb, while awakened hybrids moved with an otherworldly grace among the crowd. Andres's calloused fingers absently traced the weathered stones beneath his hand, their cool solidity grounding him as a maelstrom of emotions churned within.

Pride swelled in his chest at the sight of so many brilliant minds coming together, yet a nagging trepidation tugged at the edges of his consciousness. He ran a hand through his wavy hair, exhaling slowly. "One year, 2038," he murmured to himself. "So much progress, but at what cost?"

As if in answer, a snippet of conversation drifted up from below:

"The Crystal Skull's energy signature is unlike anything we've ever seen," a young scientist enthused, her eyes alight with excitement. "If we could harness that power—"

"Careful, Dr. Chen," interrupted an elderly man in ornate Andean robes. "Our ancestors understood the dangers of wielding such forces without wisdom to temper ambition."

Andres's brow furrowed as he descended the pyramid steps, drawn into the heart of the gathering. The hum of dozens of overlapping conversations washed over him, each one a testament to the delicate balance they were striving to maintain.

"...quantum entanglement on a macroscopic scale..."

"...the Akashic records speak of a similar convergence..."

"...ethical implications of consciousness transfer..."

He paused near a heated debate between a neuroscientist and a shaman, their words carrying clearly across the plaza: "But think of the possibilities!" the scientist argued. "We could cure Alzheimer's, restore lost memories—"

The shaman shook his head, beads clacking softly in his gray hair. "At what cost to the soul? Some wisdom is meant to be earned, not downloaded."

Andres felt the weight of his grandmother's pendant against his chest, a physical reminder of the spiritual heritage he carried. How would Inez navigate these treacherous waters between progress and preservation?

A young hybrid approached, her iridescent eyes filled with an unsettling mix of ancient knowledge and childlike wonder. "Dr. Paredes," she said, her voice carrying an otherworldly resonance, "how do we move forward without losing ourselves?"

Andres met her gaze, feeling the full weight of responsibility settle on his shoulders. "That," he replied softly, "is the question we must all strive to answer together."

As the sun dipped below the horizon, Andres found himself drawn to the Gateway of the Sun. He traced the intricate carvings with reverent fingers, sensing the whispered echoes of countless rituals performed in this sacred space. The last rays of light caught the edges of the monolithic doorway, and for a moment, Andres could have sworn he glimpsed shadowy figures moving beyond the threshold—ancestral guardians keeping watch over this tenuous new chapter in human evolution.

"We stand at a crossroads," he whispered to the ancient stones. "Guide us true."

Maya's emerald eyes swept across the gathering, her serene presence a stark contrast to the energetic buzz of conversation. She stood with Talia Elara and Dr. Elera Voss, an unlikely trio united by shared trials and transformative experiences.

"The integration of Atlantean technology with our current understanding is progressing faster than I anticipated," Dr. Voss remarked, her typically icy tone warmed by a hint of excitement.

Talia nodded, a wry smile playing at her lips. "Who would've thought a year ago we'd be standing here, discussing the ethical implications of interdimensional travel?"

Maya's melodic laughter rang out. "The threads of fate weave intricate patterns, my friends. Our journey together has strengthened bonds that transcend time and space."

Dr. Voss's brow furrowed. "I still struggle with the weight of my past actions," she admitted, her voice barely above a whisper.

Talia placed a reassuring hand on Voss's shoulder. "We all have shadows to face, Elera. It's how we move forward that defines us."

Maya nodded sagely. "In the tapestry of existence, even the darkest threads contribute to the beauty of the whole."

Their moment of reflection was interrupted as a group of eager young scientists approached, their eyes shining with curiosity and hope. Talia stepped forward, her posture straightening as she addressed them.

"You stand at the precipice of a new era," she began, her voice carrying a passion that belied her usually pragmatic demeanor. "The knowledge we've uncovered here at Tiwanaku isn't just about advancing technology or unlocking ancient secrets. It's about understanding our place in the cosmos and our potential as a species."

The young scientists leaned in, captivated by Talia's words. She continued, her eyes blazing with conviction. "We have the power to transcend the artificial divisions that have held humanity back for millennia. The Atlanteans knew this, and now it's our turn to carry that torch forward."

One of the scientists, a young woman with curious eyes, raised her hand. "But how do we ensure this knowledge isn't misused? We've seen the dangers firsthand."

Talia's expression softened. "That's where you come in. Your generation has the opportunity to shape how we integrate this wisdom. It's not just about what we can do but what we should do."

As Talia spoke, Maya observed the subtle shifts in her aura—the layers of guilt and fear giving way to purpose and hope. She marveled at how far Talia had come from the guarded, cynical hacker they'd first encountered.

Dr. Voss leaned toward Maya, her voice low. "She's come a long way, hasn't she? We all have."

Maya smiled, her eyes twinkling with ancient wisdom. "The path of redemption is never easy, but it is always worthwhile. Each of us carries the potential for both shadow and light."

As the sun began to set over the ancient stones of Tiwanaku, casting long shadows across the gathered crowd, Maya felt a ripple of anticipation. The journey that had brought them here was far from over, and she sensed that new challenges—and opportunities—lay just beyond the horizon.

Dr. Elera Voss's silver hair gleamed in the fading sunlight as she addressed a cluster of attendees, her voice carrying the precise cadence of a surgeon wielding a scalpel. "The Atlantean crystal matrix isn't merely a power source," she explained, gesturing to a holographic display. "It's a living network, capable of amplifying our collective consciousness."

A murmur rippled through the group. Dr. Voss's eyes, once cold and calculating, now held a glimmer of reverence. "We stand at a precipice," she continued. "Our responsibility is not just to wield this technology, but to become worthy of its gifts."

Her words hung in the air, weighted with the memory of past transgressions. A young researcher raised his hand. "Dr. Voss, given your... history with the Sons of Belial, how can we trust your guidance?"

Voss flinched, her composure cracking for a moment. She took a deep breath, steadying herself. "A fair question. My actions were driven by ambition and fear. But witnessing the true potential of this knowledge... it changes you. Our task now is to ensure it changes humanity for the better."

As she spoke, Dr. Voss felt the weight of her past pressing down on her. The faces before her blurred with memories of colleagues she had betrayed, of the destructive path she had nearly set humanity upon. Yet here she stood, granted a second chance she scarcely believed she deserved.

"We must approach this legacy with humility," she said, her voice gaining strength. "The Atlanteans fell because they lost sight of the balance between progress and wisdom. We cannot make the same mistake."

Nearby, Maya glided between groups, her presence a calming counterpoint to the electric excitement in the air. A circle of eager listeners formed around her, drawn by the aura of ancient knowledge that seemed to shimmer in her wake.

"The crystals sing with the resonance of the cosmos," Maya explained, her green eyes seeming to reflect entire galaxies. "But their true power lies in awakening the dormant potential within each of us."

A skeptical archaeologist frowned. "That sounds more like mysticism than science."

Maya smiled gently. "The Atlanteans understood that the two are not separate but intertwined. Just as your DNA carries the history of your ancestors, so too does the fabric of reality carry the echoes of creation."

She gestured to the ancient stones around them. "Tiwanaku stands as a testament to this unity. Its builders understood the sacred geometry that links matter and spirit."

As Maya spoke, she felt the familiar stirring of cosmic energies. The knowledge of countless lifetimes flowed through her, a river of wisdom seeking to nourish a world on the brink of transformation.

"We stand at a crossroads," she continued, her voice taking on a resonance that seemed to vibrate in the very bones of her listeners. "The path ahead requires not just intellect, but the courage to expand our understanding of what is possible."

A young physicist leaned forward, eyes wide. "But how do we begin? It all seems so... overwhelming."

Maya placed a hand on the woman's shoulder, her touch radiating a sense of peace. "By remembering that the journey of a thousand miles begins with a single step. And by trusting that the wisdom of the ages lives within each of you, waiting to be awakened."

The sun dipped toward the horizon, painting the sky in vibrant hues of orange and purple. Andres stood atop a weathered stone platform, his silhouette backlit by the fading light. He raised his hands, and a hush fell over the gathered crowd.

"Friends, colleagues, seekers of truth," Andres began, his voice steady yet tinged with reflection. "As we stand here, surrounded by the echoes of an ancient civilization, we bear a profound responsibility."

His eyes swept across the faces before him—scientists, spiritual leaders, and awakened hybrids. Each person represented a thread in the tapestry of humanity's potential future.

"We've unlocked secrets that have slumbered for millennia," Andres continued. "But with this knowledge comes a sacred duty. We must guide humanity's transformation while maintaining the delicate balance between progress and preservation."

A cool breeze whispered through the ruins, carrying the scent of sage and distant mountains. Andres paused, allowing the weight of his words to settle.

"Our actions in the coming days will shape the course of human evolution. We stand as guardians of both ancient wisdom and cutting-edge discovery. Let us move forward with humility, compassion, and an unwavering commitment to the greater good."

As Andres's words resonated through the gathering, a flicker of movement caught his eye. Amaru, the Tiwanaku elder, was approaching with uncharacteristic urgency. The weathered shaman's silver braid swayed as he strode purposefully toward the group, a modern tablet clutched in his hand—an incongruous sight against his traditional Andean poncho.

"Andres," Amaru called out, his gravelly voice laced with concern. "The Amazon speaks. We must listen!"

The group converged around Amaru, their earlier contemplative mood shifting to one of keen interest. On the tablet's screen, a pulsing graph displayed erratic spikes of energy emanating from deep within the rainforest.

Dr. Voss leaned in, her brow furrowed. "These readings... they're unlike anything we've seen before. It's as if the very fabric of reality is fluctuating."

Andres studied the data, a mixture of excitement and apprehension coiling in his stomach. "Could this be connected to the global energy grid?" he wondered aloud, his mind racing with possibilities.

Maya's eyes widened as she gazed at the screen. "The Amazon has always been a place of great power," she murmured. "But this... this feels like an awakening."

As the group huddled closer, examining the mysterious data, Andres couldn't shake the feeling that they stood on the precipice of something monumental. The fading sunlight glinted off the ancient stones of Tiwanaku as if the very site itself was bearing witness to the unfolding of a new chapter in humanity's cosmic journey.

Talia squinted at the tablet, her fingers flying across the screen as she manipulated the data. "These energy fluctuations," she mused, her voice tight with concentration, "they're not random. There's a pattern here, almost like... a heartbeat."

Dr. Voss's eyes narrowed, her analytical mind already dissecting the implications. "If these readings are accurate, we could be looking at a tear in the fabric of space-time. The risks are astronomical." She paused, her gaze sweeping across the group. "But so are the potential benefits."

Andres felt a familiar thrill of discovery coursing through his veins. "What kind of benefits, Elera?"

Dr. Voss's lips curled into a thin smile. "Imagine harnessing that energy, Andres. We could revolutionize our understanding of the universe itself."

Maya interjected, her voice carrying a note of caution. "But at what cost? The Amazon is not just a place of power; it's a living entity. We must approach this with reverence."

Jacqueline, who had been quietly studying the ancient inscriptions on a nearby artifact, finally spoke. "These texts warn of distortions in reality when forces beyond our comprehension are meddled with. The Atlanteans knew of such anomalies—and they feared them." She glanced at Andres, her expression grave. "This could be one of those rifts, and if so, we must tread carefully."

As the group debated, Andres's eyes met Maya's. In that fleeting moment, a silent understanding passed between them. The weight of their shared history, stretching back through lifetimes, settled upon their shoulders.

"We have to investigate," Andres said softly, his words meant only for Maya. "Whatever this anomaly is, we can't let it fall into the wrong hands."

Maya nodded, her eyes reflecting the same mix of determination and trepidation that Andres felt. "The balance we've achieved is fragile," she whispered. "This could tip the scales in ways we can't foresee."

Jacqueline exhaled, running a hand over the artifact's surface. "Then we'd better ensure we're the ones deciphering its mysteries—before someone else does."

Around them, the stones of Tiwanaku seemed to pulse with an ancient energy, as if acknowledging the magnitude of the decision before them. Andres took a deep breath, feeling the responsibility of their chosen path settle into his bones. The Amazon awaited, its secrets calling to them like a siren song, promising revelation, and peril in equal measure.

The group began to disperse, their voices fading into the cool evening air. Andres and Maya lingered behind, the weight of their impending journey settling between them like an invisible presence. They walked slowly toward the edge of the ancient site, their footsteps echoing off weathered stone.

"We'll need to move quickly," Andres mused, his brow furrowed in contemplation. "But discretion is paramount. If word of this anomaly spreads..."

Maya's serene voice cut through his concerns. "The Amazon has its own guardians, Andres. We must approach with respect, not haste."

Andres nodded, feeling a familiar thrill of anticipation mixed with trepidation. "You're right, of course. But I can't shake this feeling of urgency. It's as if the very air is charged with... expectation."

They paused at the site's perimeter, gazing out at the star-studded sky. Maya's eyes seemed to reflect the cosmic tapestry above as she spoke. "The challenges we face are not just physical. The Amazon is a nexus of spiritual energy, much like Tiwanaku. We must be prepared for trials of the soul."

Andres's hand unconsciously moved to the pouch at his belt, feeling the comforting presence of the Crystal Skull within. "I've been having dreams," he confessed, "visions of shadowy figures moving through the jungle, of ancient temples hidden beneath the canopy."

Maya's lips curved into a knowing smile. "The Skull is preparing you, connecting you to the energies we'll encounter. Trust in its guidance, Andres."

As if in response to Maya's words, a soft glow began to emanate from Andres's pouch. He carefully withdrew the Crystal Skull, its surface shimmering with an otherworldly light. The artifact seemed to pulse in rhythm with the stars above, creating a tangible link between earth and sky.

"It's beautiful," Andres breathed, marveling at the play of light across the Skull's crystalline surface.

Maya's voice took on a reverent tone. "It's more than that, Andres. It's a bridge between worlds, a key to unlocking the secrets that await us. The Skull's activation now is no coincidence."

As they stood beneath the vast expanse of the night sky, the Crystal Skull cradled in Andres's hands, he felt a profound sense of connection to forces beyond his comprehension. The journey ahead loomed large in his mind, filled with both promise and peril.

"Whatever we find in the Amazon," Andres said softly, "I'm glad you'll be by my side, Maya."

She placed her hand gently on his arm, her touch radiating warmth and reassurance. "As it has been for countless lifetimes, my friend. Now, let us prepare. The Amazon calls, and we must answer."

Andres's eyes met Maya's, a silent understanding passing between them. He took a deep breath, his resolve strengthening. "You're right. We can't ignore this call. The Amazon holds answers we need—answers that could protect everything we've built here."

Maya nodded, her long brown hair catching the starlight. "The balance is fragile, Andres. What we've achieved at Tiwanaku is precious, but it's only the beginning. The anomaly in the Amazon could tip the scales in either direction."

As they began walking toward their quarters to prepare, Andres's mind raced with possibilities. "What do you think we'll find there? Another hidden civilization? Or something more... otherworldly?"

Maya's green eyes sparkled with ancient wisdom. "The Amazon has always been a place of mystery and power. It's possible we'll encounter echoes of civilizations even older than Atlantis or Tiwanaku. But we must be prepared for anything."

Andres chuckled nervously. "Prepared for anything? That's a tall order."

"We have each other," Maya reminded him, her voice soft yet strong. "And we carry the wisdom of ages with us. That will be our greatest asset."

As they reached the edge of the archaeological site, both turned to look back at Tiwanaku. The ancient stones seemed to shimmer faintly in the starlight as if acknowledging their departure. Andres felt a lump form in his throat.

"It's as if they're saying goodbye," he murmured.

Maya smiled, her expression serene. "Not goodbye, Andres. They're offering their blessing. Tiwanaku has always been a nexus of spiritual energy. It recognizes the importance of our journey."

The stones pulsed once more, a barely perceptible wave of energy washing over them. Andres felt a surge of hope and purpose flood through him. "Then let's not keep the Amazon waiting. We have a world to protect."

With a final glance at the glimmering ruins behind them, Andres and Maya turned towards their future, the promise of discovery lighting their path forward.

The Crystal Skull pulsed with an otherworldly radiance, bathing Andres and Maya in its ethereal glow. Its faceted surface seemed alive, shifting patterns of light dancing across their faces as they stood transfixed.

"It's never reacted like this before," Andres whispered, his eyes wide with wonder and a hint of trepidation.

Maya's delicate fingers traced the air just above the Skull's surface, her third eye shimmering in resonance. "It senses the journey ahead. The Amazon calls to it, as it calls to us."

Andres felt a shiver run down his spine. "What do you think we'll find there?"

"I'm not certain," Maya admitted, her green eyes meeting his. "But the Skull's reaction suggests something of great cosmic significance awaits us."

The skull's glow intensified, casting long shadows across the room. Andres's mind raced with possibilities. "Do you think it's another node? Or something... older?"

Maya's expression grew serious. "Whatever it is, it's clear that the balance we've fought so hard to achieve is at stake. The Skull reminds us of our duty—to bridge the gap between our technological aspirations and our spiritual essence."

Andres nodded, feeling the weight of responsibility settle on his shoulders. "It's a delicate balance. One misstep and we could lose everything we've worked for."

"That's why we must approach this with both wisdom and caution," Maya said, her voice taking on the timeless quality that always left Andres in awe. "The Amazon holds secrets that could revolutionize our understanding of human history and potential. But in the wrong hands..."

"It could be catastrophic," Andres finished, thinking of the Brotherhood of Belial and their ruthless pursuit of power.

The Skull's light pulsed once more, as if in agreement. Maya placed a hand on Andres's arm, her touch grounding him.

"We carry the hopes of two ancient civilizations with us," she said softly. "Atlantis and Tiwanaku. Their legacies live on through our actions."

Andres took a deep breath, steeling himself for the challenges ahead. "Then we'd better make sure we don't disappoint them."

As they began their final preparations, the Crystal Skull's glow seemed to follow them, a constant reminder of the cosmic dance they were part of—a dance between past and future, technology and spirit, human limitation, and limitless potential.

The Amazon awaited, its secrets calling to them across time and space. And as the first light of dawn broke over the horizon, Andres and Maya stepped forward to meet their destiny, the Crystal Skull's light guiding their way into the unknown.

The Prophecy Realized

The ancient words of the *Scrolls of Light* have come to pass. What was once a vision seen through the veils of time, inscribed in the sacred temples of Atlantis, has now manifested in the world of tomorrow. Humanity has awakened.

Through the trials of ages and the struggles between light and shadow, the threshold was finally crossed. The echoes of Atlantean wisdom, long buried beneath the ruins of forgotten civilizations, have reawakened in the hearts of those who remembered. The ancient sites, aligned with the celestial rhythms of the cosmos, have become portals once more—bridging the earthly and the divine, past, and future, self and Source.

The *Homo Omega* now walk the Earth, no longer bound by division or fear. They are luminous beings of higher consciousness, their minds attuned to the harmonic frequencies of creation. Telepathic, heart-centered, and multidimensional, they exist in unity with nature, the cosmos, and each other. No longer are they shackled by the illusions of power and separation that once led to the downfall of Atlantis. Instead, they wield a new power—the wisdom of *Oneness*, unity, the mastery of energy, and the ability to shape reality through pure intention.

The Vesica Piscis, the sacred geometry of the ancients, shines once more as a gateway to higher existence. The Crystal Skulls, long hidden and waiting, have served their purpose, unlocking the final keys of human evolution. The Earth's energy grid hums in perfect resonance, no longer dormant, but fully activated—pulsing with the collective consciousness of an enlightened species.

The great cycle has turned. The *Great Ascension* has unfolded, and a New Earth has emerged.

As Amara once foresaw, the Atlantean dream has not been lost. It was merely waiting for those ready to claim it—not as rulers, but as stewards of the next age. The path of *Homo Omega* has begun. And with it, a new world—a world of balance, peace, harmony, and the infinite potential of the awakened human soul.

Afterword

In 2017, I became part of an international meditation group, where I was introduced to the Arcturians through the Group of Forty (groupofforty.com). This global network of like-minded souls is dedicated to spiritual collaboration and planetary healing. That experience profoundly transformed my life. It awakened me to my true galactic heritage as a Starseed and helped me realize my deeper purpose—to assist in healing the Earth and play my role in manifesting Homo Omega, humanity's next evolutionary leap.

I wish to extend my deepest gratitude to David and Gudrun Miller, co-founders of the Group of Forty, and the Arcturians, whose wisdom, dedication, and guidance have illuminated the path for so many of us seeking to fulfill our higher purpose. Their teachings and leadership have profoundly shaped my spiritual journey, providing me with the tools and understanding to step into my role in this great transformation.

I am also deeply thankful for my fellow Starseeds, brothers and sisters whose unwavering commitment to planetary healing and higher consciousness continues to inspire me. It is through our shared efforts, unity, and vision that we are co-creating a new paradigm for humanity. I see the writing of this novel as my own contribution, however small, to the expansion of consciousness—a means of bringing new awareness and possibilities to those who are ready to receive them.

Our world today faces not just potential but probable catastrophe. Accelerated climate change, global warming, and the destruction of the biosphere—along with the rapid loss of biodiversity—are pushing us toward the very real possibility of human extinction. Yet, throughout history, great cataclysms have reshaped life on Earth, wiping out dominant species while paving the way for entirely new evolutionary lineages. Traditional evolutionary models suggest that adaptation occurs slowly over millennia, yet evidence from mass extinction events tells a different story—one of sudden, dramatic leaps in biological complexity. This phenomenon, known as quantum speciation, suggests that life does not merely adapt to environmental collapse but undergoes a rapid and often radical transformation, almost as if responding to an unseen evolutionary force.

In this novel, the concept of *Homo Omega* is born from this understanding of evolution—not as a linear progression but as a quantum leap in consciousness and being. Drawing inspiration from the Arcturians and both esoteric traditions and scientific speculation, *Homo Omega* represents the next stage in humanity's evolution, emerging in response to a planetary shift. Just as the age of dinosaurs ended to give rise to mammals, and early primates evolved into self-aware beings, humanity now stands at the precipice of another great transformation.

This transformation is far more than just a biological shift. Unlike past evolutionary leaps, which were primarily driven by external pressures, the emergence of *Homo Omega* is an inner evolution—a profound expansion of consciousness, perception, and energy.

This idea aligns with indigenous traditions that speak of *Homo Luminous*—a being who has awakened their full potential and exists in harmony with the cosmic order. However, in the novel, *Homo Omega* is also shaped by an Arcturian perspective, viewing humanity's evolution as part of a greater galactic awakening. From this higher vantage point, Earth is not merely a planet subject to natural selection but a sacred crucible, a place where higher beings emerge—multidimensional beings who integrate ancient wisdom, sacred technologies, and interdimensional knowledge.

The Arcturians refer to this higher path of spiritual evolution as *The Sacred Triangle*—the unification of three powerful spiritual forces:

The White Brotherhood and Sisterhood—representing the unified teachings of the world's religions.

Galactic Spirituality—embodying higher-dimensional wisdom and cosmic consciousness.

The Teachings of Indigenous Peoples—preserving the sacred knowledge of Earth's original guardians.

This triad forms the foundation for a new spiritual paradigm—one that is essential for Earth's transformation and humanity's ascension into its true potential.

This story is more than a work of fiction—it reflects a deeper truth woven through history, mythology, and spiritual traditions. The legends of Atlantis, the teachings of the ancient shamans, and the insights of visionaries like Pierre Teilhard de Chardin, who envisioned an Omega Point of collective consciousness, all point toward the same unfolding destiny. Whether through the activation of sacred sites, the reawakening of ancient codes, or the unlocking of hidden potentials within human DNA, the transition to *Homo Omega* is not merely possible—it is inevitable.

As we stand on the edge of an uncertain future, we must ask ourselves: Are we willing to embrace this transformation? Will we cling to the old paradigms of division, materialism, and fear? Or will we step into our highest potential, activating the latent light within us, and co-create a new reality?

Perhaps, as the novel suggests, the true key to evolution is not found in the remnants of the past but in the awakening of our own infinite nature aligned with ancient wisdom and cosmic forces.

Throughout this narrative, the presence of hybrids and artificial intelligence serves as more than just a subplot—it reflects our current trajectory as a species. The fusion of consciousness and technology is no longer confined to science fiction; it is unfolding before us in real time. Initiatives such as Project 2045 and advancements in AI, transhumanism, and neural integration challenge the boundaries of what it means to be human.

In the world of this novel, the hybrids represent both the promise and peril of this evolution. On one hand, they symbolize the potential of an expanded intelligence—one that harmonizes biological and artificial consciousness. On the other, they serve as a warning against the unchecked manipulation of human essence, echoing the ancient Atlantean struggle between spiritual enlightenment and the pursuit of power.

As we stand at the precipice of a new era, where AI and human consciousness are increasingly intertwined, we must ask ourselves: What kind of future are we creating? Will technology serve as a tool for enlightenment, or will it become another means of control? The story of the hybrids is not just a speculative thread in this novel; it is a mirror held up to the choices we face today.

This book would not have been possible without the unwavering support of a dedicated group of friends. To my friend, Bruce Colbert, a writer extraordinaire, with 15 published novels—thank you for your insightful manuscript review and invaluable suggestions, which I took to heart. Your expertise and keen eye made a profound difference. You truly know your craft. To my fellow Starseed and wise friend, Cosmin Supeala, who embraced the manuscript review with enthusiasm, offering thoughtful guidance and encouragement. To my lovely wife Ellen, the best friend and cheerleader I could ever have, who supported me throughout with her keen insights, and put up with my absence, especially with the long hours away, locked in my office.

I would like to express my deepest appreciation to my dear friend and starseed, Elizabeth Heartstar, whose wisdom and dedication have been a profound source of inspiration on my journey. As a master astrologer, Earthkeeper, and sacred tour guide, Elizabeth's work has illuminated the deep spiritual significance of the Earth's power sites and their role in humanity's evolution.

Our many journeys together to sacred power sites across England—Avebury, Stonehenge, Glastonbury, and beyond—opened my eyes to the intricate web of energy that connects these ancient places. Through our explorations, meditations, and profound discussions, she helped me understand how these sacred nodes are not just remnants of the past but living, dynamic portals that hold the potential to awaken consciousness and reactivate the planetary energy grid.

Elizabeth's deep knowledge and reverence for these sites inspired me to weave them into my novel, highlighting their role in the unfolding transformation of humanity. Her unwavering passion for this sacred work has left an indelible mark on my own spiritual path, and I am forever grateful for her loving friendship, guidance, and the shared experiences that have shaped my understanding of the mystical energies of our planet.

A heartfelt thank you to the expert designers at Design Crowd for bringing my vision to life with a truly fabulous book cover. Your creativity and talent have given this novel the perfect visual expression, capturing its essence in a way that exceeds my expectations. I am deeply grateful for your work and the dedication you put into making this cover a reality.

I would like to extend my deepest gratitude to Thea Stevens and his Word-2-Kindle dedicated staff for their exceptional work in formatting and preparing the novel for publishing. Their attention to detail, professionalism, and commitment to excellence have been invaluable in bringing this project to life. I truly appreciate their hard work and expertise in ensuring that the final product is polished and ready for readers to enjoy. Thank you, Nick, and your entire team, for your outstanding support throughout this process.

Finally, I would like to acknowledge that the writing journey was enriched using modern AI tools like ChatGPT and Sudowrite. These technologies served as collaborative partners—offering creative prompts, refining ideas, and helping me explore the vast landscapes of myth, history, and imagination that shaped this story. While the soul of this book is undeniably human, these tools demonstrated the incredible potential of blending human creativity with technological innovation. I hope the result resonates with you as much as it did with me during its creation.

Robert Maldonado

Selected Bibliography

Alper, F. (1981). *Exploring Atlantis.* Irvine, California: Quantum Productions.

Andrews, S.(1997). *Atlantis: Insights from a Lost Civilization.* Woodbury, MN: Llewellyn Publishing.

Aribalo, M. (2007). *Inka Power Places: Solar Initiation: Andean Archeo-astronomy.* Peru: Shamanic Productions.

Bellamy, H.S. (2019). *Built Before the Flood.* California: The Book Tree.

Bryant, A., & Galde, P.(1989). *The Message of the Crystal Skull: From Atlantis to the New Age.* St. Paul, MN: Llewellyn Publications.

Cayce, E. (1988). *Mysteries of Atlantis Revisited.* San Francisco: Harper & Row.

Carrol, L. (2013). *Kryon—The Recalibration of Humanity.* California: The Kryon Writings.

Cooper, D. (2005). *Discover Atlantis: A Guide to Reclaiming the Wisdom of the Ancients.* Scotland: Findhorn Press.

Cooper, D. (2007). *The Web of Light: A Spiritual Adventure.* London: Hodder & Stoughton Ltd.

Childress, D. (1996). *Lost Cities of Atlantis, Ancient Europe & the Mediterranean.* Stelle, Ill: Adventures Unlimited Press.

Cori. P. (2001). *Atlantis Rising: The Struggle of Darkness and Light.* Berkeley, CA: North Atlantic Publishing.

Donnelly. I. (2023). *Atlantis: The Antediluvian World.* Zinc Read.

Gray, M. (2024). *Sacred Sites.* Arizona: Jonglez Publishing.

Hararai, N. (2017). *Homo Deus: A Brief History of Tomorrow.* New York: Harper Perennial.

Janusek, J.W. (2008). *Ancient Tiwanaku.* Cambridge University Press.

Joseph, F.(1987). *The Destruction of Atlantis.* Olympia Fields, Ill: Atlantis Research Publishers.

Joseph, F. (2004). *The Survivors of Atlantis: Their Impact on the World.* Rochester, VT: Bear & Company.

Joseph, F. (2012). *Atlantis and 2012: The Science of the Lost Civilization and the Prophecies of the Maya.* Rochester VT: Bear & Company.

Joseph, F. (2004). *The Destruction of Atlantis: Compelling Evidence of the Sudden Fall of the Legendary Civilization.* Rochester, VT: Bear & Company.

Keller, E.H. (2014). *The Crystal Skull Messenger.* Dancing with the Sun Productions.

Kingdon, K. (2024). *What Ever Happened to the New Age?* Vajra Flame Press.

Kolata. A. (1993). *The Tiwanaku: Portrait of an Andean Civilization.* Massachusetts: Blackwell.

Le Flem, M. (2022). *Visions of Atlantis: Reclaiming our Lost Ancient Legacy.* Independently published.

Litten, J. (2007).*Crystal Skulls: Interacting with a Phenomena.* Flagstaff, AZ: Light Technology Publishing.

Maldonado, R. (2011). *Children of Atlantis: Keepers of the Crystal Skull.*

Meir, M. (2022*). JoinWith.Me.* South Carolina: Palmetto Publishing Company.

Menzies, G. (2011*). The Lost Empire of Atlantis.* New York: Harper Collins.

Miller, D. (2019). Conncecting with Arcturians 3. Flagstaff AZ: Light Technology Publishing.

Miller, D. (2020). *Connecting with Arcturians 4.* Flagstaff AZ: Light Technology Publishing.

Miller, D. (2021). *Connecting with Arcturians 5.* Flagstaff AZ: Light Technology Publishing.

Morton, C., & Thomas, C. (2002). *The Mystery of the Crystal Skulls: Unlocking the Secrets of the Past, Present, and Future.* Rochester, VT & Company.

Pearce, S.(2005). *The Angels of Atlantis.* Scotland: Findhorn Press.

Stanish, C. (2011). *Lake Titicaca: Legend, Myth and Science.* World Heritage and Monument.

Tyberonn, J. (2015). *2038: The Next Quantum Leap.* Nevada: Star Quest Publishing.

Vigato, M. (2022*). The Empires of Atlantis.* Vermont: Bear & Company.

Wilson, C., & Flem-Ath, R. (2000). *The Atlantis Blueprint.* London: Delacorte Press.

About the Author

Robert R. Maldonado, Ph.D., is a healer, author, teacher, and artist dedicated to transformation, spiritual awakening, and global consciousness. A former U.S. Marine Corps helicopter pilot and Air Commando, he transitioned from military service to a life of energy healing, education, and spiritual mentorship. Holding advanced degrees in Energy Medicine, Transpersonal Arts, and multiple disciplines, his work integrates ancient wisdom, healing practices, and transpersonal arts, which he shares through his books and teachings. He resides in Fairhope, Alabama, with his wife, Ellen, and their beloved pets. Reach him at rrmaldo41@gmail.com

www.ingramcontent.com/pod-product-compliance
Lightning Source LLC
Chambersburg PA
CBHW051213130726
47988CB00001B/78